PRAISE FOR
Novel

"You will have to admit that *Novel* the novel has a novel way of attracting your attention." —*Newsday*

"[The] unchallenged king of the comic Southern short story." —*The Atlanta Journal-Constitution*

"One of the funniest writers south of David Sedaris." —*The Oregonian* (Portland)

"Read [*Novel*] outdoors if you tend to laugh out loud when you come across something that tickles your funny bone." —*Jackson Free Press*

PRAISE FOR
The Half-Mammals of Dixie

"Singleton's relentlessly offbeat stories are a miasma of flea markets, palm readers, bowling alleys, and alligators, offering a disturbingly askew—at times, downright surreal—vision of the South." —*Entertainment Weekly*

"The South will get a rise out of you again with [this] marvelously skewed and skewering collection of stories...a book by turns raucous and enigmatic, and by and large inspired and inventive." —*The San Diego Union-Tribune*

NOVEL

NOVEL

GEORGE SINGLETON

A HARVEST BOOK
HARCOURT, INC.

ORLANDO   AUSTIN   NEW YORK   SAN DIEGO   TORONTO   LONDON

Requests for permission to make copies of any part of the work
should be submitted online at www.harcourt.com/contact or
mailed to the following address: Permissions Department,
Harcourt, Inc., 6277 Sea Harbor Drive, Orlando, Florida 32887-6777.

www.HarcourtBooks.com

The Library of Congress has cataloged the hardcover edition as follows:
Singleton, George, 1958–
Novel/George Singleton.
p.   cm.
1. Autobiography—Authorship—Fiction.   2. Brothers and sisters—Fiction.
3. City and town life—Fiction.   4. South Carolina—Fiction.
5. Young men—Fiction.   6. Secrecy—Fiction.   I. Title.
PS3569.I5747N687   2005
813'.6—dc22   2004023462
ISBN-13: 978-0-15-101128-5   ISBN-10: 0-15-101128-1
ISBN-13: 978-0-15-603091-5 (pbk.)   ISBN-10: 0-15-603091-8 (pbk.)

Text set in Electra LH
Designed by Liz Demeter

Printed in the United States of America

First Harvest edition 2006
A C E G I K J H F D B

This one's for friend and coconspirator André Bernard,
publisher and editor, who didn't say the word "novel" to me, ever.

NOVEL

PART I

"For sheer nerve, there's nothing beats a woman
caught in the act: guilt fuels her fury and defiance."

—JUVENAL, SATIRE VI

1

MY BROTHER-IN-LAW should've left his car window rolled up when he chose to smoke with his mother beside him in the passenger seat, oxygen strapped to her nostrils. They were driving between Graywood Emergency Regional Memorial hospital and her home in rural Gruel. My mother-in-law, Ina—whom I called "Vudge" behind her back, insisting in my head that her middle name was Ina—had gotten released after a lung-surgery stint. According to oncologist Dr. Rolander, they should've filmed the procedure it went so textbook. A third of one lung got clipped out, no chemo or radiation would be scheduled, and Vudge could go on to live another seventy years. Rolander might've been the only good real doctor in all of Forty-Five, South Carolina. When he came out of surgery he told all of us—brother-in-law Irby, my wife, Rebekah, and me—"Man, that went way better than I ever thought!" I tried my best to sigh relief.

This, of course, all took place outside the surgery waiting room exactly five days before Irby rolled his window down, which caused the ember of his cigarette to fly off, perform some kind of trick acrobatic backflip witnessed normally during

Christmas, Fourth of July, New Year's Eve, or Confederate's Day celebrations in South Carolina when bottle rockets get minds of their own, and finally embed itself between Vudge's left nostril and the rubber tube spraying pure-tee oxygen in her face.

The resulting explosion was merciless, as you can imagine—car, in-laws, and metal canister lifting skyward like a regular Scud missile. It got mentioned on a local television station newscast sixty miles away, not just on Forty-Five's local access.

But let me get back to the surgery waiting room and explain what went on there, and what must've been a daily, ongoing routine. Evidently a six A.M. surgery admittance of a friend, relative, or long-lost acquaintance becomes the social highlight of the year for everyone in Graywood County. My wife and now-dead brother-in-law took cushioned seats between the giant-screen TV—morning cartoons, no national news—and the complimentary doughnut/coffee/hot chocolate/PayDay candy bar rolling kiosk. Blacks and whites gathered in groups of their own, and I noticed right off that one set of well-wishers dressed as if going to a funeral, the other as if on their way to a tractor pull. But I don't want to generalize whatsoever. I don't want to categorize my wife's people. I'm sure that some white people wear bib overalls and stained, bent LET THE BIG TIRES ROLL caps to loved ones' awkward eulogies.

People called out to each other from one side of the room to the other. Introductions were made and more than once I heard, "Oh, I 'member you! You went by Little Bubba when you was a boy," or "I 'member you! You had a brother in my grade name of Little Bubba, back when you was a tiny girl," or "Hey, you 'member me! I went by L'il Scooby by some. Big Stuff by some. My sister was Shonuff," and so on from across the way.

4

Not a magazine had been read on the wall rack, as far as I could tell. Both *Time* and *Newsweek* ran cover stories on Richard Nixon's daughter's upcoming wedding in the White House.

I said, "Hey, Bekah, we should've brought some cards. Or pin the tail on the donkey." I should mention that Rebekah bragged how her name got spelled exactly like the Bible woman. Then four years into the marriage she decided to go by "Bekah." Bekah thought with such a moniker she'd come across as more easygoing, sympathetic, open-minded, and friendly. She cared. It was important in her job as a debt collector.

So she went by Bekah for another four or five years. But for all I know, since the deaths of her mother and brother she's cut it all the way down to plain Kah.

Kah, Kah, Kah.

Back in the surgery waiting room my wife said, "People act in different ways when faced with diversity. Don't judge so much."

I felt pretty sure she meant "adversity," but who knows? If I'd've predicted Vudge's and Irby's demises, Bekah's inheritance, our odd investment, the hospital's willingness to settle quickly out of court, and then Bekah's departure two months into our new life in Gruel, I might've spoken up. I said, "Why you so quiet, Irby?"

Irby and Bekah weren't twins but somehow got birthed only six months apart and both of them weighed in at eight pounds, something ounces. If it matters, Bekah came out first. She and Irby looked and acted similarly throughout life, though my wife went to college and became certified to teach first graders, then got a six-week paralegal degree in order to make a living in the Carolinas. After about a year of working for lawyers she somehow got hired on by a guy who tried to collect from ex-patients with no insurance who, for various reasons, chose not to pay their medical bills.

On a side note: I watched my wife watch everyone else in the waiting room. You could tell she picked out those who'd never paid and those who never would pay. It was uncanny.

Irby, on the other hand, spent a lot of time working odd jobs in between court-ordered community service projects. I liked my brother-in-law. If I'd've been able to predict everything, I would've yelled out for Irby to either not smoke altogether or to at least roll up his window so as not to chance the spark-fizzle-boom.

Irby stared at Fred and Wilma Flintstone on the TV. He said, "I'm quiet 'cause this has got me scared, that's all. I ain't ever thought that much how you could be here one minute and gone next. I didn't study up on history, Novel. I guess *you* reminded me of here-now, gone-then all the time, what with your knowledge of the things."

I never thought about it. I said, "Lord, Irby, shut up. Your mom will be okay, and you'll probably live forever."

It's true I studied history and continued to do so right before Vudge Ina went in for surgery, came out healthy within the week, then had her face melted off like an arc welder to a sheet of Bubble Wrap. As a matter of fact I'd recently finished up a fascinating biography of famed pathological liars called *This Won't Hurt*. To this day I have no clue what was fact and what was made up in that book.

Which brings me to this: Maybe the oxygen blowup due to Irby's keeping the window rolled down occurred otherwise, et cetera. Bekah and I followed behind Irby and Vudge, and it would take one of those slow-motion stop-freeze cameras to see what happened first: a spark in the car cab *before* veering down a long steep embankment going down to Lake Between; or a veer off the road, an impact, the explosion.

Me, I said nothing. Bekah, though, told cops and coroner alike that she'd take a lie detector test about what she witnessed. Seeing as she had that debt collector job, I think she got to practice, unknowingly, for the polygraph any time she wanted.

The next thing you know, my wife had inherited her childhood home, retained two lawyers well-known for keeping athletes and wrestlers out of jail up in Charlotte, and somehow settled a quarter-million-dollar negligence charge against the hospital for its oxygen tank. Bekah said, "It's a sign that what I proved to myself during that weeklong sneezing fit last year is something I should show anyone with a weight problem. You watch and see, Novel. Watch and learn. I know what I'm talking about."

We'd gone through a dual funeral for her mom and brother. I said, "If you need me to quit my job," which I didn't want to do seeing as I loved it, kind of, "I'll quit. Whatever you want."

Listen, I kind of remembered Bekah sneezing so hard and frequently two springs earlier that she lost fifteen pounds and toned her stomach down to—my opinion—a scary, scary washboard. And I kind of remembered when she had said, "You know what, Novel? One day, if I ever have the money, I'm going to open a surefire weight-loss tone-up clinic that'll baffle scientists and dietitians alike."

My first job when I got home from work back then, outside of wading through Bekah's opinions concerning that law where she couldn't call people up before nine in the morning or after nine at night, was to fill out some mileage forms and stack that day's completed surveys in descending order from "this bites" all the way to "definitely worthwhile" in regards to revisiting what I had to offer everyday citizens and schoolchildren alike. That's right: "this bites" meant good. Anyway, it was part of my job description. I don't know everything there is to know about state-funded agencies that relied on both private and public operational monies, but my boss let all of his employees know that we required valid hard-copy documentation should the legislature cut what we had to offer in the same unwincing and reckless way it did to other unneeded agencies like the North Carolina Arts Commission, the Department of Social Services, and school bus maintenance. We needed proof, by god.

I guess my boss understood that my background in American history made me one of a dozen perfect candidates to drive the Viper-Mobile around my appointed counties. Me, I would've gone with Asp-Mobile, but no one ever listened. I drove around Mecklenburg County mostly, from pre-K schools to nursing homes, a trailer attached to my step van like some kind of circus sideshow attraction. I kept the copperheads, eastern diamondbacks, and cottonmouths in the trailer. With me in the step van, though, rode rat, corn, black-, and garter snakes. And mice. Don't think I didn't comprehend the state's mission: Most people killed snakes on principle, not knowing that my reptiles helped control everything from june bugs to rodents, illegal aliens, and Yankees. Less june bugs and rodents meant more and better tobacco plants. If p, then q. If we purchase Louisiana, then we'll have more crawfish. We purchase Louisiana. Crawfish. If we throw tea in a harbor, then the British will understand our backbone. We throw tea in a harbor. Littering.

History. It continues. It went right on up to my mother-in-law, Ina, and her son Irby dying in a straightforward and almost unquestionable exploding oxygen tank circumstance.

Bekah said, "Are you sure you won't mind someone else taking care of the snakes? I mean—and I got to be honest—I won't miss not knowing they're not out there in the driveway every night."

I catalogued more than two hundred kids' questionnaires, all of them "This bites," a percentage record. I said to my wife, "I can give up the snake job." But I didn't tell her how I could, indeed, continue the other part of my job anywhere, what with technology. I didn't mention it, for she never knew the second half of my working life.

✦ ✦ ✦

At some point between mother-in-law Vudge Ina's third-of-a-lung removal and her subsequent release—by the way, Bekah by then planned a prosecutorial argument that involved her mother's premature hospital release (only five days after major surgery!) and how, in a rational, humane amount of time, Ina wouldn't've needed to-go oxygen—Irby took me aside and said, "I'm going to the drugstore across the way. You need anything?"

He owned a look in his eye like the time he got mad at a construction foreman, then set his own miter box for forty-three-degree angles. It was Richard Petty's number, Irby told me.

"You're not planning to *rob* the drugstore, are you?"

We stood in the white smoking area, across from the black smoking area, outside Graywood Emergency Regional Memorial's downstairs Museum of Dislodged and Extracted Objects.

9

There weren't actual black and white signs, of course—this was the year 1998, which meant about 1966 for Graywood County—but gene pools kept everyone treading in their own personal waters. Irby said, "No. No. Mr. Goddamn Goody-goody. I'm going over there to either buy the patch or a box of that nicotine gum."

Mr. Goddamn Goody-goody! I swear. I said, "Good on you, Irby. Man, you're taking your momma's illness seriously. Way to go." I stifled a belch. "I don't need anything seeing as I already quit years ago. If they got some kind of booze patch now, I'll take a handful of them."

Irby didn't throw down his cigarette butt, though the filter burned. "You think you could let me borry fifty dollars?"

Lookit: Bekah and Irby's father, Sherrill, might've been one of the wealthiest non-cotton-mill-owning men in all of Graywood County. He certainly had more money than anyone in Gruel proper. Sherrill died of an "accidental" gunshot wound to the lower jaw according to family myth, before I met Bekah. He owned a taxidermy outfit and stuffed deer, turkey, bass, and bobcats for every citizen in a three-county area. It never would've made the news, but I wouldn't be surprised if he stuffed dodos and mastodons—that's how far Gruel stood from civilization. Sherrill Cathcart probably stuffed a legendary dogheaded man, cynocephalus, for all anyone knew, or any Bigfoot traveling to Florida. I don't want to get way ahead of myself or offtrack, but it didn't shock me whatsoever when professor-led groups of archaeology graduate students from Arizona, Borneo, and the Olduvai Gorge in Tanzania showed up wanting to rent long-term rooms from me once Bekah's Sneeze 'n' Tone spa in Gruel expired unnaturally.

I said—and I'll feel this guilt for years—"No. I'm not lend-ing you more money. Somewhere along the line you must've gotten a dictionary that confused 'borrow' with 'give.'" I don't know if it was tension—I didn't trust anyone else driving my Viper-Mobile route, much less handing out mice cakes the way my snakes liked them. But I reminded Irby of all the money he'd promised to pay me back, and for what reasons: interview suit, tuition money for a technical college's culinary program, banjo lessons, a used Porta-Sauna to rent out to toxin-ridden friends, new moped tires, the occasional trip to a bona fide dermatologist. Bail money, of course.

Irby said, "I don't blame you one bit, Novel. And I'll put a palm on the Bible when I say I'm going to give it up somehow, and use that money to repay you and Rebekah." He lit another cigarette, using a book of matches. "See? I'm already not wasting money on disposable lighters."

How could I have known that maybe he really would've quit, and only chewed gum while driving Ina home to the only three-story house one block off Gruel's square, filled parlor to attic with unclaimed stuffed game? Because of this: Irby had no luck. If I'd've gotten him on the nicotine gum, then Irby, nervous behind the wheel seeing as I wouldn't let him borrow money to get a New Mexico driver's license a year before, would've popped the foil gum wrapper in his mouth, chewed hard, caused a spark, and blown up Ina's oxygen tank anyway.

I might never be labeled an optimist, but by god I know rational thought inside out. When I studied American history, and please remember that I still do, my heroes included Hal Holbrook playing Mark Twain and Diogenes portraying a man who gave a shit.

Between the double eulogies and my wife's last remaining

relatives' burial in Old Gruel Cemetery, laid out next to sad Sherrill—a patriarch taxidermist so depressed by the depletion of his surrounding woods that he agreed to trust a normal embalmer to make him appear lifelike and ready to pounce—Bekah almost took my elbow. She said, "I hope my cell phone works in the back of the Brougham." I opened the back door to a family-members-only funeral home limo. "I'm going to call up work and quit. I'm going through with our plan. I got a Realtor who's agreed to sell the house."

I kind of remember nodding as I pretended to understand Bekah's train of thought. Some kind of plan . . . no more calling the destitute and demanding money . . . this snake show bites . . . Kah, Kah, Kah.

2

I SHOWED UP in my mother's bed Novel, an unplanned child brought up by near-normal and falsely diagnosed infertile parents Ted and Olivia Akers who, in their mid-thirties, had already adopted two Irish orphans, my brother and sister James and Joyce. This all occurred in Black Mountain, North Carolina, once home to the famed avant-garde Black Mountain College where Josef Albers, Robert Creeley, Robert Motherwell, and Buckminster Fuller taught. My parents met there as students in 1948, graduated, then went around the country as semisuccessful concert pianists for a good six or eight years. Finally, they returned in order to live off the land. John Cage, of all people, reportedly stood in my parents' living room as a midwife aided Mom. He may have been the first person to actually point me out in the crib and say, "James, Joyce—Novel," as my adopted brother and sister, my parents, maybe Robert Rauschenberg, stood in a circle chanting or whatever it was that prehippies did back then.

This might all be, as they say, "exaggerated somewhat." This story of my birth and welcome to western North Carolina may be apocryphal. My birth certificate proves that I got born nine months to the day after Kennedy's election. Black Mountain College had officially closed its doors in 1956 when—this is my theory—students and teachers alike received telepathic brainwash radio waves of some sort administered by both J. Edgar Hoover and Joe McCarthy. Then the legends of the art world quit performing daily chores necessary to operate a co-op institution of higher learning.

So don't quote me on anything. Joyce, James, and I were schooled in a first-through-eighth-grade setting, then high school, among both local kids and the illegitimate children of fuck-prone ex-BMC professors and students alike. I should mention that my parents—again, both pianists—may or may not have undergone hallucinatory episodes while performing a Berlioz piece in southwestern Arizona as guests of a local music professor–shaman who cultivated peyote long before the Grateful Dead took to touring. According to my mother, she and Dad *simultaneously* had *epiphanies* that rain forests died for the sake of *pianos*, et cetera, et cetera.

Me, I've come to learn that, more than likely, they got plain bored and tired. They got to where they could play "Flight of the Bumblebee" faster than anyone else and thought, What next? They moved back to their adopted home, took in the orphans, found other jobs and avocations, and spent midmorning to late afternoon wondering when someone would compose a challenging piece of music.

Then they came outside to yell us in for dinner as always, "James! Joyce! Novel!"

It took me years to understand why our neighbors—ex-colleagues of my parents—yelled *"Ulysses!"* or *"Finnegans*

Wake!" or "Read something else!" as my brother, sister, and I ran crazy for the front door, heading for our goulash.

◆ ◆ ◆

Now, I have another theory about how I, Novel Akers, went off to college, received my degree in history, got into four Ph.D. programs, then quit after a couple years. It's not in the genes, per se, like how maybe I learned everything there was to know about America's past and only needed to read the morning newspaper, *Time*, *Newsweek*, and the *Onion* in order to keep up with what future generations would view as "history." It has to do with Santayana and that whole "those who don't understand history are doomed to repeat it" dictum. Listen, you can't expect all persons in the United States to understand and value what truly happened to their ancestors. Think of most Alabamans! So it's going to be repeated regardless, no matter what we should know of, say, trickle-down economics; attacking poorer nations without thinking about how their inhabitants might later detest America; allowing industries to expel waste in the air and water; and trickle-down economics, trickle-down economics, trickle-down economics. If it's going to happen anyway, then why bother studying up to stop it? Me, I'm waiting for people to start turning into pillars of salt. You'd think it would've happened by now.

But I'm getting off subject. I'll get to life in Gruel, but it might be worthwhile to know that adoptees James and Joyce, both four years my elder—though, somehow, not fraternal twins, or identical twins, or weird six-months-apart twins like Irby and Bekah—hated my parents and me. They never showed it outwardly much, like a good born-after-1980 kid will do. I'm talking these odd Irish orphans stewed.

Here's my prognosis:

"Novel" means "new." They didn't like that one bit. It's also, of course, a long-ass piece of fiction, and fiction is only a fancy lie. My parents—I figured this out two minutes after studying symbolism in eighth grade—understood their supposed infertility to be a lie. I'm convinced that they were so drunk and stoned throughout the Eisenhower administration that they probably forgot to screw, but I never got around to asking them.

Anyway, James and Joyce were stereotypical Irish adoptee siblings. You should've seen them throw rocks! Man, from seventy yards away my brother and sister could nail anyone wearing protective headgear and holding a shield. Luckily there weren't any motorcycle cops in Black Mountain when I grew up. On Halloween sometimes, though, trick-or-treaters dressed up like baseball catchers, and the next thing you knew old Joyce and James followed kids from a distance of two houses back. My brother and sister dumped out their candy bars in order to make space for cue-ball-sized granite orbs in their pillowcases.

Needless to say, James and Joyce didn't make friends and endear themselves to the community. Most kids our age took private music lessons, except for voice, or were tutored after school in the art barn by leftover Black Mountain graduates. I never mentioned it to my dead brother-in-law Irby, but I could've offered him banjo lessons for free. Or dulcimer, steel guitar, enough fiddle to play "Turkey in the Straw," and Jew's harp. My older brother took up bassoon for two reasons: no one else did, and the instrument itself made for a better projectile. Joyce went to art class and made Jackson Pollock look like a portraitist.

And then, years later, they took off running. The last time I saw James he wasn't five-six and weighed maybe 120. He wouldn't join the high school track team, but ran the mile in 4:05 and a 10K in thirty minutes flat. Joyce was the same at eighteen, with a three-mile time of sixteen minutes. On the night of their graduation they approached Mom and Dad and me. I'm pretty sure now that they practiced their announcement, which—imagine a fast, lilting Irish brogue here—went "Ya bollocks ya, you only loved little Novel-boy, and let me say, ya bollocks ya, a sane man moves to the shore for fish, doesn't drive daily all the way to salted water. No, a sane man moves to the mountains for apples, peaches, and moonshine, ya bollocks ya. Even in Belfast the parents don't send their kids off to factories fourteen hours a day. Ya cunts ya."

I barely understood what they said. Their accents never came up in normal sibling conversations. Maybe I never was a great listener, though.

And that was it. From what any of us could tell, James and Joyce turned around outside of our high school's front lawn, ran all the way to New York, crossed the Atlantic, and joined the Irish national Olympic team.

My mother said, "Our children don't seem to appreciate us, Ted. Why would they say such things?"

"I told them they didn't need special running shoes. Look at them go in those regular dress shoes. And Joyce in high heels."

Well I knew why they would say such things and run off, but I remained silent. I only foresaw my having to double up summerly work with James gone, plus maybe take over Joyce's female duties.

Here: Years earlier, after Dad decided that he couldn't kill

17

another Steinway, he decided to buy a used U-Haul truck, refrigerate the back end, and bring shrimp from the coasts of North and South Carolina back to the mountains. Meanwhile, Mom and Joyce picked apples and peaches, and garnered white lightning to take back to some wild, inebriated fruit-eating people living on the coast. Oh, it was a great isosceles triangle of an excursion that never stopped. But we only had to work with Dad or Mom June 1 to August 31, Labor Day weekend, Thanksgiving holiday, December 15 to January 15, Memorial Day vacation, and any other days that my father got special orders worthy of keeping us out of school. Many of the Black Mountain College leftovers and reprobates didn't eat beef, chicken, pork, deer, coon, possum, or potted meat. None of them knew how to tie a fly or cast a line, so they couldn't wait to pay Dad for what bounties he brought back iced and costing twice the going rate.

And those poor scurvied fucks outposted on Ocracoke wouldn't know an apple from a lemon. If it wasn't an oyster or crab, by god, it was a fruit or vegetable. My parents made a killing, I understand, looking back on the weird operation. Sometimes we hauled otherwise goods. Sometimes we picked up hitchhikers for gas money. And sometimes my father let James out in the middle of Highway 17 and said we'd meet up with him some twenty miles up the road, usually at some unmarked beer joint.

"Do you have any interests besides dulcimer and steel pedal, Novel?" my father asked me more than once on these trips.

"I'm not all that interested in either, really," I would say. "Are we ever going to move somewhere else?"

My father smoked nonfiltered Picayunes, something he

picked up while playing with the New Orleans Symphony, he said. "I don't mind you playing football. I don't mind you becoming a lawyer." My father often drank during these family business outings. "Be honest with me."

I said, "I can tell you what I *don't* want to do for the rest of my life. I don't want to be in a loveless, make-believe marriage." I had been reading a fascinating exposé on FDR. My father thought I made an allusion—a word I picked up then in the seventh grade.

I didn't want to be a distance runner, highway construction worker, litter control worker, or botanist, I learned after Dad let me off on the berm—after he told me to think before I spoke—to meet James at the tavern in Rockingham. Or Apex, Climax, High Point, wherever.

"Ha, ha, ha," my brother said more than once. "Ha. Tell Dad you want to be a penis, like him." James would have already found ways to talk some bartender into giving over two Pabsts by the time I showed up unaware that most parents didn't let kids off in the middle of a two-lane road that intersected tobacco fields.

My father always said, "I read the want ads. Don't be a philosophy major. There's never a 'philosopher needed' section in the classifieds." He said, "Making people laugh might be the thing to do. There aren't enough people out there making us laugh."

I tried to explain all of this to Rebekah, even before she became Bekah. My upbringing came up when we met in Chapel Hill, and at my parents' odd and fearful funeral of sorts, and when Rebekah matriculated to her position at the collection agency. I said, "My father always thought I should be a comedian. He said I made people laugh."

My wife never said anything about how she needed to make people sneeze.

I got the job driving the Viper-Mobile soon thereafter. Maybe some people laughed. Maybe my wife. I know this: Either James or Joyce—more than likely James—pushed me off an overlook one time in the mountains back when Mom and Dad thought it necessary to see, hear, and delineate every waterfall in western North Carolina should we ever wander off confused. I hit my head and stayed unconscious for three days after James feigned the hero for saving me. Pretty much most of ages four through eighteen got lost because of this one episode. For me it's only dulcimer lessons, shrimp, conniving adopted siblings, more shrimp, a crazy visual artist who spoke in a Dutch accent, a supposed composer who stood around silent for minutes at a time. Driving. High expectations because of my name. I can't be sure, but I think I woke up in the middle of the night—maybe 1969—and overheard Joyce and James huddled in the corner, talking about bomb making. Not long thereafter, I heard Mom and Dad making promises: no more kids, no more lighters/matches/fertilizer/household cleaners in the house.

3

THE GRUEL INN hadn't operated since the 1950s at the latest. You know how the interstate highway system perfected by Lyndon B. Johnson destroyed motels and diners along Route 66, or Highway 1, or 301 between mid–South Carolina and northern Florida, or 29? Well those aforementioned American byways, when first constructed, caused the Gruel Inn to fold, even though Jefferson Davis, Robert E. Lee, and Charles Darwin had stayed there. William Tecumseh Sherman reportedly so feared the myth of the Gruel Inn and the wrath of its owners that he veered away toward Columbia.

I believed exactly zero of this story, of course, but by god the citizens of Gruel, Forty-Five, and most of Grayfuckingwood County found it to be what some psychiatrists and scholars might call a "raison d'être."

"I want you to trust me on everything that happens from here on out," Bekah reiterated when the final post-funeral goer left the family visitation with her Tupperware container of noodles Buenos Noches. "I don't want to reach retirement age and realize that I didn't follow my dream." Bekah went on and on. We sat in the kitchen of her parents' house. I got stuck with "to dream the impossible dream" flaring over and over in my mind—which is going to happen to you now, sorry—until I glanced around above the cabinets and saw a row of jackalopes. Sherrill Cathcart followed his dreams, too, I supposed, unless antlered rabbits roamed these parts.

I said, "I'm here for you. I've had some dreams of my own." First off, I thought it would be cool to maintain my own reptile farm—the popularity of those guys on TV had skyrocketed on PBS, Animal Planet, the Discovery Channel, and a couple of the cooking shows. But more than anything—call it middle-aged crises, and a fear that my life in this solar system was meaningless unless the basis of a meaningful existence consisted of spewing gases out into the atmosphere upon death—I felt obligated to live up to my name. Or at least my first name. Hell, I figured I could write an autobiography or memoir, call it *Novel*, and get readers buying both ways. Or I could write a regular novel—say, *Come Take a Ride in the Viper-Mobile*—which would have "A Novel" below the title, then my name. Oh, it would be what behaviorists and advertising executives might rightly call "subliminal."

Bekah bought the Inn for a dollar from Gruel township, from what I understood at the time, with the stipulation that she would refurbish and renovate the place into a respectable building in accord with Gruel's remaining businesses on the square: Victor Dees's Army-Navy Surplus store, Roughhouse Billiards, Gruel Drugs and adjacent Gruel Home Medical Supply, and so on. Well, not so much *so on*: Most of Gruel proper's square died right around my birth, from what I understood. Gruel BBQ and Pig-Petting Zoo thrived out on Old Old Greenville Road, just north of the town limits, but that was it.

The Gruel Inn, too, stood two miles outside of town to the south on Old Old Augusta Road. Here's how daring the youth of Gruel had been over the five-decade period of a vacant, vandal-ready brick establishment, a slight one-wing building set so close to the road a child who got his two arms clipped off in a thresher still could've thrown a rock or bottle and damaged a window, could've ridden by in a passenger seat with spray paint and graffitied the place up: Outside of a bad roof and water damage in rooms 4 through 12, the place appeared to be a life-like set for a 1940s Hollywood production that involved two buddies on a road trip who encounter maybe a couple hundred zombies.

I need to point out, though, that across the road stood a rain forest, desert, oasis, mountain, and part of Lake Between. Any blindfolded and kidnapped fool, flown around in a helicopter until confusion set in vis-à-vis time and space, then plopped down on the outskirts of Gruel, might announce, "So this is Costa Rica—land of the most diverse ecosystem on the planet!" But then he or she would hear gunshots within a minute, and the ruse would end, seeing as Costa Rica owns no standing army.

"I want to go on record as saying I would rather have Mom and Irby here with us today. I'm fully aware that I couldn't've started up the Gruel Sneeze 'n' Tone hadn't Momma's oxygen tank blown up. Lord knows your driving snakes around Charlotte wouldn't have ever given me the money." Bekah offered this little speech at the ribbon-cutting ceremony, a month after setting everything in motion. Here's who attended the festive event:

Novel.

I stretched the ribbon across the front office threshold and Bekah cut it in half with giant gag scissors she'd bought at an ex-beautician's yard sale down in Forty-Five. I thought about the afterlife, and how I would do my best to find and kill Irby and Vudge Ina Cathcart should I track them down.

◆ ◆ ◆

I'll give Bekah this: She researched allergies and irritants and the medical phenomenon of sneezing. Not to go backwards, but on or around 1996 something caused Bekah to start a two-week sneezing binge. She couldn't look into sunlight or fluorescent light, of course, but her seizures didn't slack off in pure dark, either. Achoo, achoo, achoo, achoo—four a minute. Two hundred forty per hour. Fifty-seven sixty in a day, eastern standard time.

She barely ate. We went to a doctor and his expert analysis went something like, "Did you accidentally inhale some black pepper?" That doctor called an allergist who stuck pins in my wife, everything from goldenrod to Charlie perfume. Nothing. The allergist—another Phi Beta Kappa genius—asked me, "Is there anything different in your household? Like a cat?"

"A cat!" I said. I popped my forehead like Laurel and Hardy. "Rebekah, this man is a *savior*." I promise on a stack of Hoyles that the doctor smiled to himself *job well done*. "Last week we took in a *cheetah*. It runs around so fast I hardly ever see it. It's *cheetah dander*, Rebekah. Thank you, Doctor. Thank you. When we get home we'll prop the door open and hope that thing runs away."

I took my wife out of there, musk of chimpanzee or whatever still stuck in her forearm. She held my arm like a blind woman might. She kept her eyes closed and mouth open—by

24

this time she didn't even attempt to cover her face, so I had to keep a handkerchief out in order to stymie the flypaper effect of hanging mucus from her nostrils.

I'd like to say that my wife ended up allergic to lawyers, bill collectors, the Department of Social Services, the Social Security Administration, and the pathetically inaccurate judicial system—she'd recently been named "Debt Collector of the Year" for the state of North Carolina, again—but that wasn't the case. There have been documented historical accounts of how one spouse became inexplicably allergic to the other. That wasn't the case, though, in the Akers's household. As sudden and unexpected and inexorable as her attacks started, that's how they stopped. Me, I don't remember it all that well because my favorite blacksnake—which I'd brought home to recuperate from an infection triggered by an overconfident, attacking mouse that caused the snake to secrete a strange milky substance at the end of its alimentary canal—finally died in its cage, right there at the foot of our bed.

Like I said, Bekah went from a hefty size fourteen to a 34-24-36 size six. From that point on, for the next couple years, she intook 2,500 to 3,500 calories a day three weeks out of the month, then spent a week snorting cayenne, baby powder, ragweed, and the contents of our vacuum cleaner bag in order to get back in shape.

Me, I feigned interest for about a year, but mostly thought up new fun facts and lies to tell schoolchildren, county employees, and 4-H clubs about the menagerie I drove around in a retired and converted bookmobile. I put up with Ina's biannual visits, her stories about how her husband could've stuffed my snakes so realistically that the state could save money raising mice. I humored Irby when he showed up at our small house off Trade Street—Irby always arrived between midnight and three in the morning—and drank my booze with him while he conducted monologues on such fascinating and diverse topics as massage therapy, spirit rocks, the police forces of south Georgia, his mother's button collection, what rehab clinic workers need to understand most, Mayan counterculture, healing creeks, milk thistle, his father's irrational expectations, how to shave properly, the secret government ingredients infused in every American cigarette, and—oddly—Bauhaus artists he admired. Irby also liked to tell me about the women he'd met in bars and jailhouse visits.

Irby didn't know that she'd been pierced down there, and five seconds into trying to pleasure her he wondered if he lost a filling: There's a possible and appropriate novel opening.

◆ ◆ ◆

This ended simple enough: The Gruel Sneeze 'n' Tone had a separate heat and air return for each room. I'm talking some crazy ductwork, an exorbitant cost for Trane or Carrier units, and so on. Bekah ran "The surgeon general and FDA won't approve my weight-loss program—because it works!" in every woman's magazine from *Ms.* to the AARP newsletter. She hired on a couple part-time old lady employees who once worked at Gruel Florists so I could spend my time over on Gruel Mountain searching out as-yet-undiscovered South Carolina anacondas.

Our eleven guest rooms—which went for two hundred dollars a day—were furnished with televisions, a single bed, the requisite toilet/shower/sink. We didn't arm the place with Gideons, but I talked Bekah into letting me place American history textbooks in every room, a book of poems by the Agrarians, *The Half-Mammals of Dixie*, and a photography book of Lisette Model's obese swimsuit wearers.

Our room — number 1 — had a vibrating bed. We didn't stay in Bekah's childhood home for a variety of reasons — I thought at the time — which ranged from my wife's superstitions all the way to my *own* superstitions.

So basically a handful of overweight women, unable to undergo stomach stapling or gastrointestinal slipknots, flew to either Atlanta or Charlotte, then rented cars equipped with global positioning devices in order to find their way to Gruel, South Carolina. If a tone-needy woman happened to be less than thirty-five years old, we found that she sneezed ceaselessly when inundated with White Linen perfume fogged into the room. Older women, some of whom lost senses of taste and smell over the years due to a combination of smoking and/or electric shock treatment, could only summon sneezes when my special sweat sock/potpourri/pre-1950 library book/ammonia-filled cat litter box concoction got piped into their quarters.

Bekah seemed delighted that I took such an interest in her clients. What the hell, I usually thought upon waking each morning. Bekah said, "I told you. I told you about this fantasy, Novel. I don't want to get all overachievement like when I thought I could go from debt collector to North Carolina's secretary of the treasury, but I'm thinking we might could start a franchise. The name 'Gruel' turns out perfect."

Looking back, I wish she would have said something about my walking off my job like a fool, and so on. I said, "There's a place in south Georgia named Porridge. That might be a place. All those rich Miami women might come up to Porridge."

The women came, the women fled—taking off all the weight they wished to shed. I'm serious. Bekah only spent advertising money once, and then word of mouth took care of everything else. We made twenty-two hundred dollars a day, for three months. The patients got two hours off every afternoon— Bekah understood that no one could undergo the sneezing rigors she'd unintentionally set up for herself. I drove my old step van into Gruel's square and let our customers out. They mostly walked around aimlessly. Some played pool at Roughhouse Billiards. All of them knew how to blow their noses farmer-style, which wouldn't gain us any Business of the Year awards from the chamber of commerce, should a real chamber ever crop up.

4

THERE'S A CONDITION in post-op circles called "adverse drug effect." Sure, anesthesiologists, surgeons, nurses, and the occasional candy striper shorten it to ADE. No one knows why certain people undergo hallucinations that would make Timothy Leary and his set come off as teetotalers, but it happens. It happened to Ina Cathcart for about one day, but all of us knew that her condition probably had more to do with no one knowing how to read scales at Graywood Regional Memorial, thus causing nurses to shoot her up with enough oxycodone to make Secretariat woozy.

But ADE can occur, evidently, without the D. You've seen these people before. The effect usually occurs after what some police officials and wives might call "seeing the light," and Jesus always comes into play. It took place with our goofball president, who supposedly gave up drinking—and all notions of social or economic theories—and found Gawd.

This has nothing to do with my story, really, but I have found that you should never befriend or hire anyone whose parents misspelled the kid's name at birth. I'm talking don't hire anyone named, say, Rusel, Howward, Andray, and so on. No woman named Juyne, Amee, or Fillis. Never, ever vote for a president whose parents named him Bubba, but spelled it George.

Okay. Back at the Gruel Inn, I witnessed the adverse drug effect minus the "drug" part inside room 3. Bekah signed in one Ms. Maura-Lee Snipes, a heavyset woman in her late thirties who ran a catering business down near Columbia. *Or so she said.* Maura-Lee said to me, "I get this feeling that no one wants to buy cakes and bread from an unfit woman. They see my cakes, then look at my hips. They put two and two together."

More like two and two hundred, I thought. Like I said, the spa stayed at full capacity right off. I agreed to give up, at that point, my dreams of owning my own reptile farm or of writing my memoir or novel called *Novel.* My job leaned toward changing sweaty bed linens, serving a light lunch, driving clients into town, and aiding Bekah in the long, long phony check-in questionnaire. Oh, we asked our dieters about previous health problems, whether they had high blood pressure or diabetes, if there was a history of heart disease on their family tree, if they were allergic to any types of prescription drugs or over-the-counter medicines, what foods they normally ate for breakfast, and so on. We went through about a thousand "Have you ever sneezed in the presence of . . . ?" questions. You wouldn't believe how many people say no to pollen, but yes to Irish Spring and Coast soap bars.

Anyway, Maura-Lee Snipes said she had no previous histories, that she went to an all-female college up in Virginia, and that she put on a good ten to twenty pounds per year there. She sat in our office—I learned on day one to reinforce our couch with an extra set of four legs—and said, "I noticed one time that

I had a sneezing fit from paprika. It was Cinco de Mayo last year. I had a big catering job for a party of Mexicans."

I wrote down "Irish Spring and paprika."

It needs to be said that, after only two months on the job, I had been anointed with the gift of envisioning these women at half their sizes and all shaped properly. If I were to actually write a memoir or novel, this would be what English teachers really stress in the eighth grade and call "foreshadowing."

I checked Maura-Lee in, sent her to room 3—which may have aided in her conversion seeing as all Christianity simmers on that father/son/holy ghost theme, or on that gold, myrrh, and frankincense theme—and set up the air-vent pipeline right away. I put my ear to the door, heard her first sneeze thirty seconds later, and went back to the office.

Some days, when the Gruel Sneeze 'n' Tone lived up to its capacity and name, I crossed the road and walked into the primordial forest to see how far I could go before not hearing twelve women a-sneezing. My strides are exactly three feet. The record distance was 247 yards, though I admit that somehow these particular women all sneezed together. You get eleven women in close confines—though in different rooms—and it doesn't take long for their clocks to readjust, you know.

I didn't get it. I thought about shelving my autobiography in order to research the idea.

"Room 3's good to go," I said to Bekah. She looked up from an ad we'd placed in *Woman's World* magazine. Bekah still insisted that we sell her family home, that we live at the old Gruel Inn. But her eyes told a different story, one that may be labeled "sleep deprivation."

She said, "I can't take much more of this. The noise! Even when I accidentally nod off I can only dream of a giant Laundromat, all the washers turned to heavy duty. The sneezing's driving me insane. Most of the day I spend my time trying to stifle sneezes in time with the clients'."

I will now admit that, perhaps, my marriage to Bekah was doomed by this point, though I didn't know that an elaborate scheme lie or lay hidden beneath it all. I could have easily said, "Yeah, I felt that way, too, for the first week. But then I went down to Gruel Drugs and bought a pair of tiny, hardly noticeable rubber earplugs."

But I didn't. I said, "To dream the impossible dream," meaning Bekah's fear of turning sixty-five and kicking herself for not following goals, et cetera, and knowing she'd now have either Jim Nabors's or Robert Goulet's voice in her head for a good ten hours, competing with the wash cycle. I said, "This new woman Maura-Lee seems like a real sneezer. I'm thinking if she works out, we might could get her to do some testimonials."

Of course we took before and after photographs. Of course Bekah got out a seamstress's cloth measure and tallied figures.

Bekah said, "Listen, I spoke with Paula Purgason earlier today. She's not a real real estate agent, but she's the best Gruel has to offer. She told me that the old Wiggins place has been on the market for nearly fifteen years. It's right at three thousand square feet."

"Same size as your dad and mom's."

"I'm glad you're paying attention. Well the Wiggins's grandkids have gone from asking a quarter-million dollars down to only seventy-five thousand. There's still been no one interested."

Bekah stuck her pinkies in her ears. I said, "There's nothing to do in Gruel, and little to do in Forty-Five outside of break a finger, go to Graywood Regional Memorial, and die under odd and sudden circumstances. Nothing against your hometown, honey, but I don't know why anyone would move here unless the government started witness protection."

My wife, I'm positive now, didn't mean for "Oh, there are reasons to live in Gruel" to come out audibly. Then she said, "Maybe I'll get in touch with the FBI. Well no, it's probably best not bringing the government down here checking out my people." Behind me all of the women responded to whatever irritant I had blowing into their vents. My wife, nearly psychotic from lack of sleep, spoke toward the window in our office.

I thought, Possible chapter 2 opening of *Novel—Essays*: It's a well-known fact that the Republican Party wants the poor poorer; indeed, with citizens unable to pay electric bills or purchase newspapers, then it's impossible for them to know what's going on, or even when to vote next. Seeing as a high percentage of Republican politicians—male and female—could never carry on a meaningful sexual relationship postadolescence, they want more poor people, which means more streetwalkers, which means it won't be so difficult to get laid.

I said to Bekah, "You need to go over to your folks' house and take a little nap. Go over there, get some rest, and think about selling it off for fifty grand. Or we could move in. I don't want to come off as highly logical and rational, but if your clients drive you crazy, then we could take out all the stuffed trophy heads and *move in, goddamnit.*"

You might have noticed by this point that not much has been said about our house in Charlotte. Had we sold it yet? No. Had we signed some kind of lease with a nice family originally from Pennsylvania? No. Did all of this hang over my head? *Fucking A yes.*

My wife began to cry. She welled up and fanned her face. "We wouldn't be going through all this if I hadn't lost weight. Why couldn't I have only started sneezing near a piano and found out I could play 'Smoke on the Water' by the way my hands flopped on the keyboard? Then I'd've had that dream."

I'm not lying. "Smoke on the Water"—which, I'm sure, a chimpanzee could learn to play during flea season. I said, "Believe me, you don't want to end up like my parents, Bekah."

I don't know if it was the crying jag or her first attempt to go by Kah, Kah, Kah, but my wife let out some noises I'm certain only B. F. Skinner ever came across.

◆ ◆ ◆

So Maura-Lee sneezed until she got orgasmic some six hours later—go look on the Internet and you'll see how it's not pure urban myth—and then eleven other fit-obsessed women moaned in unison, each from her room. It broke all records, believe me. I took out my earplugs and stepped off almost three hundred yards into the woods. Because I'm not one to hide anything I'll admit that some "ideas" crossed my mind that involved hidden cameras, tape recorders, and peepholes for the clientele of Roughhouse Billiards on the square.

Later on, long after her forty-pounds-lighter-in-just-two-weeks! stint, Maura-Lee Snipes told me it got to the point where she could no longer stand in her room, that she remained in the fetal position, sneezing and climaxing, and losing inches by the half day. Way later, she confessed to me that she often crawled around room 3 looking for a Gideon Bible in order to pray bet-

34

ter for God to stop the constant electricity that ran down there. She said she didn't want to be ruined for life, knowing that no other person (notice how I say "person" here, and not "man"—this'll come back later) could satisfy her near what a sneeze could offer.

I never said anything about how I might start off my novel one day with the labial piercing mistaken for a fallen-out piece of mercury filling.

"I have found a reason to live," Maura-Lee said upon completion of her stay with us. "I have to tell you—and I didn't mention it when I got here because I feared an intervention for my suicidal tendencies—but I planned to come here and flat-out die. I planned on never returning to Raleigh. And I *still* won't go back, except to pack my bags and move to Gruel."

Raleigh?

Bekah said, "Well I guess you got your wish. You want me to go ahead and charge your bill on the American Express?"

Maura-Lee nodded. She raised her palms upward, and sure enough it was apparent that she'd shaped up. I said, "I know of a house for sale." I said, "What would you plan to do here in Gruel?"

Now, I might not be the most perceptive man in regards to women, but because I worked with snakes for so long I could detect little subtle, secret movements that meant a strike neared. And I knew that I saw Bekah's head move to the left just enough so I couldn't see her either cut her eyes or widen them scarily toward Maura-Lee as one of those "don't say anything" international signals.

Maura-Lee said, "Never mind." See?

My wife said, "American Express has to be paid on time in

full," for some reason. I couldn't figure out that particular international signal.

"It's as if God came down and whispered in my ear," Maura-Lee said. "God said, 'You know how to bake bread. Go ye to a place where people need your talent.' As far as I can tell, there's no real bakery in this area. People need to know something better than Sunbeam King Thin. Or Pepperidge Farm pastries."

I didn't say anything about how we couldn't even get Wonderfuckingbread in Gruel, much less Pepperidge Farm, and how there had never been Sunbeam Bread since the dented-can store closed, some time back when Bekah grew up in Gruel. I said, "How about that. How about that, Bekah?"

But my wife didn't listen. She worked to keep her eyes open, to concentrate on the conversation. She'd not slept well since opening the "spa." And she'd foregone any sneeze therapy to eradicate those twenty extra pounds she'd put on since her mother's and brother's deaths, though she tried daily. Whatever it was that caused the original seizures just wasn't present in Gruel, though we experimented with Bekah's nose almost every time she returned from her utter devastation of Gruel Drugs' candy aisle.

5

IT WASN'T ONLY shrimp and moonshine growing up. Oh, I'm prone to exaggeration and habitual lying, I know—what smarter men and women call "hyperbole"—so let me confess that glimpses of my childhood reveal themselves at times much the same as that little polka-dotted man carrying a valise shows up when one ingests a gram-too-much psilocybin mushroom the night before his wedding.

Like I said, my parents were ex–concert pianists. They had long, long nimble fingers. What do nimble-fingered ex-musicians trying to raise a family of adopted and biological children in the North Carolina mountains take up in order to pay bills, put food on the table, and create college funds should said adopted children not run back to Ireland? I hate to bring up such obvious and rhetorical questions. It's almost embarrassing. You're probably way ahead of me.

Panning for gold wasn't the easy, scientific, rent-a-sluice kind of operation it is today. This was 1965 to 1975 or thereabouts. A lot of people think my parents either chewed tobacco or gnawed leg bones nonstop, what with their tiny, miniature, newborn-baby's-fingernails-sized teeth. But I say no emphatically.

Here's the possible opening to either my autobiography or novel: The neighbors didn't know how my parents tested possible gold nuggets sieved out of Rash Creek with their molars. There.

Joyce and James and I learned early on how and where to shovel. We filled five-gallon drywall buckets and lugged them to our parents' makeshift troughs onshore. We poured in the contents—mostly mud, mica, road gravel, smooth stones worthy of skipping across calm lakes near where rich kids camped summertime. My parents fished out the rubies, emeralds, sapphires—plus anything that wrongly resembled a Cherokee arrowhead—and gold. They somehow made enough money to pay off my hospital bills after James pushed me off the overhang. My parents could've put me through college had I not gotten some scholarship money, work-study grants, a loan, and so on. Once Joyce and James stroked back to their supposed birthplace my parents bought some extra land near Grandfather Mountain, built a series of tree houses for them and their new birder friends, and invested in high-tech binoculars and powerfully lensed cameras.

The last time I saw my folks, as a matter of fact, was when they said something about wanting to see a rare, rare purple sandpiper, or a rare, rare yellow-breasted chat, or a near-extinct American pipit, or some kind of lesser nighthawk. They needed to take a field trip down to south Florida in order to witness such ornithological oddities. According to both wildlife rangers and deputy sheriffs, a slither of alligators evidently wanted to see a mythical pair of humans down there in the Everglades.

It's the truth. It made the newspapers. And now it's on the Internet if you Google pianists/Akers/ornithology/severed limbs/overhead Miami weather crew/Cuban refugees found hiding/American pipit/binocular straps used for tourniquets/ Black Mountain College/James, Joyce, Novel/"Flight of the Bumblebee"/the sunshine state.

Look it up. Let me know if you get a "Your current search did not match any documents." I'll kill someone. I'll go find Google and beat the shit out of whoever collects info.

Or exchange "American pipit" with "Lesser nighthawk" and see what happens.

I'm okay. Back to the mining venture: When it wasn't worthwhile to head east for shrimp, et cetera, my parents and I hit the Second Broad River, creeks off Thermal City Gold Mine, Little Meadow, and all the Rash tributaries. Mostly we showed up two days after floodwaters peaked. Then my brother, sister, and I dug two or three feet below the beds of these shin-deep waterways, brought up our rocks, and hoped. Word was some fellow unearthed a seventeen-pound nugget once, but my parents might have only belittled us. I think the largest chunk any of us ever found wasn't much bigger than a brook trout's eyeball. My father said more than once, though, "We don't need a seventeen-pound nugget if y'all excavate 544 half-ounce chinks."

I think it was James who always coughed out, "Racist!" when my father made this claim. Or Joyce said it. Or me.

◆ ◆ ◆

Maura-Lee Snipes went home to Raleigh or Columbia, sold off what she didn't need, packed a long U-Haul, and returned to Gruel in order to unintentionally close down the Gruel Sneeze 'n' Tone spa. I'm here to say that we would've closed anyway. Bekah would've gone more nuts and killed a high-pitched sneezer within the month. Or she would've killed me had I been more persistent in keeping our marriage intact.

Through Paula Purgason—a woman who scoffed at sneeze therapy, and followed her own regimen of counting calories, exercising regularly, and downing bottles of No-Doz—Maura-Lee bought my wife's childhood home furnished. Then she rented what was last known back in the 1960s as Gruel Vacuum. Gruel Vacuum, from what I learned from the owner of Roughhouse Billiards, didn't stay in business more than a year seeing as people like Bekah's parents understood how brooms cost less, lasted longer, and took about the same energy. Plus, brooms didn't run up the electric bill.

Maura-Lee Snipes opened Gruel Bakery, and started right off baking everything in the form of a cross—gingerbread men, crescent rolls, pecan pies. I'm pretty sure she ordered pans from a Christian organization out of Lynchburg, Virginia.

She baked a special Jewish rye covered in what she called "Jesus crust."

Jesus crust, I swear! You'd think that people would view this as sacrilegious, but the opposite occurred. Even known heathens like Victor Dees from next-door Victor Dees's Army-Navy Surplus store popped in each morning and said, "Give me some Jesus crust. I need Jesus crust. Fill my belly with Jesus crust!" and whatnot.

I'm not sure how much real butter this woman used, but when I drove our Gruel Sneeze 'n' Tone women into town daily, and when they discovered the bakery, something happened. It was almost as if Bekah and I saw our clients gain five pounds upon their return. It's as if we saw happy, slimming, orgasmic women lose any ground they'd gained—or lost—once they got back in my step van.

"We have to keep them here twenty-four hours a day. That's it. There's no other option," Bekah said.

Me, I couldn't believe that it was our only choice. I'll admit now that maybe I wasn't a 100 percent team player in regards to my wife's business venture.

Oh—I need to tell the story about how my debt collector wife wanted to call it simply the Gruel Sneeze 'n Tone. I said, "If you want to call it that, then you have to put an apostrophe after the *n* also. An apostrophe stands for missing letters. If you call your place what you want to call it, there's a missing *d*," et cetera. I wrote it out on a piece of paper, right after writing my resignation letter to the state of North Carolina. I said, "Let's just go with the entire word 'and.' It won't take any longer to understand. And we won't be grouped with places that sell biscuits 'n' gravy, liver 'n' onions, fun 'n' games, you know. It takes the same amount of time typing out, anyway."

So much for my powers of persuasion.

"I can't believe that our best client would turn on us," Bekah blurted out, back to our story. The bags beneath her eyes fell down past the point where her lips would've turned up, should she ever smile. "Jesus crust. That's just not right."

"I think it's funny. Crustians. It's funny."

My wife looked at me as if I'd projectile vomited on her blouse. She looked down at the old-timey ledger we kept for lodgers. "This is not how I foresaw everything happening. Maybe I haven't had time to grieve Irby's and Ina's tragic deaths. This isn't how it should be."

I looked down at the ledger. I'd made a point not to get emotionally attached to these women, and tried not to even remember their names. I didn't want to be crestfallen should one lose hope, or get sick, and so on. I only knew that, at most moments, there was at least three thousand pounds of quivering women in my midst.

But let me say two things: I had noticed how Bekah strode through her brother's and mother's deaths as if they'd only taken a Caribbean cruise and would return presently. And when I met Rebekah, I truly fell in love. That's two things.

I'm not sure how it happened, but my odd parents instilled a "stick with it" mind-set in my adopted siblings — *obviously* to them, seeing as they took off — and me, no matter how difficult the situation. I had long ago talked myself into waiting Bekah out. I had converted, so to speak.

"Malleable" might be the word.

Bekah said, "It was free money. My father's three-story house. I don't care about the heads. I miss Charlotte. I need some time. And space."

I didn't say anything about Heidegger or Sartre. I said, "Ham and cheese on Jesus crust. Corned beef on Jesus crust. Roast beef on Jesus crust. Pimento cheese, chicken salad, tuna, braunschweiger. Jesus crust."

Bekah said, "I knew you'd take her side. I knew."

I didn't say how maybe I'd been looking down at the CD player, how maybe Irby didn't flick his cigarette out the driver's side window, how perhaps I touched his back bumper in a way that would cause him to veer over an embankment and cause Vudge Ina's oxygen tank to explode. I said, "What're you talking about, Bekah?"

She said, "It's all paid for. You can stay here and do what you want. Take room 1. Take room 3. You need to find your own way. What happened to your dream of a giant snake farm? I know how much you love those vipers."

I shrugged. I didn't say anything about *Novel*, the novel, or *Novel*, the autobiography. I said, "You're leaving? You're letting go of everything we worked so hard to put together out here in this no-man's-land?"

Bekah didn't look me in the face. "When's the last time we had sex? I don't need to have sex. I've sneezed more sex than we've ever had in twelve years. No offense, Novel. But that's the way it is."

Luckily we had two cars. Bekah left in the Jeep. Me, I got stuck with the old step van. Behind me, a good eleven women sneezed. I knew that I wouldn't shove allergens into their air vents again.

Now, a lot of you people will think that I let Bekah go for the money—kind of like a person would quit writing short stories exclusively to write a novel—but that's not the case. This story's about reptiles. It's about snakes. It's about slithering animals, and my attempt to write a life story. My parents did the best that they could do. They played piano, sold shrimp, and panned for gold.

I'm not making excuses.

6

I HAND-LETTERED the sign back to its original moniker: The Gruel Inn. After a month of answering the telephone, of telling desperate women that the Sneeze 'n' Tone took no more customers—and I'll admit that I spent most of that month calling Bekah and pleading for her to come back, plus my old boss in Charlotte pleading for my Viper-Mobile job—I went out with a bucket of latex and opened for business. This was February, the shortest month, so it's not like I groveled myself away. No, I pretty much aired out the rooms constantly, got the various odors out—except that god-awful roomful-of-old-women White Linen that worked as one of our most productive sneeze enticers—and tried not to think of Anthony Perkins in *Psycho*.

I caught a couple of nice blacksnakes, a couple corn snakes, and a baby rat snake. I kept them in separate aquariums I bought from some lost fellow named Drew Gaston passing through on his way to a convention of exotic fish salespeople.

I drank daily at Roughhouse Billiards.

"Say, that woman put y'all out of business," Jeff the owner said every late morning when I arrived. I had no clue as to Jeff's last name. He always stuck out his hand and introduced himself as "Jeff the Owner."

"Pretty much. In her own way. Maura-Lee and Jesus crust. That sounds weird. That sounds about right."

I started off each day with a shot of Jim Beam and a can of Pabst at this point. I always kept an open notebook, should some kind of novel or memoir idea hit me. Mostly it never happened, outside of "After the sneezing drove my wife crazy—within a year of her mother and brother getting killed from my accidentally hitting their back bumper and shoving them over into old Forty-Five landfill—there was nothing left to do except close down our spa and wait for answers."

Jeff the owner said, "You gone reopen the Gruel Inn as the Gruel Inn? I hope so. Gruel's growing, man. We need us the motel."

Roughhouse Billiards never held more than two other customers. These guys were always covered in flecks of paint and practiced trick shots on the one pool table. If I had a case quarter for every time I overheard, "Around three banks, up the cue sticks, down the cue sticks, bounce off the saltshaker, light the pack of matches, eight ball in the corner pocket," I'd've been able to add another twelve rooms to the Gruel Inn.

I pointed down to the cooler for another beer and looked across the square at Gruel Bakery. "It's growing, all right."

"Man, there's gone be some kind of art car show here next year. You ever seen those people paint up their station wagons with macaroni and such? They coming *here*. I don't know how our chamber of commerce pulled it off—well, Paula Purgason's our entire chamber of commerce, I suppose—but they did. I wouldn't be surprised if we hosted the next Olympics, you know."

One of the pool players said, "Well if that happens we got the gold medal in trick shots. Hey, watch this: around the banks, up the cue sticks, down the cue sticks, bounce off the salt-shaker," and so on.

"That Maura-Lee woman ever come in here after work?" I asked Jeff. "I mean, after she's done with baking for the day?"

"She bought your mother-in-law's place up Old Old Green-ville Road, didn't she?"

"I guess. I ain't seen any of that money. My crazy wife, Bekah, took that money."

"That *dough*. Get it? Maura-Lee Snipes started a bakery up." Jeff the owner wiped down an already-clean countertop. He slicked back his already-slick-backed hair. "Jesus crust."

I took a beer on the house and tried not to think about Maura-Lee in a roomful of stuffed heads. I said, "We'll have to put a stop to all this," which I knew made no sense in regards to the conversation at hand. But it was the exact same thing one of those Native Americans supposedly said when Custer's forces reached a hilltop.

History!

✦ ✦ ✦

She'd installed the only ding-door in all of Gruel. When you opened the front door to Gruel Drugs, Victor Dees's Army-Navy Surplus, and the Gruel Home Medical Supply stores, nothing happened, but at Gruel Bakery a loud *ding!* sounded to let Maura-Lee know she had a carbo-loading customer.

I walked in and said, "Maura-Lee, I want to talk to you about how you helped ruin my marriage."

She came out of the back room wearing oven mitts. Maura-Lee said, "Well it's about time. What're you feeding those women over at the spa? It ain't bread. Don't you love me anymore?"

Maura-Lee looked great. I said, "Where've you been lately? We're out of business and Bekah up and left me."

She took off one mitt, then the other. I should mention that she wore her hair in two braids, and that those braids ended right at her nipples. She looked like an off-blond woman posing for a Swiss Miss commercial. "Oh, I'm sorry, Novel," she said. "Hey, you wouldn't want any jackalopes over at your place, would you? They're kind of freaking me out all over the walls."

You would think that a place that prided itself on Jesus crust would play Billy Graham loops over and over, or Amy Grant, or any of those gospel quartets. Maura-Lee had the Clash blaring. I said, "What the hell."

"Come on back here, man." In my head I heard her going on to say *I've loved you since we first met.* I saw her juke her head, and I went around the counter as if on autopilot. She put the oven mitts back on—could this be for some kind of kinky hand job? Maura-Lee said, "I have no clue what you're talking about with Bekah leaving you. Hey, are these cockroaches or palmetto bugs or some kind of mutant silverfish nesting back here under my sacks of flour?"

◆ ◆ ◆

Maura-Lee lived up to her name, as it ended up, to my disappointment. I was lying on the cement floor of what was once

47

Gruel Vacuum, beside a giant dough mixer, Maura-Lee not straddled across my torso. She said, "Victor Dees said he kept too much Vietnam jungle bug repellent to ever have a need to know insects. I thought maybe you'd know something about these things."

I said, "I thought you were going to bring me back here to tell me how much you loved me, that we should get married. I thought by now you'd have those hips gyrating like all of you women did in a middle of a good sneezing fit."

Maura-Lee walked past the flour sacks and opened the back door. She said, "I'm not that way."

"Maura-Lee. Morally," I said.

She untied and retied her apron. "Yep. Well I guess not completely, but I don't want to talk about it right now."

Maura-Lee looked like Vivien Leigh. She looked like skinny-waisted Scarlett Fucking O'Hara with some loose skin. *Ding!*

"You better get the door," I said. "I'll stay down here pretending like you don't have a roach problem. Someone just came in the door."

"Jesus crust," a woman yelled. "You got any Jesus crust rye bread back there?"

I heard Maura-Lee say, "I've got two more loaves till tomorrow."

Down there on the floor I thought about how rye bread had little seeds in it that looked similar to chopped-up cockroach body parts. When Maura-Lee came back and said the coast was clear, I didn't get up. I didn't ask her if she'd wish to reconsider dating me, or at least fucking me. I said, "I'll take as many of those jackalopes as you want to give up. I'm working on some new ideas, and it might be good to have a beady stare honing down on me from every room."

Maura-Lee turned on her dough mixer and leaned back against it in a way that reminded me of my sister Joyce when the family dryer ran. I know I might rationalize, but it made me feel better about myself.

◆ ◆ ◆

My history of philosophy professor, a guy named Dr. Harold Simkins, said I had a quirky mind. He said that I should either join the CIA or get a job inventing crossword puzzles. I had taken a hankering to Hume and that "blocked habit of expectation" notion. Dr. Simkins said it was an unnatural choice on my part.

"The problem with people like Hume is, he tears down the canon, but never offers a rebuilding plan," Dr. Simkins told me one day in his office. Looking back, I'm pretty sure he had his pants around his ankles there behind the desk. "You, Mr. Akers, need to involve yourself with a philosopher who takes chances—a man who can rightfully tear down his predecessors, yet construct new foundations."

I remember this day fully—outside of Simkins's exposed thighs—because the dogwoods bloomed and a slight breeze kept the campus aglow. I held a pint of bourbon in my back pocket. "Yeah, yeah, yeah," I said. "Let's talk about people who constructed new foundations: Mussolini, Tito, Lenin, Stalin . . . who'm I missing?"

I pulled out the bourbon. Simkins took two glasses out of his desk drawer. "Okay," he said. "I still think you'll go into the CIA, or work for the *New York Times* crossword puzzle division."

We clinked glasses.

"I don't think I'll be doing any of those things for a living, with all due respect," I said.

"What could be worse? Say, what're you doing tonight? My wife's gone to see her sister in Wisconsin."

I'd already met and courted Rebekah. I said, "Maybe we'll come by your place later. Maybe."

"You're a spy from way back when. You're a spy. Also, I'd like to see you quit drinking for at least a few weeks out of the year. Do you think you can do it?"

I thought about this little scene as I left Gruel Bakery, on my way across the square to Roughhouse Billiards. In a way Dr. Simkins foresaw my future—I'd torn things apart with no aim to rebuild them. Marriage. Jobs. Future plans.

And I haven't even admitted to the other part of my snake-driving duties, the part that may have affected every citizen in North Carolina at one time or another.

7

I CAN'T KNOW for sure if my wife immediately called Joyce and James, but they appeared at the Gruel Inn within a week of my repainting the sign. They brought no spouses or children, though they came armed with family photos and stories. I had stayed in touch with them slightly over the past twenty-plus years—mostly we sent cards to each other on June 16 and St. Patrick's Day. My brother and sister sent a sympathy card on the occasion of our parents' exotic and supposed deaths.

"We, the both of us, almost made the Olympics in 1980 and 1984," James said. He had a beautiful, lilting accent now. We sat in what I considered my new office at the inn. "So. What have you been up to, Novel-boy?"

Joyce worked for the *Irish Times*—she had become a real writer—and James spent his days in a Dublin pub due to "disability." He'd evidently blown out his knees from distance running and, though he'd been a secondary school teacher and cross-country coach, talked the government into believing his frailties.

I said, "My wife talked me into this place. I quit my job and cashed in my retirement, stupid. This motel used to be a motel, then we turned it into a spa of sorts. Now it's something in between."

James said, "What happened to those snakes? You're not still scaring people with the snakes, are you?" What should've tipped me off that my brother and sister weren't true, true Irish orphans back in the day was their noncommittal attitude toward what mountain snakes lived in our midst growing up — copperheads, timber rattlers, northern water snakes, and the like.

"I had to hand over my job snakes, but I caught some other ones over there." I pointed across the street toward Gruel Mountain. "I got them in aquariums out back in a shed."

But maybe returning to Ireland brought back James's once-lost cultural instincts, for I have to say this: once a runner, always a runner when it's time to choose flight or fight. It was a good thing that his disability officer hadn't traveled with them to Gruel, because as soon as the words "caught some other ones" came out of my mouth those Irish "blokes" took off like Democrats in search of free government cheese during a Republican administration. And when they found themselves outside — in the land of snakes — they rushed back in. Joyce said, "Well that goes to show how long it's been since we've been to the States."

I wish I had remembered the truth. My snakes were no longer in their aquariums. The last time I'd seen them they coiled at the ready for a patch of field mice that nested in the wall between rooms 3 and 4. I said, "I wish y'all had brought your families. Can you stay awhile? James, why don't you take your suitcases and bed down in either room 3 or 4. Joyce, you take the other. Those are the cleanest right now."

There was no talk as to the length of their stay, or if indeed Bekah had invited them to look after me. "We're only traveling around," James said. "We both felt like we needed to come back down to the South and revisit our old haunts. What with the IRA and England getting along better, it's not as much fun living in Ireland. I might even look for a job."

I handed my brother two keys. "We only have one bar in town. But it opens early. There's no Catholic church anymore until you get to about Atlanta."

"You sound like you don't want us here," Joyce said. "One bar."

Even though I did want to be left alone for a good year or ten, I said, "Not at all. I mean, no, y'all are welcome to stay forever. It's just not going to be as exciting as Black Mountain, and you remember how boring that place was after the college shut down." I said, "Go put y'all's suitcases up. Then I'll take you to the square." I figured they wouldn't need to clean up, really. They'd only been in transit for two days, not an overly extended period of time between baths for a typical European, I thought.

While they hung up their clothes I backed the step van right up to their rooms and waited. Joyce came out of 3 in a few minutes. She got in the passenger seat next to me and said, "You've obviously done well for yourself, Novel. I've been thinking about writing a memoir about how our parents adopted us, and how he and I were such buttholes. I've always regretted running away back to my homeland. Our parents did nothing but love us, you know. In their way. We shouldn't have driven them toward bird-watching and their ultimate deaths."

I shoved an early Pogues CD in the player. It still hadn't occurred to me that my new snakes might have James cornered and/or fainting. "Tell me about your job at the paper."

Joyce rolled her blue eyes and shook that black, black hair of hers. "I mostly deal with local news, but there's talk of sending me to Paris. Wouldn't that be something? The Paris bureau chief for the *Irish Times*."

We sat in the van for what seemed to be another fifteen minutes. Joyce told me all about the flight to New York, then to Charlotte, then the rental car and how they spent an hour in Forty-Five, South Carolina, trying to find a person who knew how to get to Gruel. I said, "I better go check on James. Maybe I forgot to put toilet paper in the bathroom."

Like that would matter, now that I think about it.

Joyce told me to hurry up, that she was so thirsty she could drink a St. Louis beer.

Okay, so this American history professor I had back in undergraduate school, he specialized in William Henry Harrison and made all of his students take a YMCA-sponsored CPR course, so I thought I knew how to find a pulse, feel for breath, et cetera. There was no way I could count on an ambulance showing up within six hours or thereabouts in order to take my brother James all the way out to Graywood Emergency Regional Memorial.

So I found James flat on his back beside the bed, seemingly gone. I looked around, thought about those mouse-hunting snakes I'd scattered around the motel, and so on. I yelled for Joyce, who helped me get James in the back of the step van. She said, "It must've been a massive heart attack."

I drove so fast my windshield wipers blew right off. On the way, over the noise coming in my open doors, I said to Joyce, "This isn't the best hospital in the world, but I guess it's better than nothing. I'd trust taking James to a vet, but I don't know of any around here."

She looked straight ahead. Thinking back on it now, I kind of glimpsed a smile on her face.

I wheeled into the emergency room entrance, ran to the back of the van, opened the doors, and found no brother there. Had we forgotten to load him up? Was his heart attack so massive that it imploded his body? Joyce sashayed back to where I was right about the time a young black orderly came out and said, "The cafeteria entrance on the other side. Take the bread there."

To Joyce I said, "Did he fall out the back and somehow the door closed behind him? Get in, get in." Again, she seemed to be in no rush. Was this some kind of last joke on a little brother? Did James hear me say those bad things about the hospital, come to, and feel that he'd be better off rolling down the asphalt than being treated for a heart ailment by some doctor who couldn't find a sink to wash his hands in?

We backtracked three or four times. "This is some kind of magic trick y'all played on me," I said.

"Maybe not us," Joyce said. "Maybe us, but probably not us. And don't ask why, 'cause we don't know either."

◆ ◆ ◆

My wife blamed neighborhood kids back in Charlotte, but looking back I now understand that she probably added another V to the beginning of the Viper-Mobile, thus making me drive the Wiper-Mobile for two days before noticing the practical joke. I'm not even sure I would've noticed it at all had I not gone to the Piedmont-Charlotte Retirement Center and had a dozen octogenarian women come out to the parking lot ready to change their adult diapers. Yes, I got sent out to retirement homes on occasion seeing as a harmless, innocent snake's worst foe, oftentimes, is an old woman armed with a hoe. Halfway houses for our unfortunate retarded comrades also ranked high on the Viper-Mobile's places to visit.

"Somebody changed the name of my step van," I said one afternoon to Bekah.

"I didn't do it. It wasn't me. It wasn't me or I—I always forget the correct English. I don't know anything about it," Bekah said.

This was a month before her mother's hospitalization and subsequent death of questionable means. For the record, I had wanted Ina Cathcart treated in Charlotte, not Graywood County. Irby got drunk, called me up, and said, "Between me and you— or I and you—it might not be all that bad for Mom to have some shoddy care. There's a lot of money tied up in the old homestead. I'm thinking fifteen, twenty thousand, not counting the deer heads and stuffed turkeys."

I said, "I'm not following. Do you need to borrow some money? I can lend you a few hundred or thereabouts."

Irby cleared his throat and tapped the receiver with something. He said, "I'm not in jail."

"Hey, your brother's not in jail," I yelled back to Bekah in the bedroom.

She said, "Good." She said, "That's something worth writing down in a diary."

I said to my brother-in-law, "You haven't been down here any lately, have you? Somebody put some graffiti on my step van as a joke, I guess. I don't know how long it's been on the side panels, to be honest."

Irby said, "I'm serious as a cup of lye, man. She'll die one day anyway. She's got to die some time. I figure Rebekah and I could split the money up equal, bury her right, and still have a bunch left over."

I had no other choice but to say, "Irby, you're out of your mind. What would you think if you had kids who wanted you in a less-than-respectable hospital? It's your mother, by god. It's your momma."

"You're right," Irby said. I heard him stomp his foot down, or pop himself upside the temple. "Goddamn I'm glad I got you on the other line. What am I thinking?"

At the time Irby was in between a regular construction job and serving four to six months in jail for destruction of private property. Me, I always liked him. He couldn't make it to our wedding for reasons that changed over the years, but he did send a picture of himself wearing a blue tuxedo and said he'd be honored if Bekah and I propped it up where a best man might stand. "I can send you a thousand dollars," I said. "You'll be able to pay it back someday, right?"

In the background I heard Ina Cathcart yelling for Irby to get off the telephone. He said to me, "Two thousand could get me out of Gruel and back to the United States."

8

I STAYED IN TOUCH with Bekah weekly while I made new plans. She called, she apologized, she blamed it on premenstrual syndrome, post-traumatic stress, premenopausal depression, post-401(k) shock once her retirement plan proved to be slow moving. Notice how there was no present. Every one of her problems either dealt with an unfair past or a bleak future. "I've gone back to my old job. I'm living back in the old house, too. Let's just say that the renters decided to break their lease."

Let me point out that the times we spoke she started off every conversation with, "I've gone back to my old job," and so on, like she suffered some kind of Korsakov's Syndrome.

I didn't know if she meant any of this to be a lure, a sign that her mental health had stabilized. I always said, "Well getting your job back should take your mind off things. That should lift any depression, hanging out with people who prey on poor remission-ridden cancer patients." I had long believed that half of all female nurses went into the field only to meet doctors, and all female hospital bill collectors only to meet administrators and lawyers. But I also believed that all male mechanics had a need to grasp their greasy tools eight hours a day.

"Gene Weeks here thinks I've let you off too easy. He says you ought to be renting the Gruel Inn from me. Or that I should be getting upwards of 50 percent of net."

Remember that all of this situation took place in less than six months. I don't care that it sounds unrealistic — that if this were my autobiography *Novel*, you might yell out "I'm not willing to suspend my disbelief!" Not everything moves at a twenty-year-old crankcase oil's pace in the South.

I said to Bekah, "You can have 90 percent of the gross, for all I care. As far as I can tell it doesn't cost more than fifty dollars a month to live in Gruel. I can make that with two lost truckers a month."

I didn't tell my ex-wife — or, technically, my estranged wife — that I'd not had a boarder since my sister and brother checked in for a quarter hour. And I certainly didn't tell her about my future plans that, ultimately, would put me precariously close to both prison sentence and extended stay at the asylum in Columbia. Look, I had noticed in those back pages of Bekah's women's magazines a cluster of "artists retreat" and "writers haven" places for rent, usually in Vermont, Colorado, western North Carolina, northern Georgia, both coasts of Florida, New Mexico, Arizona, the Sierra Nevada, Maine, Tahiti, and Belize. There were so-called writers and artists out there willing to spend twenty-five hundred dollars a month to live in a cell and cook on a woodstove as long as there were "scenic views" and "lush trails."

Well I got out my machete and Weed Eater and blazed a good one-mile lap across from the Gruel Inn almost immediately. Then I paid for this advertisement in the back pages of all those magazines: "Writer's paradise: come live and study with secluded Novelist in quaint, uncluttered, pristine location. There's nothing else to do but hide out and write with Novelist."

At least that's what came out. I had written "Novel Akers, secluded in quaint, uncluttered, pristine location," but the copy editors in the ad department saw it otherwise. I offered no grants or stipends, no Grand Master Writer-Teacher/Master Writer-Teacher/Teacher/Upcoming Writer/Writer/Sycophant/Waiter type of hierarchy. It would cost prospective "students" five hundred dollars a week, with only a continental breakfast provided, a cash bar happy hour, plus a change of sheets every other day.

It took me a good eight hours to think this through, no lie.

One day after my ad came out I got fifty calls. By the end of the month I had reservations going into the next year. These were mostly wives of the wealthy, scattered across the country, all ready to bear down on a reader with tales of their pathetic, boring lives. I didn't care. I "couldn't have cared less," as they say in the "writers haven" field.

But I kind of wondered why more than a few of them asked if I was Thomas Pynchon, J. D. Salinger, Cormac McCarthy, or Charles Portis.

Maura-Lee and I met about the plan and devised a bagel/croissant/biscuit breakfast when the would-be novelists showed up. I talked to Jeff the owner and he said the cash bar happy hour didn't sound too promising as far as his business dealings were concerned, unless I let him sell me minibottles of booze and a special Bloody Mary mix he'd learned from, of all people, Sherrill Cathcart.

I called about everyone in Graywood County in order to get Internet service lines installed for the laptops I foresaw being brought in. Most people said, "What the hell's Internet? You mean like badminton and volleyball? You might want to call up Graywood Hardware and Sporting Goods."

I drove to Atlanta, found a used bookstore, and bought every available text on writing fiction, nonfiction, poetry, and screenplays should any of my guests ask a difficult question that involved plot or character. This one book I got offered a hundred anecdotes about famous writers hating each other and the fights they endured both physically and emotionally. I buried my machete.

◆ ◆ ◆

Well it didn't take my first night with nine old women and two old men—I put myself in room 3 what with my brother's possible specter living inside, plus the possible snakes, and kept the office open with coffee urns and ashtrays—before I knew that plagiarism might be in my future. If I wanted to live up to my name, what would be a better way to start than, "My slutty daughter isn't going to go far in life seeing as she dropped out of eighth grade on the third go-round, then got a job at the carpet factory as the official carpet burn tester"?

This is, word for word, what one Mrs. Donna-Rose Green told me while waiting for her special decaf to brew. Donna-Rose Green said that she didn't intentionally marry her husband of twenty-seven years so she'd have a memorable, Christmas-colored name, though ever since she had a vision to tell the story of her life she knew that the name would be an asset. "It means 'beautiful rose green.' In Italian. Well officially I guess part in Italian and part in English."

In fucking Crayola, I thought. "Carpet burn tester, huh?"

"She gets to wear short pants to work every day. You can't say that about anyone else still working up in Dalton," Donna-Rose Green said.

I didn't ask her why she didn't go to a writers retreat closer to her home, for I knew that she'd worn out every other director or innkeeper. I didn't ask where she got the money, either. She had slipped-on-the-Wal-Mart-floor written all over her giant blank face. I made a mental note not to mop during her stint. "Okay. Your coffee's ready, Ms. Green. Now get on back to your room and finish up that manuscript. You owe the reading public. Hurry up, hurry up, hurry up!"

"Yes sir, Coach Novel! Them's the kind of butt-kicking words of encouragement I don't get at home, goddamn it."

I locked myself up in room 3 and called Maura-Lee. I said, "How much would you charge me for making a special laxative-glazed doughnut for in the morning?"

She laughed. "You want to come over here and spend the night? I'm talking like brother and sister spend the night, not the other. Your guests will be all right by themselves."

In room 4 I could hear a Mr. Burnett typing about two hundred words a minute. In room 2 a woman who said she could only be known by her pen name—Anonymous—cried uncontrollably. I said, "I've made a big mistake. I've screwed up. Somewhere in a previous life I must've killed sacred cows willy-nilly."

Maura-Lee said, "Been there, done that, got a scrapbook of torn stubs to prove it." She sneezed a few times and said she'd gained an inch or two around the middle. "Listen, you're an adult, Novel. Get out that notebook of yours and write everything down. I'll come by and visit you for a longer stretch of time when you get to about chapter 10."

I hung up and opened a bottle of Old Crow. I wrote down, "I'm not sure what kind of séance correspondence course my ex-wife took with the Marquis de Sade, but I would figure it out before she got me killed, too."

9

ONE OF THOSE books I got for my needful writers explained how all kinds of literature could be classified either ab ovo or in medias res. Old-timey novels, like those of Charles Dickens, tended toward the ab ovo. More modern pieces went straight to the middle of things, got right to what this particular writing professor—who had published forty-seven novels, none of which I'd ever seen in a normal bookstore—called "conflict." I reread his first chapter twice, and memorized entire passages.

I'll say this: The people who shelled out five hundred a week for quiet and solitude, for the most part, worked hard for three days in a row. Over the long months that the Gruel Inn became the Gruel Inn Writers Retreat, almost every so-called would-be writer holed up for seventy-two hours before coming out to talk.

And then they *talked.*

Maybe there's some kind of mechanism in the brain that clicks on after three days, telling the body it needs human inter-action. Or maybe people who spend good money to find writing time don't really have much more than three days of ideas. It seems to me that it wouldn't be all that difficult to take pictures off your wall at home, tell the kids and spouse and dogs to shut up, and get about the same effect as what you got in Gruel. Someone should do a long-term study.

The women emerged from their rooms ready to talk about their interesting characters, how difficult it was for a woman to get published in New York City, their one-of-a-kind plots that are keeping them from their just dues on the *Today Show*, how a famous writer up in Vermont said that he'd tell his agent about such interesting characters and plot, how their adolescent kids will one day be great writers, et cetera.

The few men circled these women in my registration office turned smoking lounge, only thinking about getting some strange. I knew that look: I'd witnessed it twelve years running at the annual convention for lieutenant governors' speechwriters.

So much for ab ovo. I probably need to backtrack again.

Driving the Viper-Mobile happened to be what is known in some circles as "a cover." In North Carolina there were a good twenty or thirty Viper-Mobile drivers, lower-level zoo officials, pig farm run-off inspectors, black bear trackers, and so on, all of whom really got paid by taxpayers to write speeches for those who needed to but couldn't do it themselves, namely governors, lieutenant governors, the superintendents of education, state senators and representatives, and so on.

Going further backwards: one thing I learned while living in Gruel and watching local news—South Carolina could've used such a system.

Anyway, and I don't know about my colleagues, I got paid ninety grand a year to supposedly showcase snakes to the public. And I did that part of my job well. But at night—and most every day in the step van—I wrote out five-hundred- to three-thousand-word speeches for the lieutenant governor that both outlined and offered specific details on such topics, urgent and diverse, as school lunch menus, hurricane evacuation routes, the proper place to tie yellow ribbons on trees during state and/or national emergencies, four-way stop sign etiquette, the list goes on. It used to be part of a plan to flash my lights toward oncoming traffic when driving on I-85, I-40, I-95, or I-77 so that other drivers thought a speed trap lay ahead, but once state funds dropped dramatically due to decreased speeding ticket revenue, the lieutenant governor decided we could all live with out-of-control "vehicular operators."

All right. I feel better now that I've admitted this part of my life, one that *Bekah never knew.* Hell, she thought I only earned hourly wages and a nice benefits package as a Viper-Mobile specialist. I had a hard time staying quiet when she piped up about something stupid the lieutenant governor said on the six o'clock news like, "If we all recycle our outdated telephone books, then there will be more trees available in the future for telephone poles."

I wrote that one on purpose one day when I was angry at Jesse Helms for one reason, or another thousand reasons. I'm contrite about taking it out on our lieutenant governor. Another day when I felt like I couldn't take it anymore I wrote out a speech detailing how North Carolina welcomed new businesses to locate in the Research Triangle, from burgeoning nations such as Chad, Rwanda, and Niger. His mispronunciation of that last country really got him scolded, and maybe lost him a few votes the next election.

"The role of the writer is to tell his story in a less convoluted and more mesmerizing way than the average man on the street. We could all learn from the dolphins and whales," I announced during happy hour of day three. I'd rehearsed this little speech straight out of one of those how-to-write-a-novel-in-your-sleep textbooks.

My campers and I stood around outside the office, listening to what may or may not have been howler monkeys in the forest across Old Old Augusta Road.

Of course it was Donna-Rose Green who said, "In my novel, I have dolphins swimming with my main character who's got cancer. These dolphins come out of the Atlantic Ocean, swim up the Savannah River, cross into North Carolina via the Chattooga and Ocoee rivers, cross the mountains, and end up at Frozen Head State Park outside Oak Ridge, Tennessee, right there next to Brushy Creek federal prison. Believe me, I had to do the research. I had to find a *atlas*."

Mr. Maurice Gall, a retired junior high English teacher from Kansas who worked on his novel about a large family of Christian do-gooders living on a prairie, said, "I have witnessed pods of dolphins as far north and west as Omaha, right on the Platte River. Come to my room, Donna-Rose, and I'll show you pictures."

Donna-Rose Green said, "Okay!" like that.

Listen, out of plain meanness I said, "Why, again, would dolphins—that must live in salt water—find their way to Tennessee, through all of those category four rapids in order to swim with a girl with cancer?"

Maurice Gall said, "It's *fiction*. Anything can happen." He tried to put his arm around Donna-Rose's shoulder.

"Because the little girl's there to see her grandpa, who happens to share a cell with James Earl Ray, the guy who killed Martin Luther King," said Donna-Rose. "So this little girl *knows* some things about what *really* happened in Memphis, and she's got to live long enough in order to expose everything once all the old-school FBI men either retire or die off. The dolphins have curative powers, you know. And they are all-knowing about what went on, and goes on, in the human world."

"The FBI had something to do with MLK? I thought it was JFK and RFK," said Gall.

"That was the Mafia in those cases," Donna-Rose said.

"Tell us how you would handle the scene, Novel the novelist," Anonymous said. "Most of your books are a little more realistic, I know. Because I've read them all."

Anonymous had cried all three days up to this point. I had a feeling that she once owned a palm-reading venture near where Reagan lived during presidential vacations. Anonymous knew some scary things, I could tell, outside of contemporary American fiction.

I topped off everyone's Bloody Marys and said, "No charge. This round on the house." I stalled and tried to think of another little aphorism from one of the books on craft. "Throughout the first draft of your story, keep one finger on the pulse of your rising action, and one finger on the jugular of your reader. Neither let you or the reader fade out entirely, or have a stroke. Always be careful not to go too far."

I'm not exaggerating when I say that it looked like I was surrounded by a gaggle of baseball bobbleheads. It looked like those brainwashed victims at an Avatar Basic Attention Management weekend seminar, nodding up and down relentlessly to such drivel as "Your beliefs will create your life events."

Man, I have to admit that I was into it. I kind of wanted Bekah to witness this power I hadn't felt since making the lieutenant governor come out looking like pure enlightenment personified by plagiarizing William Hazlitt's "Rules and models destroy genius and art," while addressing a troupe of visiting ballet dancers in Winston-Salem. Hell, I'd've taken Ina and Irby for witnesses.

I reached behind my makeshift wet bar—which most people would've called "the Xerox Document Centre 220DC Photocopier"—and pulled out a bottle of bourbon, ready to regale.

10

"Let me get this straight," Jeff the owner leaned across his bar to say. It was two o'clock on Saturday afternoon of my first week with dilettantes and I had already vowed to sell off the property and send the money to Bekah. I asked for a six-pack of Goody's powders from his hangover relief shelf, stacked between pickled pigs' feet and a paperback book filled with graphic photos of "male body parts" suffering from long-untended sexually transmitted diseases. "Novel. You're running a whorehouse in outer Gruel, everybody there wants you to sit around and tell war stories about a publishing career that you've never experienced, and you're thinking about *moving*? Son, we might need to FedEx a psychiatrist in here to tell you what's what. I got a supposed trick-shot pool player who's come in here every day for I don't know how many years—ever since the sand and gravel place shut down and turned into a school—and he's never made one *shot*. I saw him play straight pool one time and he had seven balls left on the table at the end of the game. Against a guy in a *wheelchair* who had to use a *periscope* to even see the table."

I unwrapped the box of powdered aspirin, curled up its cellophane, opened the box's lid, pulled out one wax-paper-covered strip of crushed aspirin, read the box's list of ingredients—520 milligrams aspirin, 260 acetaminophen, 32.5 caffeine, all active; lactose and potassium chloride, inactive—unflapped the wax paper and remembered writing a long, long speech for the lieutenant governor one time concerning the problem of coke in our cities' poorer areas and how he ad-libbed how he'd always been a Pepsi man seeing as Pepsi got "discovered" in North Carolina. I stuck out my tongue as inconspicuously as possible, lay that strip of medicine down on my tongue, and washed it down with three swigs of PBR. Then I took another.

I said, "I just finished reading a whole chapter on how step-by-step description's a good thing in writing fiction and/or nonfiction. When I try to explain it all, though, I get too impatient. If I were going to write a good southern scene about childhood friends who went to a hunt camp every weekend before Thanksgiving it'd go something like 'Larry shot the deer two miles away from the cabin. After supper, everyone said it was the best venison ever.' I wouldn't take the time to go through pulling out the dressing knife, filleting the buck out, building a fire, whatever else goes on. People have fucking things to do."

Jeff the owner said, "Hey! Y'all keep it wise back there," yelling toward the back of Roughhouse Billiards. The pool hall wasn't ninety feet deep, twenty-four wide. Jeff and I were the only ones present. "I like to keep in shape," he said. "I try to be ready should we ever have a packed house rush of redneck scallywags."

Scallywags! I thought. Who says *scallywags*? I said, "Kind of like testing your smoke alarm every few months. Kind of like that emergency broadcast system that used to beep every day on radio and TV, back during the cold war."

Jeff said, "I have no clue what you're talking about. But listen—I have a bunch of stories. What say I come over every once in a while and you tell everybody I'm a famous author. From what you told me they'd never know. Then I'd tell them a couple stories about my stories. I've read Louis L'Amour! I've read Louis L'Amour and the Bobbsey Twins! Shit, Novel, I could just tell those book reports I done at Gruel Normal back in the day, you know. This'll be fun. This'll be easy."

I'd made the mistake of telling him how, on average, the Gruel Inn Writers Retreat would hold nine women to two men weekly, all the way through Armageddon. I'd screwed up and recounted my they-can-only-write-three-days-in-a-row theory, how the women then have nothing to do but tell their pasts, the men nothing but chase panties. I said, "It would be nothing but mean, Jeff. Man, these people have hopes and dreams and aspirations and hopes again of one day being on that bestseller list. They're the kind of people who wait for *Publishers Weekly* to bring them a grand prize check. It wouldn't be right for you to prey on them."

Jeff slid me a beer, then a shot. He said, "What do you think *you're* doing, fucker?" He pulled my shot back and downed it himself. "Speaking of which," Jeff the owner said. He bowed his head once to the door. Maura-Lee Snipes walked in popping her hips stool to wall in a way that she never demonstrated while enduring the Gruel Sneeze 'n' Tone. She wore her brunette hair back in a bun, wore rouge to accentuate her risen cheeks. I noticed how her shoes now fit better.

"I figured I'd find you here, Novel," Maura-Lee said. "Any complaints with the continental breakfast?"

Jeff said, "Redneck scallywags. It could happen at any moment."

To Maura-Lee I could only say, "No complaints whatsoever. Have I told you how much I love you lately? I can't believe the ways of fate—if my dead ex-brother-in-law hadn't flicked his cigarette, then I wouldn't have met you." Jeff made a big production of finding his blender, putting in ice, slicing up a banana, pouring in rum, and making Maura-Lee a daiquiri.

She said, "If I'd've known what weird dark spots those dead animal heads made on the wall once I took them down I'd've offered less money for your mom-in-law's house. For paint and that Kilz stuff that covers bad stains. Hey, you want to buy some jackalopes for the motel? I think they'd look good in each room."

Jeff the owner popped his upturned blender pitcher with the back of his fist to properly unclog the blades. He said, "It might give them some safari ideas. Maybe the writers would look up into those glass eyes and feel like they should write some adventure items. Kind of like the ones I got stored up here." He touched his temple.

I thought for the first time in my life, I wish I still drove the Viper-Mobile. I said, "I don't know. I don't know." Was I about to cry?

"Are you writing down everything in your notebook like I told you to do, goddamn it? Come on, Novel, you've gotten dropped into a giant vat of pure sugar spinning cotton candy, boy," Maura-Lee said.

Those two trick-shot hopefuls walked in all cocky, dragging their cue sticks behind them like petrified prehensile tails. I had a feeling that some of my guests wouldn't wait till I got back before they hitchhiked to the square. "I got a new one I thought up this morning," one pool player said. "It involves four rusty nails, three Bic pens, two severed fingers . . ."

"And a tampon in a pear tree," the other guy sang out. I looked over at them. Again, they were covered in dark, dark specks of paint. What mausoleum hired them out? I thought.

"Write that down," Maura-Lee said. "You got shit all around you, Bo."

Maura-Lee, as a baker, of course, worked one in the morning until about two in the afternoon. She'd not done much to this point with her Jesus crust outside of providing breakfast to my sad clients and pissing off everybody else in Gruel who still had at least one Bible verse within them. She wore a flour-dusted red apron, but seemed neither harried nor withered. I said, "You've done a good job keeping that weight off. That Raleigh or Columbia weight off. I know it's not cool to bring up a woman's figure or weight, but you're looking fit and trim, still." I figured I said all of this in a delicate and complimentary manner. I waited to see if she'd let on where she once lived.

"'Fit and Trim's' a dog food brand, you stupid fucking fuck. What an asshole, prick-face. I can't believe you'd say something like that to me." Then she muttered something that I think she meant not to be heard. I'm almost sure I heard her say, "No wonder I love women."

I said, "Excuse me?"

Jeff the owner said, "I've been thinking about inventing a kiwi daiquiri, but too many of my regulars don't like to see the outside of that fruit harmed, you know. What with the way it looks and feels."

I had no idea what Jeff meant, nor had I witnessed Maura-Lee's mouth as such. I'd never heard such cussing since my own wife told Vudge Ina that we'd never take over the taxidermy operation in Gruel; since one of my lieutenant governors got mad at my writing the word "fecal" instead of "fecund"; since one woman calling up to reserve writing space asked why I wouldn't take performance poets; since James and Joyce called me "Novella" when they caught me with my pants down around my ankles one day prepuberty; since my own father cursed the non-gold-producing rivers he waded, and the non-shrimp-producing oceans he gazed upon; since I came out of the womb as my mother screamed out "Novel Akers!"

Maybe I heard such cussing in a previous life, too, but like I said before, I won't go into that Avatar I-am-me business.

"Here I am," Maura-Lee said. "We've known each other—what?—four, five months?"

I said, "I threw away my calendar when I moved to Gruel."

Maura-Lee seemed to have a bone to pick. She rolled her eyes and said, "That figures. Just like everybody else around here, everyone I've ever known forever here."

Notice how I didn't say, "I thought you moved here from Raleigh," and so on.

Jeff the owner yelled out, "Hey! Y'all keep it wise over there," and looked at us. "I got a special on champagne today. Hey, Novel," he looked at his wristwatch, "you ain't ordering no special Bloody Marys today? Y'all'ses happy hour commences in thirty minutes."

Maura-Lee slid off her barstool. She said, "Sorry. I don't know what's gotten into me lately. Let me come look at your people outside of what they wear for breakfast. I'll help you."

She held up her chin in a way that she tried back when she weighed two hundred pounds. And she'd go back to that weight once she committed, again, to Jesus crust. But I didn't care at that moment. There were secrets I needed to ferret out. "Come on," I said, but in my mind I only wanted to see her hold my favorite rat snake.

◆ ◆ ◆

I unloaded two ex-pickle jars filled with tomato juice, vodka, the normal spices, and Jeff's "special ingredient"—I saw him try to hide it behind the counter when he thought I looked away—which was only pulverized habanero. Maura-Lee rode back to the motel with me, and when I got to the office door with her I announced, "Y'all know Maura-Lee Snipes. She's the woman who provides us with her fresh-baked goods every morning." I carried the booze through and set it atop the photocopier wet bar. "Start handing me your glasses, please."

"Are you a writer, too?" Donna-Rose asked Maura-Lee.

"Not a writer. I'm a baker, and that keeps me busy enough."

Maurice came shuffling up wearing an ascot. He'd spent his writing hours this Saturday drenching Grecian Formula into his hair, evidently. Or he'd polished his head with good old-fashioned Kiwi black. "You should write a novel about a baker-ess, and every chapter could be a different loaf. Pumpernickel. Rye. Sourdough." Maurice had also found my stashed bourbon, I had a feeling. He looked Maura-Lee up and down and said, "I like your oven. I like your rack."

Maura-Lee smiled, but said nothing. But then this woman named Rowena—who planned on writing a sequel to the sequel to *Gone with the Wind*—said, "I don't think it's a great idea to have people from the community intermingle with us writers who pay good money to be around each other. *As God is my witness* I'll demand a refund from you, Novel."

I said, "Now, now. Come on over here and get your sixteen ounces of near vitamins and essential herbs."

Rowena'd signed up for an entire month and—I'll give her this—did try to escape the three-days-and-done pitfall. Her sequel to the sequel involved descendants of Rhett and Scarlett living in the year 2165 on another planet, and having a family reunion on the tricentennial of the Civil War's end. Get this: She called it *Gone with the Solar Wind*, and incorporated a lot of scientific information she garnered from a NASA Web site.

Maura-Lee said, "I'm just here to help. Novel wanted me to come over here and show some of you people the kind of character you're supposed to care about."

That wasn't true, but it sounded good. Five minutes later Jeff the owner walked in with one of his Louis L'Amour paperbacks—*Last of the Breed*—that he'd redesigned with colored markers so it read "by Jeff" and some last name I couldn't make out. The title, too, became *Last of the Bread*. "I'm a local author," he said to everyone. "I heard about this place and thought I'd come over and help out any way I could." Jeff wore a cowboy hat and fringed vest. He said, "Howdy, ma'am," and so on. He held up his book. "I brought along my last novel, a kind of historical piece I wrote about our own Maura-Lee Snipes over there."

Maurice Gall yelled out, "It should be *List of the Bread*! Like my idea!"

I looked over at sad Maura-Lee, who backed her way out the door and returned to my van. The expression on her face advertised nothing but years of taunting, from elementary school days on up to what customers may have said too loudly in the presence of an obese baker. I tried to get out there to see her, but someone started tossing drinks at someone else.

Then everything blurred. I asked Maurice Gall to go out to the shed for more booze, hoping that the snakes would only scare him. That much remains clear. And I kind of recall Rowena accusing someone of poisoning her croissant. The next day she got a ride out to Graywood Regional Memorial, where she evidently disappeared. At least she never came back to the writers retreat to pick up the manuscript for *Gone with the Solar Wind.*

I read through some of it, later on. The maid was some kind of cyborg named Butterfly McC-3PO. She couldn't deliver a baby, either.

11

WHEN I WAS in the sixth grade I won first place in our tiny school's science fair, then went on to the state finals and would've won that had not some freakish kid from Durham built a rocket. The only reason I placed so high was because some of the judges were health food nuts, and another worked for Pepsi. My lame demonstration involved that age-old experiment of dropping things into a glass of Coca-Cola in order to watch their inevitable demise. I lined up baby teeth, unshelled hard-boiled eggs, chicken bones, oyster shells I collected on shrimp expeditions with my father, roadkill skulls, pennies, eating utensils, and so on. Coca-Cola—or any soft drink, including Pepsi—will eat through, erode, and decay any of these things over enough time. I had a Duke's Mayonnaise jar collection of gruesome rot. My second-place prize was a hundred-dollar savings bond, which I'm pretty sure my parents cashed in years later and used for their bird-watching habit.

The rocket-boy freak had two parents working at Duke, and I would be willing to bet that they helped their kid out. My ex-piano-playing parents knew nothing of science, and thought that my experiment should involve peeing through a charcoal filtration system, then drinking what came out. They said that they used to do it all the time at Black Mountain College, then sell the charcoal briquettes to visual arts students, for some reason.

The truly imaginative science project participant, I thought, was this tiny, mop-haired girl from Asheville who wore dreadlocks twenty years prior to white people taking up this odd and culture-wrong hairstyle. She had written a story, one that ran through my head for years:

"A 102-year-old man lived way out in the country, and one morning he awoke at three o'clock to find out he'd smoked his last cigarette before the late news. He looked in all of his coat pockets and found nothing. He searched his ashtrays only to find butts already smoked down to their filters. The man went out to his old pickup truck and looked beneath the bench seat for a half-smoked pack that might've fallen beneath his feet while driving. But he found nothing. He looked in his refrigerator because, at age 102, sometimes he got confused and put things in the wrong places. One time he found his cat in the freezer.

"Well he began the first stages of nicotine withdrawal. Since he lived in the country, it was a good forty-minute drive to the nearest open-all-night store."

At this point in her story I thought she might've been better off at the yearly math fair. I sat in the front row, with my parents, trying to remember all the details—102, three o'clock, late news, zero cigarettes, forty minutes. I thought it was going to end up one of those famous "word problems."

"He got in his pickup truck and backed out of his long, long gravel driveway. Then he turned onto the state road that ran right through his property. It being only three fifteen in the morning, he saw nothing but unlucky possums and raccoons that hadn't made it through the night.

"As he slowly meandered through back roads he thought of his wife, and how she had died twenty years earlier. He knew that if she'd still been alive she would've reminded him to get cigarettes before the Corn Crib closed—a crossroads grocery store only a mile from their farm. He turned on his AM radio and listened to an all-night station where callers from across the country talked to the DJ host about UFOs they'd personally witnessed landing, or at least hovering."

I was twelve. I thought, This girl's nuts. Asheville wasn't all that far from Black Mountain, I thought. I wonder if I can ever find a way to get her up my way. I could show her some waterfalls. I could take her outside our house in order to peek in through the window at what James and Joyce do to each other on James's bed.

"The old man drove and drove. It was winter, but his truck's heater didn't work. He reached behind his seat to grab for a scarf, because his neck felt a chill. At this point he wasn't but about two miles from the all-night convenience store."

My father leaned over and said, "You got this thing won hands down." The idiot rocket boy hadn't gotten on stage yet and explained how one day he wanted to be the first man to tread upon Uranus.

"When he couldn't feel his scarf, he reached further—or maybe farther—over behind the passenger's side. This caused his left arm to jerk the steering wheel."

Let me say now that this little girl's face looked a whole lot like one of those babies you see born without eyelids, like a zombie child. I might've gotten my very first full-fledged erection staring at this girl as I sat between my parents inside an auditorium that could've housed Black Mountain's population times a hundred.

"His truck veered off the road just enough for him to hit a cement bridge abutment over the French Broad River. Half of the truck went down the embankment and into the water, while the other half—carrying the 102-year-old man—flipped over down the asphalt. He was dead on impact, but the part of his car he was in didn't stop skidding until the convenience store parking lot could be seen."

The girl waited. She stared at a point above the last person's head in the audience. "My science experiment shows that smoking can kill you." She curtsied. "Thank you very much," she said, and walked off the stage like a robot.

People clapped, sure. They had to. She was a weird, little mop-headed girl. But even the health food nut judges in 1972 understood how the North Carolina Science Fair would lose all of its funding if it selected an antitobacco contestant.

I applauded harder than anyone. She should become a speechwriter for the governor, I thought.

My father grabbed my hands. He said, "There might be an applause meter on something like this, so you don't want to cheat yourself out of an award, Novel."

The girl came in last place, as it ended up. Maybe she should've had the old man live at least another day.

◆ ◆ ◆

My first love faded from the pack—both literally and figuratively—and I knew that my entire existence depended on making her feel welcome to the human tribe. (That would make a good opening to a how-to-feel-good book, I'm thinking, or maybe a sci-fi novel.)

Like I said, I thought of the poor mop-headed science fair reject off and on, and then, of course, she showed up at the Gruel Inn Writers Retreat all those years later. I recognized her immediately.

"My name's Novel Akers," I said to her in the office. "We've met before."

She introduced herself as Patty Anderson—a name that didn't fit whatsoever—and said, "No, sir. I've never been down this way."

I explained everything about the science fair, the 102-year-old man, the smoking addiction. I said, "I had a hard-boiled egg that's shell looked like tooth rot. A Chinese boy made a rocket ship of sorts."

Patty Anderson came equipped with two laptops, three suitcases, and an umbrella normally used by professional golfers' caddies. "That could be true," she said. "I'm not contradicting you. What's your name again? I've gone through many stages in my life and tried to forget about them all. You wouldn't believe. Anyway," she picked up one laptop, "where's my spot?"

Oh I put her right in number 1, next to the office. I said, "You're from Asheville, and you used to have this nappied-up hair. You told stories."

Patty Anderson said, "I don't know. Are you saying we went to school together? I'm sorry. I don't remember school very well."

The term "electric shock treatment" occurred to me. I said, "Maybe I'm mistaken. Anyway, my name's Novel, and I'm a novelist, and although I expect that you know everything you need to know, I'm here if you should have any questions concerning plot, action, character, subplot, pacing, or dialogue. Dialogue's my forte. I find that dialogue's the toughest part for writers who have to spend money in a place like this."

"I just need help putting up my things," Patty said.

I gave her the key. These were regular keys, by the way, not those credit card–looking things used at Hyatts, Ramadas, Hiltons, Radissons, Holiday Inns, and the wonderful O. Henry Hotel in Greensboro where I stayed once during a speechwriting/herpetology convention.

I carried Patty's other bags. When we got inside I acted like any bellhop I'd ever met for real or seen in a movie. I pointed out the sink and toilet, the bed and lamp. The electrical outlets. I went through a brief history of the Gruel Inn, the Sneeze 'n' Tone, and now.

I set her suitcases on the foldout aluminum stand with sturdy webbed lining.

And then Patty Anderson pushed me on the bed, which— I'm proud to say—had a completely washed spread as opposed to those semen-stained things exposed by *60 Minutes*, *20/20*, or *Dateline*. She said, "As soon as I read the ad in *Southern Living* I hoped it was you."

I couldn't make this up. For some reason I said, "Hold on, Patty. I might still be married. You don't have a rubber by any chance, do you?"

She rolled over and said, "You're right. It's been a long day. Hell, it's been a long life. But let me tell you this: During that whole science fair presentation—and I don't know if you noticed it or anything—I focused on your face. We were both, what, twelve? But I don't think I could've gotten through my spiel without your face."

Let me go ahead and say that Patty stood about five-ten and might've weighed 130. It didn't take a visionary to understand how she'd done runway work in Paris, Milan, London, and New York, that she had undergone heroin treatment twice in the best rehab centers that Sweden offered, that she'd tested the waters of Lake Lesbos, that her last chance was probably a tell-all exposé she would ultimately write in Gruel, South Carolina. I said, "I've had a pretty interesting life, too." Then I tried to pull her back on top of me.

"No, no. You're right. I shouldn't come out of the blue here and take out my insecurities and inadequacies on you." Patty walked over to the desk and flipped open her laptop. "I've paid up for a month, right? Come back and see me in thirty days. Give me that. I swear."

My First Boner, My Last: that could've been the subtitle of my memoir *Novel*. I got up off the bed and started to say, "Be nice to the morning continental breakfast woman if you see her. She may or may not be a serial killer." I said, "Are you writing an autobiography about your experiences as a supermodel?"

"I wasn't a supermodel. Where'd you get that idea?" Patty said. "Nope. I'm writing a regular book. It's about a woman who's obsessed with money. She's the main character. Her name's Mona Tara Lee. Get it? *Monetarily*. And she's married to a rich guy who's in the seafood business named Sebastian. Get it? *Sea bass chin*. Anyway, she doesn't want to have kids, and he does . . ."

Patty kept talking. She should've been a speechwriter for state reps who prided themselves on filibusters. Me, I noticed how I did indeed need to use those jackalopes Maura-Lee offered, or any of the heads my dead ex-father-in-law I never knew stuffed. I stared at myself in the motel mirror and counted cracks in the ceiling. What, again, were the state capitals of North Dakota, Maine, Missouri, Oregon, Michigan, Delaware, and Wisconsin? If Jeff the owner wanted to bring in new business, he should offer a big sandwich better than what Gruel BBQ had to offer. Carpet or wood floors? Should I feel bad about charging so much money for a week at the writers retreat seeing as lightbulb engineers now had their products lasting over a year?

"...and then, in the end, this guy comes out of nowhere and she realizes that she's been missing a little thing called Love the entire time, even when she was hanging around the Mafia guys. Or the retarded kids she worked with on a volunteer basis."

I nodded. "That sounds good. That sounds like a bestseller. Listen. In the morning don't forget that there's a free continental breakfast. And, God forbid, if you fall and hit your head in the bathtub just let me know. There's a hospital not fifteen or twenty miles away."

◆ ◆ ◆

Bekah called and said she needed to come down on the first anniversary of her mother's and brother's tragic fatal deaths. I said, "Wasn't that about ten years ago? You mean to tell me that hasn't even been twelve months?"

Bekah said, "Gene Weeks said I need to come down there armed with a subpoena, change of locks, alimony papers, and a gun."

I didn't say, "We're not even divorced yet, so it would make no sense to have alimony papers." I said, "Man, if you're coming with all of that, you might need some more arms. Or a wheelbarrow."

"Well. Whatever. He said I'm getting the short end of the stick."

"You left me! Why's it always the goddamn husband's fault? I fucking followed *you* down here on your screwball sneeze dream, and then you chickened out and left. *I'm* the one who should have at least eight armfuls of papers."

Bekah made a big point of sighing into the receiver. She said, "There are some small-print clauses in our state's marriage and divorce codes."

I didn't think she told the truth—what codes could there be, seeing as most of North Carolina didn't have zoning laws—but said nothing. "Well come on down here if you want. I don't think you could stay here, seeing as I'm full to capacity. I guess that Ms. Snipes woman could let you stay in your parents' house. Or maybe Jeff the owner will let you crash on his pool table."

Bekah said, "Oh there's a code, my friend. How's about this, Novel: Gene Weeks has a new client he's collecting debts for. And he happens to be the ex–lieutenant governor. I've been dealing with the guy—gee, I have a feeling that you know him—and you wouldn't believe what I'm finding out. Yep. I introduced myself as Bekah Akers, and then he started talking about how he once had a guy on staff named Novel Akers, and then I said yeah, with the snakes, and he said . . ."

Again, I started wondering about state capitals, state birds, state flowers and mottoes, how far the stock market had gone up since the last Republican dynasty, how every dog in existence looked funny with painted-on eyebrows, how too many small-town visual artists got interviewed in one form of the media or the other and whined, "I can't make a living here, what with the small amount of people who buy artwork"—like they could make it in New York City or Los Angeles or Lexington, Kentucky—and every movie I'd ever seen where the camera showed a scary house up on a hill.

"Are you listening to me? Novel, are you attuned to this conversation?" Bekah yelled into the receiver. This, by the way, was six thirty in the morning. I awaited Maura-Lee's continental breakfast delivery, and feared that Patty Anderson might traipse in and yell out something about her character Mona Tara Lee.

I said, "I'm here. There's a pterodactyl or something in the road eating a stray hyena."

"The lieutenant governor said, 'Akers. I used to have a speechwriter named Akers.'"

"Yeah. So what? There are a ton of Akers in the Carolinas." I could feel my face redden out of embarrassment.

"He said, 'I had a speechwriter named Novel Akers.' How many fucking Novel Akers are there in the United States, much less North and South Carolina, you sandbagging dickhead?"

Sandbagging dickhead! I actually wrote it down on a piece of brown paper bag as a possible title for my memoirs. "At least two, I guess."

"Two my ass. You weren't a Viper-Mobile driver. You were on the inside, Novel. He told me all about it. He told me about Niger, and recycling telephone books."

Listen to this story: I was in the middle of handing over docile, gorgeous corn snakes to a group of Daughters of the

American Revolution descendants—all nice women—when my phone rang inside the step van. I wasn't happy, as normal, seeing as I'd just gotten into the part of my rehearsed speech concerning how snakes can't really turn themselves into giant hoops and roll down the road. I excused myself, picked up the phone, and the lieutenant governor kind of screamed, "I need something immediately about the funeral home industry. I'm about to talk to the Greater Greensboro Optimist Club."

I remember that speech verbatim: "If we get a true gift from someone, then we should be able to do with it whatever we want. For example, if we get a rare Tiffany lamp for a wedding present, the giver should not be appalled when—for some sacrificial and superstitious reason—we decide to throw said lamp against the wall, shattering the shade into a thousand pieces. No giver will question the fate of a true gift. Now, what is the greatest gift God has given each of us? The answer is Life. And if it's a true gift—and God would only offer up true gifts seeing as God must be benevolent—wouldn't God allow us to do whatever we wanted with this gift? Therefore, suicide and euthanasia should not be considered immoral, pessimistic actions."

Who knew that a news crew would've shown up at such a picayune event? The Optimists were happy, sure. But the medical community got extremely upset—their whole livelihood depended on people hanging on forever throughout Lou Gehrig's disease, multiple sclerosis, cystic fibrosis, Hodgkin's disease, blindness, infertility, chronic pain, cancer, massive strokes, and plain old outré manic depression. If I'd've known what I learned later, I would've only directed people with an ache or pain to Graywood Regional Memorial in Forty-Five, South Carolina, you know.

I said to Bekah, "When did you start cussing so much? I don't remember your cussing. I thought you told me that before we met you were Junior Miss Graywood County. I'm thinking the sponsors of that pageant asked their winners not to cuss and to never wear pants. Are you wearing blue jeans right now?"

My wife hung up the phone. Because I lived in Gruel, South Carolina, I wasn't able to hit star 69 and find out that she wasn't calling from our old house.

12

I SAT AROUND HARD for three days hoping to attain that famous "recovered memory syndrome" in order to remember something worthwhile and significant, any little episode that might be beneficial and meaningful in regards to my life story. It was like I had writing retreat dyslexia—when everyone else didn't think within my square rooms whatsoever, I *did*, and vice versa.

I waited for Bekah. I got out my calendar and checkbook to figure out the actual date of Vudge Ina's and Irby's miraculous deaths. When Bekah didn't show up on that date, when she didn't show up three days later—like in the stupid Bible story—I let myself breathe. I quit hanging out at Roughhouse Billiards drinking nonstop, quit thinking about what advantages I might gain from wandering into Gruel Jungle for forty days and forty nights, quit expecting a long-range flood like Jeff the owner did.

"She's a regular-looking woman with shoulder-length hair and high-heel shoes," I said to Jeff one night while expecting Bekah. "You and I have to come up with some kind of code whistle, in case I'm in the men's room when she arrives, so I can stay in there." Jeff filled out a parlay card some small-time old boy bookie from Forty-Five brought over weekly. Jeff said, "Novel. I don't know how pickled your brain is, but you might recall that I'm *from* here, and Rebekah was from here. I know who she is and looks like. It's *you* I don't know."

"Oh. Yeah. I forgot you knew her. Hey, was she ever Junior Miss Graywood County?"

Victor Dees walked in from his army-navy surplus store across the street. I'd only run into him a couple times before. Dees always had a look on his face like someone chased him, and on the sidewalk he turned his head around about every sixth step. He looked at Jeff and said, "Jeff." He looked at me and said, "Speechwriter for the criminally insane."

I smiled and shook my head a few times. "I take it Bekah called you up to say I was some kind of bad person. I can hear her now. She said our whole marriage was a sham, built on a foundation of half-truths. She said something about how I should've been a Hollywood actor, the way I pretended to love snakes and all. Well, good. Good for her. For the record, she won. She's back in Charlotte, and I'm ass-deep in Gruel. She's got her old job back taking money from poor people, and I'm stuck running a goofball writers haven that I have no interest in whatsoever. If I sell out, technically, the money's hers, I guess."

Victor Dees sat down on the vinyl stool beside mine. He pointed at the bourbon shelf, then waffled two fingers in the international sign to say one for him and one for me. Jeff the owner poured two straight shots and placed them on the counter. Dees said, "She said none of that. Rebekah called me up and asked how much I would charge to kill you. I said that I probably couldn't do such a thing unless there was good valid reasons. Like if you went around fondling little girls and old

92

women. Or boys. Domesticated farm animals." He held up his glass for me to clink.

"Well I'm proud to say that I've done none of the above," I said.

Victor Dees held his eyebrows high and cinched up his camouflaged balls. "Are you sure about that?" he said. "Do you have proof?"

Where were the trick-shot pool players when you needed them? I wanted some kind of distraction. I could've used the new clan of writers to find Roughhouse Billiards en masse and take me away for a series of private consultations about the overuse of adverbs and adjectives. I said, "I don't have any photos of me fucking any of those people you mentioned, if that's what you mean. Bekah doesn't have any photos, unless she doctored some up the way that can be done nowadays."

"That's right. I don't have any photos, and Bekah doesn't. But *you* might. Of course you're going to lie about not having pictures of yourself with sheep, Lolita, and Grandma Moses, unless you're criminally insane."

I would've gone ahead and punched Victor Dees in the nose if he didn't have two bayonets strapped to his thighs. I said, "Jeff, could you please hand me the phone? I need to call Cape Kennedy and see if my spaceship's ready to return to Earth."

"You wrote a speech for the lieutenant governor up in North Carolina about how the nuthouses in Morganton and Raleigh could be operated better if more ex-patients were on the boards of directors, right? You wrote a speech about how there was nothing more depressing for a manic-depressive than having happy people run the asylum, correct?"

I thought, Goddamn, how much did the lieutenant governor tell my wife? "I never liked any of our lieutenant governors. It was a joke."

Victor Dees clinked my glass again. He said, "Do you know what's the best thing about teaching at a school for the blind?"

I tried to make the connection. I couldn't remember writing a speech pro or con the North Carolina School for the Deaf and Blind. I said, "No sir, I don't."

"No dress code! You can go to work naked!"

I bought the next round. Victor Dees said he was running a special on old-fashioned two-man canvas pup tents he'd gotten at an estate sale up in Sylva, something about a survivalist who didn't survive. I said, "Put me down for two of them. I might have someone writing a war novel who needs to act the part. I could send him across the road from my place into Gruel Jungle, or whatever y'all call that primordial acreage."

Jeff the owner said, "We used to call it Boy Scout camp a thousand years ago. You remember, don't you, Vic?"

"I've seen more two-headed toads back in those woods than I've seen regular ones. No one believes me, but I saw a unicorn up on the hummock one time, right across from Gruel Inn." Victor Dees held his forehead high.

"Those were the days," Jeff the owner said.

I said, "Hey, Vic—Jeff here's a famous writer. Did you know that? He wrote a little paperback novel one time. Show him your novel, Jeff."

Victor Dees took my arm and said, "Don't ever, *ever* call me 'Vic' again."

◆ ◆ ◆

Maura-Lee Snipes started catering Jesus crust bread to every white-flight private school in Graywood County, plus schools right across the border, which numbered about a hundred elementary, middle, and high schools that "taught" how hatred was a bad thing, how the Golden Rule was a good thing, and how God would want to charge exorbitant yearly tuitions so no black person could ever afford transferring from, say, Forty-Five High to Rock of Ages K–12. Maura-Lee started off using my old, empty Viper-Mobile, then had to lease two nearly new models and hire a couple delivery drivers. Each slicked loaf cost $1.66. The average school went through four hundred slices per lunch, especially on Deli Meat! Sandwich! Day! Loaves, minus heels, got cut into thirty-six slices of bread. I don't know what Maura-Lee's overhead ran, but outside of the lamb's blood dripped into each vat of dough for authentic Jesus crust, she wasn't hurting in regards to net and gross. Do the math. Because Irby Cathcart flicked his cigarette — or didn't — and killed Ina Cathcart, because my wife used her inheritance to start the Sneeze 'n' Tone, because Maura-Lee wanted to lose twenty or thirty pounds and somehow had an orgasmic conversion, et cetera, et cetera, et cetera, I made the woman who would never love me become a millionairess.

I said, "What're you paying your bread drivers? I spent a dozen years driving my step van. Maybe I'll close down shop and service the Graywood/Abbeville/Ware Shoals private school region. I can read a map." This was later on, on Victor-Dees-Makes-a-Threat Day, inside Roughhouse. Dees went back to his store in search of Brasso to "shiny up" his bayonets — his words.

"Normal. Better than normal. A dollar more than minimum wage per hour, plus a loaf of misshapen. I'm thinking about giving dental insurance if they stay six months."

Gruel minimum wage had been $2.35 since the 1970s. I'm not sure how no one knew the difference or cared. I said, "Never mind."

"I got a call from one of those evangelists the other day saying he wanted me to appear on his show."

I said, "Ernest Angley?"

"The other one."

"Billy Graham or his son?"

"The other one."

"Not that prison dude—Jim Bakker?"

Maura-Lee sipped from her Manhattan. "The other one."

"Leroy Jenkins?"

"How do you know about so many TV evangelists?"

I said, "The guy with the hair—Benny somebody?"

"The other one."

"That woman who played Ellie Mae on *The Beverly Hillbillies*?"

Maura-Lee said, "No, it was a man. You know. Goddamn, I can't think of his name. I think he might've had something to do with wrestling, too."

I looked over at Jeff who tried to pull off a trick shot on the pool table involving a Zippo lighter and a tiki torch. It was a good thing no insurance agents ever traveled into Roughhouse. "Senator Newt Gingrich? Senator Orrin Hatch? Jesse Helms? Senator John Warner? That dickhead out in Missouri, Ashcroft? Reagan. Bush. Nixon's *dead*."

Maura-Lee said, "I want some boiled peanuts. Hey, Jeff, you got any boiled peanuts in the cooler?"

He shot his cue ball into the air, lit the Zippo, which lit the torch, which fell on the table and knocked the eight ball into the corner pocket. He said, "It's not all that hard. I keep telling those boys it's not all that hard."

"I know who you're talking about—that guy who had his face blown off in Vietnam. That evangelist."

"No more boiled peanuts," Jeff the owner said.

"Not him. Damn it to hell." Maura-Lee looked up at the punched-tin ceiling. "It doesn't matter. I'm not going on. Say, you never did answer me as to if you wanted those jackalopes for the Gruel Inn. You want those things? I've got them stacked up on the back porch."

I said, "Ollie North. Any of those guys who did prison time due to the Watergate break-in."

Maura-Lee turned on her seat and faced me. "I thought you were going to write a novel, Novel. What're you doing? You know how to write, if speechwriting counts for anything. Vic Dees told me that much. How come you're not with your people, working on a manuscript?"

I said, "Oh. I know. That guy who ran a Kansas mile in 3:51 when he was still in high school. Him. Does he have a TV show now?"

Maura-Lee said, "What kind of good southern bar doesn't have boiled peanuts anymore? That's like Gruel BBQ running out of coleslaw."

I said, "It'd be like you running out of yeast. Or flour. Or eggs." I couldn't remember what else went into bread.

Maura-Lee got up, rounded the counter, and made her own new drink so as not to disturb Jeff, who now attempted a trick shot that involved a yardstick, two dog collars, and a giant rattrap that may or may not have held vermin not two minutes earlier.

◆ ◆ ◆

I called Bekah and let her know that I learned of her hired assassin, but that he and I worked things out. She said, of course, "What're you talking, Novel? Are you out of your fucking mind? Go run the motel and quit hanging out at Roughhouse Billiards."

I moved away from the office window. "So you've already talked to Vic Dees, I take it. How else would you know that I've been 'hanging out,' as you put it, at the pool hall? Huh? Answer me that one, if you don't mind."

Bekah sighed hard. In the background I heard a knot of tele-marketers calling up poor people in order to yell at them about hurting the economy, being sad excuses for human beings, et cetera. Although Bekah could do her job from home, she still went into Gene Weeks's office more often than not. "I was brought up in Gruel. Anybody unable to speak without a slur in his voice has been sitting in Roughhouse a little too long."

"Well that may be," I said, "but it doesn't excuse you from trying to kill me."

Bekah said, "Yessir, yessir, yessir," to someone in her office. To me she said, "I don't need to hire anyone, Novel. You've been doing a fine job all by yourself. Snakes. Making politicians look the fool when they talk to an audience in front of cameras."

I said, "Well I just want to get it straight that I know. That's all. Now if you'll excuse me, I'm leading a little impromptu seminar on the importance of lists in all forms of writing."

Bekah said that maybe she should start writing bestsellers immediately, seeing as she had a list of things to say. "Maybe you should tell those people how important it is to be historical, Novel. Maybe—in the state you're in now—you should talk to them about sci-fi, Novel."

I wondered how long she'd been waiting to use those sentences on me. She was still laughing when she hung up.

13

My mother carried on a yearlong affair with a man who could've become one of the most recognizable abstract expressionists in the twentieth century. At the time, though, he carried around his own easel and copied from the masters, charcoaled boring still lifes, and so on. This is according to my mother's journals, dated 1949–1952. She never wrote down his name, or used any initials, code words, or nicknames. You'd think that a person would slip up occasionally, maybe write, "Today Splash said he wanted to go for a drive, but I told him he was too drunk."

I learned all of this in a haphazard way: When my parents died they left a couple boxes of what I considered useless "ephemera"—a word I didn't know until Bekah forwarded a letter addressed to me that had made its way to the lieutenant governor's office. When I was eighteen or twenty I referred to "ephemera" as plain old "useless notebooks." Anyway, these personal items landed in the Black Mountain College Research Archives, which, in the year 1999, lost its funding due to government cutbacks. I had two days to come pick up whatever boxes still belonged to me, in a lawful and technical sense.

I borrowed back my step van and took off, made my way up I-26 eventually, and learned that, had my parents ever made a name for themselves in the music world, their belongings would probably be transferred to the North Carolina State Archives in Raleigh, with most of the general files, faculty reports, and photographs stuck in Black Mountain. Some of the materials were donated and accepted at the Smithsonian, according to the archivist.

"Nothing against your mom and dad," soon-to-be-unemployed registrar Milson Willets said to me. "They didn't live long enough to make what we might consider an 'eternal impression' on the arts. I'm sure that these catalogued notebooks and letters will be invaluable to you, but they're not up to par in regards to a state repository much larger and more complete than poor old Black Mountain College Research Archives Center and Storage."

I said, "No need to apologize. I'm kind of excited about getting these back. I probably shouldn't have given everything up back when my parents got killed. I guess I couldn't understand value back then."

Milson Willets parted his hair in the middle, I supposed, but the part was a good two inches wide. It was as if he sported a reverse mohawk. "Now, there could be extraneous circumstances. For example, the letters of Faulkner's mother are quite worthwhile in the archival world. What have you made of yourself, Mr. Akers?"

I almost proudly announced my Viper-Mobile and speech-writing days, the Sneeze 'n' Tone abetment, the Gruel Inn Writers Retreat. "I'll just go ahead and take these back home. Maybe between now and my death I'll do something worthwhile and lasting. Then I can donate everything back to someone."

I had snakes living in four-sided habitats larger than the box filled with my parents' important papers. There were four notebooks, two of which seemed to be an unfinished experimental composition my father wrote titled, "RE: Quim for Mozart." Some snapshots of James and Joyce settled down at the bottom. There were none of me, though maybe I had "purloined" my Polaroids in hopes of showing a prospective girlfriend in the history department how cute I was panning for gold or popping the heads off shrimp.

When I got back home to Gruel I noticed immediately how Dr. Bobba Lollis—whose given name was "Bobby," really, and who didn't have a medical degree or Ph.D.—moved his free portable blood pressure machine out onto the sidewalk in front of Gruel Drugs. He'd taken the three vinyl chairs out there also, the ones that stood against the wall next to the pharmacist's station, beside the systolic-diastolic device with *Heart Rate Feature!* I returned from Black Mountain as I went—prodigal son in neither direction—at dawn after getting Jeff the owner to watch my writers for a night.

Certainly I could've made it up there and back all in daylight hours, but something told me that I might not be in the best mental shape. Maybe I'd seen too many afternoon talk shows. Perhaps deep down I knew that I would be scarred for life should I open the marbled covers of my mother's notebooks. It could've been the wood nymphs that called me nightly from deep in the woods across the road, I don't know.

I made it to a KOA campground outside Pumpkintown, where a slew of Wally Byam Caravan Club Airstream freaks parked. I paid my campsite fee, parked, and got out my mother's secrets.

Remember that my parents thought they had no children

because of dual infertility, that they "adopted" James and Joyce from early Irish Republican Army instigators, that I came along more or less—this wasn't a grand surprise to me—as an accident, a novelty. One: Joyce and James were as Irish as my corn snakes. Two: Joyce and James sprang from the loins of a modern dancer who didn't want her career ruined with children, right there at Black Mountain College.

I'll give my parents bonus points for taking on my brother and sister. Oh, I'm as pro-choice as they get, but I'll applaud my folks for taking in unwanteds—kind of like what I do at the Gruel Inn, though on a smaller scale.

Three: My mother had exactly zero respect or faith in my father's ability as a composer.

Four: My mother had a half-dozen "miscarriages" before Joyce and James, then not another between their arrival into the Akers fold, then mine. That's how she wrote it. "Perhaps I thought more about my once-promising career than I did about checking the calendar monthly. God those 'miscarriages' hurt. There should be a law . . ."

Well I don't know about you, but I'm all fucked-up finding out that my mother probably stuck hangers up there.

I read and reread, then joined a crook of Airstream enthusiasts who invited me over for a delicious supper of creamed corn, whipped potatoes, mashed yams, and lime Jell-O. We drank sweet tea and listened to some banjo music a fellow named Lloyd picked up on his super-duper AM radio. Everyone camped around me enjoyed their last flickers of life, and when I left at dawn *I hoped that someone would shoot me in the head before I ever spent twenty minutes commenting nonstop on creamed corn and banjo music.*

Which gets me back to the blood pressure machine. My favorite geezers, Conrad Hulsey and Swenson T. Jones—both of whom hated me because I wasn't born and raised in Gruel—went inside the pharmacy daily and checked their blood pressure. I'm talking mid-1970s until Maura-Lee opened her bakery. For some reason these two men never thought to make who-buys-the-beer bets over at Roughhouse Billiards. Once Maura-Lee's Jesus crust became all the fashion, though, Hulsey and Jones got competitive. Maybe they liked her looks better than Jeff the owner's.

As it went, whoever had the worst blood pressure got a free coffee or bagel from the other. I witnessed their bickering many a morning—then noon and night—when I went into the drugstore to buy condoms for my miserably hopeful and confused male novelists, usually Wednesdays and Saturdays.

"One ninety-one over 90 is worse than 170 over 100," Hulsey might say. "Do the math. You owe me a bagel." They both probably couldn't remember the day they retired from Gruel Sand and Gravel, back when it still furnished much of Graywood County with driveways and horseshoe pits.

I puttered my step van into the square and saw them flipping a case quarter to see who went first. "When did Dr. Lollis move this out of the store?" I asked.

Maura-Lee waved through her plate-glass window next door. "This ain't none your bidness," Swenson T. Jones said. He insisted on being called Swenson T. I asked him what the "T" stood for only once. He said, "Tongue," but the look on his face let me know that any other day it might be "Tumultuous" or "Tallywhacker."

"You can't play," Conrad said. "This is our little game."

They stood in the half-light, across from a statue of Colonel Dill, Gruel's second founder and Civil War hero. I'd not lived in the area long enough to appreciate the annual Dill Day celebration. "Y'all should see who can have the lowest blood pressure," I said, seeing as I was a nice, normal, sane ex-speechwriter. "Y'all should see who can pull off a 120 over 60 or thereabouts."

"I'm eighty years old," Swenson T. said. "You going to tell me how to live a longer life?"

Conrad lifted his cane as if to strike me. "I'm eighty-one, goddamn it." He reached in his denim shirt pocket and pulled out a pack of Virginia Slims Ultra-Lights, lit one, and inhaled. "I'm ready to take the test."

I looked down at the orange extension cord snaking through the misaligned front door of Gruel Drugs. Swenson T. took a bottle of schnapps out of his hip pocket and took two swigs. He said, "I'm feeling mighty tense this morning. I'm about stroke-ready."

I wanted a gun. It was like living on the set of a cowboy movie solely made up of character actors named Cookie. "Kill yourselves," I said. "Y'all should eat some fatback sandwiches more often. It's men like you that're causing health insurance rates to rise every day. Start smoking real cigarettes and drinking real liquor, for god's sake. Hurry up and die. You're costing the rest of us too much money."

Well I'm sorry. I didn't really want anyone to die, but human beings could still be nice to one another, I thought. I said, "I got a couple vipers over at the motel. How much will one of you pay me to get you bitten on the forearm? You want your blood pressure up? A good dose of copperhead venom will do the trick.

I'm betting that with my help I can get either of you old fucks up to 250, maybe 300, over 150. I can get your heart rate right up there to world-record status before you keel over with your free cup of coffee."

They didn't look at each other. Jones and Hulsey stared at me, their foreheads raised, mouths open. "World War II didn't scare us," Swenson T. said. "Being in Boy Scouts on jamboree didn't scare us, and neither do you."

Nowadays I realize that I didn't want to get back in the step van. I didn't want to go to a place I didn't call home. I said, "Y'all ever thought about writing your life stories? Y'all ever think about helping other people write their autobiographies? I don't know that I could pay you much, but I could get you free continental breakfasts. I'm talking, just to be advisers of sorts. Just to be available."

Swenson T. Jones said, "The 'T' stands for 'Take a Hike, Son.'"

◆ ◆ ◆

As best I could make out my father's—if indeed he was my father—musical composition, there were parts in his "RE: Quim for Mozart" that employed Jew's harps, combs wrapped in toilet paper, a handsaw, and a manual typewriter's return ding. In the margins he wrote things like "Play fortissimo, as if killing an abstract expressionist," and "Barely audible, like Olivia sneaking out of the house on Wednesday nights."

My mother's last entry ran, "I'm hopeful that Novel turns out all right. He never gained the backbone of either James or Joyce, but that might be genetic. Novel didn't exactly spring from dancers. The most athletic I've seen his father act occurred while running from a stirred nest of yellow jackets. I sure hope there aren't many flying insects in Florida. There's no telling how many heart attacks Ted might have."

I have no clue as to what made my brother and sister such great rock throwers and distance runners, and for all I know their biological parents were Irish dancers, like early Riverdance idiots.

I pulled into my parking lot at seven fifteen and noticed every light on. I imagined all of my guests smoking cigarettes and drinking coffee, typing out masterpieces that may or may not have begun with, "I'm supposed to get my free continental breakfast at seven o'clock, no later."

Jeff the owner came out of the office. "All is well on the southern front." He grabbed his crotch and pumped it a few times. "Man, if you ever need any more help let me go ahead and volunteer now."

"Thanks, Jeff. I just saw Maura-Lee up on the square. I don't know why she's late."

Jeff lit a cigarette and asked what I had in the cardboard box. He said, "You got this woman took a semester off teaching all-girls' college so she could write her a novel? And last night she come in the office asking advice, you know? She had it in her mind that I'd been publishing all along."

I sidestepped Jeff and set my mother and father's recrudescent testimonials on the photocopier, shoving aside two bottles of Jim Beam. "Where'd she get that idea? Are you talking about Dr. Culver?"

"Yeah. I guess she got the idea because I told her I had one book out. Anyway, the next thing you know she's asking some serious questions about how to write a sex scene without it sounding either sappy, unbelievable, trite, melodramatic, old hat—hey, I found your thesaurus back on the shelf; I hope you don't mind my *perusing* it—and the next thing you know we're aping the fancy metronome."

I thought to myself, Do not forget to call your memoir *Aping the Fancy Metronome.*

I envisioned my parents' metronome, on their near-priceless piano, before giving up music altogether. I envisioned Joyce and James's real parents, clippity-clopping, dressed like suspendered leprechauns. I said, "Maura-Lee knows how to set things up. Let's you and me go find her, and then start drinking early today."

We found Maura-Lee outside Gruel Bakery, conducting CPR on Swenson T. Jones. From what we learned soon thereafter, he had regained consciousness and his heart pumped a strong seventy beats per minute resting. He said, "That was a close one."

Unfortunately, though, his best friend called an ambulance, which showed up an hour later and took Swenson "the 'T' is for Thrombus" Jones to Graywood Regional Memorial hospital over in Forty-Five. There he supposedly contracted pneumonia and a staph infection, but died when he was accidentally drowned during a sponge bath.

Possible first sentence to chapter 1: My Gruel confederates grasped instinctively the despair a gambling man underwent when forced to test his blood pressure alone daily.

14

I FIGURED IF my rich writers retreat guests made it this far in life with little or no talent, and pipe dreams that only appeared in surfer documentaries or Cheech and Chong movies, that they could figure out how to spend their days in a room with faulty thermostat settings. I helped Jeff open his pool hall three hours early, then we pulled down the blinds and took to the bottles like thirsty Tangiers bandits. I said, "I've come across some unsettling news that has me thinking the future, Jeff the owner. I need some straight answers about this town, in case I decide to give up altogether."

He said, "I'm keeping tabs, Novel. I can't afford to have people come in here drinking free. Word'll spread and then everyone'll want it for nothing."

I nodded. I raised my glass. "First off, what's your last fucking name? Everyone just calls you 'Jeff the owner.'"

"It's *Downer*. You must've heard it wrong the first time and kept going with it. Some of the boys and me had bets as to when you'd realize your mistake. I guess I lose. I said never, because I predicted that Victor Dees would kill you beforehand."

I got up and pulled some Goody's powders off the shelf before I found myself too drunk to remember. "These 'boys' you're talking about. Where *are* they? How long have I been in Gruel now, anyway?"

"Since you got here." Jeff the owner shrugged.

Possible roman à clef opening: "I'd never met anyone last-named Downer. Who would go by that name voluntarily before legally changing it at age eighteen?" I said, "I can count on ten fingers the locals I've met from Gruel. Nine now that Swenson Jones got taken to the hospital."

"T. You forgot to say the T."

"Swenson T. Jones, and the 'T' stands for 'Time's up.' Where is everybody? There are houses up and down Old Old Greenville Road. There are curtains in the windows. Nobody's shutters look half unhinged."

The bar strobed. "I need to get me some lightbulbs last more than a week. I might need to drive over to Georgia someday." Jeff said, "Guess how old I am."

I knew better than to answer this question when a woman asked. The first time I met Ina I thought she was Bekah's grandmother. I said, "My age."

"Well if you're sixty, then yes. Listen. Gruel could have a sign at the town limits that says FIRST COTTON MILL TOWN TO DIE. Graywood Mills had a big operation here that went bankrupt in 1946. Every other town in America flourished. Shit, there could be a sign that says LAST TOWN TO SEE THE EFFECTS OF RECONSTRUCTION, seeing as it ain't happened yet."

I couldn't help but laugh. Jeff the owner spoke so slowly I was sure he turned sixty-one midway through his explanation.

"It's not funny," I said. "Sorry. It's so true, though, it comes out funny."

One time when a matchbook factory opened up somewhere in the middle of eastern North Carolina I wrote a speech for the lieutenant governor to give at the ribbon-cutting ceremony. He said, "I'm predicting that this here company will light a fire under our economy's butt." Everybody laughed and appreciated the lieutenant governor's colloquial metaphor, until a sulfur fire caused a major evacuation, the unemployment rate returned to 25 percent in the county, and what few hog farmers remained lost their livelihood once all the meat-packing plants complained of a hideous stench that emanated off the affected pigs' "other white meat," meaning snouts to buttholes.

Jeff poured us more bourbon, this time without the lemon slices we both set to the side earlier when we thought it looked bicoastal.

"Most people up and died. A few people got out. You ever hear of the actor Grainger Koon? He's from right here in Gruel. Oh I know he got all bigheaded later on and claimed to be from Claxton, Georgia—the Fruitcake Capital of the World—but he was brought up here. You might've seen him on *The Munsters* or *Mr. Ed*. He was in an assortment of those scary movies. He played 'Scary Man on Dock,' you know, and 'Drunk Man Falls off Park Bench.' His family only moved to Claxton 'cause Daddy got a supervisor position at the fruitcake factory."

I said, "I don't know him." I thought about my father wildly searching a pan for gold, my mother looking toward the mountains' nonexistent horizon.

"Some left, like I said. Some died. A *bunch* of us have stayed on seeing as, ironically—now there's a word I bet you didn't think I knew—we never seemed to age much, and we're waiting for something to happen. Kind of like your Gruel Inn thing. We actually got excited about that."

"Well you've had a weird way of showing it. Nice welcome wagon, fucker."

Jeff the owner said, "We didn't like Rebekah moving back, if you want to know the truth. We didn't need another from the Cathcart clan. You see, her daddy only dealt with death in one way or the other. First, his taxidermy operation. Then some stuff in between you'll find out sooner or later from someone wiser and more loose-lipped than I am. Then Sherrill Cathcart's death. He's the only man or woman ever took his own life in Gruel, supposedly. We might not be the most Sunday-religious folk in all of South Carolina—you may've noticed no churches left in operation—but we got our convictions. We've never had our own funeral home, and we've never had our own doctor. Most people wouldn't even want Gruel Drugs, I'm thinking, if they had a vote."

I said, "I get what you're getting at," though I wasn't really sure unless my fellow citizens believed that every purported good thing was bad, and vice versa. Or maybe I landed in a town of Christian Scientists. But I did catch that "He's the only man or woman ever took his own life in Gruel, supposedly." The "supposedly" might've been placed strategically, on purpose. If Jeff the owner knew the word "ironically," he might've toyed with me some here.

"One day everything will change, though. One day Gruel will store urban sprawl. How far are Atlanta and Charlotte away from us—150 miles each? We'll become a bedroom community within the next hundred years, I'm predicting, with our own train station."

I thought, My memoir *Novel* could begin: Since pickling is a preservative, the townspeople of Gruel and I attempted to can our brains forever. I said, "I see where you're coming from."

Jeff the owner looked at himself in the mirror across our way and said, "Now what's your next question?"

✦ ✦ ✦

I learned that Jeff Downer's wife turned out "to be a real Downer." He didn't mean that she walked around the square maudlin, sourpussed, recessive, and aggrieved. He meant that she turned out to be a first cousin left on the front stoop of a successful young couple over in Forty-Five, who adopted her South Carolina–style—no judge or social service worker, just an announcement in the newspaper. Jeff's wife, Carla, received Skinner for her last name, went through public schools, got a job as a bookkeeper, met her husband-to-be at a square dance, then later learned of her once-orphaned status when some do-gooder relative stood up at Gene Skinner's funeral in order to report a blow-by-blow account of the highlights of Skinner's life: third place in the county track meet, Insurance Agent of the Month four times, wedding, oh...and that cardboard box of baby found on the front porch back in 1942.

"It was one of Carla's great-aunts. She assumed that Carla's parents had told her the truth by then. They hadn't. They were Presbyterians. The great-aunt couldn't have known. She lived real far off, like in Spartanburg, or Richmond," Jeff said.

"I'm following you. That had to be a real shock to Carla."

"It was what economists might call 'devastating,'" Jeff Downer the owner said.

I made a mental note as to where the restroom was, plus the best route around the pool table. I foresaw falling off the barstool, becoming confused, then peeing outside on the sidewalk. But I still held enough rational faculties—thanks to years of speechwriting—to say, "This doesn't explain how she realized that she was related to you from the get-go."

The proper Roughhouse Billiards opening time came an hour earlier. The trick-shot boys knocked at the glass door and tried to peer through cloth pull-down blinds every fifteen minutes, their cupped-faced shadows recognizable.

"She had the smarts to know that no one in Gruel could afford a child, more than likely. And we lived here, understand. I had opened up the bar by then, though it went by Roughshack Pool. Anyway, Carla went straight to a woman who kind of kept track of everything Gruel, you know. She went to the woman who kept a makeshift scrapbook of historical facts."

I was way ahead of him and felt my face blush, as if I were a part of this tragic, Sophoclean truth. I said, "My ex-mother-in-law Ina Cathcart."

Ina liked to corner me and give me the "Jefferson Davis once slept here" monologue. She told stories of long-lost gold mines, of Confederate money cached beneath where Paula Purgason's house now stood, of the Siamese quadruplets who lived in Gruel from 1898 until they found out about a circus that paid good money. Ina claimed to know everything that happened in this sad section of Graywood County. I said, "Wow," to her more often than I said, "I love you," or "Pass the corn bread" when I visited those few Thanksgivings, Christmases, Labor Day weekends.

Jeff got off his stool, rounded the counter, and returned with a cribbage board. He set the four pegs in the game holes and said, "I've been looking for more of these little metal men. And I've been looking for the rules to Chinese checkers."

I couldn't tell if Jeff joked or not. I said, "I don't know. I used to play poker once a week with some buddies."

"It wasn't Ina Cathcart. I mean, that was who Carla went to see directly. And I'm still of the belief that Ina lied in order to protect the innocent, as they say. So Ina said, 'Lordy, Carla, I don't know of anyone having a baby and then boxing her up all the way out to Forty-Five back the time you was born.'"

I said, "Well that's good," because I didn't know what else to say. Jeff Downer the owner started to look a little like Victor Dees from the army-navy store at this point, and I—paranoid—began to wonder if my getting locked up inside this bar happened to be an elaborate scheme to eradicate me as if I'd gone to Graywood Regional Memorial hospital's emergency room with an earache.

"It was Sherrill Cathcart gave up the news," Jeff said. "He stood there with a squished groundhog in his hands and he said, 'I know what happened, I bet. You the daughter of old Quarry and Ulena Downer, Carla. I know this 'cause Quarry come home with a dead twelve-point buck and a newborn baby girl. He said he didn't have money for the mount, so he wanted to trade. I said it didn't seem right and sent him on his way.'"

I picked up the cribbage board and said, "You need a deck of cards to play this game."

"I was there, you know, supporting my wife. She said,

'Downer?' She said, 'Quarry and Ulena Downer? Hey, Jeff—that's your daddy's brother, Quarry.' Well I sat right down there inside the Cathcart home, atop a cougar-hided settee."

I poured us two more drinks, which I thought might be the last two I ever saw. Jeff Downer the owner's eyes showed more white than iris and pupil combined. I said, "I tell you a good game—it's a dice game they play up in Wisconsin called ship-captain-crew. Now that's a good game."

"Carla left me for good within the day and never let me know. I'd been having relations with my own first cousin for twenty-two years, eight months, and more than a couple days. No wonder we couldn't have childrens!" Jeff slugged down his drink. "I guess it's a blessing. The more people move off or die, the less people know around here."

I said, "It's not a sin or anything," like I had a notion of the sin market. I said, "That name—Quarry?—that's an interesting name." I thought of a novel opening that went something like: Quarry had a speech impediment, but that didn't stop him from having the largest and most diverse rock collection in the South. "Well I'm about full of booze. I better get back to the inn."

Jeff Downer the owner grabbed my left forearm and clutched it like a C-clamp. "I'll put the weenies on. We can eat hot dogs. Listen, I don't want to sound like a pussy or nothing, but I kind of feel good talking all this out. Pretty much it's been Carla found out her DNA, she left, and I've either hid out or shut up since 1981. Reagan got sworn in on the day my wife left. I've always held that against him. It snowed here that day, too, and it don't snow here much. All these people looking up at the sky with their tongues stuck out, and I'm looking at the ground hurting."

116

I told myself not to start thinking about Jeff Downer the owner as Jeff Downer the Owner Moaner, seeing as he started wailing about this point. He blubbered, blurted, and gagged. I would've known how to act if stupid and cold Bekah showed any emotions at her mother and brother's double funeral.

I put my arm around his shoulder like I'd seen men do in TV movies. I knew not to say, "Okay. Let me check back with you in a couple days after I look in on my writer guests."

"I didn't mean to," Jeff Downer the Owner Moaner bleated out. "I know that everyone thought it was suicide, but I didn't mean to."

I pulled my arm away. I said, "What?"

Jeff stopped. He slapped his palms down on the bar. He said, "I'm sixty, goddamn it. I'm sixty and I'll live to be a hundred ten like everyone else who sticks in Gruel."

I said, "Are you telling me that Sherrill Cathcart didn't really kill himself? You need to tell me the truth, buddy. My wife needs to know the truth."

I'm not one to believe in karma—that would be a great opening for some kind of serial killer's autobiography, I thought—but Jeff Downer cocked his head upward like a South American jungle bird, stared at the ceiling, and said, "I've never owned a shotgun. I've never taken a geometry class. How would I know how to stick a rifle upward at a certain angle and make it look real? You can't get me on this. You can't get any of us in on this."

◆ ◆ ◆

James and Joyce told me later on in my adolescence that my parents lied, that my first word wasn't "Daddy" or "Momma" or "car." I didn't say anything until I hit three years old, and must've bottled it up like a noxious gas. My brother and sister complained throughout my growing up how Mom and Dad doted on me, how they pulled out a Brownie camera every time it looked like I might smile, frown, or tilt my head angelically. Meanwhile they talked to me incessantly, I was told, hoping that I would absorb state capitals, the periodic table, Roman emperors, Shakespeare's tragedies, the presidents in order, winners of the Academy Award, French, pi out twenty decimals, art history, botany, planets and stars in the Milky Way, *Don Quixote*, World Series winners, poker ranks, third-world countries that they knew would get worse once Republican administrations started screwing them over in the future for oil, the short stories of Flannery O'Connor, a list of bourbon brands out of Tennessee and Kentucky, even a list of past boxing champions.

I only remember all of this because I was told more than once. To be honest, there's no recollection, really, of my being flat on my back in a crib with big faces looking down at me listing off things they wished I'd remember later in life. James and Joyce told me all of this behind our house in Black Mountain, when I was seven, nine, eleven, and thirteen, as they pinned my shoulders against the heart pine exterior. That's what seeped in.

My first word, according to everybody, was "Shutup!" I could walk and run by this time—I could ride a trike—and evidently I finally screamed out "Shutup!" Nowadays I like to say my first words were "Shut the fuck up!" or "Could you please shut your goddamn grits-hole up!" but probably I went for brevity.

"Shutup!" was what I yelled at my writers retreat participants when I returned home and found them suddenly pissed off and unionized. "Go back to your rooms! Don't y'all have any ideas whatsoever?"

Man, I saw this as a James/Joyce/Jeff Downer/Bekah/Victor Dees/Maura-Lee conspiracy of sorts. I had a brand-new woman who'd paid dues named Tania who purported to write a novel about three generations of office supply store owners. When she checked in and signed her name in the guest book—I made a big thing about how I would one day sell this guest book filled with famous writers' signatures—I said, "Like the SLA Tania. Like Patty Hearst." She looked at me as if I'd spoken in one of the *Star Wars* dialects. I said, "Welcome to the Gruel Inn Writers Retreat. If you need anything, pick up the phone and dial zero. Or the number for Roughhouse Billiards listed on the 'Things to Do in Gruel' laminated handout."

I shouldn't have wasted a whole sheet of paper for the handout. I could've listed everything on a fortune cookie slip.

"You are not a real novelist you lured us in I've gotten on the Internet and can't find one item about you or your books on Amazon or even Google there's no Novel Akers listed this is a hoax and sham I'm going to expose and sue you for everything you got *Writer's Digest* will hear about this in order to warn people about you."

I thought, Boy, that's a good example of run-on sentences, because I had read all about their use and misuse in one of those *Write Now!* textbooks. According to some professor, it was okay for Latin American writers and Faulkner to use such convoluted structures, but no one else. So of course I said, "Tania, I can't let you leave Gruel sounding like that. The New York publishing industry will not allow for such subject-verb-object-subject-verb-object-subject-verb-object construction." I didn't say anything about how I had no clue what she meant by "Google."

This took place in my office/smoking room space. Every other participant stood there, too. *Women* wore ascots and smoked pipes. Everyone stood there with arms crossed over their chests, like offensive linemen between plays, like diplomats tired of détente, like parents unbelieving of their children's tardy stories, like rap stars. I said to Tania, "Wait a minute. Go through all of that again, please."

"You're not who you advertised to be," an effeminate man named Rico from Kentucky said. "You advertised how a novelist would be running the show."

He'd actually been crying. I said, "Somebody go get Rico a paper towel to get off that running mascara." I said, "No I didn't. The stupid magazine ran a misprint. My name's plain Novel, nothing else. I dealt with snakes before getting stuck in this business. Anyone want to go look at the largest blacksnake I've ever seen?"

Rico raised his hand.

I said to Tania, "Listen. I'm sorry that you can't write a fucking sentence without someone looking over your shoulder. Fucking quit. Give it up. Go on to something else. Learn how to knit. Run for a spot on your local school board. Take up swimming to prove you won't drown. And *shutup*."

I needed to steal Dr. Bobba Lollis's blood pressure machine and hook it up in the Gruel Inn office.

Tania said, "I'm going to take my three generations of office supply store owners elsewhere. I could've gone to Bread Loaf! Come on, friends."

I could've gone to Bread Loaf! my dick. Listen—and I have nothing against people having big dreams and/or unrealistic ambitions—but the people who entered the Gruel Inn's writers

120

retreat couldn't have gotten into Pita Slice. I said, "Well go on then. As a matter of fact, I want all of you off these premises by sundown!" I think someone said that in a famous movie western once, so I can't take credit.

I didn't think about reverse psychology or child psychology or of Jeff Downer the Owner Moaner when I pulled out my reservation ledger and called up every other would-be novelist to say that they needed to find another haven, that I closed down, that I about had it with rich people who had no talent or direction. Pretty much I only said, "Have you been reading?" and then said, "*Shutup*" when they said they didn't have time, or that they didn't want to be influenced, et cetera. Even I knew better.

I called up Roughhouse Billiards next, and Jeff answered without a tinge of booze in his voice. He said, "Roughhouse Billiards. Home of the Trick Shot," like the pope might say.

I said, "This ain't right."

15

I THOUGHT MAYBE the constant trudge I heard happened to be my last guests. In the night I sat up off my cot hungover and slightly lonely. The beginning of the Sex Pistols' "Holiday in the Sun" might best represent what I heard, the incessant foot-stomping of irreconcilable teenagers. Don't ask how I know that band or song. In my previous life as the lieutenant governor's speechwriter I tried to know everything about pop culture.

I sat up off the cot alone and cocked my head. Due to a high blood pressure I'd never acknowledge, I thought that maybe only my ears pounded. But this was different. I walked outside in my boxer shorts and looked across the way at what I had begun calling Gruel Jungle. The *pank-pank-pank* of clomping came from there, barely.

It sounded like ten thousand men marching from afar, is what I'm saying. I had no other choice but to hit the Xerox machine and get me another drink, then go back outside with my battery-operated Coleman lamp complete with clock light. The onward stomping definitely moved in my direction.

I went inside, called Maura-Lee, and said, "Hey, what's that goddamn noise?"

She said, "Your voice?"

"Stick your head out the window and listen. Do you hear a bunch of people marching by? Is there a parade going on downtown? I'm not fucking around. Tell me what you know."

Maura-Lee said, "You can just come over if you want a little company, Novel. I thought I'd made it clear before that I might be a little more than interested in you. Where's your hand? You're not beating off, are you, and that's the sound?"

First off, of course I thought, What the hell is she talking about, all that "I thought I'd made it clear"? I thought, I've got the wrong number. I locked the office door and turned off the lights. "Can you hear it through the receiver from this end?"

"I hear cicadas. I hear crickets. I hear a man who might've lost his mind earlier in the day, seeing as every one of his guests has stopped by my house asking directions to the nearest hotel."

I said, "Idiots. Too bad one of them didn't write a travel book."

Maura-Lee said she needed to work anyway, and told me to meet her at the bakery if I wanted. It might have taken me two minutes before I showed up wearing my drinking clothes from the day before. She shook her head and handed over a hairnet. "You can either make yourself useful or stand out of the way. This gets messy."

I washed my hands, then walked over to the forty-quart mixer. I said, "What's a machine like this cost?"

"Your life," she said. "So did you make up the ghost-soldiers-advancing story just to come see me? Please say that you're not in the throes of auditory hallucinations. That's what happened to every man in my immediate family. They thought they heard younger women beckon them to Texas. Or California, Washington State, the middle of Florida."

Maura-Lee looked as if she'd not eaten since opening up Gruel Bakery. I'm talking she now couldn't have weighed more than 120, and almost appeared somewhat emaciated due to her height. I said, "Goddamn, Maura-Lee, are you taking care of yourself? You're not still sneezing away the pounds, are you?"

"Hand me that boat paddle. Sometimes the dough clogs up the blades." She wore a thin white tank top, and her biceps bulged as she worked the mixer. Her nipples hadn't receded from weight loss yet.

I handed her an oar cut in half lengthwise. She pulled off the safety guard from her mixer. I said, "I'm thinking you could put a meat-grinder head on this thing and run Gruel BBQ out of business."

Maura-Lee stroked and prodded deep inside the machine. "You know, Novel, you've only tried to be with me once, and then you never came back. Probably sobered up the next day and have felt embarrassed about it. Went on your way. Felt guilty, so threw me the continental breakfast bone. Well, well, well."

She spoke the truth and I felt horrendous about it. I wanted the subject changed and said, "You don't have any paper hats around here instead of hairnets, do you?"

"Maybe that phantom sound you hear was my remaining self-esteem advancing on your position."

"I've made many mistakes in my life. If I hurt you, then I count that as one of my biggest. I'm serious."

Maura-Lee turned the machine back on and changed gears twice. "If it weren't for my Jesus crust loaves going out to school-children I'd really be pissed off. Your halting the writers retreat knocks me out two-fifty a week. Thousand a month. Now I'm going to have to go beyond my sales region. Hey, are you even keeping track of expenses? Do you have a business license, or tax ID number?"

I said, "No. This is Gruel. You're not reporting all of this either, are you." I waved my arm, then readjusted my hairnet.

Maura-Lee told me to roll a baker's rack toward the table and asked if I was smart enough to figure out her automatic slicer. She said, "You fool. You're right—if you weren't such an outsider you could probably get away with it. But you're not from around here and these people hated the Cathcarts, in case you haven't figured that much out yet."

I said, "Hold on a minute, Snipes."

"Now you've gone and closed down the only business that brought business to the square. Way to go. I guess you can now stay away from the IRS, but how're you going to live? Don't tell me you plan to write a goddamn memoir. That's all America needs is another fucking memoir, candyass."

I walked out, crossed the street to Roughhouse, found it closed, and didn't know whether to wait on the step until daybreak or drive home. By now, I supposed, the advancing regiment more than likely encamped across from my place. From my vantage point I could watch Maura-Lee scoop and shape dough into pan after pan, transfer just-made dough to a walk-in refrigeration unit, and so on.

She'll have to hire on workers, I thought. A one-woman operation might've been fine for bagel-eating scribblers, but not for an entire region of staff-of-life-devouring kids being taught racism indirectly.

If I still held bourbon in my veins I would've volunteered to help out. But I didn't. I walked to my step van, started it up, and drove home bravely. No soldiers ambushed me, this time, literally.

I looked above Gruel Bakery, to its second floor. Did I see two human shadows cross the windows? Did I hallucinate?

At dawn I released my few snakes from their shed, asked them to always live nearby if possible, apologized for my past feeble attempt at stroking and nurturing unpublishable vanity writers instead of them. I checked each room's doorknob from the outside, made a mental note to buy a sledgehammer and handsaw from the army-navy store, and almost wished that I owned a Gideon for an odd comfort I foresaw needing.

I looked across the road. Was that Ina and Irby half hidden in the trees, waving, showing off their clogging shoes?

PART II

"Though talent be wanting, yet indignation will drive me to
verse such as I—or any scribbler—can manage."

—JUVENAL, SATIRE I

16

IF I STOOD four-ten or less I could walk from my office at the Gruel Inn all the way to the far end of room 12 without bowing my head or bending my knees. Of course, if I were less than four-ten and still dealt with snakes professionally I could be the star attraction at any midlevel traveling county fair freak sideshow. If I were a little person with a large snake I would fear being swallowed whole every minute of my life, and could never offer the world *Novel: Autobiography.*

I knocked holes in all of my walls with the sledgehammer and cut two-by-four non-weight-bearing studs. I drug each mattress, box spring, and frame out and stacked them in the ex-snake shed—not knowing that it would soon return to its original purpose. I ripped up short nap indoor-outdoor carpet, rolled it tightly, and room by room pulled it outside. After every trip I washed my hands seeing as the carpet industry saturates "floor-covering fiber" with enough formaldehyde and "other man-made essential chemicals" to kill off a midsize third world nation. Then I drug said carpets across the road on the second day of my self-imposed reclusion and rolled them out like a Hollywood entranceway to Gruel Jungle.

Listen, if I knew back as a speechwriter what I learned reno-vating the Gruel Inn, I would've had my lieutenant governor offer up another long-winded discourse as to how the United States could conquer Cuba, Bolivia, Uganda, Cambodia, Nicaragua, Chile, Iraq, Iran, Colombia, and Alabama only by dropping 24' × 24' sections of Dalton Orlong carpet from B-52s maybe every hundred yards onto these lands, thus rendering them scorched and useless.

I exaggerate, or "hyperbolize." With Chile it would have to be carpet runners, what with the country's slight width.

I took out every nightstand, chest of drawers, telephone, wire hanger, TV, and free paper shoeshine rag from all the rooms, except number 3. Here was my thinking: If I wanted to write a great memoir, then I needed to cleanse the place of my last tenants, the idiotic good-intentioned men and women who couldn't help themselves from starting any story with "It was a dark and stormy night" or "Call me *Put Name Here.*"

Listen, if any Buddhists or exorcists lived in Gruel back then I would've offered up half the twenty-four grand I still had in cash money saved from the writers retreat people, in order to come smoke out all the bad juju karma from my abode.

I knocked a trail through my walls but each one owned elec-trical lines, for some reason, right at the four-ten mark, and I don't know about you but I won't touch a wire. When I was a child our house in Black Mountain had a cement-floored back room that my parents pretended to one day turn into a music room. This room stood against a mostly clay embankment, and it flooded with every downpour. Because James and Joyce formed some kind of union with stipulations that ruled out any kind of manual labor outside their normal allowance chores—

scattering shrimp heads off in the woods for feral bears, cats, coyotes, cougars, panthers, dogs, and hermits—I got forced to "mop" the supposed "studio."

This was 1971 or thereabouts. I'm not sure where my parents obtained a prototypical, cylindrical, metal Shop-Vac. I walked into the room, mop in hand, barefoot. I thought, This might take some time. I thought, Them sons of bitches Irish adopted bastard nonworking fuckers.

I'd learned how to talk and think this way from Willem de Kooning, or somebody who taught earlier at Black Mountain College. So I held the mop and toed the bucket forward. Then I went into the kitchen and shoved that metal canister into the flooded room. This'll be so easy, I thought. I can suck up the water, dump it in the bathtub, and suck up some more. I remember plugging in the prong, and how it felt when I turned the toggle switch to *on*. That kind of vibrates, I thought. I watched the standing water shimmer as if a school of minnows frenzied on a lake's surface.

Where were my parents? Did they travel alone for shrimp and other shellfish? Did they pan for gold on Rash Creek? Because I might have stored up a certain amount of paranoia over the years since—writing speeches for various politicians tends to cause such a condition, I'm betting—sometimes I think my own sad impatient parents, unable to weather the crescendos and diminuendos of the music world, set up an "accidental" electrocution trap. It all hit me one day as I cleaned out our gutters during a lightning storm, part of my "chores." I thought about it again during tornado warnings when Mom and Dad asked me to sit with our neighbors down the road who lived in an ancient trailer.

Anyway, I moved the Shop-Vac a second time and my left ring finger stuck to the switch. My arm undulated like a rabid surfer's dream wave. I think I yelled out, "Hey, hey, hey!" or something nearly as helpless. No one in my childhood home ran to my rescue. I stood barefoot in standing water with an electrical appliance that played for keeps.

Somehow I pulled away.

At age eight I didn't think about how it was my *left* ring finger, my wedding band finger—how maybe it would all haunt me later on in an area so appropriately named Gruel.

But I stray.

Back at the motel, I knocked out Sheetrock, cut studs, and did my best at making it look like a professional job. When bent down in the office I could look all the way down to the last room. I tried not to think of portals, or tunnels, or looking through a telescope backwards, or my subconscious.

Notice how I left the hot plates, by the way.

My original plan—which I hadn't outlined even though a few of my how-to books suggested writing out a step-by-step procedure to follow—was to write a twelve-chapter memoir, using each room. I would start on the far end, deal with the first memories, leave that section on the desk, then move one room closer to the office until I finished.

I would sleep on the floor and know that work needed doing until I reached the office holding at least 240 pages of manuscript to be sent off to a publisher that specialized in psychological treatises that directed parents how *not* to bring up a child, and states how *not* to treat employees, and spouses how *not* to push their mates into actions unbefitting of the human race. I foresaw my autobiography *Novel* being taught in both American literature and abnormal psychology classes. If I did well in chapter 11—"The Gruel Year"—maybe even sociology and economics departments might push it.

I ordered MREs from Victor Dees's army-navy store and paid him cash money. I asked Jeff the owner to drop off a bottle of bourbon and a bottle of vodka once a week. Toilet paper, little soap bars, shampoo, and toothpaste—I had enough of all those things seeing as I'd thought the Gruel Inn Writers Retreat would last forever. I postdated water and electric and insurance bill checks, and mailed them off. I thought about cutting off my phone service, but didn't—just in case.

We're getting somewhere, I thought. I thought, Now dickhead Milson Willets will be sorry he didn't keep my parents' invaluable papers that would help explain little Novel Akers.

I started on a Sunday morning. I sat down at room 12's desk and stared at the mass-produced landscape on the wall, a wonderful desert scene that, off in the top left corner, showed an ancient cowboy hiking out of the mountains, leading his horse by the bridle. I'd never noticed it before! That's how the mind works! I thought, and knew that I had to remember this moment when I got all the way back to room 2, "The Gruel Year."

I laughed and laughed. This is going to be *so easy*, I thought.

Then I heard a noise outside room 12's door that could've only been a hognose snake scraping its scales together, trying to sound like a western diamondback rattler. I went outside and spent most of the day looking for that particular serpent. I followed up my ex-carpets well into Gruel Jungle, checked beneath each edge—snakes like to warm up beneath flat, flat pieces of lightweight covers (go stick a piece of tin roofing out in the yard late summer; pick it up two days later; notice the good coiled reptile)—but found nothing.

Then that goddamned marching sound started back up and I ran like hell back to my room. By this time it was dusk. I looked at my notebook, where I had written, "I don't remember my actual birth." There was nothing left to do but heat up one eye on the hot plate, boil water, and eat some delicious freeze-dried stew, then curl up on a cement floor still swirled with glue remains that couldn't hold down nap forever.

17

I'M NOT SURE what gold went for in 1969, but I'm almost certain it was more than a dollar an ounce. My parents offered up that much money at the end of the day, divided by three. Me, I used that money for gum down at Black Mountain Candy. James and Joyce—I'll give my adopted brethren this—socked their profits away, saying, "Who needs gum when we got free tar on the road?" They chewed tar! I'm talking they stood around the roadside on hot, hot days, waited for the asphalt to bubble, then thumb-and-fingered out their warm black nuggets.

Who chews tar?

Lookit: Dealing with the shrimp might stick in my memory more than gold panning in Rash Creek, but for the most part my family probably stood shin-deep in water more often. Oh our parents gave us galoshes—*rubbers*, they called them—but I'd be willing to bet any DSS worker would say that James, Joyce, and Novel would be classified as abused children these days.

And even though I say my dad worked the pans, et cetera, he really set up illegal seines upstream, caught rainbow and brown trout, and hauled them down to Charleston chefs before picking up shrimp, oysters, and clams. And live jellyfish for the more adventurous snakehandler members of the Black Mountain Pentecostal Holiness Church.

"You'd think that people who lived on the Atlantic Ocean would get their fill of spots, blue, and snapper. It doesn't make sense, my taking mountain trout down there. These people pay upwards of twelve bucks a meal for rainbow," my father said most afternoons. My mom normally said something like, "James, Joyce—quit torturing that frog," or salamander, or box turtle.

I always said, "Can I start taking oboe lessons? Can I take violin lessons? Can I start taking ballet lessons? Would one of y'all teach me how to use a sewing machine? Can I get an Easy-Bake oven for Christmas? Can I take a correspondence course in interior decorating? Can I spend my afternoons down at Black Mountain Beauty Shop and learn how to mold a bouffant?" I said about anything that would be less embarrassing than living with parents who gave up their music careers altogether in order to scrape by in ways they now saw fit. If I'd've been brought up in the aluminum years I would've said, "Can I scrounge around Dumpsters and pick up beer cans to turn in at the scrap metal recycling center?"

My mother slogged across the creek, laden down with maybe a half ounce of speckled dust, most of it between her molars because of the chew test. "James, Joyce—have you got any homework tonight? I want y'all to study more and quit babbling."

My brother and sister never answered. They limped toward the car, playing blind, running into trees, holes, the occasional authentic miner. I yelled out more than once, "Could I please learn how to play the harp?" and, looking back on it, I'm pretty sure it was only a premature death wish.

◆ ◆ ◆

Victor Dees came over and knocked on every door until he hit 11. I woke up and opened it. "I'm just making sure you ain't dead," he said. Victor wore fatigues, an olive green T-shirt, mirrored sunglasses, and a World War I German helmet with that spike on top.

I said, "Come on in. You want a drink? I got bourbon and vodka, but I don't have but one glass. And only one chair. Come on in. I mean it! What's with the outfit? Did you get another call from Bekah and you come to kill me?"

Victor Dees walked in not as rigidly as he should have. He said, "I thought you only joked. I didn't think you meant it."

"Welcome to my humble abode," I said.

He looked at my blank notebook, the blank page riveted into the Smith-Corona typewriter, the blue, blue screen of my computer. "I'll take vodka. It's not as predictable. It's almost odorless. I got to talk to the ROTC people over at Forty-Five High later tonight."

I handed him an unopened bottle of Smirnoff. "Do you know the day and date? I've been so submerged. *Submersed.* Man, I haven't felt like this since trying to memorize the Roman Empire one night before exams."

"You've been holed up three days," Victor said. "Those MREs I sold you were more for show and less for chow. To be honest I thought you only wanted to decorate the office or something. I've been selling those things like crazy to every Cracker

Barrel on interstate exits near military exits. Fort Jackson. Camp Lejeune. Edwards Air Force Base. Parris Island, you know."

I took the bourbon and swigged three Adam's apples' worth. "Very cool. Hey, you sit in the chair. Be my guest, my first guest! I'll sit on the floor. If you have any stories, feel free to type them in." I pointed at my unused Mead marbled composition book. "Or pick up the pen and handwrite it down. I bet you got some good stories, Victor."

Victor Dees sat down and spread his legs out in a way that made him look like an effeminate commandant. "I don't want you getting botulism. You *have* eaten some of the MREs, right? I'm just thinking—hell, sixty years—some air might've found its way in the package. I know no one else cares about you in Gruel, but I don't want you dead. I don't want that on my limited conscience."

I held my Old Crow between my legs. I said, "What do you mean by all that?"

"I don't want to be the cause of your death, you know. I don't want me or anybody else coming over here and finding you laid out flat stiff dead because of poison. Goddamn. Though I guess we could send your body to Graywood Regional for an autopsy and it would come back that you had, what—I don't know—cancer of the vagina."

I stood up and paced the room just like I'd done in room 12, like I would do in 11 through 1. I said, "Is it 'laid' out stiff or 'lain' out stiff?"

"I don't want to be the discoverer of dead bodies," Victor Dees said. He hit the vodka. "I was never really in the armed services, you know. One day I'll show you what's wrong with my feet."

What else could I say but, "They're flat?"

"No. Cleft." Then Victor Dees finished the quart of vodka in one long slug, and disappeared.

◆ ◆ ◆

Bekah and I didn't marry in Gruel for a number of reasons, all hers. First off, there was no standing church left. Gruel could've been the only town south of the Mason-Dixon with a population over three—preacher, preacher's wife, one congregant—without a standing house of worship. We didn't want to ship in either preacher or judge to stand on the porch where her daddy committed suicide. This old boy named Sammy Koon, Bekah was convinced, would try to interrupt the proceeding, too. The list went on. She had undergone nighttime visions, et cetera. She'd read somewhere how it was bad luck to be married in a town that General Sherman didn't find fit to burn down. Migratory birds often lit in Gruel, and their squawking would ruin the moment, according to Bekah.

Why didn't I gather all of this information back in my twenties and cancel the entire operation, you might ask. Or *someone* might ask. The fucking lieutenant governor at the time up in North Carolina might've pulled me aside and told me to skip town if he had any ideas as to what the forecast held. My few friends—mostly herpetologists and mechanics who specialized on the step van's motor—surely noticed Bekah's insecurities and lack of commitment. If anything, one of my less weight-sensitive buddies from the bars could've spouted out, "Your fiancée seems to be letting herself go, Bo. She's putting on the *pounds*," not knowing that she'd have sneezing attacks however many years later, lose all the weight, regain a hard stomach worthy of a handball court, and so on.

But I got no help from friends. My most unpredictable rat snake had a better chance of turning Mr. Ed and telling me what I couldn't see in the future.

We drove down to a wedding chapel halfway between Conway and Myrtle Beach, South Carolina, where no blood tests were needed. I paid for the deluxe ceremony, which included two potted palmetto trees flanking the altar, twenty-four photographs, and rice that fell out of the ceiling as long as I stepped on the special button on our way out the door. We had our choice of Elvis, Willie Nelson, the Supremes, or the Beatles before and after the wedding marches in and out.

Listen, I clearly remember saying "I do," but I think Bekah only moved her lips, and then Lester Clark — owner-operator of the wedding chapel — said I could kiss the bride.

You would think that we'd've driven the twenty miles south down to Myrtle Beach for our honeymoon. Instead, we backtracked to North Carolina and up to Virginia, because Bekah wanted to see Luray Caverns. There was some kind of stalactite pipe organ she'd heard all about, *which she thought actually worked*, like a player piano.

I don't need to go into my wedding night, obviously, at the Cave Inn.

Victor Dees left and I sat down in front of the computer with my bottle of bourbon. I lit a cigarette for the first time since leaving North Carolina. Up until this point I had not felt obligated to keep that state's economy going. I tilted my head back and counted 252 ceiling tiles. I got up, hunched myself all the way down to the office — something I'd promised myself not to do — found a tape measure, came back, and indeed learned that a crack in the east-facing wall was more than forty-eight inches long. It was fifty-two. I got out my hawksbill knife and chipped through eight inches of paint, the last being yellow.

Back in the office I called Maura-Lee and woke her up. She said, "Remember, Novel, I work third shift basically. I always will. Third and most of first, then I come home from hours of kneading Jesus crust, and sleep."

I might've yelled, "How long have I been here? Oh god, how long have I been here in this self-imposed exile in order to write my autobiography?"

I'm not saying that I cried or anything, but maybe the bourbon got me overly distraught and somewhat confused. Maura-Lee said, "Not that I'm x-ing off my calendar waiting for your return to civilization or anything, but I think it's been either two or three days. I'm not keeping track. That's your job."

Then she hung up, like she should have, of course, indubitably. I made a point to remember this occasion, should Maura-Lee ever decide to write some kind of old-fashioned bread and pastry cookbook, become frustrated over having to use the word "yeast" so many times, and call me up in the middle of the night asking for a synonym.

The answer's "single-celled ascomycetous fungi," according to my dictionary.

18

THE STUPID PLAY PRODUCTION!

In the eleventh grade I got forced to audition for a part in a theatrical extravaganza that my English teacher wrote based on the life of Thomas Wolfe, the excommunicated Asheville novelist. My English teacher went to Black Mountain College as a *poetry* major, of all things, and then underwent experimental electric shock treatments from some guy named Thigpen down in Augusta, Georgia, before matriculating to a normal women's college in Greensboro and obtaining her degree in secondary education. Her name was Miss Margaret Dickel, heiress to the Tennessee bourbon empire, and she spoke freely of her time with battery cables on her nodes almost every class period. Miss Dickel said things like, "I'm thinking that if Mr. William Butler Yeats underwent shock treatment like I did, he might not've written rubbish the last years of his life."

I'd done well enough on my PSAT to get named a Furman University and UNC scholar. College reps from schools I'd never heard of said that I, alone, could bring their averages up fifty points, though I think they meant "mean," not "median." Or vice versa—I never learned what that stood for in math, or why it mattered. Math, though, played a part in my later years, as I'll explain.

"The Sad Boy Inside the Boardinghouse Blues," Miss Dickel's play, attempted to portray young Thomas Wolfe as a precocious lad intent on making a mark on the planet. I would play the part of young Tom, Miss Dickel the part of Tom's mother, our assistant principal—I forget his name, but he, too, had spent time at Black Mountain College as a sculpture student—as Mr. Wolfe the dad, then as Thomas Wolfe the grown-up. *Every other student and citizen* of Black Mountain had what's known as a "walk-on role" as a boarder, shop owner, neighbor, or literary figure from the canon who showed up in young Thomas Wolfe's dreams: Shakespeare, Marlowe, St. Augustine, Cervantes, Lord Byron, Emily Dickinson, Mark Twain, Charles Baudelaire, Dickens, the Apostle Paul, Harriet Tubman, Plato, Melville, Queen Victoria, Phillis Wheatley, Voltaire, Carl Gustav Jung, Dante—everybody. I'm talking Miss Dickel got out the *Norton's Anthology* and found a way for Thomas Wolfe to hear the voices of about anyone who'd put pen to paper. She even went into a sci-fi mode and got living writers to show up in Thomas Wolfe's dreams. Truman Capote spoke up, as did Kerouac and that Allen Ginsberg celebrity. This was 1977 or thereabouts. Joan Didion showed up, Susan Sontag, the guy who wrote *Jaws.*

Needless to say, the entire house had a part, which meant there would be no audience. My lines pretty much went, "Who's there?" I was to sit up in bed, say "Who's there?" and then someone, let's say playing Oscar Wilde, would say, "You must go open your mother's chest of drawers, inspect her panties, then write about them in full detail!"

I was supposed to nod, maybe raise an index finger in the air, and go "Aha!" like that. Then I would roll over and write—using a Bic pen that didn't exist at the time, by the way, in 1910—in a Mead composition notebook that didn't exist at this point either. The play ended with my pretending to type about four hundred words a minute, and then I would rip out the last page of *Look Homeward, Angel.*

Notice how I've used the verb "was supposed to."

In the prefarming old days, oysters weren't good unless the month had an *R*. That meant September through April. The school play was set for the last week in April, and my father—who had agreed to play Faulkner in one of the sci-fi dream sequences—decided that I needed to help him down in Charleston more than I needed to lay on a boardinghouse cot and entertain the history of literature. He said, "I got forty people wanting a bushel bag apiece. Summer's coming and they don't want to wait, son. What with Joyce and James running back to Ireland, I have no other choice."

I knew right away not to put my wants first. I said, "But how can Miss Dickel run her show without Faulkner? Nobody but you could play Mr. Faulkner, Dad."

He lifted his can of beer. "Well fuck that Faulkner, Novel."

✦ ✦ ✦

Jeff the owner showed up in the middle of my wondering why room 10's ceiling held only 228 tiles. The bathroom wasn't any larger, I'd figured out with my tape measure. I counted and re-counted the ceiling at least a couple hundred times, both east to west, then north to south. I found the midpoint tile and swirled around it clockwise and counterclockwise twice. Every time I ended up 228. I went back to room 12, then 11, and counted them again.

Something was wrong. I didn't like this at all.

"Whoever done your grouting put too much grout in this room," Jeff said. "It's not hard to figure out. Look, man—let's say you got you twelve one-by-one-foot tiles, and you grout them an inch apart. What's one inch times twelve?"

I said, "A foot."

"You damn right. Twelve inches. One times twelve equals twelve, even in Gruel. Now. Let's say you got twelve one-by-one-foot ceiling tiles but you only grout them a *half inch* apart. What's that come out to?"

I should mention that in my preliminary memoir itinerary I knew to stack clean socks, underwear, shirts, and pants in order in each room right atop the toilet bowl reservoirs. On this day I wore a pair of blue work pants and a yellow shirt, plus a cap I'd gotten somewhere that advertised Square Books in Oxford, Mississippi. I said, "Six. Six inches. Half a foot."

"Why're you dressed in blue and yellow? Is that some kind of school colors for cold feet and chicken backbone? Don't fuck up on me, Novel. We got bets going on down at the Roughhouse."

I shrugged. "Have you heard from Maura-Lee? Has Bekah called up Victor Dees?" I asked. "Hey, that rhymed. Maybe I should be writing poetry in here instead of my autobiography."

Jeff the owner said, "Maybe you are, boy." Then he popped me upside the head. "Okay. Let's say you have twelve one-by-one-foot ceiling tiles. There's a five-eighths grout inch between half of them, and a three-eighths grout between a third, and a one-inch grout between the rest."

I said, "I'd kind of like to know whatever happened to Miss Dickel. I assume by now she's taken over her ancestors' bottling company, you know."

Jeff hit me upside the head again, twice in a row. "You're not paying attention. I knew this might happen. I've seen it before! What do you think happened to the previous owner of this place, back in 1940? You have to concentrate, boy."

"Did you bring me any more booze? I got the money. People keep coming over here and drinking on me free. I got money," I said. "What time is it, anyway? Shouldn't you be back running the bar?" Pop-pop-pop-pop-pop-pop-pop up the side of my head happened before I could raise my hands in self-defense. I said, "I'm going to kill you if you do that again."

"Now *that* sounds like my little Novel. Now you're talking. I just wanted to make sure you hadn't drifted off to Alabama-land. I only wanted to make sure you knew the difference between pain and glory. Please tell me you ain't planning on moving out to Wichita to think you deserve to have this work of yours printed up just because you lived in the middle of nowhere for a spell, like some kind of poet."

I had no idea what Jeff the owner meant. I said, "No," because it seemed more likely that I wouldn't get hit. "If all that grouting was the way you said, it would still average out an inch wide between. It would end up the same as an inch wide."

Jeff the owner held up a finger and backed out of room 10, Gruel Inn. He returned with a quart of bourbon, a quart of cheap vodka, and a bottle of red wine. "Wine's on me," he said. "Stay the way you are. Don't give up. Write the truth. Or at least write. And remember me well. I'm not asking for any kind of dedication or epithet, goddamnit. I only ask that you speak of me well when it comes to the Gruel years."

I said thanks. He left. In my notebook I wrote down, "Jeff the owner said 'epithet,' then cursed."

◆ ◆ ◆

We weren't brought up in a religious household, though everyone outside of me spoke in tongues. My parents made us go to every area church once, and drove us down to a synagogue in Asheville one Saturday. "If something sticks, then go with it," my father said. "I don't care. It doesn't matter, if you ask me." He'd been brought up Episcopalian somewhere in Maryland; my mother grew up Church of Christ in Connecticut. Grandparents on both sides didn't seem to notice how their own children were a little more than fucked-up, and even Grandpa Akers came down to visit one time and said, "James, Joyce, Novel—you'll end up nothing but confused. *Stupidity* is better than *confusion*." To my parents he said, "How many *stupid* people live long lives? The answer: a lot. How many confused people—and I'm talking confused early on, not being old and stupid—how many confused people end up *not* taking their own lives? The answer: zero."

We all sat in the common area of our stone house during Grandpa Akers's little speech. Joyce and James kept their arms crossed, but gave my father's father the finger, you know, like in a high school yearbook. Mom said, "We want them to grow up open-minded, Dad. We want them to grow up having experienced the world's religions."

I'm not sure how my brother and sister rehearsed their little skit, but both of them blurted out in tongues simultaneously, yelling out what I found out later to be an Arabic translation of the First Amendment to the United States Constitution. They waved their arms and throttled their necks.

My grandfather waited, and watched them run outside after finishing their diatribe. He said, "I believe it was Gandhi who understood all the world's religions best. He ended up skinny wearing diapers most of this life."

My grandfather got up and limped his way to the car. He drove off, as if for cigarettes, and never returned. When my parents got killed and I hired an auctioneer for everything, I found my grandfather's suitcase in the would-be music salon, shut tight, his worn leather-bound Bible on top.

No: My parents died, I got an auctioneer, I found the suitcase and opened it to find a bunch of *Playboy* magazines on top.

Wait: teen porn and a whip. That's what I found.

Anyway, we went to all these churches and one synagogue, and pretty much we only learned that everybody hated each other. We learned that, for a thousand dollars apiece, we could go down to Bolivia or Brazil and build thatched-roof bungalows for the natives as part of a mission trip. We learned the intricacies of church league basketball games, how to run a hot dog sale and car wash, and the importance of giving up 10 percent or more of our weekly allowances. I bet I heard half the preachers tell a story about how they threw their collection plate money in the air and asked God to keep what He wanted, ha ha ha. When the rabbi told this story he used the terms "manna" and "Yahweh," I think.

I learned early on that organized religion wasn't something I required or wanted. I yelled out pseudo-Aramaic slang whenever Miss Dickel asked me to lead the drama club in prayer, et cetera.

This was a time before ACLU-led litigations against mandatory convocations. I would come home, my parents would ask what I learned in school, I'd tell them the truth, they'd ask how I felt about it, and I said, "Yella-yella-yella-yella-yella-yella-yella."

I should mention that although my parents Ted and Olivia Akers had given up the classical music concert business, they had a somewhat alarming and constant habit of playing air piano regularly, right in front of people. My parents often looked like they tried to hypnotize the person with whom they spoke. I would bet that when I screamed out, "Yella-yella-yella-yella-yella-yella-yella"—with Mom and Dad playing imaginary keys—it looked like I would either levitate or be successfully exorcised.

Maybe that's what ran my father's father back to Maryland, I don't know. Maybe he knew better than to print out and keep nudie photos of James and Joyce, showering behind the stone house, oblivious to what the outside world might think.

◆ ◆ ◆

Miss Margaret Dickel lived way up Black Mountain Road, as I remember, in a house her family bought and maintained a century before. She said, "Novel, I don't have much hope for my students and never have. I've gotten to the point where I can only hope that my students will learn to *appreciate* dramaturgy. Like if they somehow go up to New York, maybe they'll attend a play instead of visiting the Statue of Liberty."

I said, "Yes ma'am." I had been summoned to her house in order to learn my lines. Miss Dickel, it seemed, didn't trust my saying "Who's there?" like that. I said, "My parents want me to go to Carnegie Hall one day, if I ever go to New York City."

Miss Dickel's house was like no other I'd ever seen. She'd decorated the inside with a bunch of paintings by de Kooning, whom she must've known. In between were empty bottle after bottle of George Dickel Tennessee Sour Mash Whisky Old No. 8 brand. Even back then, without looking up to count ceiling tiles and run multiplication tables through my head, I understood that her place ran in the thirty-six-hundred- to four-thousand-square-foot range. I should mention that I'd never had sex with a Black Mountain girl at that point in my life. "Foreshadowing," according to one of my writing textbooks, "isn't a bad thing."

"Say your line," Miss Dickel said.

I said, "Who's there?" but didn't quite get the gist of it, evidently. I kind of let it trail off, as if I knew who was there and didn't want her to come inside. Looking back, it was kind of like when Bekah went off to see a tributary of Luray Caverns, forgot her camera, then came back to find the motel room locked with me inside. I said, "Who's there?" knowing it wasn't the maid.

Miss Dickel said, "You have to be more excited, Novel. Imagine a ghost coming to see you. Imagine a *vampire*, or *burglar*, or gigantic pointy-headed *Martian*."

She wore a sequined dress that stopped midthigh. She'd gotten a haircut recently down in Asheville so that she looked like the woman playing Peter Pan. I said, "Who's there?" even worse.

"No, no, no," Miss Dickel said. She threw her ermine wrap to the slate floor. "Maybe you need to loosen up a bit, Novel. Have you ever had a drink?"

A drink! I thought. While my parents played air keyboard and my brother and sister ran laps around the mountain, I often drank. "Yes ma'am," I said. "I wouldn't mind some bourbon, vodka, Scotch, or anisette. Or all of the above. That might loosen me up."

"I have it all!" Miss Dickel screamed out. "Me, too! I'm going to drink some, too! Maybe that's what I need so's not to be so hard on you. Expectations, you know. Expectations, expectations." She ran out of the giant room going, "A-ha-ha-ha-ha-ha-ha-ha-ha," like that. I won't say that I didn't have a gigantic, big, monstrous hard-on. Miss Dickel came back with two sixteen-ounce tumblers of bourbon and Coke. She said, "Now try your line."

I drank some, then said, "Who's there?" in a way that almost made it a question.

This might be hard to believe, but Miss Margaret Dickel punched down her booze, unstrapped her straps, slid off her dress down to the navel, and said, "Now."

I'm talking her boobs hung out there like two off-kilter beacons. I could say nothing else but, "*Who them?* Hotdamn, who are *those* big fellows?" And then I went into one of my uncontrollable speaking-in-tongues "yella-yella-yella" monologues.

Miss Dickel took my hand and led me to the couch. She said, "I might not be here next year. Let me give you a premature graduation present."

"Premature" ended up being the right choice of words. I'm not sure she even got fully reclined on the couch before I said, "Hey. Where's the bathroom? I'll go get some toilet paper for your leg." Miss Dickel knocked on the end table a few times. I don't know why. I yelled out, "*Who's there?*" perfectly.

19

MY NEW TOWN might find ways to survive, I finally told myself inside room 9, unable to think up anecdotes outside lies that involved snakebites. I thought, If I hide out long enough then maybe something will happen around here worth reporting. One of my how-to textbooks pointed out that the main character must cause the action, not pray that the action come his or her way. This particular author wrote, "It's better to have your protagonist kill somebody, as opposed to his being killed on page one."

What a fucking genius, I thought. What a fucking genius. And then I thought, Show, don't tell; Show, don't tell; Show, don't tell so many goddamn times—and it could be that I underwent some kind of "alcohol-saturated amnesia"—that the mantra lulled me into automatic pilot, for all I know (it's not like I could drive over to Graywood Regional Memorial and seek out a qualified psychiatrist and/or liver specialist), but pretty much I regained full consciousness all the way back in the Gruel Inn office, my mission complete.

Well, fuck me. All I'm asking is for a little of that "willing suspension of disbelief." There were bits and pieces that came back to me, most of which involved bad memories of my child-hood, marriage, job, and past "important decisions," but that's about it. Snakes—I remember turning back to snake collection.

And I kind of remember talking myself into—this is the weird part, at least how it came true—how the good citizens of Gruel would believe that I was some kind of famous writer, and how they should indubitably set up a paid position for me at their private school.

Foreshadowing!

Here's a little: "I've changed my handle to Beethoven," my dad said to me on one of these trips. Joyce and James had fled to their supposed homeland by this point, so I must've been fifteen or sixteen. "You know why?"

"Because you're going deaf?" He kept that goddamn CB squawking so loudly on Highway 64 that live shrimp in back died of trauma. "Because you want a trucker to beat you up?"

One thing about concert musicians, ex- or not: They won't hit children or walls out of anger seeing as they don't want to chance breaking knuckles. Back in Black Mountain with my parents' friends—all violinists, violists, and cellists—when we went fishing they wouldn't bait a hook or take off a caught fish, forever paranoid of accidentally snipping their finger pads.

My father *looked* like he wanted to hit me. He said, "Bait oven. It's my little joke. Truckers think I'm saying 'Bait Oven' instead of Beethoven. Let me tell you, Novel—if we ever had the cold unit go out on one of these back roads that's exactly what we would become. A bait oven."

He drove ninety miles an hour down the two-lane. *Beethoven.* I should mention that both of my parents believed in karma, yin-yang, what goes around comes around, good and evil, apples and oranges, serendipity, Sodom and Gomorrah, ham and eggs, you name it: They believed that every action had an inevitable reaction, et cetera. And that's why, most Friday and Saturday nights when I should've been out parking with Wickie Portis— the love of my then life and daughter of two ex–Black Mountain College students who, like my parents, flat out gave up in order to run a produce stand filled with peaches and pecans—I had to sit in my father's refrigerated shellfish truck, CB on, and warn truckers of phantom Smokies running radar on I-26, or I-40, or up and down 74, 108, and any four-lane road that went in or out of Asheville.

"Weekends are when most accidents occur, Novel," my father told me, as if he'd gotten the statistical information from a soothsayer. "You got your just-paid drunken construction workers, and your high school sweethearts either celebrating or grieving their high school football team's game. So if we can somehow get everyone thinking the highway patrol's out there, I believe we can save some lives. And if we save lives, then we'll go to heaven if indeed there's such a place."

I didn't know why he couldn't do it himself—why he wasn't concerned about reaching fucking heaven, you know. I always said, "Truckers will know it's a trick. They'll hear my voice and know it's a kid talking."

My father said, "This'll be a great time to practice voices. Miss Dickel thinks you have a talent. I'm of the belief that this little exercise might help you get a college scholarship, Novel. Try some different accents."

I realized later that my parents spent Fridays and Saturdays *smoking dope and fucking* while I sat out in the driveway going,

"Breaker one-nine, this is the Carolina Kid—a Smokey's over on the exit ramp taking pictures," in my best Clint Eastwood, Edward G. Robinson, Humphrey Bogart, Clark Gable, Richard Nixon, or Mr. Ed voice, over and over, occasionally agreeing to a made-up rendezvous with a woman trucker down in Asheville at the Sambo's parking lot. I never thought about how some male transvestite truckers might've envisioned a life in Hollywood, too—that they disguised their voices in hopes of meeting another trucker in the parking lot for a little something other than what I supposedly offered.

And there's a snatch of Jeff the owner showing me up to say, "Barry and Larry finally made a shot on the pool table."

I said, "I don't know Barry and Larry."

"Your trick-shot brothers. Well they kind of made one. Barry had three balls arranged at a weird part of the table. I'm saying they weren't in the center of the table, or on the rack dot, or in front of a side pocket, or up against the rail." I nodded, nodded, nodded, and waterwheeled my hand for him to get on with the story. "I think Barry used the one, three, and five. He used odd numbers for this one. He had some kind of theory about how evens hadn't worked out for him. Anyway, these three balls were in a triangle, you know, way off in a no-man's-land of the table. Then he had some those Matchbox cars circling his balls. I think they was all Corvettes, you know."

Room 9 had the same number ceiling tiles as room 11. The wall behind where the bed stood held veins that, if you squinted, looked like a giant cannon. I said, "I get it" to Jeff.

He twisted off my Old Crow cap, got up, and walked to the bathroom. "Where's your glass?"

I think I had broken it into little bits and flushed the shards down the toilet in case my upbringing brought up suicidal, wrist-slashing thoughts. "Oh. I don't know."

I thought, I'm going to kill Bekah, more than a few times, and sometimes wondered if I already had done so.

Somewhere along the line between room 9 and my reemergence into the world of real Gruel I began writing Hallmark greeting cards, and my first one went "Roses are Red / Violets are Blue / So are My Balls / Get on Over Here as Soon as You Can."

Jeff the owner must've been there at the time, because he said, "This place when it was the original Gruel Inn," he waved his arm, "used to be the midpoint between here and there, you know. Greenville and Augusta. Asheville and Savannah. Charlotte and Atlanta. I'm talking before 1960 or thereabouts. New York and Miami. Boston and Los Angeles."

I said, "China and Japan. North and South Pole, in a way."

"That's right. Mercury and Mars, almost. Well what you don't know is, when the Gruel Inn finally folded, these do-gooder people took it over. They pretended to run a farm back there, and over there." Jeff the owner circled his arm meaning everywhere. "Cotton. Corn. Beans. Everything."

I said, "When?"

"A long time ago. Anyway, they died off or whatever—they had enough with people dropping in unannounced—and the next thing you know these folks come up from Charleston wanting to buy up the place on the pretense of getting unwanted orphan kids to help run their farm. You know what I'm saying? This man and woman went down to the coast, brought up newborns to feed, clothe, educate, and work. Twelve rooms, twenty-four babies. Me, I saw it all. I was there, Novel. Me, I think that that marching sound's a load of unwanted children stomping through."

I took Jeff's tiny Ancient Age bottle and held it behind my back. I shook my head to let him know that I didn't buy this story. "You can't scare me," I said.

Show, don't tell—like the books say.

"It's *true*. From somewhere's near after World War II until right before Kennedy, I swear, this place was run by a mom-and-pop operation running orphans. I'm talking the mother made the girls learn sewing machines—they's talk that they single-handedly ran old Gruel Cotton Mills out of business, but it ain't true seeing as Gruel Cotton made fabric and these folks bought it; so really they might've kept Gruel Cotton in business longer than it should've been—and the daddy farmed. He had his boys planting and harvesting, and shucking later, you know what I mean."

I said, "So?" I tried to make a mental note to relay how my father taught me how to tie my shoes, which involved chopsticks—both the eating utensils, and my mother playing that song on the piano over and over as some kind of torture until I learned how not to knot my laces.

"Be honest. You don't know this story?" Jeff the owner asked me.

I thought about how I needed to write down how, one time, the lieutenant governor asked me to write him a speech pro roadside flowers on the interstates. I went through a whole thing about daisies, cosmos, daylilies, and hostas, and how what gasses these plants exuded let us live in a more healthful environment. I wrote about how travelers coming through would look around, feel good about North Carolina, then both spend money at Stuckey's and consider moving from Maine on down to Virginia, or Texas on up to South Carolina. This happened to be a taxpayer option.

Unfortunately, I wrote down, "Oh, this'll be beautiful. Think about motoring down the highway and seeing Carolina jasmine over and over." The lieutenant governor—right on the Charlotte, Greensboro, Wilmington, Raleigh, Asheville, and Durham six o'clock news—said, "Jism." He went improv, too: He said, "What would be a better advertisement for our state than for motorists to go back home and say they became entranced with Carolina jism?" Somehow I got in trouble over all of this.

I said to Jeff the owner, "I'm sorry. What?"

"I think you can figure it all out, Bubba. It'd explain some things."

I shrugged. I said, "I don't feel like playing this game. I failed recess third grade because I told the teacher I didn't play around." I said, "It was the Cathcarts, wasn't it. My wife's parents ran this place. That explains how we got it so fast. It wasn't even for sale, really, right?"

Jeff, I think, said I didn't hear any of this from him. There was talk that a bunch of the orphans died here on the premises. One way or another, you know. Natural and unnatural causes, as it were. I believe he told me that Mr. and Mrs. Cathcart ran an abortion clinic, too. He said he didn't want to be the boy what only brings tragic news, but this is the truth. That stomping sound I heard at night? Dead babies and lost orphans. Jeff said, "And there's talk that somebody bought Gruel Inn about 1980, stayed one day, then fled. He still has all the original keys. Word is he might come back one day, madder than hell."

I tried not to think about how, maybe in the fifth grade, my teacher insisted that we all write an essay about how we got scared once. I didn't think about how she made us write one day about someone we missed, though I thought of another Hallmark card: "Oceans are Deep / Deserts are Dry / So is My Vagina / I Wish You'd Hurry up and Get Back Here, Goddamnit."

◆ ◆ ◆

Who could stick a key through Superglue? I figured out. When Jeff the owner finally left, I humpbacked my way to the office and called Victor Dees. I said, "Do you sell Superglue? Or do you think Gruel Drugs might?"

Victor said, "He told you the story, didn't he. Goddamn it. I told Jeff not to go off scaring you that way. And I'm willing to bet you're going to glue shut every window in the motel."

I hadn't thought of the windows. My father had tried to glue shut James and Joyce's windows one time so they couldn't sneak out on nightly Black Mountain forages. The glue didn't take, with the help of a cat's-paw, putty knife, and crowbar. "I need some nails, too," I said to Dees. "Maybe four or five pounds of tenpenny nails and a good six tubes of Superglue."

I went straight to my computer and, within the hour it took Victor Dees to show up with my provisions, wrote, "On the night that I awoke to find my piano-playing parents shackling James and Joyce in the back room where they—my folks— would never have a music studio, I decided to never further my banjo career, never run away, and never believe what my parents had to say vis-à-vis ways to live one's life." It seemed a good beginning, at the time, though I knew deep down that I could never use it in a memoir, seeing as I didn't want to cast aspersions on siblings or parents.

Victor Dees must've shown up at some point, seeing as I found all of my windows glued shut later.

◆ ◆ ◆

Evidently I brooded somewhere between rooms 9 and 1 about the time my father unsuccessfully tried to raise beef-flavored crayfish. This was the summer of 1972 and, much like the Democratic Party of that election year, Dad—of course we called him "Crawdad" at this point—tried about everything. He dammed a creek on the back section of our property and installed wire mesh screens to keep the crayfish more or less penned in. Although a crayfish can crawl out of its habitat, trek across land, and dig a new den miles from its birthplace, my father believed that his experimental pets wouldn't stray, for some reason. He threw butcher-cut rib eyes in the pool. He netted individual crayfish and injected them with bovine blood. My father said that he sent letters to the Food and Drug Administration, the U.S. Patent office, and the *Guinness Book of World Records*. He found and called a union of lobstermen up in Maine.

And everything went fine. Crayfish with metal plates in their tiny heads couldn't have been drawn to giant magnets as fast as these four-inch armored crustaceans hit Dad's steaks. They pinched, nibbled, and scoured. They scurried backwards to the creek edge, mated, and went for more.

"The thing about it is," my father said more than once as I stood there with a crayfish attached to my finger, "I'm thinking about beef-flavored catfish. Beef-flavored shrimp. And when that money comes in, your mother and I are going to buy some farmland out by Boiling Springs. Shrimp-flavored beef."

Every week the five of us sat down and did a blindfolded taste test that involved a one-inch cube of sirloin and a chunk of crayfish. Looking back on it all—and with what I've read in various psychology textbooks—I'm pretty sure that the entire Akers family suffered from "self-absorbed delusional high hopes." Jefferson Davis, Robert E. Lee, Stonewall Jackson, and Bob Denver from *Gilligan's Island* underwent similar problems. Anyway, we were all convinced that Dad's scam worked. My mother announced one night, "This will transform the entire restaurant industry. Surf 'n' Turf will no longer be!" Then she went down to Asheville and bought a fake fur coat. Even Joyce and James got excited. They helped me dig an auxiliary dam upstream. When we all went to the coast a few days later my father bought upwards of a thousand live shrimp, and dumped them straight into the creek water before nightfall. Unfortunately, concert pianists attend conservatories and don't pay attention to the biological world. My father didn't study up on ichthyology, to be more specific.

"I'm going down to Black Mountain Feed and Seed," he told us after we'd undergone this particular eight-hundred-mile round-trip. "I'm thinking one salt lick should be enough for the shrimp. We'll do a little trial and error. I need to stop by Mr. Fitzgerald's butcher shop, too."

These were happy, enthralling times, even though—far, far away—our troops got massacred, our president ordered break-ins, and so on. Some nights we sat in the den spouting out other beef-flavored products we might want to invent: Dr Pepper, Bazooka Joe, baby aspirin, sunglasses, postage stamps, pacifiers, ice cubes, toothpaste, and envelopes. My father yelled out, "Panties!" one night right in the middle of *Laugh-In*. My mom screamed, "Fingernail polish for women who bite their nails!" I yelled, "Tar!" for my brother and sister.

I don't remember if James said, "Douche" or "K-Y jelly," but it certainly caused my parents to reconsider his curfew.

The shrimp might've lived a grand total of two days. Their collective mass death and the subsequent stench attracted panthers in the area. Turkey vultures circled our home nonstop. My father couldn't get to his still-thriving crayfish—or perhaps he feared what food chain catastrophe might occur back there on the creek—and they eventually died, too. I think they'd become so accustomed to free daily steaks that they couldn't hunt for themselves anymore. Kind of like dolphins and whales raised in captivity from birth.

Our neighbors weren't happy with Dad. The telephone rang nonstop, and a couple of ex–drama instructors threatened to burn our house down. The unofficial mayor said he would look into condemning our property, that both the short- and long-term effects of our dead shellfish-thick stink wouldn't help him out when he tried to obtain state and federal grants that would jump-start Black Mountain proper's tourist industry.

We smelled like a bait oven, of course.

My father gathered the family one evening and said, "Goddamn it to hell, you can't blame me for trying. At least I tried to help Americans enjoy beef-flavored fish." My mother fashioned kerchiefs for us to wear over our mouths and noses. I'm talking we looked like the Akers Gang sitting around the table, going over a Wells Fargo stickup-to-be.

I don't want to come off as maudlin, sentimental, eager, embarrassed, cosmic, family-oriented, or whorish, but as I sat there looking into the eyes of my adopted siblings and my misdirected parents, I decided to write a long, heartfelt, pleading letter to the governor of North Carolina in order to explain our plight and past aspirations. I don't remember the entire plea, except for the final, strongest point: "Wouldn't it be great to entertain foreign dignitaries and tell them how we also had beef-flavored tobacco in the works?"

I don't think the governor ever read my opus. One of his interns sent me a flyer advertising the annual lieutenant governor's essay contest. That year's topic went "Something I Love about North Carolina that Everyone Should Know." From what I learned later, every other kid wrote about his or her teacher, parents, or preacher—all sucking up. Me, I wrote about our timber rattlers. I won first place. The judges, evidently, didn't understand what, years later, my Gruel Inn Writers Retreat textbooks labeled "satire."

◆ ◆ ◆

I must've stared at the computer screen a good hour one day, then typing paper, my empty composition book, until I realized that room 8's cracks on the front wall looked a whole lot like America's interstate system. So I waddled to the office, opened the front door, made sure it was wedged open so as not to lock myself out, sprinted to the shed where I once held nontrainable snakes, picked up a spray can of black Krylon, got back to the room, and stood back. I got a pencil out first and outlined the continental United States, then, meticulously, spray-painted a third of North America. Because I knew I might need to remember major ideas in my memoir *Novel*, I had a variety of highlighters, and used them to trace out Interstates 65, 40, 95, 10, 77, 85, 5, 20, 94, 90, and 15. I could've done parts of 1 and Route 66, but didn't. I didn't know enough about Alaska and Hawaii, but they would've ended up on the ceiling and shower wall anyway, which would've been weird.

And I don't think it was a dream when Maura-Lee said, "What're you doing?" from the passageway between rooms 7 and 8.

Needless to say I had three heart attacks and streaked a new freeway between Las Vegas and a point seven hundred miles outside San Diego somewhere in the Pacific Ocean. "Goddamn. How'd you get in here?" I could feel my body shudder uncontrollably, not unlike the first time I got bitten by what ended up being a velvet-tailed rattlesnake, not unlike the first time I asked Bekah to marry me.

Maura-Lee laughed, walked through the threshold, and said, "I came through the trapdoor, fool. Hey, your door was wide open. I thought maybe it was an open house."

I walked directly to room 8's bathroom and peed. I yelled back to Maura-Lee, "You scared the hell out of me. What's been going on?"

"I came to see how you were doing, Novel. Nothing else. I'm taking it that you're serious about holing yourself up forever. Jeff and Vic have come by to get fresh bagels in the morning, and they're both a little concerned." She walked straight into the bathroom right as I waggled myself. "Talk about *little*."

I said, "Ha ha," and flushed.

"Listen to me. I wanted to warn you that a new friend of

mine's on her way over here. I think you'll like her. Her name's Nancy Ruark. She's been teaching drama over at Forty-Five High for about ten years, but before that she did a commercial for one of those banks up in Greenville. I mean, before that she went to college, and I think she tried to make the big time in Louisville or someplace. She's all right."

I motioned for Maura-Lee to sit down. I would've offered her some of my MREs but I understood that she only appreciated fresher, better food groups. "You look like you've lost even more weight," I said. It might've been the last thing I remember seeing on TV, some talk-show host explaining to men what good things they could drop into a conversation every so often.

"I haven't even been trying!" Maura-Lee said. "But I'm down to a size eight or ten, depending on the designer." She wore what looked to me like a long tan T-shirt, a giant blue fish lacquered on the front.

I didn't say how I'd not gotten to eight or ten lines on *Novel*. "I don't want to meet a theater person," I said. "They're a little too 'on' for me, if you know what I mean. Or if they're not 'on,' then they're way past 'off.' They're so beyond off they're not even invented."

"Surprise!" this woman yelled out, popping from room 7 to 8, obviously Nancy Ruark. I didn't jump as much as when Maura-Lee snuck in and I became some kind of international road designer. But I gripped somewhat. I even thought, This isn't good for my writing schedule.

"Nancy, Novel. Novel, Nancy," Maura-Lee said.

Nancy might've stood five feet tall, and she had a five-foot-wide smile of tiny white teeth that didn't look unlike rows of special-order scrimshawed chess pieces. You had to love her on sight. She held a stack of booklets and said, "I'm selling coupons to help the Forty-Five High Drama Club travel up to New York City and see four plays in three days. There's a Sunday matinee."

I hate to say that I fell in love with Nancy Ruark immediately. It was like having a clothed jumping bean enter my life. I said, "Okay, then. Maybe I'll buy a couple those coupon books."

"You don't even know what we got, Novel! Look here," she said, approaching me. "*Shew!* It smells like someone's been drinking nonstop in here! It smells like a big *bar!*"

I didn't say, "I will quit drinking altogether if you rescue me from Gruel and take me to the metropolis you call Forty-Five, home of the fine Graywood Regional Memorial." I said, "You've caught me on a day when I've spent all of it writing my memoir. I've been so caught up I haven't even taken a shower."

Maura-Lee said, "Show him what's in the coupon book."

I flipped through the ads quickly: Buy twelve two-by-fours and get the thirteenth free from 45 Lumber; buy one pizza and get another half price from 45 Pizza; buy 45 45s from 45 Records and get a free record player stylus; buy a wedding dress from 45 Debs and Brides and get a free veil, et cetera. I said, "I try not to go into Forty-Five. Fuck, I try not to go into downtown Gruel anymore."

Maura-Lee went sneaking off into rooms 9 through 12. Nancy Ruark jerked her head down and put on a sad-face look. "You can buy one of these for your friends, couldn't you?"

Let me go ahead and say how mean I know I can be. I'm not proud of this, but so what. Kill me. I said, "Are you one of those people who says your body's your instrument?"

Nancy Ruark pogoed up and down. "That's the first thing I say in Drama I: 'Y'all have to understand that your body's your instrument!' I think they say that down at Kayren's House of Dance, too. I think dancers say their bodies are their instruments. I'm not sure who came up with it first."

I no longer had a hard-on for tiny, tiny ecstatic Nancy Ruark. I had *minus* erection. I owned less dick than Miss America. I said, "Well you don't want to be a plagiarist, dear heart," even though I pretty much labeled all actresses as plagiarists, every performance stealing from Bette Davis, the Hepburns, Ingrid Bergman, Elizabeth Taylor, Mae West, et al.

"There's a coupon for Gruel Bakery," Nancy said, flipping through it. "Buy three Jesus crust loaves and get another for nothing. Here's a second one: Buy twelve disciple rolls and get the thirteenth free." She hopped up and down. Her blood could've been transfused into coma patients in order to bring them back to being alert. "Buy a can of Vienna sausages and get a free pack of crackers from Rufus Price's Goatwagon store. Free chili on any cheeseburger from the Dixie Drive-In. All told, the coupon book offers over five hundred dollars in savings, all for twenty dollars."

Maura-Lee walked back in and said, "You aren't writing. You're doing anything *but.*"

I blurted out, "A prostitute says her body's her instrument, too. That's what a prostitute says."

I think that Nancy Ruark burst out in real tears. You can never tell with community theater actresses, though. Nevertheless, it was enough to make me buy ten coupon books and remember how this particular scene in my life couldn't show up in *Novel: The Unlikely Life of Novel Akers,* or whatever my title might be.

20

I KNOW THAT I called Roughhouse Billiards and got no answer. The same went for Gruel Drugs and Victor Dees's army-navy store. No one in Gruel had purchased, or perhaps *heard of,* an answering machine. I paced in an inward gyre once, an outward gyre once, then north to south a hundred times before calling Maura-Lee's house. No answer. Gruel Bakery. No answer. *Jesus crust,* I thought.

I talked myself into believing that it didn't take a city manager with special seminar certificates in supernatural communication to understand that everyone left in Gruel met up together somewhere past Gruel Jungle and atop Gruel Mountain in order to re-create the marching banter of a thousand unborn children killed at the hands of a taxidermist turned abortionist. They wanted to drive me out of town the same way that the lieutenant governor wanted me out of North Carolina, how snakes wanted St. Patrick out of Ireland, how Bekah and Gene Weeks wanted me off the planet.

With the incessant stomping going on one ridge away, I came to realize that when Irby Cathcart flicked his cigarette ash, he'd intended for it to hit *my* eye, which would cause me to veer and career down the embankment toward Lake Between.

Oh I figured it all out, buddy.

I opened the door and yelled out, "You can't scare me off, people. You ain't going to scare off old Novel Akers this easy. This *easily*."

At one point in college I considered being a world religions major until I took a physics course from a professor who convinced us all that beings existed in other solar systems, and that they probably had thousands of religions, too, trying to explain life as they saw it certainly. This professor believed that we'd meet up with aliens before the year 2000, in a jovial, nonthreatening kind of way. Man, it was too much for me to grasp. I couldn't even name off all the goddamn *Protestant* denominations, much less the religions of the universe. My roommate—a country boy from Haw River, North Carolina—said, "Maybe you should concentrate on American history. Then when the aliens come down you can tell them what they've missed. Stuff like when the government repealed that antidrinking law."

Perhaps I thought of all this some time in the motel, and that's why I stuck wads of toilet paper in my ears to block out the marching Gruelites, and/or vengeful orphans, and/or confused fetuses—in addition to my memories. I must've unscrewed the cap of an Old Crow quart and poured four fingers in a motel bathroom glass a few too many times. I'm saying I probably poured it to the brim, pretty much. I looked at the wall, for the millionth time, forgetting that I had no clock, approached my typewriter, and clacked out, "My college roommate might've talked me out of Buddhism, indirectly."

That much I know for sure. It showed up, on the floor, written in cursive.

◆ ◆ ◆

I won't say that my sister Joyce never wandered far from James, that she didn't slide me over in my single bed, that she didn't take her index finger and thumb to pinch my tiny divining rod and pump it up and down seven times before saying in her fake Irish accent, "You tell anyone about this and I'll kill you."

It wasn't a dream back then. And it wasn't my mother, father, or James. Remember that my siblings weren't but four years older than I, and since this all started happening prebreast Joyce, I could tell, even with my eyes shut, that her hands were softer than mine, or James's, or Mom's. Dad tended not to wear perfume. James always smelled of a weird sweat I later learned exuded from bipolar sufferers. Mom and Dad kept that Lysol/ Life Savers/incense/marijuana smell. Joyce only smelled like Joyce. She slithered into my bedroom haphazardly, pumped my pecker enough for me to wake up and wonder why I wanted more, then steal away after making threats.

It might've been the highlight of my life, of course. When I got older I said to myself, "It's not like incest: She's adopted." When I got my parents' individual diaries I said to myself, "It would be like only having my parents' college friends' daughter sneaking in every once in a while to check out my goober."

Joyce only put her mouth down there a few times, but that was right before she left home. I don't think it affected me whatsoever.

◆ ◆ ◆

I heard nothing emanating from Gruel Jungle. Then I bandy-legged my way to the office, opened the door, plugged a stray brick doorstop against it, walked to the shed, found my hammer and chisel, got back the brick, fashioned five nice one-by-one-by-one-inch cubes out of it, got out my pen, turned the cubes into dice, took the glass out of the room, shook my homemade dice, and wondered how many times it would take to roll out five boxcars. Or five snake eyes.

I never took a mathematics course in college. I took logic, but I never underwent one of those probability and statistics classes. It didn't take much brains, though, to figure out that one die had a one-in-six chance to roll a six, and that the other four dice had that same chance. When it all got multiplied out—as I spent a few hours figuring—a person should roll five of the same numbers every 7,776 rolls.

Evidently it could've taken me more times than that. I spent at least four successive days in that room. I got up once and wrote in my notebook, "Rolling dice isn't anything that could be labeled mathematically pure."

I made sure not to bastardize standard written English and, more importantly, to tell the truth.

◆ ◆ ◆

Lookee here at what I know happened one day: I got distracted writing because I heard two people talking outside the room in accents that made Victor and Jeff the owner come off as Pennsylvania Dutch. I peeked out the blind and saw a U-Haul truck parked lengthwise about a foot from my building.

"Sorry about all the noise," the man said when I came out of the office door. I propped it open with my computer. "The dag-gum truck's transmission seems have mind its own."

"And the muffler," said the woman. "It seems think it's machine gun previous life."

They were both dressed in blue jeans and T-shirts that advertised Rex and Randi's Reaths. It seemed to be intentional, the spelling. They were leathery-skinned people aged anywhere from thirty to forty-five, though Randi looked incredibly toned. I noticed that the rental truck held a Florida license plate, but that didn't mean anything. I said, "You need some water for the radiator?"

They looked at me like I slithered out of Gruel Jungle. I wore boxer shorts, no shirt, a cardigan sweater, and some large high-heeled shoes that one of the near-writers left by accident. I think a man left the shoes, but that's another theory. My entire defense concerned trying out anything that would bring forth more than one sentence per room for my autobiography. One of the how-to textbooks said a man should always wear a dress when writing from a female point of view. This fellow also believed you had to rob a bank in order to write a novel about a teller's everyday fear. I wore a baseball cap from Upstate Waste, a little present from Victor Dees back about room 11.

"I wanted a phone but don't know now," the man said. He pulled his hood up. "Randi, open up back get me socket set." I held my arms up and said, "Oh! I normally don't dress like this. It's a little joke I play with people coming through these parts." I went back inside, threw on some Dickies, and kicked off the shoes.

"See? You can trust me now. I'm normal."

Randi pulled the U-Haul's door back down. I barely spied

stack after stack of wreaths. Rex took three steps toward me as I approached. He stuck out his hand and said, "We're not from around here. Sometimes you hear stories about these small southern towns. These back roads."

I nodded. Randi handed Rex a toolbox. She *might've* arched her back, blown her blond bangs back, pulled her T-shirt all the way up to mop her brow, and asked if I would mind scrubbing her bare backside with a sea sponge. She *might've* mouthed, "We're brother and sister, not husband and wife. Fate, destiny, and karma have landed me here to meet you, oh great auto-biographer." I said, "There's a phone inside. Where are y'all from?"

"Middle of orange groves in the middle of Florida, some-ways south of Orlando and someways north of Miami," Rex said.

I looked at Randi and said, "I'm Novel. I'm writing my life story inside," as if that would impress anyone.

Randi said, "Hey." Rex got up on the front bumper and stuck half his body over the motor. Randi might've mouthed, "Go slam the hood down and kill Rex. At least knock him out. Me and you could have some fun on one them Vibro-beds."

Rex yelled out from beneath the hood, "Open the back back up and see if Mr. Novel might be interested in a wreath." He said, "I think it's only a loose belt. Loose belt and a time chain. Time chain and clogged carburetor. Clogged carburetor and about ten other things I can fix with one socket, a pair of Channellocks, and a screwdriver."

Man, I thought, this guy can list some things. I made a point to make lists when I got back in the room, maybe list everything I knew right on the wall. Randi said, "We gone lose our load we don't get New York by Thursday, sell it all at once."

I said, "I don't really need a wreath. I'm not planning on celebrating Christmas. Wreaths kind of spook me in the first place. I don't think anyone's planning to die in here, you know, how they put wreaths on the front door."

Randi kicked off her leather clogs, unbuttoned her pants, and shimmied out of them. She wore *no underwear*, not even a thong! And she owned no tan line, which meant she truly lived in Florida buck naked, or visited one of those fluorescent salons almost daily. I never understood tanning salons thriving between Texas and North Carolina, between Florida and mid-Tennessee.

Randi began a series of gymnastic maneuvers that involved the U-Haul's back bumper and the roadside stripe of Old Old Augusta Road. I watched her cartwheel naked straight up into Gruel Jungle, up Gruel Mountain, on the carpet path I'd rolled out sometime before room 12.

Or maybe she reopened the back and said, "We got pine wreaths, palm frond wreaths, palmetto wreaths, orange twig wreaths, lemon tree wreaths, and kudzu wreaths." In a lower voice she said, "Are you a smoker? Rex and I kind of have to be careful. Behind the wreaths we got about nine thousand cartons of cigarettes. All-flavors Marlboro, all-flavors Camel, all-flavors Winston, all-flavors Virginia Slims, Kool, Doral, and even some special-order Picayunes, Larks, everything you heard of."

"We even got Tareyton!" Rex yelled out. "L&M—you don't see those every day."

"Up in New York City, they pay twice much what we pay down here. Gas money in a U-Haul ain't great, but what can you do?"

I wanted to say, "I didn't just fall off the turnip truck," but one of those books warned to avoid clichés whenever possible. I tried to multiply nine thousand by twenty bucks, or by forty. But I quit trying when I remembered how I'd taken logic, how cigarettes in Florida probably cost more than twenty a carton, the average going rate in both North or South Carolina. I said, "You all are transporting cocaine from Point A to Point B. I didn't just fall off the turnip truck. I'm not still wet behind the ears. North Carolina's the state to buy cheap cigarettes."

"Wrong-o," said Rex. "Show him, Randi. We might have to stay here and I don't want him thinking we're drug smugglers."

Randi said, "Fuck. Excuse my language." She raised the back again, and started stacking wreaths away from the real haul.

Rex said, "There's something called import-export. We get our cigarettes in North Carolina. You're right. Up in New York we get real bagels and bialys and knishes. We bring those back down to Florida. You may have heard or read how a bunch of New Yorkers live down Miami way, and they miss the old days. Then we pick up wreaths, or seashells, anything. We do what we got to do. Today we had to make a detour from Asheville down this way, 'cause we heard about a mighty nosy highway patrolman on the interstate."

I said, "Goddamn. My father used to—"

"I'm betting this fixes it," Rex said, tightening a nut.

"Hey, there's a woman in town who makes some nice authentic bagels. And some kind of bread she drops lamb's blood into and calls Jesus crust."

"Get in, Randi. Is the back closed back up? Close the back and let's try this out. We need to get."

I thought, Don't start, don't start, don't start. I thought, I could deal with Rex and Randi as friends. What Gruel needed,

I thought, were more scam artists. Any underdeveloped town could use such new citizens.

At the time I didn't know what really went on in Gruel, understand.

Rex and Randi didn't wave or throw a wreath out like some dog biscuit to a roadside stray. I still stood at the edge of my property, looking down Old Old Augusta when Maura-Lee and Nancy Ruark drove by, going maybe seventy miles an hour. They yelled. They hooted. I might've heard, "My voice is my instrument," from one of them.

A couple hours later, back in my high heels, I admitted to myself that Randi never acted all supermodel. I got out my notebook and must've written, "Sometimes, even now, I don't know what I should fear."

✦ ✦ ✦

I've never purported expertise in the realms of the paranormal, science fiction movies, parallel universes, or abnormal psychology, but I would be willing to bet that a government panel of behaviorists might conclude that a town inhabited mainly by ex-college arts professors and ex-artists across the board can only result in a foot-dragging, wild-eyed, misshapen-haired populace that roamed around shouting non sequiturs.

My belief in communication with the dead began in front of the Black Mountain Candy Store one afternoon, maybe the summer between sixth and seventh grades. My parents and James and Joyce and I had just come back from Rash Creek where we'd sifted through about two tons of river grit and gravel in order to steal out a half ounce of flake and dust. This was a dry, dry season, and what nuggets held fast below the Rash

Creek current couldn't have been pried out with Caterpillar scoops and biblical floods.

I had about three quarters to my name and wanted a paper bag of Squirrel Nut Zippers and Mary Janes. This ghost man stood two feet from the doorway and said, "The dentist is not in. The dentist only works from afar."

A polite and mannerly child, I said, "Excuse me." I didn't say it with a question mark. I meant, I'm going inside the store and you're in the way, geezer.

"The dentist is not in. The dentist only works from afar."

As much as I knew there were no dentists in Black Mountain. My parents took us all the way into Asheville once or twice a year. So in a way zombie-man spoke the truth. I said, "Yessir," and tried to squeeze past him.

"I have come from afar myself, young man, in order to save you from a life of pain," he said. The zombie didn't wear a halo like an angel, or tattered, dirty brown clothes like a normal walking dead person. No, oddly, he sported a painter's smock, a beret, and chinos. I can't remember for certain now, but I think he had high-top Converse All-Stars on his feet. He hadn't shaved in a week, though. And one eye wandered like a North Pole compass.

Listen, two or three grown adults walked right through this supposed apparition into the candy store. And they came out, armed with Russell Stover mixed boxes, seeing as Father's Day neared. Nowadays I understand that I only suffered a temporary astigmatism. I said, "Hey. I got seventy-five cents."

The man shrugged. He said, "If you had a dollar and put it in the bank, you'd have well over a thousand dollars by the time you retired. If you had a hundred dollars, you'd be a ten thousandaire at age sixty-five, Novel."

That made no sense to me, but then again I didn't understand prime interest rates and had no clue in regards to mathematical options. But I knew enough to say, "How you know my name?"

He said, "Go on, now. You must leave the premises if you know what's best. *Go on!*" He stomped his zombie foot. I ran like hell without tripping—which might happen in the movies—thus proving I *did* have some athletic ability.

Let me say that for an entire year I encountered such ghosts, always at the candy store, movie house, other convenience store, and a place that sold dirty magazines in the back. These men stood in front of our few dress shops and women's shoe stores, too.

I took it seriously. I put my extra change in Black Mountain Bank and Trust. How do you think I have enough money to sit on my butt and almost write my memoir, outside of Bekah's "generosity" and my leftover savings from writing specious lieutenant governor speeches?

My mother, as far as I could tell, never bought a new dress or wore shoes, except the galoshes during gold mining adventures. Somehow I understood how that image would make me a better person later in life—kind of like it would for a man from, say, Arkansas who dreamed of making it in the world of politics.

21

ONE OF THE *So You Want to Be a Writer!* texts I kept in the office offered this advice: Go into a bare room, close your eyes, pick a season, and remember scenes that occurred for you at ages five, ten, fifteen, twenty, and so on.

Give me a break. I picked winter and thought sleet, sleet, sleet—at age twenty I had a roommate from Florida and an eight ball of coke.

I picked fall and thought leaves, leaves, leaves—at age twenty I took a course on the Civil War first semester, and my girlfriend at the time said to me, "If you continue not planning to make anything of yourself I'm going to leave you faster than body mass left Andersonville prisoners." It's true.

I don't think I ever tried spring or summer. More than likely I counted cracks in the wall, ceiling tiles, the frequency of drips in whichever bathroom sink. I listened for specters, heard none, and opened the door, even at night. "The next car that comes down Old Old Augusta Road," I said to myself constantly, "I'm going to write furiously whatever comes into my head until the next car comes by. Then I'll look at what I have, find an idea in there, and go with it." I said to myself, "That's it! I should've done this back in room 12."

Maura-Lee came over once and said, "We took a vote and decided that we're almost kind of worried about you out here," she said. "Over at Roughhouse Billiards we drew cue sticks and I lost. I got that damn fifteen-ouncer. So here I am. We're worried about you. Jeff's decided to donate a week's worth of tip money to get you help at Graywood Regional Memorial. They got a man there. And a pretty decent rehab center program up on the third floor."

I couldn't believe it, of course. I said, "I know this trick. Y'all just want me out of here so you can buy the old Gruel Inn from my ex-wife for, I don't know, a couple dollars. You think I don't know how South Carolina's legislature will soon vote casino gambling into existence, and the Gruel Inn would make for a wonderful resort?" I stood up. Maura-Lee shook her head side to side slowly. "Or a tattoo parlor. The legislature's going to legalize tattooing one day. This place would make a great parlor." I sat back down.

Maura-Lee said, "Damn you, Novel." She looked like she was about to cry. "I don't think there's been a secret between us. So I don't think you're so out of it to know that I've almost loved you ever since enrolling in the Sneeze 'n' Tone program, you know? Even when I finally understood that you weren't attracted to me, I tried to hook you up with my friend Nancy just so you'd stay in the area. That's how I am—pathetic! Maybe this is just the yeast talking, but by god I can't watch you dwindle away to nothing trying to remember why your life turned into such a pitiful existence. You have to get out of here fast. Come back to Bekah's parents' old house with me. I rode a bicycle built for two all the way out here."

Looking back on all of this, the only terms that come to mind are "reverse psychology" and "child psychology." But I didn't know it at the time. Maura-Lee pulled it off well, I'll give her that. She went on and on in her monologue, by the way. I could see how Nancy Ruark affected my friend Maura-Lee Snipes. I said, "I'm serious. You should wear a helmet. I know there's no traffic, ever, out this way, but you might have to swerve from some ghosts, and then you'd fall over in a ditch, and then you might break an arm. Next thing you know you're at Graywood Regional Memorial hospital getting it set and you die from the Ebola virus."

Maura-Lee wrenched her neck a few times. "You're in some kind of fantasy, Novel."

I might've handed her my bottle of Old Crow—which, I'd like to fake believe, I'd not touched for days on end. Maura-Lee threw the bottle up against the wall with such force that I would need a five-gallon bucket of compound to patch the dent. Luckily, though, the Old Crow people used the thickest, best glass possible, and my quart only bounced and skittered across the cement floor. I said, "*Taming of the Shrew! Who's Afraid of Virginia Woolf! A Streetcar Named Desire!*" I tried to think of other plays wherein crazy female characters got violent. I said, "Bekah!"

I would like to say that Maura-Lee broke down, that I held her there at my nearly unused computer, typewriter, and Mead composition book until she settled down. "A good, happy ending to a scene," one of the textbooks points out, "involves two star-crossed lovers either kissing each other, or killing themselves."

Maura-Lee, obviously, had taken private lessons from Nancy Ruark. Before I could even offer up one or two coupon booklets as some kind of booby prize Maura-Lee's tears dried up, she walked out backwards of whatever room I had recently settled in, and she mounted her bicycle built for two. She said, "Later on, when people from town ask, you have to admit that I tried. Right? I tried to get you out of here."

I said, "I'm sorry that my mission's to have a mission."

"We're straight on this."

I said, "Okay. Yeah, I'll back you up on whatever you need."

Maura-Lee pulled up her camouflaged shirt and showed me her no-bra tits. She said, "Are you queer?"

I got a good look and conjured up all self-restraint ever possible. "You know that I'm going to have to write about all of this. It's an autobiography. It's about everything that's ever happened to me."

Maura-Lee said, "I think you have some problems."

Then, as far as I recall, she rode off alone. She sang a happy song—at least that's what I planned to write later. I would start off with, "There were women in my life who didn't leave unsatisfied," which was a blatant lie.

In the New Journalism, according to my books, exaggeration wasn't *not* permitted.

◆ ◆ ◆

My next-to-last lieutenant governor didn't need a speechwriter when he got voted out of office. He went back to cattle ranching. Moo-moo-moo—that's about all I'd had to say for him. I called up Jeff the owner and said, "You come over here and say

182

all that to my face, I'll kick your ass," because I had it in my mind that he'd set me up somehow, and said some things otherwise behind my back.

He said, "You and whose army?"

You and whose army? Who said that anymore? *You and whose army?* I said, "Me and my army of one," like that.

Well in a weird way, looking back on it all, I got my wish. Jeff the owner closed down his Roughhouse Billiards. He showed up within thirty minutes armed with Larry, Barry, two cue sticks, fifteen balls, a cue ball, an armload of bricks, two old Texas Instruments hand calculators, a roll of nickels, two six-packs of PBR, and quartered oak logs. Jeff said, "You sounded a little depressed on the phone. I thought the boys and me might come out here and try some trick shots on the cement floor."

I know that I didn't daydream or fantasize this much.

Barry walked all the way down to the last room. He yelled to Larry, "It hasn't changed much, has it? I didn't think I'd ever stop back in here again."

I looked at Larry. He peered into room 1, but you could tell he was scared. I said, "Do y'all know the real truth about this place? Y'all know that I was a history major, right? I need to know about history."

Larry pointed down the long, long room-dividing corridor I had made. He set his balls on the photocopier. Barry yelled back our way, "We're your brother-in-laws." He yelled again, "We're your brothers-in-law."

Larry said to me, "If these walls could hock," I swear to God.

Jeff the owner looked at me and smiled. He held his shoulders up toward his ears and squinched his forehead. "You'd've known all this if you'd've been friendlier to my daily customers. And not threatened me."

Barry yelled out to ask me if I had a bowling ball to roll from one end to the other. I said that I didn't. He remarked that it might be something fun to do, if I ever found time to goof off.

I made a point to say how I never goofed off, that I was all work and no relaxation, that I would be finishing up my long-awaited memoir before the publishing world knew what hit them.

Then, I'm afraid, I starting humming, "Mares eat oats, and does eat oats, and little lambs eat ivy . . ." like a fool.

◆ ◆ ◆

So something oddly illegal—between child labor and flat-out slavery—occurred at the Gruel Inn back in the old days. Pregnant unmarried teenaged girls came in, delivered babies, and gave them up to Bekah's parents who, as far as I could figure out, either took care of the kids or sold them off to childless couples in Kansas, Iowa, Indiana, Nebraska, and every other state that required farmhands. Their favorites remained in Gruel, according to Barry and Larry the painters who relentlessly tried trick-shot cue-stick eight-ball eight-rails before knocking a shot of bourbon onto the five before going into the side pocket. Rebekah, my wife, for example. She got to live in the Big House, among the deer and antelope heads.

"I can't believe that your wife never let on about all this," Jeff the owner said there with the trick-shot experts he brought to my motel. "Nice marriage. To have and to hold, in sickness and in health, for richer for poorer. In secrets and in more secrets."

I don't know why it seemed necessary for me to say, "Bekah thought I only drove around with that van full of snakes. She didn't know how I really worked in an advisory capacity to the lieutenant governor. It's not like I had to sign any kind of oath with the state government."

Barry and Larry left, saying they had work to finish up. Jeff said, "Oh. Well that makes it better. Two people keeping gigantic secrets from each other makes it okay." He poured tomato juice in a bathroom glass halfway. "I didn't bring eggs. I figured you couldn't take eggs." Jeff topped off the six-ounce glass with warm PBR, then plopped one Alka-Seltzer in. He handed it to me. "Hold this."

The Alka-Seltzer fizzed near red on my forearm hairs. Jeff the owner felt his shirt pockets twice, pulled out a bottle of Tabasco, a six-pack cardboard sleeve of Goody's extra-strength headache powders he'd brought along, and a giant vitamin B tablet. He dashed the hot sauce in my glass. I said, "I feel fine, Bubba. I don't need all of this. As a matter of fact, I need to get to work on my work."

I didn't say, "You would've brought along some milk thistle if you really cared."

I won't say that I didn't trust Jeff the owner, but it would've been easy to take the safety cellophane off the Goody's, pour out the aspirin, acetaminophen, caffeine, lactose, and potassium chloride, replace it with arsenic and/or strychnine, refold the flat wax paper strip, reglue the safety cellophane, and so on.

Jeff said, "Years of dealing with hungover customers brought me to this remedy. Raw chicken used to work until someone got a bad case of worms."

I said, "You go first."

Jeff did so and handed me the leftovers. He said, "I'm glad I'm not you. Always wondering what you don't know."

I drank my share of PBR/tomato juice/Alka-Seltzer/Tabasco and washed down one powdered aspirin. "Don't worry about me, buddy. Well I take that back. There's something going on around here that no one wants me to know about, I know. Fuckers."

Jeff popped another beer. I thought, Why does everyone in Gruel drink so much nonstop? for about two seconds. He said, "What're you working on today? Are you going from birth to death? It seems to me that anyone writing his memoir would have to have some kind of special talents knowing when he'd die, so that he could write 'The End' right before his last breath."

What else could I say except, "Uh-huh."

"Well," Jeff the owner patted my shoulder eight or ten times, "you finish up this work and come back to see us, you hear?"

I didn't like or trust that country "You hear?" one bit, certainly. I said, "You're way too old to've been brought up by Mr. and Mrs. Cathcart. You weren't brought up here. Don't try to tell me that you were brought up here, buddy-ro. I know better. I can tell. I've been around."

"I'm almost the same age as your dead in-laws," he said. "And my doctor's all confused about how long I've lived. He said I should've hit middle age at about twelve. I remember that day when I had my midlife crisis. I bought a brand-new shiny Schwinn ten-speed bicycle. Get it? Do you get it? I think about all this time as way past my postlife."

I didn't say anything, but I thought about a time when I went out and bought a brand-new reclining chair at the age of twenty-four or thereabouts, and about how I neared the end of my life.

◆ ◆ ◆

For two days, I think, I walked off whatever remedy Jeff the owner had me down. I *thought* the whole time, understand. Man, I remembered crap that happened I'd not remembered in years. Here: I had a slight crush on a girl named Sherry Dalton who sat beside me in a Philosophy of Sports class. Don't ask me how I thought this was going to help me understand history. This New Jersey linebacker named Bobby Monica lived on my hall and he said he wouldn't beat me up in the community shower if and only if I sat next to him, enough said. So Sherry Dalton, the women's swim team's number one backstroker was on one side, and Bobby Monica on the other. Sherry held a pen in both hands at all times, but she never took notes. No, she windmilled her arms backwards constantly, like some kind of dyslexic paddle wheel. The professor—a tenured guy in the philosophy department who had some theories about long-distance runners, squash players, hockey goalies, placekickers, and volleyballists—brought Schopenhauer into every lecture. I don't want to tell tales out of college, but I think the guy secretly hated athletes and wanted to get his students to quit. Bobby Monica said to me midterm, "What the fuck's this guy mean about Plato's cave and the wishbone offense? Did Plato have a big bonfire out front and he was cooking chicken? I don't get it."

I said, "I'll write it for you. You get me two tickets on the fifty-yard line next game and I'll write your next paper for you." Me, I'd chosen to write on satire and Ping-Pong. Being and

Nothingness. Nausea. I said, "What's with the Windmill Girl next to me on the other side?" meaning Sherry.

My buddy Bobby Monica said, "You like her? She's from New Jersey, too. Well, I mean, she's from Chicago but that's just like New Jersey. You can have all the backstrokers you want, Novel. Me, I'm looking to nail her roommate. She's a *breast*stroker."

"You shallow fuck," I said. Oh, I said it!—I knew that he depended on looking at my test.

Bobby Monica punched me once, that I know of. I awoke naked in the community shower, faceup, water pounding my face. There in room 4 I wrote, "One time in a community shower I either lied or laid." I wrote, "Sometimes in college it felt like I'd been filleted."

✦ ✦ ✦

If I know anything about orphans and bastard children—and I'm pretty confident that I do, seeing as I spent fourteen years of my childhood with James and Joyce—I realize that they stashed contraband inside walls, above ceilings, and beneath floorboards. When I convinced myself that Jeff the owner only cared about the restricted veins transversing my brain and that I wouldn't have to rush toward "The End" so as not to die from "accidental" poisoning before completion of *Novel: My Life and Times,* I returned to room 12 with claw hammer, cat's-paw, crowbar, and a vacuum cleaner I'd never used. I took out room 12's bathtub first and here's what I found beneath it: an entire unopened carton of Picayune Extra Mild Class A unfiltered cigarettes—the Pride of New Orleans. By the time I had the ceiling, walls, and floor torn out and haphazardly stacked outside, I had discovered vintage melted lipstick tubes, a cache of silver coins, what appeared to be a crude zip gun that shot straightened paper clips, a few empty bottles of Rudd's gin and Old Schenley bourbon, a couple Bakelite bracelets, one feather hat, an ashtray that advertised Gruel Apothecary, a teddy bear with a metal stob in its ear, a dozen makeup compacts, a slew of makeshift diaries, and the perfect bones of what I understood to be a puppy. I found real silver silverware, plates, and booklet after booklet filled with S&H Green Stamps. I found baby teeth behind those walls. Man, I skittered my way back to room 4 and wrote down, "Don't ask me how I knew that unhappy children would hide their cherished things."

This took days, of course. I stacked my treasures, then transported them from one room to the next. Make a mental picture, I ask—room 12's treasures into room 11's. Then that stack into 10. Twelve, 11, and 10's into room 9, and so on.

Every so often I wrote something like, "There, in the floorboard, I found what must've been a gumball machine ring." And so forth.

Oh, I'm guessing that I must've averaged three rooms a day. It's not all that difficult tearing things down and eyeballing what had been hidden forty to sixty years earlier. It's not that much different than a manic-depressive charting a family tree, finding that incomprehensible uncle, and making rational conclusions. Building—creating—ends up being somewhat harder.

No one from Gruel interrupted me, as far as I recall, during my deconstruction phase, which made me wonder a little later how they knew I would come across a book of matches with "Help! R.C." written on the inside flap, for instance.

I didn't figure out "R.C." until I had already destroyed the entire motel. I had stripped the place down to beam, joist, and stud on the inside. "R.C." only stood for a Coca-Cola competitor as far as I knew, at the time, obsessed with collecting geegaws stolen away by unwanted children.

Again, no one visited. No one warned me. Bekah didn't call up to tell me how her new life with top-notch collector Weeks made her believe in a dozen good gods. I neatly stacked my collectibles and slept well on the floor each night. Then I found a torn-out sheet of Blue Horse filler paper with "Save my sister and me, God" written on it, signed "Irby C."

More than once the lieutenant governor at the time let me know that I lacked the ability to connect dots when it came down to political career-on-the-line pressure situations. I think that's what he said. He might've been talking about the Department of Transportation, not dots.

Finally, I found an unused receipt pad, the carbon paper still stuck in back. The first page read "Cathcart" in mean, scratchy, rushed printing. The next page read "Rebekah." The third read "Right."

That made no sense, I thought. The fourth read, "Not," and the next "Is."

Fucking lieutenant governor tells me *I* can't connect the dots.

I turned straight to the last page, found "Please," and flipped the pad like an old-fashioned cartoon. I don't want to say that I caught everything on that first go-through—there was an enormous amount of asbestos particles floating in the motel room, clouding my vision—but pretty much the gist of it went, "Please, someone, get us out of here We're not prisoners, exactly, but our daddy keeps us against our will We did not ask for this life My brother seems to be injured both mentally and psychologically There are dead animals and scary mean children everywhere who aren't our relations Barry and Larry keep touching me The girls don't like sewing They make guns that shoot needles The mommas living here cry all the time The other boys run away into the woods You must believe that it is not right Rebekah Cathcart Why Why Why Please help us now please."

I flipped through it about six thousand times. I believe that my exact words out loud to myself went, "Well this kind of explains some things." I didn't place Rebekah's order pad for help on top of my other auction-worthy treasures.

If she'd been famous, I might've. If she were married to a famous person, I might've. If her dead mother and father ever accomplished anything worthwhile—like committing history's worst examples of infanticide—I might've sent the booklet straight up to Sotheby's, or that other house.

I'm not proud to say that I thought about calling Gene Weeks's house and saying, "Goddamn, Bekah, you really had a problem with run-on sentences back in the day," on his answering machine.

But I didn't. There were more important things on my list. I waved my arm, wondered if Victor Dees sold masks, found my notebook, and wrote, "I married a woman who never told me her unfortunate upbringing." I wrote, "This probably explains why we never danced in our marriage. She wouldn't go to parties. She wouldn't invite people over to our house. A boys-only night was out of the question. At night she either curled up at the foot of the bed, or got up completely and slept on the couch. I'm sure a certified psychologist could explain why I never heard her singing."

191

I figured that I could go back and rewrite this passage, make it sound more lyrical. One of my textbooks called this type of writing "heat-of-the-moment nonstop regurgitation." It didn't escape me that Bekah's flip-book stood in this same genre.

I coughed and coughed, thought about going outside for fresh air, heard the oncoming army approach, and turned off the light. I stood in the middle of my hidden-prize-filled room, wearing short pants and kneepads.

It's not how I foresaw my life, back when I promised strangers how the shellfish weren't tainted yet.

22

I DON'T WANT to say that Irby Cathcart strained to grasp simple concepts, but the only college that would take him in was tiny Anders College over in Forty-Five, an institution of "higher learning" that forever teetered on legitimate accreditation. Irby chose General Studies as a major because he'd seen the movie *Patton* and figured he had a head start.

It took until his senior year, after he'd taken every 101 class in every department as part of the General Studies program, before realizing that no one on the faculty planned to offer in-depth seminars on Washington, Grant, Lee, Eisenhower, or MacArthur.

So he dropped out and took over his dead father's business. Irby did pretty well in some of the General Studies courses: He made As in Volleyball 101, Badminton 101, Bowling 101, Board Games 101, Shuffleboard 101—Anders College administrators believed that their Leisure Studies graduates would matriculate to productive and successful lives in the cruise-ship industry— and Culinary Arts 101, all of which were one-hour credits. He squeaked out Ds in English, history, psychology, sociology, economics, finite math, and so on. Irby failed Philosophy 101 because he misunderstood his "professor" and kept writing, "I think there, four-eyes Ann," whenever possible. He misquoted Socrates with, "The only thing I know is that I—no!—nothing."

Irby had saved even his failed tests and papers in a box he kept in his mother's house, along with a list of animals he wished to stuff one day. "Unicorn" held the top spot.

In every part of life where Irby spun his wheels, his sister drove full speed. And vice versa. Irby would've been a wonderful, trustworthy, loyal, levelheaded, committed, faithful husband had he not flicked cigarette embers carelessly.

"Irby was one of a kind," Jeff the owner said to me ten minutes after I chiseled out the last piece of Sheetrock, pulled out asbestos packed tighter than inch-thick felt, and found an evaporated bottle of perfume, atomizer intact. "If he could've lived longer I believe he might've made a mark in this world. Well, like, I mean, if he could've lived to be three hundred. I remember one time Vic Dees brought him a big old largemouth bass to get stuffed. Irby shoved giant glass eyeballs usually reserved for sailfish or bison on the ten-pound fish, which gave it an overly surprised look. It was perfect. Dees had to get rid of the thing it spooked him so much." Jeff the owner looked around my naked, unadorned, skeletal motel.

I said, "When, again, did Mr. Cathcart kill himself?" I didn't say it in a way where Jeff the owner could hear me italicize or "double-quote" the word "kill."

"A long while back. I don't know. I guess you should ask Rebekah about that. You can't ask her momma or Irby. Hell, I can't imagine anyone around here remembering for sure." Jeff pretended to examine the roof trusses, I thought. He wouldn't look me in the face. "We've all tried to erase that day out of our minds, here in Gruel."

I said, "I heard that. I *knew* it. Somebody killed Mr. Cathcart." I asked Jeff the owner to hold on. I found my notebook, dusted off the cover, and wrote, "I married a woman involved in patricide." Back to Jeff I said, "Hey, did you bring any booze with you? I kind of have a hankering for a vodka tonic. Usually I only like vodka drinks on the first day of spring. But for some reason vodka feels right right now."

Jeff the owner walked to the end of the Gruel Inn. He passed my stacks of found contraband and said, "Hotdamn. You got yourself some antiques here, son." He said, "No. I didn't bring you any vodka. I didn't know. I brought beer and bourbon, per usual. You need to pay up your tab, by the way."

"Beer and bourbon's good," I said. I said, "Don't touch anything over there, it might be contaminated." At the time, too, I cared about fingerprints, in case some fellow showed up later on and declared, "I'm a detective, Novel."

◆ ◆ ◆

"No one could prove anything. You got to remember that first off. How many cops you seen in Gruel? Zero. How many sheriff's deputies you see driving on the square in a normal day? Zero. How many real coroners? Zero. We don't even have our own funeral embalmer anymore now that Mr. Blythe died. Shit, he had to be sent all the way over to Forty-Five when he passed. It's kind of like the riddle about a one-barber town and who has the longest hair."

My plans changed. It wasn't exactly working the way I'd set

out, anyway. I held up a finger for Jeff the owner to hold his thought. In my notebook I wrote, "It was hard to distinguish truthful people in Gruel from the ones who lied."

Jeff the owner said, "Let's pretend that you're going to finish this little project of yours. Let's pretend it gets published. Well what're you going to do then?"

I didn't let on that deep down I knew the entire notion was a farce, a joke, a pipe dream—that at best I should try to write short stories. I said, "I don't know. I never thought about it."

"You goddamn right you never thought about it. Are you planning to stay here in Gruel, in this place? Look around." Jeff the owner waved his arms around my now naked hovel. "I didn't think anyone could lower the property values of Gruel proper, but you've managed. Way to go, fucker. For all of us."

Somehow I had the ability to make people hate me, I thought. I thought, Write that down. "When I sell my autobiography, I'm thinking about settling down here and opening up a junk shop. An antiques store. Believe me when I say that I'm committed to helping our community prosper. Go ask Maura-Lee. I've told her all about it."

Jeff looked at his wristwatch. "I put Barry and Larry in charge of the bar. I better get back. But I'm holding you to everything." He tapped my sad chest with his finger, just like a movie gangster.

I called Maura-Lee at home, then at the bakery. I got no answer at either place. On both answering machines I blurted out, "I'm going to stay in town I have all this old paraphernalia People will make special trips to Gruel It'll help our economy What do you think about my renting the old vacant Gruel Five-and-Dime building?"

Then I sat on the floor. I'm sure I must've written, "As a child, it wasn't hard for me to understand the importance of synchronicity."

✦ ✦ ✦

Here's a funny thing: I began to wonder if my orphans and bastard kids buried things out in the yard, and then Victor Dees brought by a metal detector soon thereafter. I'm talking twenty minutes after I conjured up the idea. I kind of wondered if I had said aloud to myself, "I sure could use a metal detector," and Victor Dees heard it through secret devices, or if he had a telepathic communication ability. Victor Dees showed up with what looked like a Weed Eater and said, "I got this on sale back at the shop. You want me to put it on your bill?"

This was a ten o'clock in the morning episode on a Sunday. I walked out back, hit the switch, and right away scanned earth as if I ran a floor polisher.

Victor Dees pushed me to the right, out behind room 9. He said, "I'm thinking this might be the place."

Later I would understand that he knew something I didn't know.

The little Geiger counter beeped nuts, that's all I have to say. "There might be something valuable down here somewhere," I said.

Dees nodded. He said, "You got a shovel? If you want, I can go back to the store and get a collapsible entrenchment shovel. They're handy." I set down the detector, jogged to my shed, and pulled out an old-fashioned spade.

Let me say right here that I stood transfixed for a moment, that I noticed a ton of snakes in my shed, all balled up in aquariums that I thought I'd thrown away. Somewhere along the line I'd gone back out and, using my knowledge, *recaptured* either the snakes I *had released*, or *caught* new ones hiding beneath stumps, and caged them up in my old shed. They all had lumps midway through their bodies, which meant I'd thrown mice in there, too.

I didn't come back and say any of this to Dees. No, at the point in question I might've gone six inches into loam before hitting a clanky-clanky hard substance. Victor Dees pointed at the back gutters at the Gruel Inn. He said, "You might want to check up there too. Later on, you know."

Within the hour I found a cache of butcher knives buried behind my motel. By "cache" I mean a good dozen, all at least ten inches long, rusted—I think—or bloodstained. In the gutters, oddly, I found two shotgun shell casings.

◆ ◆ ◆

Maura-Lee showed up either a minute or week after Victor Dees left. She brought along a loaf of pumpernickel, which may or may not have had the drop of lamb's blood Jesus crust. Maura-Lee hadn't seen the motel skeletonized. She said, "You look like shit. Victor Dees ordered white coats for us, and a straitjacket for you in case it comes down to our needing to come pull you out of here. You're nuts."

I tore off a chunk of bread and ate it. "I'm fine," I said. "Thanks for the update, though. You look great, M-L. You look better than ever, dear."

This conversation occurred, maybe, in room 2, where I'd been holed up between four and ten days, I estimated. The knives and shotgun shells sat scattered in a circle around my desk. I had tried to work on my story but couldn't get an image of Bekah, or Irby, or Vudge Ina—or a combination of them— killing father, husband, taxidermist Cathcart.

"My parents wouldn't've approved of how my life turned out," was the only thing I could get out on paper. I don't want to sound paranoid, but it became obvious that a giant mean trick got played on me, that everyone in Gruel participated, that the entire Ina and Irby death scene and funeral was a setup, a hoax, a grand plan to teach Novel Akers some kind of lesson.

I believed that my last lieutenant governor, somehow, orchestrated the entire operation.

He might've had good reason: One of his last speeches, covered on the Greensboro/High Point Fox affiliate by morning anchors Brad Jones and Cindy Ford, occurred at a paper mill located somewhere in western North Carolina on the Pigeon River, near Canton. The lieutenant governor had received undying support from the region, both nonunion and union-friendly workers who thought that they needed less environmental standards and more job security.

Well let me say that I felt differently, seeing as my father and I'd discovered more than a few three-eyed trout, two-headed salamanders, and half-witted slope-headed local fishermen in the area when we ventured for gold dust on what Dad hoped were unchartered creeks worthy of de Soto. Oh I swear I didn't want anyone losing his or her job—I've never wanted such, except for hospital debt collectors, telemarketers, Republican strategists, overpaid and whiny professional athletes, attorneys who represented the health-care industry, anyone with a lame Ph.D. in education, insurance company CEOs, pitbull puppy farmers, most advertising and public relations executives, and so on.

From what I saw on the news, all the way over at my home in Charlotte, my lieutenant governor was saying what I'd written, namely, "To heck with people who believe in evolution. If we as a species progressed like the scientists say we do, then why don't we have a tiny water-squirt mechanism right below our tailbones? Am I right or am I right? Why aren't we equipped, by now, with an inboard bidet so we don't have to wipe ourselves? I'll tell you why—it's because God wanted us to cut down trees and, among other things, make toilet paper out of them. You doggone right!"

The audience members, all right-wing conservatives, "erupted in laughter," as they say. More than a few slope-heads yelled out, "You damn right!" and "We been wiping our butts for years!" although I doubt any of them had ever seen or heard of a bidet.

My lieutenant governor said, "I don't care if we cut down the last tree in our planet's forest as long as good North Carolinians have a fine two-ply roll in which to unsully themselves. How many trees do y'all see over there in the Arab countries? None. It's a giant desert. Do we want to be part of a populace unconcerned with people who have to walk around all be-nastied? I don't think so."

My lieutenant governor never got such an ovation. I kind of felt bad about it. But after the news spot, boy, levelheaded people started calling in to the station, wrote letters to the editor, and stood up at school board meetings throughout the state. It seemed that no one cared to be represented one way or another by a man who even *visualized* a ready-made squirting bidet popping out of the human spinal cord.

I feigned innocence when the lieutenant governor called me up two days later in the middle of my snake show at an inner-city after-school boys club. I said, "Did the paper mill people boo?"

"No. But the state's not made up solely of paper mill workers, Novel. We got tobacco farmers. We got white-collar workers in Durham and Chapel Hill."

I said, "Well. You might've brought up your concerns on the first read-through." The lieutenant governor never read copy before the actual show. "The governor might have been able to foresee such a predicament."

I had glued that line — "The governor might have been able to foresee such a predicament" — to my Viper-Mobile dash. I knew to say it regularly. Here's how I kind of lost my job, right before Vudge Ina kicked off anyway: Every incoming lieutenant governor thought that if it weren't for my speeches, he'd not've been elected. See, every brand-new lieutenant governor realized that I wrote bad, weird speeches on purpose in order to get the sitting lieutenant governor deposed. Then the new lieutenant governor rehired me, thinking I was on his side.

This takes too long to explain.

What matters is, no one understood that—as a history major—I recognized every unrelenting supposed statesman's urgent and needful downfall. The next hammerhead elected felt convinced that I wouldn't abandon and sabotage his undulating and flimsy platforms, beliefs, platitudes, and promises.

You'd think that I'd've been stressed out during these years, that I needed to attend cheap weekly YMCA yoga classes or hire out certified massage therapists each Wednesday afternoon. I didn't. There's no sociological, or anthropological, or neurological evidence concerning my beliefs, but I'm of the thought that constant shrugging kept my blood pressure, conscience, and alimentary canal settled, not to mention regular knotty, stress-filled shoulder blades pounding from lactic acid.

All of that happened to most of those Roman emperors, by the way, from what I figured out during my postgraduate reading of the great satirist Juvenal.

Not that any of this matters. No, to stay on the subject, Maura-Lee showed up with a loaf of pumpernickel. She said, "You can't sweet-talk me unless you almost mean it. I didn't want to imply that you've aged since we met, but you've become more unkempt. You have to know what I mean."

I said, "Where's that community theater woman of yours? Did I scare her down to Alabama?"

"Now you're just being mean." Maura-Lee cinched her blue jeans and tucked in the thin light green blouse that she wore. "I don't know about your standards, but right now I'd like to say that the number one toilet manufacturer in the United States is called American Standard."

That all probably made sense. At the time, though, I didn't follow Maura-Lee's little analogy. Me, I had to worry about a big wind blowing away my tin roof, seeing as I'd peckered away even the particleboard underlayment—which shouldn't have been there in the first place, seeing as it kept the roof from breathing—in hopes of finding, I don't know, say, hidden newspaper clippings.

"Give this all up and let's shoot some pool," Maura-Lee said. "I got some time. Did I ever tell you about how I'm now selling to some private schools? I got their bread contracts."

"Are you insane? Didn't you borrow my step van when this all started way back when? I didn't dream that up, did I?"

Maura-Lee tapped her head. "Oh." That's all she said: "Oh."

I could read her face, though. It showed, *I have to get out of this area pronto.*

I said, "Hold on," found a scrap of paper nearby, and wrote, "I finally noticed how I had to get out of Gruel."

At the time I didn't envision this simple statement as being pure-tee "foreshadowing."

Maura-Lee said, "With the chance of sounding desperate, I want to tell you something. Sometimes in the middle of the morning, when I go home and try to sleep, I imagine us leaving here and starting a new life together elsewhere. I'm not daydreaming about Alaska or Costa Rica, or even Florida. Just *somewhere.* There's exactly nothing to do here, or over in Forty-Five, outside of drinking away two livers. Outside of staring at that statue of Colonel Dill in the middle of the square and wondering when the Civil War will really end." She picked up my bottle of Old Crow off the sill and uncapped the screw top. "Outside of wondering about your real mother and father. Didn't your brother and sister come visiting here once? They should've stayed. They'd've been perfect for here, making up trick shots with Barry and Larry."

I said, "Stop."

"Have you ever seen your birth certificate? I mean, have you seen your *original* birth certificate?"

I said, "Hand that bottle this way. And be quiet. I don't like to think about all this."

Maura-Lee walked circles. She said, "Not that I believe in predestination, you know, but *I* was adopted. You got all these people living here spawned from the Cathcart orphan farm. James and Joyce kind of visiting, but getting out in their own way. I would wonder, if I were you."

If Maura-Lee had been a man I would've shoved her up against the exposed studs supporting my naked ceiling. I said, "I have work to do. I'll see you after I get done."

"There are secrets to be discovered, Novel," Maura-Lee said on her way out. "Enjoy the pumpernickel. And if you ever want to get married, I'm here. Don't let some other man grab me up. Or woman. You and I could have kids who weren't orphans."

Here's a *really* bad one: The lieutenant governor, for some reason, accepted an invitation to address the Gay and Lesbian Alliance over in Asheville right before I had to come down to Gruel with my wife in order to watch her brother and mother explode. I wrote the lieutenant governor's speech. He said, "I'm all for a legal marriage between same-sex partners. As long as they're taxpayers. No, wait—either we legalize marriages between same-sex partners or we abolish the institution of marriage altogether. I have come to the belief that the act of marriage is the number one cause of divorce in America."

Ding-ding-ding-ding-ding!—he didn't get reelected after *that* one became public record.

And I haven't been completely truthful in all of this. Maybe I kind of got fired, and took off behind Bekah, stealing the step van loaded with its wares.

◆ ◆ ◆

On my last day of writing the memoir, sobering up, I thought about how I could write *The Southern Kama Sutra* next, and only include naked men and women doggie-style with different settings in the background: a patch of kudzu, the grits aisle of Winn-Dixie, Myrtle Beach's pavilion, a Clemson-Carolina football game, in a deer stand, atop the roof of Thomas Wolfe's ancestral boardinghouse, amid alligators at that St. Augustine wrestling pit, in the middle of cotton or tobacco fields, on the sidelines of a cock or pitbull fight.

I need to make it clear that my intentions after about sophomore year in college were to complete a master's degree, perhaps go teach in a poor, rural mountain area for a few years, and decide whether or not I wanted to tackle a dissertation. I envisioned regaling Appalachian children with stories of the American Revolution, the Bolshevik revolution, the people's revolution, Castro's revolution, and the Monroe Doctrine; of English kings, Roman emperors, European philosophers, American inventors, and Russian czars; of Ponce de León, Marco Polo, Francis Drake, Lewis and Clark, Admiral Byrd, Erik the Red, and—on a lighter note, maybe right before Christmas vacation—women who followed men out to California during the gold rush. I would spend an entire day on the emancipation proclamation. I wouldn't mention Christopher Columbus, seeing as how I learned early on about his misdirection. My parents were dead, my siblings had emigrated, and I was a serious young man who tried to stay away from the Cat's Cradle punk bar at least half the week.

And then I found out how goddamned graduate school's about nothing more than area and focus. Whereas I'd been able to jump around junior and senior years—a little Chinese history here, a little American South there, a class on imperialism and another called Babylonia to Idi Amin—I needed to pick a mentor and grasp everything he or she knew so that (I figured later) when he or she retired I could offer up the same "facts."

I'm no mathematician or psychologist or neurologist, but I've always thought that you can't *know* everything that someone else knows. If generation after generation gets taught and taught by mentors, in time it'll come down to a full-fledged professor only being about to call the roll and say, "Uh, like, the Louisiana Purchase meant *a lot* in the United States' development, man."

I sat in the office drinking refried coffee. Because I wanted to be highly symbolic, I planned to gather all scraps of paper at noon—starting with room 12 and ending in room 1. I would collect my ephemera from typewriter, notebooks, computer printer, and what scraps I had tacked to walls, then retacked to exposed studs.

The marching continued down Gruel Mountain, by the way. Whatever wayward ghost troops that haunted me from the beginning now approached, it sounded, right across Old Old Augusta Road. I didn't peer out the window. I didn't recheck all of my glued-up doorknob keyholes.

Here's what I gathered together finally, in scraps, of *Novel: A Memoir,* in no particular order:

> I came from a line of ex-musicians
> who never planned having a child.
> Vudge Ina had waved to her cancer physician
> then the fireball I saw was no less than wild.

Oh it went on and on. I don't want to embarrass myself with the entire opus; it ran more than a couple hundred pages, most of which I didn't remember writing, but—as best as I could chronologically piece it together—some of it went thusly:

> I don't remember my *birth.*
> Jeff the owner said "epithet," then *cursed.*
> A series of lieutenant governors ruined my life, *maybe.*

In college I considered being a world religions major until I took a physics course from a professor who convinced us all that beings existed in other solar systems, and that they probably had thousands of religions, too, trying to explain life as they saw it *certainly*.

How embarrassing is that? What an idiot I am, I thought. *Show, don't tell!* Where's my bourbon? It went on:

When the zombies spoke to me, I understood how my life
     might have a *reason*.
I've never been the kind of person who had a favorite *season*.
There were women in my life who didn't leave *unsatisfied*.
There in the Gruel Inn I worried about *cyanide*.
One time in a community shower I either *lied* or *laid*.
Sometimes in college it felt like I'd been *filleted*.

Like I said, this went on. It continued. My goofball memoir made the *Odyssey's* length look like a fucking public toilet limerick:

I married a woman who never told me about her unfortunate
     upbringing.
This probably explains why we never danced in our marriage.
     She wouldn't go to parties. She wouldn't invite people over to
     our house. A boys-only poker night was out of the question.
     At night she either curled up at the foot of the bed or got
     up completely and slept on the couch. I'm sure a certified
     psychologist could explain why I never heard her *singing*.
I married a woman involved in *patricide*.
It was hard to distinguish truthful people in Gruel from the
     ones who *lied*.

Somehow I had the ability to make people hate *me*.
As a child, it wasn't hard for me to understand the
    importance of *synchronicity*.
My parents wouldn't've approved of how my life turned *out*.
I finally noticed how I had to get out of Gruel, and to drive
    away no matter what *route*.

I'm talking it went on and on, with too much in between. I finished it off by saying something about having a goddamn master's degree. I wished that I'd've had some kind of good editor inside the Gruel Inn back when it was a writers retreat, some guy who could've looked me in the face and said, "You kind of have a little too much idle chitchat in the middle of your story, Novel."

I walked outside. The sky might've been twelve feet off the ground. I exited the Gruel Inn, raised my hands upward, and yelled, "That's not a goddamn *memoir*—it's a fucking *poem*. It's a series of barely connected *rhymed couplets*. This is not how I wanted *Novel: A Memoir* to end! This is not how I wanted *Novel: My Big, Fucking Fascinating Autobiography* to end!"

My voice echoed back from Gruel Mountain. I unzipped my pants and peed my name out in cursive—*Novel*—right there in the Gruel parking lot.

Then I heard nothing. I'm talking a silence enveloped Gruel and its sad, tragic, doomed, haunted environs as if a nuclear catastrophe occurred right as I read the last word of my "autobiography." *Disasters.*

PART III

"One small dose of venom . . . dropped in that receptive ear, and I'm out, shown the back-door, my years of obsequious service all gone for nothing. Where can a hanger-on be ditched with less fuss than here . . . ?"
—JUVENAL, SATIRE III

23

WHEN I TURNED the step van's ignition it didn't make a click. Dead battery, I thought, which wasn't unnatural. After Maura-Lee purchased her own bread trucks to transport Jesus crust loaves to white-flight private schools, I totally forgot to crank up my own van during all of those days and nights of cranking out nonstop the fifteen couplets I'd amassed like an idiot.

I went to open the flat hood to find that I no longer owned a battery. Nor did I own a radiator, carburetor, alternator, or entire engine block. I thought, Those marching ghost orphans stole my motor.

I released the hood and began walking into town. For a minute I considered going into room 3 in order to look at myself in the mirror, to see what I appeared like under undue duress. Maybe I needed to see if my face and hair and eyes looked like those of a "bewildered madman." But I didn't do so, seeing as one of the how-to-write-books books said you should never have a first-person narrator haphazardly stray by a mirror, stop, glance at it, then describe what he sees. That's too amateurish, according to this particular writing scholar, who'd never published a book of fiction, but had three textbooks to his name and had chaired a number of panels at the AWP (Associated Writing Programs) annual conventions, which had to mean something. Me, I didn't go look in the mirror because there was still a chance that I'd write another autobiography and then would have to say, "After I wrote a two-hundred-page poem, I found out that someone stole my engine; then I went inside to view my bloodshot eyes, sea anemone hair, grizzled chin, and worried forehead."

I didn't want to do that. "Poem" and "engine" kind of rhymed, again.

I turned to silent Gruel Mountain, the four-hundred-foot-high hill above Gruel Jungle, and yelled, "At least it wasn't a fucking *haiku* you forced me to write. My life's been longer than a *sonnet*."

"Well I'm done," I said to Jeff the owner when I walked into Roughhouse Billiards some ninety minutes later. "I've finished writing my memoir, and let me say that you show up on page one. Could I please have a quadruple bourbon on the rocks, three vodka chasers, two shots of tequila, one Pabst Blue Ribbon, and a pistol stuffed with bullets?"

"Page one! Did you hear that, boys?" Jeff the owner turned toward omnipresent Barry and Larry, my goddamn unknown bastard brothers-in-law. I looked over and saw them standing by the pool table with a fire extinguisher, a five-ounce plastic bottle of Ronsonol, one box of Ohio Blue Tip wooden matches, and an old-fashioned Hot Wheels loop-de-loop track set out for one of their purported shots.

"How long did your story end up to be?" Barry said. "Hold on a minute; I need to go pee."

That rhymed, I thought. Fucker. Fucking fuck.

I said, "It didn't end up as long as I thought it would. Long enough, but not as long as I thought. Not an epic. Not a tome. But longer than I thought, seeing as I ain't yet seventy years old."

"I didn't hear you even drive up," Jeff the owner said.

"That's because I walked here." I didn't go into all the details. I didn't say how I didn't look in the mirror at myself.

Jeff the owner got out what's usually used for a pitcher of draft beer and made my quadruple bourbon. He said, "Walked?! Well I guess that explains your bloodshot eyes, crazy hair, sun-damaged forehead, and stubble. Cheers."

"Thanks." I looked around and noticed a slew of red hearts dangling from the ceiling or taped to the walls. "Are you turning into a blood drive bar?"

Jeff the owner said, "It's Valentine's Day, idiot. We're expecting a crowd tonight. Maura-Lee's coming. I don't know how to tell you this, but I think Bekah might show up—she's been in town a while. Nancy Ruark's showing up seeing as the Forty-Five Little Theatre's production of *Oliver!* closed down after only one night."

"Valentine's Day? How long have I been at the Gruel Inn?" I should've counted my bottles and divided by two. "I thought it was something like New Year's."

Barry squeezed the fire extinguisher handle and emitted a jet stream of white powder. Larry said, "I told you so."

"You've been gone ten years," Jeff said. He handed over my three vodkas. "Naw, I'm just japing you some, boy. It *is* Valentine's Day, but still 1999."

I pointed toward the tequila bottle. I should mention that, at the time, South Carolina still served booze in airline minibottle-fashion. It was the law. Jeff the owner—in keeping with the

Gruel community—didn't cotton to the law. "This would be a good place for a bar if you could find a barkeep worthy of getting his customers what they want."

"Ha-ha," Jeff said. "Page *one*, man. Hey, the beer's on me."

I said, "Rebekah's here? Bekah's here? Kah's here? Why is she still here? Don't tell me I've been gone so long that everyone pays their hospital and doctors' bills. Have I been gone that long? Was there some kind of legislation I missed?"

Larry took his cue stick and knocked the Hot Wheels track off one pool table as if he played T-ball. Barry said, "I got one that involves a run of dominoes, a roll of quarters, the game Mousetrap!, an amber vial of penicillin pills I picked out of Paula Purgason's garbage can, my ant farm, a bull's skull, two hummingbirds' nests, a series of Holiday Inn plastic flyswatters, an empty Penrose pickled sausage jar, and"—Barry pulled this out of the back of his pants—"this here catalog of the religious paintings housed in the permanent collection at Bob Jones University."

Larry said, "Stick that Bob Jones back in your pants," with some urgency that I didn't grasp at the time. No, I felt too busy feeling good about being back in civilization, I'll admit.

Victor Dees burst open the door to Roughhouse. He gave Jeff the owner two fingers for whatever he wanted. Victor looked at me and stared, then to Barry and Larry's new trick-shot conglomeration. "What you need," he said. "What you could *use* is a battery, carburetor, radiator, and entire engine block. Now that would make for a great shot on a table. And I just so happen to have those items over at the store."

Then he laughed and laughed. I said, "You fucker."

He said, "Happy Valentine's Day! Happy VD! V. D.'s Army-Navy Surplus store! It's my day!"

I thought he might kiss me, but he only grabbed my jowls and shook my head hard with excitement.

Jeff the owner said, "Two Bloody Marys? Did I get that right?"

"Two," Victor Dees said. "Hey. Hey. It's Valentine's Day. What're you doing here, Novel? I'd think this would be your least favorite day of the year. Well outside of St. Patrick's Day what with that old man running snakes out of his country."

Lookit: Victor Dees shouldn't have known about my snake-handling days, really. I made a note. I thought to myself, Remember this, remember this, in case I ever tried another autobiography. I said, "I didn't know the date."

Dees punched my right bicep forty times, swift and easy. He said, "I didn't expect to see you here today."

"No one did."

"Well here we are. Hey, could I get you anything?" He looked behind Jeff at the bar's selections. No, wait—he looked behind the bar, into the mirror, at his falling-locks hair, his wide eyes, his full wide nose and perfect lips.

I said, "My motor. You could get me my step van's motor. Peckerhead."

When my first punch knocked him off the stool I'm almost certain every witness said, "Oh!" or "Ooh!" But when I kicked him in the head and ribs those same people screamed out, "Hey!" They yelled out, "That's enough!" and "Good goddamn Gruel doesn't need this kind of reputation seeing as General William Tecumseh Sherman decided against burning down our town and houses seeing as he was Colonel Dill's friend at West Point," or something like that. I know that I heard people screaming something about Sherman.

I'm talking I fucking waylaid poor Victor Dees. Hell, I punched my buddy Jeff the owner in the nose when he came around the bar to stop everything. "Happy Valentine's Day," I said, but I don't know that anyone understood my words, seeing as my voice shook uncontrollably. I said, "Would anyone like to tell me the truth regarding the Gruel Inn? Would anyone here like to tell me what went on where I've been spending time aimlessly?"

One of my how-to-write books said that a main character couldn't be hated, couldn't be the bad guy, the "antagonist." I understood that notion, and felt bad about punching out people. Let me say that Freud might've been right when he wrote about how a man's pent-up emotions will get the better of him before he dies. Well Freud might not have said anything about that. It might've been in a biography I read about either porn actor John Holmes or sacred Mother Teresa.

Victor Dees got up off the floor and said, "You're lucky we don't have an insurance agent or dentist here in Gruel anymore."

Jeff the owner said, "You're cut off. From now on you can only get a triple bourbon."

The jukebox came on playing Merle Haggard. I thought to myself, Man, what're you doing punching out people? You promised not to do this anymore after that fiasco at Cat's Cradle when you tried to get up onstage and sing "Little Opie Taylor" with Black Flag. I thought, Bubba, there are probably still homeless people in the United States and you're worried about—what?—the ex-woman in your life?

Not that I'm any kind of soothsayer or seer, but I thought *this* on Valentine's Day, 1999: There's a chance that Bush's son will become president, and that means that he'll invade one of those Arab countries in order to make up for his father's fuckups, and then the stock market will go down drastically, and if you ever have any money, Novel, you need to keep it in a CD that'll only garner .0109 percent interest at fucking Bank of America. I thought, But .0109 percent will be better than stocks falling nonstop due to fear, and a deficit that seemed unimaginable, caused by war costs and weird "tax cuts" with which the father promised but didn't follow through.

Gas would reach two bucks a gallon, even in South Carolina, I thought.

Santayana! History!

I had stood with my heel atop Victor Dees's neck—my buddy Victor Dees—and thought about how things weren't right, until Victor Dees screeched out, "Okay. Okay. You're one of us, man. You're one of us."

Jeff the owner said, "You a goddamn liar! You been hanging out in the Gruel Inn taking punch and jab lessons!" He held a bar rag to his nose.

I could do nothing else on Valentine's Day but hold up my arm and declare, "Drinks on me."

◆ ◆ ◆

Bekah walked in pretty as a petit four and said, "I take it you're finished, finally. I want you to know that we've all been behind you on this one. On this little autobiographical 'challenge' you've set upon yourself. Tell him, Jeff."

Jeff the owner had a tampon up his nose. He said, "If I get

toxic shock syndrome somebody's going to pay. I ain't behind *anybody* as of this moment forward."

Maura-Lee walked in with Nancy Ruark. They wore matching red taffeta dresses. Nancy said, "I got these from the wardrobe room at the Little Theatre. I think they're from *South Pacific!*"

Listen, I expected that dude Milson Willets from Black Mountain College's archival room to show up and say something about all of this.

I said to Bekah, "I knew you were in town. What happened—did everybody in America decide to pay their bills?" I didn't tell her how I thought about all of this earlier.

Bekah said, "I know you knew." She said, "I can work from anywhere, as long's there's a phone. I could work out of my car, if I wanted. But I wouldn't. Guess what the percentage of accidents occur nowadays while a driver's talking on the phone. You wouldn't believe it. It's worse than drunks."

Let me say that I felt more duped than the time the lieutenant governor asked me to write a speech for the North Carolina Daughters of the American Revolution, I did, and he said the *opposite* of what I wrote. Oh he'd caught on, evidently. To Bekah I said, "A hundred and one percent."

"You're close," she said. "It would be more if the people in Gruel didn't get in wrecks driving over their tin cans attached with strings holding cans together to talk, ha-ha."

Maura-Lee, Nancy, Jeff the owner, and Victor Dees laughed. Barry and Larry held their cue sticks and looked our way. I said, "Happy Valentine's Day, Kah." I wove my hand around. "Drinks on me!"

I won't lie and say that I didn't lead people on to believe I had finished a much-anticipated, full-length autobiography called *Novel: A Heartbreaking Memoir of Incredible Philosophical Depth* that would be published up in New York City by, say, Harcourt. Oh, I acted all fool and played the rogue.

Somewhere along the line, evidently, I whispered drunk out of my mind into tiny Nancy Ruark's scalloped ear, "I've always thought I could be an actor. You know, in college — in undergraduate school — I almost took a course called The History of English Theatre, from Liturgy to Reformation, Minus Shakespeare. I didn't, but I almost did. Say, let's you and me go outside and do some improvisation." I only know this because I woke up in room 3 at the Gruel Inn later, on the floor, surrounded by Bekah, Maura-Lee, Nancy, Barry, Larry, Jeff the owner, Victor Dees, a woman who swore she was Mrs. Victor Dees, a fellow who said he owned Gruel BBQ and Pig-Petting Zoo, some old ne'er-do-well boy named Sammy Koon who said he'd buy anything off of me I wanted to sell, and Paula Purgason the amateur real estate agent. It wasn't an orgy situation. We all seemed to fall out while in our clothes, and I can only assume that I invited everybody back to my abode in order to drink whatever leftover booze I had while writing my memoir. When Victor Dees said the next morning, "Yeah, you'll be the perfect history teacher and lacrosse coach over at Gruel Normal," I remembered what happened, kind of.

Nancy Ruark said, "Oh, Novel. Say that soliloquy again."

My half-wife said, "Be warned."

24

THE COMMUNITY, without my knowledge, gathered money and donations in order to renovate the Gruel Inn. I'm talking the nonelected town officials decided that the Gruel Inn deserved new Sheetrock in each room, new tile floors, a paint job throughout, and perhaps a terra-cotta roof. "My people waltz to a different Jew's harp twang," Bekah told me inside the bare office. "They think you might be their economic savior, you know. They believe that once your opus comes out, pilgrims from all over will want to come here and hang out. They'll want to pay their respects. Like they do for Faulkner or Thomas Wolfe or that bar down in Key West for Hemingway."

I had, of course, told exactly *no one* the truth about my "opus." To Bekah I said, "Did you kill your father? Did you have a hand in the death of your mom and brother?"

"I thought Graywood Regional Memorial would do *that* job for me," she said, which didn't quite answer my question. She said, "If people come to see where Novel Akers holed up to write his autobiography, then they'll certainly have to spend money on the square. Victor and Jeff are looking into how to get a Motel 8 or Econo Lodge franchise maybe over on Old Old

Greenville Road on some farmland owned by Paula Purgason. Oh, they have plans."

There stood no booze bottles in my skeletal abode. After losing my temper two days earlier I vowed the wagon, at least until St. Patrick's Day. "Let me get this straight," I said. I held my right hand with my left, lifted my knee against them, and tried to bring a coffee mug to my mouth in order to stop shaking. "You've been living with Maura-Lee for, what, more than a few days?"

"A few months, more like it. I sold Mom's house to Maura-Lee, of course. There were no hidden deals. No strings. I went back to Charlotte like I told you. Then I realized that A) I didn't like my job; B) it might not've been exactly moral; C) I could continue my job anywhere what with e-mail, faxes, and cell phones; D) Maura-Lee could rent me out a couple rooms from my own house, et cetera, and so on."

I wished that I'd've known all of this while writing my memoir. It couldn't have been all that difficult to tag this on toward the end. "That makes sense," I said, though it didn't. My main concern that morning, for some reason, dealt with controlling my shakes. "What's your boss think about all that? How's he feel about having a mistress 150 miles away?"

Bekah stood up and stretched her arms upward. She looked at the missing ceiling and rafters. "Technically, I own the motel. We're hoping you'll agree to let us auction off everything you found tucked up in the walls or buried out back. We could use the proceeds for building supplies. Until the project's done you can either live here, or take a room at my old house. At Maura-Lee's. I won't bother you. She certainly won't. As a matter of fact you can move into Maura-Lee's for free and I'll move out here. Maura-Lee has agreed to move out here with me, too."

I spilled coffee on my knee. "Are you and Maura-Lee lesbian lovers? Is that what's going on?"

I cocked my head because I thought I heard marching across the road. It ended up being a sad-mufflered Chevrolet driving by at thirty miles an hour. Bekah said, "You'll have enough money. Gruel Normal's prepared to hire you out as their historian in residence. You don't even have to show up every day. Basically, you'll be available to students who want to ask questions about politics, Gruel's role in the Civil War, and proper college application essays. That's it. Well, and I told the guy in charge that you'd be happy to show off your snakes whenever possible."

One of those how-to-write text scholars admonished trick endings. This guy wrote, "Don't write a fantastical story only to have the main character wake up at the end and find it all to be a dream." He said that it was okay to do this in the old days, like in the 1800s and before, but not in the "fast-paced society of modern men and women."

I said, "Nice joke. Ha-ha-ha. Don't think I haven't figured out y'all's entire scheme." I made eye contact and didn't blink. Somewhere along the line I'd read where liars either blink uncontrollably all the time or shift their gazes to the left and downward.

Bekah sat up and turned her head twenty degrees. "You're not *dead*. Some people have argued that the Gruel Inn would be a better tourist trap if you died unexpectedly, before you wrote a second book. They say there has to be some tragedy to bring people here." She stood and looked through all of the opened walls, all the way to the end. "Have you sent your memoir out yet? Are you sending it to an agent first, or straight to an editor? I'd love to read it. We all would. Nancy Ruark said she'd like to try her hand at turning it into a screenplay. She says

Gruel could become the next Manteo. You know, that story about the Lost Colony where Andy Griffith got his start out there in the Outer Banks of North Carolina."

Man, I needed a drink. I wanted one goddamn thimbleful of bourbon, which I knew would set my nerves down to nothing more than irritating twitches. "I'm pretty sure that my autobiography might do that. But I swear to God, Bekah, y'all don't want to kill me off before I finish a novel. *Novel* by Novel! I've got it all right up here," I said, popping my temple.

Bekah said, "I'll tell everyone. I agree that one book's not enough. One novel by Faulkner or Wolfe wouldn't have attracted people to their houses, right?"

One textbook writer thought that outlining an entire novel might be a great idea, but he'd never written a novel. The other tenured professors believed that the whole fun of writing waned once a template to follow got established.

Right away I figured that the people from Gruel would expect an outline.

I said, "You tell them—or I'll tell them—that I'm writing a group of stories about the good people who revive a small southern town, and how they succeed without succumbing to irrational actions."

Bekah said, "I have to go. I have to make some calls. Guess how many people only answer their phone calls after you let it ring once, hang up, then call again? The answer is 'most.' I got this woman who's had cancer four times, among other things. Then her husband and two children got killed in some kind of freak motorboat explosion. I have to make some threats."

My still-wife. She raked a hand through her hair. Bekah pulled at her jeans down twice from the tops of her thighs. I said, "I'll think about that job. I'll believe it when I see a contract. *And tell everyone in your club I'm busy on another writing project.*"

"Do you want to live here, or there?"

I said, "We'll see."

"Do you think I'm getting fat?" Bekah asked. She turned around ninety degrees or thereabouts.

✦ ✦ ✦

Victor Dees drove up in his camouflaged pickup truck. He backed it in close to room 6's front door, got out, and opened the tailgate. "I have it from quality sources that you're willing to donate what you've found," he said as I moseyed up from the front office. "I'm in charge of picking it up, inspecting the goods, and deciding prices. Then I'm taking it all up to the Pickens County Flea Market Wednesday morning. You're welcome to come along."

I knew this trick. It's the last thing Jimmy Hoffa heard, too: You're welcome to come along. The followers of Jim Jones, the residents of Easter Island. Wile E. Coyote. Jesus of Nazareth. I said, "I can't go. I'm in the middle of writing a novel. I'm waiting to hear from a number of agents, editors, and publishers. I have to work on a syllabus as the glorious and wonderful historian-to-be over at Gruel Normal."

Victor Dees pulled his red polyester-and-mesh hat brim down low to the forehead. A stitched-on emblem advertised Gruel BBQ/Petting Zoo. "I've eyeballed what you got and I'm thinking I can get a good couple thousand dollars out of it if the right gay antique dealers and collectors come around. From Atlanta, you know. Savannah and Charleston. I once sold a box of octagon Holiday Inn ashtrays and another Hefty bag filled with green and white Holiday Inn towels to this old boy down Montgomery way who lost his virginity in one them hotels. He paid, I believe, three hundred bucks for the lot. Timing plays a part. Luck."

I said, "Predestination. I've been thinking a lot about predestiny these days."

Victor Dees nudged room 6's door open. "I got some special alcohol at the store that'll denature your Superglued keyholes, if you want. I ordered it right after you made that paranoid decision."

"'Denature' isn't the right word, you idiot."

"You know what I mean." Victor Dees held his open palms toward me, in front of his face. "Don't hit me again."

I shook my head. "I apologize again, Victor. I guess I got all stove up with testosterone and adrenaline. Look at my arms," I said. My biceps, as always, weren't much more than miniature versions of swaybacked Shetlands. "Here. Go inside, find that stack of knives, and stab me. I don't care. I know it's what'll happen eventually, if I don't get kicked out the passenger side of a car going seventy down the road first."

Victor stuck his hands in his green cloth janitor's pants. He said, "I've changed my ways. I saw this documentary a couple nights ago about a Buddhist monk woman. She couldn't touch money. She wouldn't touch men or food. People had to take her from here to there. Basically she couldn't interact. I'm thinking about turning that way as soon as it's feasible."

I thought, That's not a Buddhist, that's a fucking mooch. "It'd be hard to run the army-navy store and not touch money," I said.

225

"Not as hard as you'd think. It ain't exactly gangbusters down there, if you know what I mean. I could use an ice storm once a year or so to sell Sterno, at least. Anyway, that's why I wanted to see if you'd help me sell off this shit at the flea market. So I wouldn't have to touch the money. So I could get a head start on my Buddhism."

Of course, I thought, who would lie about wanting to become one with the Buddhists? Who would lie about the most peaceful religion in the world? I said, "What the hell. Wednesday. Come pick me up."

Victor hauled a box of ancient safety razor blades into the bed of his truck, those double-edged kind best used against a sad wrist. He said, "I might be wrong, but I'm thinking that a hardcore orthodox Buddhist believes that he should walk into the woods and *die*, become one with Nature, forgo any kind of food or aid. He must become something called an ascetic."

I said, "That might be Hinduism. It's one or the other. Buddhism or Hinduism." I'd never had the opportunity to research these sects in order to write speeches for a lieutenant governor, unfortunately. "I don't know for sure."

"Well I ain't going that far. I want to go on record as saying I won't go that far. If it looks like I might be leaning toward starvation, I'm putting you in charge of beating some sense into me." I thought, I know this trick.

◆ ◆ ◆

Of course there wasn't enough room in Victor's truck for everything I'd unwalled. So we loaded up the step van. In a strange cause-and-effect sort of way, the overabundance of orphan-hidden gimcracks required Victor Dees to drop my engine back in, et cetera. We drove in tandem up Old Old Greenville Road, to a left on Due West two-lane, meandered to Highway 25, then drove north to Pickens County. I should mention that this journey began at two thirty in the morning. We'd spent the previous two days poring over antique and collectible price guides from 1989, then doubling everything. I drove my old Viper-Mobile armed with a carved hickory stick, a butcher knife, and a two-foot-long, two-inch-thick piece of rubber-coated copper wire I'd discovered in the shed. These were my weapons should Victor Dees renounce Buddhism and try to kill me.

We arrived at the flea market two hours before daybreak and backed our vehicles up to three of the last one thousand tables. Men and women roamed the flat, flat red clay field adjacent to a twenty-foot-wide creek, surrounded by hills that fed the southern reaches of the Blue Ridge Mountains. Most everyone carried flashlights. A couple old-timers walked from table to table armed with burning torches.

"If we can sell enough by, say, nine thirty, we can get out of here without having to pay the man for table rent," Victor Dees said. He unpacked his truck and arranged our wares neatly.

I said, "That doesn't sound too Buddhistic. I guess it'll keep you from having to touch money, though. Or from my having to stick my hand in your back pocket to fish out a wallet."

I swear to God Victor Dees said something that sounded like *"Nom yoho rengay quo, nom yoho rengay quo,"* over and over, like a personal mantra.

"How much you want for the truck?" a man with a torch asked Brother Dees. The man's beard didn't look unlike abolitionist

John Brown's. He walked behind our tables to inspect the vehicle better. "This would be a good truck to take hunting, the way you got it camouflaged realistic-like."

I set down packs of Picayune, empty bottles of Rudd Ultra dry gin, the coin collection, one gold tooth, and a stack of early *Playboys*. I put out one of the knives. Across from us a man sold shotguns, VCRs, and a goat. On the other side of him men sold push lawn mowers, yellow root, and cheaply framed portraits of Elvis in velvet. I might've misheard a hawker down the row, but it sounded like somebody pushed child slaves on one side and first-edition half-mammals on the other. Let me say that it wasn't unlike being in hell.

A woman came up to my table and shone her light slowly around. She said, "Picayunes. You don't see them every day. Did you quit smoking?"

I said, "Yes, ma'am. I quit right after my mother, father, and wife all died from the lung cancer. I had to. These packs of Picayune got pulled out of my daddy's estate, as a matter of fact." Fuck it. I tried to conjure up a crocodile tear. We should've brought Nancy Ruark with us, I thought.

"Wha'chew asting?"

I said, "Five bucks. That's a deal."

The woman picked up one pack and inspected the tax stamp. "This here package probably went for something like less than sixty cents. I'll give you a dollar."

I was about to say, "What the hell, okay," but Victor Dees whispered, "I just sold my truck and everything in it. I'm glad I thought to bring my title! Say, do you think touching a personal check's the same as touching money?"

By the time I finished unloading Victor's pickup, then looking over his buyer's check and driver's license, most of my table had been cleared. Evidently it's flea market etiquette to haul off whatever you want should the seller not respond to, "How much you asting for this?" if and only if the prospective buyer repeats it twice, or must wait more than thirty seconds.

I pulled more found collectible merchandise from the step van. As the new owner of Victor Dees's camouflaged truck drove off I said, "Are you donating the money you got from your truck to the Gruel Inn renovation project? Hotdamn. That's something. I really misjudged you. Way to go. This might be the beginning of a new Gruel era. Maybe all of us should look into this religion of yours. It couldn't be not beneficial for all of us, what with Gruel's history."

And at that very moment—as if a Hollywood director staged everything—the sun broke through low-flying horizontal gray February clouds into a brilliant, angel-song-inducing morn. A hush fell over both sellers and buyers alike at the Wednesday morning Pickens County Flea Market. I looked eastward and allowed a new warmth to envelop my feet. For a second I thought about how I could write a series of stories that involved the intricate lives of flea market vendors, but figured that some idiot had probably done it by then.

Victor Dees turned to me and said, "Who *are* you? I don't know about you, brother, but I have church tonight, it being Wednesday." Off in the distance I heard, again, someone hawking half-mammals.

25

BEFORE ANYONE could learn the truth of my pathetic endeavors I stopped exactly three hundred paces across the road, followed my ex-carpet, then turned west three hundred paces. Unfortunately, a creek stood there. I walked another three hundred measured steps north. Mind you I held a compass bought at Victor Dees's army-navy store. Man, I wanted to be accurate. When I got to that point, though, there stood a poison ivy thicket I didn't care to unburden. I turned west until, sadly, a patch of quicksand stood. Quicksand! Who's ever really seen a slough of quicksand?! It didn't ever occur to me that, perhaps, I should consider four- or five-hundred-yard lengths. I went northwest and stopped at what appeared to be the mouth of a volcano, then from there northeast only to discover a bottomless swamp. I didn't look up in the trees to establish whether, indeed, howler monkeys followed me, swinging through the canopy of trees usually known to South American rain forests. Finally, afraid that I would become lost forever, I took my entrenching tool, dug down a good three feet, and buried *Novel: A Memoir*, my less-than-epic poem. I covered the hole and placed a midsize rock on it the same way that, I was sure, any man or woman might do if embarrassed, so that no one would ever find the thing.

◆ ◆ ◆

I found an old tie from the speechwriting days—this will sound a little Stanislavskian, but I used to dress up in wardrobes that I foresaw the intended audience wearing: starched shirts when the lieutenant governor addressed lawyers, overalls for eastern North Carolina hog farmers, a simple pastel pantsuit ensemble for members of MADD—and drove to Gruel Normal, a private school housed inside the cement block outbuildings and office of ancient Gruel Sand and Gravel. The headmaster, a fellow named Mr. Ouzts who lived all the way up in Powdersville and commuted daily—he knew better than to mingle or commiserate with the locals at Roughhouse Billiards—met me at the door.

I said, "This wasn't my idea. I have no idea who's behind this."

"We're down to twenty-four students, grades one through twelve. Our endowment's over a million dollars. We can afford a historian in residence. Gruel Normal never needs to prove its commitment to education. We need viability, you might say."

I thought, Hire Henry Kissinger. Hire Jimmy Carter. "I'll do my best, should I get hired," I said, and handed Mr. Ouzts my vitae, about the only thing I'd really written over and over while secluded in the Gruel Inn. I said, "I've probably written a hundred speeches for more than a couple lieutenant governors of North Carolina about viability."

I'd not put a single lieutenant governor down for a reference, though, of course.

"I know. My wife's from Black Mountain."

231

I said, "I'll be damned," just like that. Already I knew that the whole episode wouldn't be beneficial to my health. "What's your wife's maiden name?"

Mr. Ouzts might've been ten or fifteen years older than I. He said, "Haughey. Her name was Nora Haughey. She's our PE teacher here at Gruel Normal."

I did my best to keep a blank face. That was the dancer's name—according to documentation I'd found up in Black Mountain when the pinhead guy wouldn't save my parents' ephemera—who gave birth to James and Joyce. For a *slight nanosecond* I thought, She might be my mother, too.

Ouzts stared at me, and I knew he searched my eyes for recognition. I said, "She might know my parents. I don't know. She might know my parents. I don't know." This went on for a good ten minutes, I bet.

"She might. We'll ask her. Say, I understand that you know our drama teacher, Ms. Ruark. She works here as an adjunct, Tuesdays and Thursdays."

I said, "Not really."

✦ ✦ ✦

I got housed in the ex-sand silo. It reminded me of the joke about driving a Clemson graduate crazy by putting him in a round room and asking him to piss in the corner. The school would build bookshelves and buy me as many history books as I wanted, starting with Thucydides. "My wife used to use this room for something she called 'ultimate handball.' We had to give it up when one of the Dill boys lost an eye."

I said, "Tell me again what my duties are? I'll be more than happy to bring in my collection of copperheads, timber rattlers, cottonmouths, and what may or may not be a baby anaconda I found out in the middle of Gruel Jungle. But do I really have to teach lacrosse? Somebody said I had to teach lacrosse, and I really don't know that game. But I understand that a bunch of rich kids get scholarships to places like Johns Hopkins and UNC because of it."

"No. Sit. Read. Listen. Advise. We're not asking you to teach a course. Every once in a while one of our teachers might happen by wanting advice on Genghis Khan. Or Nixon."

I said, "And y'all are paying me for this, right?"

"It's fifty grand. But everyone will have to give you the details. Everyone who's part of the deal. Part of the foundation, as it were. I haven't done the math. We don't have summer school. It's a ton of money per hour, I know that. The job only lasts as long as it lasts, which shouldn't be more than a month."

We left the silo and looked at the longest building, which might've been sixteen hundred square feet. I said, "How many people do you have on the faculty? These few students—how does it work?"

"Work?" Ouzts said. "That's a good one. Ha ha ha. Our kids get accepted to colleges, that's all that matters. Well, they get accepted."

✦ ✦ ✦

Victor Dees, Jeff the owner, Barry and Larry, Bekah, and Dr. Bobba Lollis pitched in to renovate the Gruel Inn. Maura-Lee brought over free lunches—bialys and croissants that no one else would ever buy in town, seeing as the words "bread," "biscuit," and "bagel" were not mispronounceable.

Also, a good dozen men I'd never seen before showed up,

233

strong, sinewy fellows who spoke little and wouldn't make eye contact. I figured them to be recent convicts, if anything. I said to Bekah, "I'll just stay here, if you don't mind. I mean, I feel comfortable here, and I need the room to write my next book. If you don't mind. Are you ever going back to Charlotte? What's with our old house, anyway?"

Bekah said, "Okay. I understand. Say, when do you start over at the school?"

Jeff the owner said, "I found a man in Virginia who specializes in bronze plaques. He did one for when Walt Disney came through here back in the sixties. It's over on the side of the road on Highway 72 going out to Calhoun Falls."

I said, "Walt Disney didn't come through here. Goofy might have, but not Walt Disney."

Bekah nodded. She said she'd heard the story and seen the plaque. Jeff the owner said, "We were this close to being the Magic Kingdom." He held his thumb and index finger five inches apart, which must've been about right on a regular Rand McNally page one.

"The Magic Kingdom," I said. "Gee, I wonder why he chose Florida. Anyway, you found the plaque guy in Virginia."

Jeff the owner refilled his nail pouch. I stood around kind of wondering why all these people wanted to make the Gruel Inn look like a proper abode. "Yeah! We're going to set up a roadside historical marker out front saying you lived and wrote here. When your book comes out, you know."

I tried to keep eye contact. Back when I wrote speeches with big lies included I researched how liars acted, how they became shifty-eyed, or stared at their hands. When I delivered my speeches to the lieutenant governor in person on occasion, every time, I reminded him to either fix his gaze one foot above the head of the backmost spectator or straight into the pupils of a dark-skinned African American in the front row. When dealing with a roomful of handicapped citizens it wasn't a great idea to stare at their wheelchair handles. With blind people it wasn't smart to blurt out something like, "Man, I wish I worked here—what's the dress code? You could be buck naked and no one would know!"

Maybe I've already said that one, before. It's the booze, it's the booze, it's the booze.

I said to Jeff, and to everyone inside room 1 holding hammers, nail guns, Sheetrock, drywall tape, drywall buckets, and/or paint brushes, "Well that's quite an honor."

Bekah said, "Your students at Gruel Normal should feel proud and honored to have you grace their campus. A letter of recommendation from you's going to be a coup!" As she spoke, though, she squinted—in Facial Expressions 101 that means she didn't mean her words.

I understood that either my time on this planet was limited or my time in Gruel would have to cease presently. "Yeah, we'll see. Mr. Ouzts wants me starting fourth nine weeks. That's the beginning of April, I think. I'm going in now, though, free of charge. From now until my official first day I'm going to work hard on the new book. And this time I'm just going to sit myself down in the office out there in the silo and forget about chapters per room. I'm calling it *More Gruel, Please*. It's all about us, in a fictional way."

Jeff the owner said, "Make me a little younger, and a lot more muscular, but not in a gay way."

Maura-Lee and Bekah only stared. They kept eye contact.

Barry said something about how he knew he could make a trick shot involving a box of dominoes, a Charles Chips potato chip canister, two sock monkeys, a series of empty glass Aunt Jemima pancake syrup bottles, and a Polaroid One-Step camera — using a swizzle stick instead of a cue. Bekah and Maura-Lee stared.

26

FEW CHILDREN STILL lived in Gruel. I never underwent a full-fledged sociopolitical-anthropological demographic survey, but it didn't seem far-fetched to believe that the average Gruel household consisted of retired ex-textile workers who never escaped. Maybe their children did, I don't know. For the most part, 1999 Gruel consisted of vacant Victorian homes, vacant antebellum homes, and regular rock houses still lived in by the sparse shopkeeper population that held hope for an economic rebound.

Gruel Normal's student body hailed from Level Land, Due West, Donalds, Forty-Five, Antreville, Cheddar, Spruell, and Gig. I didn't know what their parents did for a living, but by god the kids arrived in fancy late-model sedans and at lunch ate the best Jesus crust bread between Atlanta and Charlotte.

Now I don't know why Gruel Normal's philosophy of recess and physical education never outgrew the 1940s, but Mr. Ouzts's wife, Nora Haughey Ouzts, only went up to kickball. Those kids, from first graders to graduating seniors, underwent daily lessons in skipping, hopscotch, dodgeball, kick the can, four square, and jumping rope. There were no monkey bars or basketball courts. The field held no grass, only a fine silica ground down over the years since Gruel Sand and Gravel's demise.

I met the faculty, which consisted of Ouzts, Nancy Ruark, James and Joyce's birthmother whom I would allow to confess, a man named Pink Sluder who taught all sciences and math, a woman named Gloria Riddle who specialized in French, Latin, social studies, world history, civics, bad English lit through Charles Dickens, and home ec. I couldn't follow the class schedules: something about an A-B schedule certain weeks; twenty-minute classes on alternating Wednesdays; Bible studies twice a semester from a bona fide Yale seminary graduate who traveled between Richmond and Oxford in order to teach the supposed gospel.

We sat in Mr. Ouzts's classroom—he taught shop, of all things, in addition to his counseling/paperwork duties. Mr. Ouzts leaned his left forearm on a chop saw. He said, "I'll go ahead and tell you, Novel, that not all of our faculty's keen on hiring you. They think there's something morally wrong with someone getting paid for not really teaching a class."

I said, for some reason, "I wouldn't mind taking up some of the slack. I feel comfortable teaching geography, essay writing, history, civics, social studies, and anthropology." I threw anthropology in there only because of the things I'd heard over on Gruel Mountain.

Gloria Riddle yelled out fast, "Daggum it you just stick to your job in the silo giving our students advice in an advisory capacity." I'd never heard anyone from Gruel speak faster than six words per minute.

She reminded me of one particular lieutenant governor's

wife screaming at me during a fund-raising function because she thought I made her husband "look and sound like a Mongoloid re-tard." Those were her highly politically incorrect words.

I said to Ms. Riddle, "I'm just trying to help. I'm just trying to help. Can't do enough for my brethren in chalk."

"We got the money, and we need the money," said Ouzts. "What I'm saying is, to make more money, we need more students. And the only way we'll get more students is if we keep someone on faculty with a name. Later on it might be an ex-president. Or Truman Capote, John Steinbeck, Ernest Hemingway." I'm not omniscient so I don't know if Ouzts sat in on Riddle's Lit-up-to-Dickens class. All of my how-to-write texts said that a first-person narrator couldn't be all-knowing. Ouzts said, "I'm not the mathematician here, but if we get twenty grand a student, and we get ten more students due to Novel Akers, and if y'all in the room keep getting twenty to thirty grand a year—well, figure it out. We'll be better. Think if we get, like, seventy-seven new students. This is a new day! Here we are!"

My comrades-to-be erupted in applause. The deal seemed done. Ouzts took me to my silo. There were no books, even though shelves now rounded the continuous wall. I said, "Did you do this? How did you do this?" I'm talking round, rounded twelve-foot-high bookshelves.

"Me and my students did it. A T square, compass, and jigsaw can do about anything, boy."

Like I said, there were no books. But each shelf held ancient newspaper clippings and tons of eight-by-ten black-and-white photographs. I said, "I need to get my books out of storage. I can fill about a quarter of this space."

No windows stood inside the silo, of course. I looked up a good hundred feet and imagined sand and/or gravel plummeting my way. Ouzts said, "I have to make a confession. We have to confess. Your salary isn't coming directly from Gruel Normal. No. No. It comes from the Gruel Association to Sanctify History. They paid the money."

I said, "What?"

"It's a select group of concerned businessmen and -women who want to see Gruel become a town where people would want to visit and stay. Oh, it's all legitimate. Don't think this is some kind of scam."

I said, "GASH? Do they call themselves GASH?"

"Uh-huh. But it doesn't mean anything one way or the other. It just came out that way. GASH. So what? It had to come out something."

I almost said, "Something came out of your wife's birth canal that ended up being my mean, distant, conniving, ungrateful brother and sister."

"What we're hoping you'll do is sift through all of this material and come up with a beautiful history of Gruel that would be of interest to our people, of course, but also to anyone living in a forgotten small town south of the Mason-Dixon Line. What we're looking for is part southern history text and part coffeetable book."

I reached to the closest shelf and picked up a yellowed eight-page *Graywood Gazette*—long since defunct—and read the 1923 headlines: TWO BROTHERS SAY THEY FLY. It didn't take a historian well-versed in North Carolina lieutenant governor speeches to know that Kitty Hawk's maphood occurred twenty years earlier.

"You can either get paid monthly, biweekly, or weekly. It doesn't matter to us. Right now we know that we have enough money to keep you on for two years, if things don't go right for you. With the way the mutual funds are going, hell, we might be able to keep you on forever. Interest, you know. But in reality, we'd like a book before 2001. That's Gruel's unofficial bicentennial."

I tried to not figure math in my head. "That sounds about right. Y'all already have the pictures. I promise to work hard and fast and do my best." What else could I say? I kind of envisioned one of those bigger-than-a-breadbox books sitting between a couch and a TV set, maybe with a photograph of Roughhouse Billiards on the dust jacket, *Gruel!* on the top and Novel Akers below.

Mr. Ouzts clapped my shoulder blade twice. He said, "That's the answer we expected and wanted."

"Who, again, is in this GASH?"

"Everyone you know. You've known everyone except for me since you've been here. Now you've met me. There you go."

"My soon-to-be-ex-wife, Jeff Downer, Victor Dees, Maura-Lee Snipes, Barry and Larry. Dr. Bobba Lollis. Everybody in between whom I never see on a day-to-day basis. That's what you're saying?" I thought about asking if it would be too much to ask for a space heater. The ex-silo wasn't exactly warm.

"My wife says she owes you. Or that she owes your parents. She won't go into details with me, but she says since your parents have passed on, she needs to explain some things. Nora won't go into it any further. I trust her."

I said, "Do I have to call you Mr. Ouzts every time I talk to you?"

"We like for the students to only hear us by our formal names. You'll always be Mr. Akers."

I didn't say, "You didn't answer my question." The wind whipped up outside, which caused an instant tornado inside the silo. "This won't work out," I said as everything flew off the shelves.

Mr. Ouzts said, "I guess if we should ever meet in Forty-Five you could call me Derrick."

I thought Derrick Ouzts, Derrick Ouzts, Derrick Ouzts, Dairy Coots, Dairy Coots, Dairy Coots. "I'm good with addressing you Mister."

"She won't go into it any further. Anyway, I trust you have your own typewriter and/or computer to disseminate all this information." Mr. Ouzts looked at his watch. "Oh. I have to go. I'm teaching the third and fourth graders how to use a pneumatic nail gun."

◆ ◆ ◆

I drove straight to Roughhouse Billiards and strode in like I meant business. Jeff the owner said, "I'm surprised you ain't driven over to Forty-Five and traded you in for a more desirable luxury automobile than that step van of yours. You being the newly appointed local historian and all."

Barry and Larry—I'll say right now that I'm convinced they practiced and waited, waited and practiced—said at the same time, "You ought to go get a Lincoln, seeing as he was a man from history." I looked at my brothers-in-law. They didn't hold cue sticks, which I should've taken as an omen.

"Tell me what else I don't know."

Jeff slid a PBR my way. "I'm not going to live forever. Don't burden me down with such a request, Bubba. If I told you everything I know, then you'd be as smart as me."

Larry and Barry stared for a ten-beat, then emptied their pockets on the pool table, readying for a new trick shot.

I sat on a stool near the door and told Jeff the owner everything I'd learned about my new job, which, of course, he knew already due to his position with the Gruel Association to Sanctify History. "Well I bet you don't know that the fucking PE teacher over there's the biological mother of my brother and sister. How about that? How's about a little of that, man?"

Jeff the owner pulled back my beer. "I knew it'd catch up with you before long. I'm not one to make any judgments, but I took note of all those bottles you emptied while writing the autobiography. And it occurred to me that one of two things might happen—either you'd fry up all your brain cells or you'd become both paranoid and delusional. I've seen it happen before. It's what became the downfall of Mr. Cathcart before that fateful day."

Larry yelled, "I want y'all to be witness to this. One ball in each pocket, plus the can of lighter fluid will turn over and spray out a replica of a shotgun that'll catch on fire after the cue ball lights that Zippo over on the far bank."

"Do *not* light my pool table on fire, Larry," Jeff the owner turned to say. He remained leaned toward me. I noticed how his Vitalised hair looked similar to a topographical map I had once seen on North Carolina's lower Blue Ridge Mountains. I said, "Give me back my beer, peckerhead."

"You take that back about Mr. Ouzts's wife. They're two of our most successful and solid citizens. Even if they choose not to live in Gruel, or take part in any of our community functions."

I said, "I'm not delusional. I'm here, aren't I?"

"You didn't take it back. Take it back now."

The pool table, somehow, erupted in a giant blaze. At least that's how I saw it.

27

I PLUNGED DELIBERATELY into my historical research within the silo's continuous wall. I'm talking I left my cot inside the Gruel Inn—it didn't take me long to realize that moving in with Maura-Lee or Bekah wouldn't be rational, fruitful, or beneficial to my self-esteem—before dawn and remained there throughout the school day. I blocked out the singsong escapades of Gruel Normal's students during their outdoor phys ed classes, kept the door locked, and sorted. I borrowed six folding picnic tables from the so-called lunchroom, and stacked what clippings I found in epochal stacks: 1801–1860, 1860–1900, 1900–Depression, then in decades up to the present. The 1960s and 1970s, for some reason, stood highest.

I learned of "Civil War hero" Colonel Dill, and how he fended off, then finally captured, a dozen Yankees up in Tennessee. I learned of Gruel's "bustling era," wherein people traveled by horseback in 1900 in search of fabled Gruel Springs—a pool of mushlike water located, it seemed, somewhere up the hill from across the Gruel Inn. The springs held curative powers, of course, much like an oatmeal Fountain of Youth. In one issue of the ill-fated *Gruel Times* an item quoted a woman from

Charleston saying, "I not only feel twenty years younger, the mosquitoes no longer bite me!"

I sorted through glossy black-and-white photos, mostly of townspeople standing rebar-erect in front of their prize vegetable gardens, newly opened stores, and dead twelve-point bucks. I kept an eye out, of course, for Bekah and her parents, but found nothing. Bekah didn't participate in the Christmas cotillion like some of the other debutantes. Her father, I thought this odd, never showed off a stuffed twelve-point buck mounted for, say, Victor Dees's father, or Jeff the owner's grandma.

And I almost slung over a 1974 copy of the *Forty-Five Platter*—the *Gruel Times* had long been deceased—but peripherally I made some connection between a pair of skinny, skinny preteen's eyes and two people I encountered almost daily. GRUEL NORMAL BROTHERS ANOTHER DA VINCHEE? read the headline.

I'm not making this up: It was a misspelled front-page article. And it read:

Barry and Larry Dill both say that there talent comes from God. The brothers just won a national contest held for high school students in America. They will receive an all-expense paid-for trip to New York City. They will get $500 each, to. "I want to go to art school," said Barry. "I want to be a artist!" said Larry.

The brothers, sons of Mr. and Mrs. Dewey Dill of Old Old Greenville Road, say they have to thank a number of people along the way. They say there are to many people to thank along the way.

"We love our boys," Mr. Dill said. He's the great-great-great-grandson of Colonel Dill, Gruel's most famous resident.

"We don't know if the Colonel painted pictures during his war time, but we feel sure he must have."

Barry's oil painting depicts a bunch of well-dressed people sitting down to enjoy a picnic lunch on the grass. Larry's painting shows a crazy man yelling, his hands up to his face. After high school Barry and Larry believe that they will either attend Clemson or maybe a art school up in New York. "We will always remember our time in Gruel, though," Barry said.

I should mention *sic*, *sic*, *sic*, *sic*, et cetera, to all of those gaffes in the journalist's article.

The next article—above the crease—was about a local U.S. representative's attempt to have a Livestock Day passed in Congress, some time between Mother's and Father's Day. I said out loud to myself, "Paint. This makes sense."

Deep down I knew that it *didn't*, really, and I hoped that none of the students outside my silo heard me talking to no one. That would blow my reputation. I was the historian in residence! I was the famous Novel Akers, a man whose autobiography—though buried way down in Gruel soil—would one day be published and subsequently lauded nationwide in the *New York Times Book Review*.

I neatly folded this one page and shoved it inside my back pocket. I would've photocopied the thing, but this was only 1999 and Gruel Normal still operated on mimeograph machines that purpled out sniff-inducing copies.

I thought about yelling "Gotcha!" but one of my how-to-write books told me to never use dialect interference seeing as it had been perfected by Mark Twain and William Faulkner. Alice Walker. Flannery O'Connor. The rest.

I yelled out to myself, in my step van with no one listening, "I have you, Barry and Larry. You have some kind of secret that I'm going to uncover. You will one day tell me everything that I want to know."

I circled the square like an idiot, and dodged what few people crossed between Gruel Drugs, Victor Dees's army-navy store, and Roughhouse Billiards.

I yelled out at them, "I know you're all hiding something. I know there's more to know here!" and honked my bleatful horn. I'm not sure what woman gave me the finger—Paula Purgason, the amateur real estate agent maybe?—but she did, professionally.

◆ ◆ ◆

"You two aren't really trick-shot specialists hoping to appear on ESPN, the Discovery Channel, the Learning Channel, any of Ted Turner's broadcasts about legends and liars in the South, ESPN2, ETV, *60 Minutes*, *20/20*, *Dateline*, or the Food Network. Y'all are great artists gone wrong," I said inside Roughhouse Billiards. I'd just come from my work as historian in residence at Gruel Normal where I'd figured everything out. "You fuckers. Y'all are geniuses."

Barry and Larry stood at the pool table. On it stood a bag of marbles, two packs of safety matches, an assortment of colored putt-putt golf balls, a Kutmaster pruning knife, an unopened pack of Picayune cigarettes that probably came out of my walls, one of those tiny boxes of Kleenex tissues, a carved Coco Joe lava figurine, a bag of boiled peanuts, two Boston Clip #20s, a GE 900MHz cordless phone, and a Joe Camel calendar from

1991. Barry said, "I don't know what you're talking about. I thought you and me were brothers-in-law."

"That was y'all I saw that night up above Maura-Lee's bakery. I'm on to y'all. You're doing something against the law."

Jeff the owner said, "Hold on, Novel." He grabbed my right forearm. "Don't you go doing nothing you might be sorry about tomorrow when you can't even see what you're sorry about because Barry and Larry beat your eyes shut."

I said, "Come on. I'm supposed to be writing the history of Gruel. Y'all got to let on what's happened in the past. What's happening now. What's going to occur."

Barry and Larry held their cue sticks like soldiers bearing crossways rifles. Larry said, "I was against you getting that job the whole time."

"Me, too," said Barry. "I take it you seen our artwork photo, back in high school."

Jeff the owner continued to hold my arm. He clamped down better than a crab on steroids, is what I'm saying. He said, "We're all in on this, Novel. What you'll find out and discover won't be something you can pin on one person. Outside of Bekah's daddy and momma. And later on you'll wonder how it could've gone on so long without you ever finding out the whole time you been in Gruel. Let me say that we've been in practice hiding things from people a lot longer than you been in practice of digging things up."

I looked at the brothers. "Did y'all end up going to college?"

"We didn't need to," they said simultaneously, and it appeared as if they'd answered thusly more than a few times. "We didn't find a need to."

Jeff the owner walked around the bar. On his way past me he put his hand on my shoulder for what might've been considered a tolerable time if we drank in a gay bar. He locked the door and pulled down its vinyl shade, testing it three times on the bottom for hold. On the way back he tapped the top of my head six times. I took note. This meant something. I might have to put this occasion down in words, I thought.

Larry and Barry didn't turn and consider their supposed trick shot.

"Y'all aren't *only* housepainters," I said. I stood up from the stool. "I mean, don't take it that way. Housepainting's an honorable profession. What with vinyl siding these days, y'all are kind of like relics. Kind of like archaeologists. Kind of like old explorers. De Soto. Vasco da Gama. Y'all are kind of like what Ronsonol lighter fluid is to Bic lighters. Kind of like hand-roll cigars in the land of machine-manufactured stogies. Like Maura-Lee baking white bread with Jesus crust for two bucks a loaf when you can get Sunbeam or Bunny Bread at a dollar fifty in the store. Like monks to typewriters, or typewriters to computers. That's what I'm talking."

Jeff the owner pulled four beers from the cooler. He said, "You know I normally don't drink during the day. On the job. You know. Here I am." Barry and Larry walked over and accepted their bottles. "This is a different kind of day, one that I admit I figured might happen sooner or later."

Larry said, "Yeah, we went to college. I stayed an entire year and Barry went for a year and a summer school. Both of us had professors who said we were unteachable. No, that ain't right— both of us had professors who said they couldn't teach us anything new."

Barry said, "Something like that. Neither of us would cotton to the new school of thought. We wouldn't experiment. We weren't brought up to experiment, you know. Both of us were born realists."

I didn't say anything about all their goofball trick shots. Jeff the owner said, "In the old days we were all realists. *All of us.* Well Bekah wasn't. Her brother Irby wasn't. Mrs. Cathcart was, though."

Barry said, "Irby sucked. He couldn't draw a stick figure. He would've been better off getting a degree in business from Anders College and opening up an accounting firm here in Gruel."

I drank my beer and wondered how long it would take before they offered up the whole story of whatever it was they talked about. I checked the door lock. There had to be a way to jump up, turn the latch, and run away like nervous water should they never get to a point. "I didn't know Irby all that well," I said.

"He was no Leonardo da Vinci," Larry said. "Oh, he tried. He tried Michelangelo, like his sister did. He tried Rembrandt. Nothing." Larry looked up at his brother. "I got one—four banks, one shot glass, and a bottle of gin."

"Irby was no Monet. Remember?"

"Shit," said Jeff the owner. "None of us could do Monet. It didn't matter! Nobody would buy Monet at the time anyway."

I said, "I have no clue what y'all are talking about. What are y'all talking about? Even knowing that this might be something that will end up getting me killed for knowing, I want to know."

Barry and Larry said, "Forgery, you dumb peckerhead," at the same time.

"What you may or may not uncover during your time in the Gruel Normal silo," Jeff said, "is that our whole entire town is founded on what we trick people into believing's real. We're the best they is."

I nodded. I raised my bottle. "You probably don't want my writing all this down. For prosperity's sake and whatnot."

Barry said, "We've had some discussions."

"We've had some discussions," Larry said. "Even old Mr. Sherrill Cathcart told us long ago that we should have some discussions. Before his untimely demise."

I said, "Y'all are orphans. No offense, but y'all are bastard children, right? I thought Sherrill Cathcart made you work a farm."

"A farm. A farm," Jeff the owner said. "Ha ha ha ha ha. Cotton. Beans. Tobacco. A farm."

Barry and Larry took their free beers and went back to the table. One of them said, "We orphans made so much money. We made so much money."

"You saw us," Larry turned around to say. "That night—you looked up and saw us. We were in the middle of printing. Hey, Barry, what were we printing that night?"

"I don't think it was hundred-dollar bills. Those ain't worth it."

28

I QUIT UNCOVERING. I stacked and restacked photos and newspaper articles for no reason. I shifted my chair from one spot to another at least ten times an hour. An envelope filled with ten hundred-dollar bills appeared on my desk every Wednesday morning with a note pointing out, "This is only to tide you over until you get paid in full." I didn't even try to deposit them at the nearest bank, in fear that I would be charged with passing counterfeits, and so on. Jeff the owner never questioned the bills, though. Neither did Brother Scott at Gruel BBQ and Pig-Petting Zoo, Victor Dees, Dr. Bobba Lollis, or Maura-Lee. I requested all my change back in one-dollar bills and case quarters.

Finally, one Friday afternoon in mid-April, Mr. Ouzts knocked on the corrugated metal door. "I'm wondering what you've come up with so far."

"Seven hundred twenty-three is not a prime number," I said. "It can be divided by three."

Mr. Ouzts didn't step in my office more than one stride. He said, "What's that?"

"Look," I said. "I'm not as stupid as everyone thinks. I've got it all figured out. First off, Mr. Cathcart's orphans weren't forced to work in the fields. No. They took art classes here at Gruel Normal and they forged famous paintings. I don't know where they got sold, but they got sold. Number two: Your wife's the biological mother of my brother and sister, James and Joyce. I don't know if you're aware of it or not, but I don't want to be in the same 'secret keeper' category as everyone else in this so-called town. Three: Barry and Larry only try trick shots in order to cover themselves from making fake money, when they're not painting fake masterpieces. They run a printing press out of the old *Gruel Times* office, which was also the old Gruel Printing office. I'm still not sure what that stamping, marching sound is that shows up on the hill above my house, but it's something. So. How about that?"

Mr. Ouzts said, "My *wife* had *children?*"

"Bring her on in here. You bring her in and let's have a little sit-down. I'm still not sure how come I got sent to Gruel, what role I play in this charade." I waved my arm to all the clippings and photos. "I'll figure it out, though. I mean, how sad a town is it that chooses me as a messiah, you know?"

"Have any of the kids talked to you? I keep telling them to use your services. That's why you're here, partly, I tell them. My *wife*? Nora is your stepmother?"

I moved my chair to the middle of the ex-silo. "No. No, no children have visited. And Nora's not my stepmother technically. I know you know. You can't bullshit an old bullshitter. Me—I used to write speeches for the lieutenant governor! Who can pull one off on me?"

"Nora's never had any children, Novel. She had another husband once, but he died in a tragic accident down in the Everglades."

I didn't say, "There you go," or "That was *my* father," or "He was one of the up-and-coming ballet stars at Black Mountain College," or "You poor, dumb, stupid fucking man." I said, "I appreciate the town giving me this job, Mr. Ouzts."

Then I took the rest of the day off, even though I thought up an entire great speech for any sitting lieutenant governor who wished to tackle the stray dog issue.

◆ ◆ ◆

"You're not supposed to write about all that. We want you to portray Gruel as a perfect retirement community. Or the perfect place to raise children, far from danger. We aren't looking for trouble, or for people to think this is a place loaded with crime, Novel. We only want to be recognized." Bekah said all of this to me in the aisle of Victor Dees's army-navy store, between racks of camouflaged jackets and insulated underwear. I showed up to buy a canteen and helmet should I ever feel endangered and decide to camp out in the hinterlands. I had waited until coming up with an excuse, in case Dees got nosy, that I had a nephew whose birthday approached.

I said, "Those kids at Gruel Normal are *sharp*. Hotdamn. I can see how come you did so well in college. Gruel Normal's a case for not going to public schools. Why, just the other day I had a fascinating conversation with a young woman, a senior, who plans on either going to the University of Miami in order to study Cuban refugee infiltration and the subsequent rum and cigar shortages back in the homeland, or she wants to attend the University of North Dakota and conduct an in-depth study as to why anyone would live there, what without its sense of history"

I possessed an overflowing Rolodex of declarative statements, alibis, theories, and deflective questions for every Gruel occasion. I don't want to say that I only conjured these up during my memoir phase, but it seemed true. Bekah said, "You're lying. The students at Gruel Normal have been asked not to talk to you. Ever. If you came out of the silo bleeding from a neck wound they have instructions to run away."

I looked Bekah hard in the face. In the past her eyes shifted back and forth and she looked downward during big lies—her eight or twenty "pregnancies," those job promotions, how she didn't have a fling with Gene Weeks before we moved to Gruel, how she really felt sorry for the people she harassed for payments, my "lost" or "accidentally dropped" bottles of bourbon, how she thought snakes weren't embodiments of evil.

But this time she didn't blink or waver.

Victor Dees came out of the back room and said, "I didn't hear y'all in here. Sorry about that. I was doing inventory of things I can't put on display. Hey, Novel, guess how many working claymore land mines I got."

I said, "Hey, Victor Dees." To Bekah I said, "I don't pretend to get any of this trick being played on me. And I've gotten to the point where I don't care. I could just leave, you know. Nothing's stopping me from going back to Charlotte. Or Black Mountain. Not that I'm a visionary or anything, but I'm betting the state of California's governor's office will need a speechwriter within the next few years. And you might remember that I chose all my retirement funds to go into that NASDAQ tech-heavy Putnam Voyager fund. Have you been keeping up with it? There's no way I won't be set for life."

I kept up with my retirement fund by calling a 1-800 number once a week or thereabouts from a pay phone in front of Gruel Drugs, seeing as my home phone still worked rotary-fashion. The *Forty-Five Platter* ran stock quotes on Saturday afternoons, and then it only chose selected companies as opposed to the full array. I was never a financial wizard, but I had a feeling that the newspaper printed the same week's results over and over. Here's what I'm saying: Did Eastern Airlines even exist in 1999?

Victor Dees said, "I got a special on gas masks. I don't want to say that I'm being psychic or anything, but people are gonna want extra gas masks before long. I'm keeping them on sale until Valentine's Day, 2000, man."

I pulled a camo jacket off the rack and tried it on. It fit heavy, but perfect. "How much is this?"

Bekah walked one step closer to me and said, "It's you, and it's everyone else. You should feel honored. It's like being Jesus! Or Chairman Mao! It's like being Lenin, Franco, Mussolini, Castro, and Nixon all rolled into one! Buy this coat. You know history!"

Well of course I didn't like that comparison or company with Nixon whatsoever. I said to Victor Dees, "If a man wanted to hide in the woods here, he'd need more green than tan, if you ask me."

"He would," said Dees. "There's no need for you to hide in the woods, though."

"Of course that's what you'd say. I was testing you. I know that you're on their side, buddy. And I accept, respect, and understand all of this."

Victor Dees rolled his neck around six times. "I'm still not proud of the way you beat my ass in Roughhouse that time. I ain't saying I could do anything about it now, but I vow that it'll never happen again. Me—I might have to change my ways."

"Don't believe him," Bekah said. I didn't know if she meant Victor or me. "Hey, listen, what you should do is buy a bulletproof vest right now, here. That's what I would do if I were as paranoid as you've become, Novel. Buy a bulletproof vest and not worry about what people might try from now on."

"You damn right," I said. "I want a canteen, a camouflage jacket, a helmet, *and* a bulletproof vest."

Victor Dees shrugged okay.

Bekah said, "You want to see upstairs? I'll show you upstairs if you promise not to write about it. Upstairs here, upstairs from the bakery, upstairs from Gruel Drugs. From what I understand you already have a feeling about it."

Being the investigative reporter I had become I had no chance but to say, "You can count on me. Back when I worked for the lieutenant governor writing speeches, I had to make this promise daily."

Victor Dees said, "Do you want me to gift wrap any of this?"

I looked at him. He had one eye squinted. I knew that he owned more power in Gruel than anyone else, that he probably played stupid more than once on fifty occasions since I'd made his acquaintance. I said, "Separately." I said, "I want to buy some bullets in back, too. Some them bullets'll go with my twenty-two, and forty-aught-six, and four-ten, and twenty-twenty. I need me them bullets go with a good thirty-eight caliber pistol, and my Colt."

Victor Dees said, "You ain't got none them firearms, according to our results."

I said, "Yes I do."

"You're lying," said Bekah.

"Maybe I dug them up behind the Gruel Inn, or I saved my money and bought one of each. I'm not lying! Give me ammo for everything I listed off."

"Okay. Sorry to have questioned you on all this. How much you want, Novel?"

I stood tall as possible, as if I knew what I did. "Well. How about three of each, by god."

◆ ◆ ◆

Bekah held my hand and walked me up the square. We left Victor Dees's army-navy store and went north, toward Gruel Drugs, toward Gruel Bakery. I looked across the street past Colonel Dill's statue at Roughhouse Billiards. Bekah said, "We figured you'd figure, finally. And to be honest we don't know if you know already, or if you're just playing possum to see when we'll confess everything."

Maura-Lee came out of her storefront looking svelte as ever, wearing an apron and hairnet. She said, "Show-and-tell time?"

Then I felt sure she said, "Have a nice day."

Me, I said, "You too, Maura-Lee."

Man, I felt like a regular pathetic nimrod infantryman asked to march through his fallen comrades. I walked up the sidewalk and entered a door I had never noticed, to a place I thought I had only imagined that one night. Bekah said, "You can't write about all of this you're going to see. You just can't. It'll get you

259

killed, first off. And secondly—more than likely—no one would believe you. This is Gruel. This is South Carolina. All of us in the Gruel Association, though, we believe that you might need to know what I'm about to unveil to you as a way of understanding the town's people better, at least over the last half century or so."

On our way up the thin, narrow steps to a loft above what ended up being a quarter of the square, I thought, What do you have to show me, Barry and Larry's attempts at forgery?

And then I saw a dozen perfect *Mona Lisas, American Gothics, Campbell's Soup Cans, Guernicas,* and *Haystacks* stacked up against the wall. I'm talking these fakes were as cracked and crazed as any close-up detailed inset I'd seen in an art history text. There was *Whistler's Mother, Christina's World,* van Gogh with a bandaged ear, those Tahiti paintings by syphilitic Paul Gauguin, even those Pollock monstrosities.

Then there were about a hundred images of Jesus: Jesus on the cross; Jesus talking to strangers; Jesus hitching his ass to a tree; Jesus surrounded by fish, bread, and wine; Jesus as a baby looking up at the Magi. In another corner were as many stretched canvases of Madonna and child.

These weren't prints available at museum gift shops. These weren't cheaply framed prints available at Roses, Sky City, and Woolworth's department stores. Bekah said, "Most of these have been finished off by Barry and Larry. Some are still left over from the mass production years—mostly the seventies. Mom took the most talented orphans and put them to work."

I said, of course, "*No fucking way.* There's no fucking way. Somebody would've been caught by now. There's no fucking way someone could hang *American Gothic* in his living room and not have someone come over to visit and call him on it. The *Mona Lisa*? Give me a break."

Bekah said, "I did the Pollocks. I had zero artistic talent—as you might remember when I tried to paint that Carolina jasmine border on our kitchen wall—so Mom let me do those. No one in North or South America wants to buy them, though, so as far as I'm concerned I'm mostly innocent in this little cottage industry. I did sell one of the Josef Albers pieces to a woman down in Bolivia. Look, Novel, how do you think it was so easy for us to put down a down payment on our first house? And why do you think I came home to see my mother and brother so often? I was in charge of shipping and of collecting accounts receivable that didn't appear in a timely fashion."

Hell, my parents had been long dead. I figured that good grown children must've visited their parents at least twice a month if they lived within a one-day's car journey. I'd seen it on TV. Again, every one of those how-to-write-a-novel textbooks claims, "*Do not* have your novel turn out to be a dream. *Do not* have the main character wake up on the last page and remark, 'Golly gee, *that* was a weird nightmare (or coma).'" Let me say right now that I didn't dream all this up, though I wish I had.

"Just goddamn tell me the truth and why I'm here. I feel like this has been so predestined, you fucking weird siren. I have no free will! I have no free will! Is that what you're telling me?" I'm not too proud to say that I almost cried.

Bekah laughed. She put hands to knees, bent over, and shook her head. "Don't even talk to me about predestination, you idiot." She said, "Here's the God's truth: There was a time when we sold our works as originals. This was long before the

Internet or global knowledge. It wasn't hard to find a man in Idaho or Canada who'd believed he got an original, say, Rembrandt. He couldn't conduct any kind of research so easily and see that the original hung at the Tate, or Louvre, you know. Then came the time where we are now, where Barry and Larry admit that it's a one-of-a-kind reproduction, et cetera. Perhaps, *mon mari*, that's why we're down to two painters trying to keep Gruel afloat. Good lord, in the past we had twenty or thirty kids and young adults whipping these things out. My dad paid them 10 percent of whatever he got—10 percent of a quarter-million-dollar sale ain't bad. Do I need to go on? My father and mother kept a percentage, and the rest kind of went into a fund to pave roads, run water and sewer, everything a large town has."

I said, "What about Irby?"

"Irby—as you know—was stupid. He could only do Miró. They didn't sell."

"Okay. What makes the paintings look so old and cracked?"

"Heat and steam from Maura-Lee's bakery downstairs. Before that, when her father ran the place."

"I thought she came from Raleigh or Columbia. I thought she showed up to the original Sneeze 'n' Tone to lose weight."

"You would. Dope. There's going to be so much left unanswered that you won't know whether to rub your own butt on the carpet or sniff your finger. There's no way you'll figure out everything. No one will."

I didn't know what any of that meant. I asked, "Who killed Irby, Ina, and your father?"

"*Namaste. Namaste. Namaste.*"

Oh it wasn't "Have a nice day" that Maura-Lee said on my trek up to the little shop of forgers. It was one of those weirdo yoga terms. One time the lieutenant governor talked to a group in Asheville and I had him say both *"Ahimsa"* and *"Ojas,"* which meant "nonviolence" and "life energy." He got a standing ovation. To be honest, I thought the guy would mispronounce those sacred words so execrably that he'd be placed in the untouchable caste forever. So much for my knowledge of karma.

"What's with all the religious paintings?" I asked Bekah. I said, "I don't know if you're drinking much anymore, but I could use a bourbon or six about right now. Let's you and me go drink. Let's do some hard drinking like the old times."

Bekah walked across the creaking floor atop Maura-Lee's bakery, the downstairs of ex–Gruel Printing, the loft above Gruel Drugs—this space must've been six thousand square feet—and finally stopped. "We sell all of the religious paintings religiously—forgive my pun—to Bob Jones University up in Greenville. They boast the largest sacred art collection in the world. I guess that it is, if you count what Barry and Larry do as sacred. What a slew of other people have called sacred. That's been our major buyer, that college, since way back when. If you think back over the years you might remember that I've never said anything bad about a Christian, Novel. Those people have made us a fortune in their need to fool the public."

A slight steam rose through the floor, but it didn't smell like regular white, sourdough, or pumpernickel bread. It didn't smell like rye. I said, "I smell garlic."

"Maura-Lee. Come on. Let's go downstairs and see what she's up to. It's nan. It's pita. We've all decided that once you're gone Gruel can become an ashram for yoga lovers." My wife said, "My fault totally. When I ran the Sneeze 'n' Tone—those women were either too pessimistic or too cocky. And when you began the writers colony—good god I thought you'd've had enough sense not to do anything like that—those participants ended up too pessimistic or cocky. There's not a ton of difference between a fat woman wanting to lose weight and a want-to-be writer wanting to gain the weight of Truth, Justice, and the American whatever."

I began walking downstairs. Bekah followed. On the sidewalk Maura-Lee stood there smiling. She said, "Have a nice day," again. But of course this time I heard her right.

On our way over to Roughhouse Billiards I said, "Let me see if I can get this right, part two: Y'all have saved all your money—as a tiny town—over the years. You've all lived off these proceeds, I take it. For some unknown reason y'all have gathered together and voted me in as town historian, but I can't write about what's ever gone on."

"It's kind of like the Cherokee nation's descendants getting money off those bingo parlors and casinos. Well it's *exactly* like that, now that I think about it. And maybe we had too much money left over, money we didn't know what to do with. Town historian sounded good to us, as opposed to anything else. We toyed around with the idea of an airport, but too many people feared noise for one, and crashes into our houses for the other."

I still didn't trust my wife, and wondered if I ever did. I said, "You could've started up one of those outlet malls."

"It's kind of like Atlantis. Our number one export's drying up fast. Otherwise we wouldn't have the overstock. We're looking ahead, Novel. Don't judge us for foresight. We tried my clinic. We tried your stupid writers thing. Now we're going to turn Gruel into a regular full-time ashram. Maura-Lee's adding traditional Indian breads to her list. Before long you'll have to move out of the inn so we can make room for all the yogis we got on order."

We passed Colonel Dill's statue. I'd never noticed before how much he resembled my father. "I feel damned either way," I said. "If I write what I know, y'all will kill me. If I decide to not write at all, y'all will kill me. It all comes down to my knowing the past secrets."

Bekah said, "Let's play a drinking game. We haven't played a good drinking game since Chapel Hill. Like quarters. Like that you're-the-captain-of-a-ship game, and you decide what everyone gets to take aboard."

We crossed the street and I held the door open. "Turning this town into an ashram won't be beneficial for anyone involved. Believe me. I once wrote an entire speech about it."

29

MY PARENTS practiced yoga long before it became an American necessity. They got stoned every Wednesday night, and their friends came over in gym shorts in order to salute the sun or do the crow, cobra, and facedown dog. James and Joyce jumped out of their bedroom windows, snuck around the side of the house, and tried to take photographs of my parents' friends' butts without using a flash. Me, I stood in my upstairs room with a yo-yo above everybody, trying to do tricks.

What pisses me off about neophyte yoga enthusiasts is the same thing that gets me about people who come back to the United States after visiting Paris for a year. It's not impossible, I believe, to just say the fucking English word that you mean. It's easy to say at a sit-down formal dinner in Charlotte, "Oh, this duck is great," as opposed to "Oh, this *canard* is *magnifique.*" In terms of syllables, the English wastes less breath.

So about the last thing I thought Gruel needed was a slew of thin-headed women and men whose years of psychoanalysis didn't work, showing up to say things in front of Gruel Bakery like, "Boy, today I sure enjoyed my sixteen hours doing *Sarvangasana*" when they could've A) said, "shoulder stand"; and B) done something goddamn constructive like plant tomatoes on the square for everyone to enjoy. I didn't want to come across a woman saying, "I'm having problems doing a perfect *Upavistha Konasana,*" when she could've said, "wide-angle seated forward bend," or when she, moreover, could've gone, "I'm having problems helping my elderly wheelchair-bound neighbor understand that it's imperative that I clean her chimney flue so's not to cause a fire this upcoming winter."

Hell—call me stubborn, unyielding, and old-fashioned—I wanted to punch out about anyone who said, "This here clarified butter will enhance your *Ojas*" even if he or she translated it. By god, just say, "Eat this shit, it'll make you feel better." Why say, "Oh, sorry, I didn't mean to fill you up with my *Shukra Dhatu,*" when you could as easily say, "Oops, I just came inside you"?

That's my theory.

Don't ask me how I know these words. Once upon a time I tried to balance my *dosha.* Obviously it didn't work out.

◆ ◆ ◆

I ordered my wife a triple. Barry and Larry, covered in paint, sat up at the bar for once. They used their cue sticks as swizzles. Bekah said, "You boys can let your shoulders down. I told him everything."

They said, "We know."

"Not *everything,*" I said. "I still have all kinds of questions." To Barry and Larry I asked, "Do you boys run a Monotype press sometimes?"

"Our work is all hand-painted," Barry answered.

"Do you have some kind of machine that makes a noise

nightly, over and over and over—kind of a stomp-stomp-stomp sound?"

"Our kerosene heaters make a noise in the winter. We got a fan that sucks out fumes yearlong," Larry said. "That's about it, as far as noise. We're not up there listening to rap music, if that's what you're asking."

Jeff the owner shook his head and smiled. I asked him what he knew. "I'm pretty sure what you hear at night are the descendants of descendants of descendants of descendants of Vicksburg." I thought he'd taken up a stutter for a second. "They're like gypsies or Irish Travelers. Is that what you're talking about?"

My wife downed one shot. She said, "Vicksburg, Mississippi."

"What? Y'all are quite aware that I've freaked out on more than one occasion, hearing a stomping sound across from my place. But I haven't seen any gypsies. This isn't fiddle and mandolin music I'm hearing."

Barry and Larry said, "It's those people, though. Those people aren't us."

"At one point," Jeff said, "they tried to reinvent themselves back in 1866 or thereabouts."

"It's been going on since then," Bekah said. She downed her second shot and sang out, "M-I-S-S-I-S-S-I-P-P-I."

"You'll find out all about it if you take your job seriously and read some them newspaper articles closer," Jeff said.

Larry yelled out, "I got one! Six sets of deer antlers, six spent shotgun shells, and a goldfish bowl holding one of those purple Siamese fighting fish."

I turned back to Jeff the owner. "I'm sifting. I'm going through shit. I think I came across a picture of you the other day. Did you ever own a little plastic doll with only one eye?"

Bekah got up and walked toward a poster on the back wall listing the 1978 NASCAR season. Richard Petty grinned and grinned.

"No," Jeff said.

I drank my beer. I drank Bekah's last shot. I said, "I think it's you. But go ahead with your story."

"Back in 1866 a bunch of my ancestors, as a community, invited everyone to move east."

"Don't tell him, Jeff. Don't tell him. If indeed he puts it in the book we won't like it—I mean, it won't better us any. And certainly the people living there won't like it," Bekah said with her back still turned. I looked to see her pointing in the direction of Gruel Mountain. "They're melungeons, and they don't like to be bothered."

I should've brought a tape recorder, I thought. There was no way to keep track of these stories. I said, "What?"

"You a historian. You know the Civil War."

Of course I didn't go into how that wasn't my area of competency. I said, "The Civil War. The War between the States. Gettysburg. Andersonville. Shiloh. Chancellorsville."

Bekah returned and sat beside me. "We let them vote up there. That's how you got hired in a number of ways. We all voted for the painting project years ago. We voted for my Sneeze 'n' Tone, and then to allow you to run whatever kind of operation you wanted to run afterwards. Town historian. We're a democratic community, Novel. I think it came out 111 to 5 on hiring you over at Gruel Normal."

I looked back at the trick-shot kings. "In all my time spent in Gruel I've maybe seen thirty regulars on the street, or in this bar. Not counting visitors."

"That'll tell you how many people are still hiding out in the caves of Gruel Mountain. There's a bunch. They're pretty self-sufficient, they probably intermarry, and not many of them have the wherewithal to escape," Jeff said.

I laughed. "What're they doing up there all night long, making that noise?"

Jeff the owner said, "Sooner or later we might take a vote to see who'll take a machete up there and find out. There's the co-nundrum, though. I doubt they'll vote for it. And, like Bekah said, we're insistent on giving everyone a vote, even for little things like whether or not to plant azaleas on the square. Well everyone gets a vote who's lived here at least six years. It's all fashioned after most universities' procedures and laws. It's like gaining tenure."

We sat there for five minutes. I tried to make mental notes of the high points. I could think of no mnemonic device to remember, and thought about this great essay by Mark Twain called "How to Make History Dates Stick." It didn't work. "Who're the five voted against me?"

Jeff the owner picked up the phone and said, "Hey, Maura-Lee. Get on over here so Novel can see the five people who didn't trust him writing a biography of Gruel."

He hung up. I said, "Victor Dees voted *for* me?"

My wife said, "No. He was out of town that day on business and forgot to turn in his absentee ballot."

◆ ◆ ◆

Not unlike a fugitive dictator I took to sleeping in different rooms every night, and in different corners of each room. I moved more furniture per day than North American Van Lines. Barry, Larry, and the town's master carpenters came in while I was gone, re-

Sheetrocked the motel, and made it more habitable every day. These guys could've been top-notch developers had they lived in a place where people wished to move into tract housing, out in the suburbs. Every morning I felt blessed to wake, then drove halfway to Augusta, over toward Atlanta, and back to Gruel Normal so as not to circumvent downtown Gruel. I didn't answer the telephone. I finished off my overordered MREs.

Now, y'all of the most rational mind might say to me, "Novel, why didn't you just fucking *leave*? Why didn't you get out of Gruel? It's not like you wore magnetic shoes in a land covered in cast iron."

Oh I could say that I wanted to get to the bottom of things, especially if I resorted to clichés. Or I could say that I had nowhere else to relocate, what with no family in the continental United States, a few ex–lieutenant governors who would never write positive letters of recommendation, et cetera.

Or, like an idiot, I could say that I wanted Rebekah Cathcart back in my life as she was during our normal marriage, where we sat in our Charlotte backyard, telling stories to each other about how our workdays went: me lying about how I only dealt with vipers, she lying about how she only went down to Gruel to see her mother and brother.

◆ ◆ ◆

In my converted silo I shoved Gruel's history aside, off to the far arc. I set my desk up, and opened one of the many unused composition books I'd bought anticipating an autobiography longer than rhymed couplets. In my mind—to save both Gruel economically and my own self medically—it seemed right and logical to devise reinventions and renovations that would work better than inviting yogis, gurus, and double-jointed show-offs to a town that—I felt certain—couldn't sustain a dog pound.

I thought and wrote down, "BBQ Festival—there aren't any of those going on around here." There was the Catfish Feastival up in Ware Shoals, which thrived mainly because the fish got definned and thrown in the town fountain so kids could jump in and gather bellied-up nonswimming lake-bottom scavengers to win biggest catfish and most catfish prizes withdrawn from their croker sacks. Adults participated in a bobbing-for-catfish competition out of fifty-five-gallon drums supplied by one of the local heating and fuel companies. Emergency room doctors readied themselves on these days with enough catgut—of course—to suture up the sliced victims. Or there could be an art car fair: enough insane people covered their Pintos, Mavericks, Darts, Yugos, Malibus, Monte Carlos, Volkswagens, Fairlanes, Galaxies, Coupe de Villes, Audis, Peugeots, Opal Mantas, Bonnevilles, and Le Sabres with Jesus statues, Virgin Marys, macaroni, peace signs, sod, gargoyles, gum balls, Easter eggs, Hershey's Kisses, jelly beans, oyster shells, Barbie dolls, postcards, bottle caps, Matchbox cars, plastic googly-eyes, razor blades, phone books, transistor radios, paisley fabric, license plates, inoperable black-and-white TVs, miniature plastic army men, wine corks, miniature plastic Native American warriors, eating utensils, miniature plastic dinosaurs, fake jewels, bowling trophies, Marilyn Monroe figurines, baseball girls, Hawaiian women in hula skirts, Ping-Pong balls, cacti, copper pennies, beads, buttons, fake fruit, 45 singles, fast-food giveaways that feature Ronald McDonald, Cracker Jack prizes, and parking tickets in order to register their masterpieces at a number of art car fairs, most of which took place in Taos, Santa Fe, Albuquerque,

Phoenix, Flagstaff, Tucson, and the entire state of California. My theory went that the South didn't hold art car aficionados only because we entered our automobiles in stock car races, and drove them too fast to apply knickknacks on the hood, trunk, roof, and/or side panels.

Or we could invite anthropologists and historians to come interview our Vicksburg residents.

Or Gruel might want to hold a live-action poker tournament for people who would never want to be seen playing poker; a weekly tough-man competition; a nudist colony for the shy.

I wrote down more, too, all within an hour, but got my concentration broken when, without even a knock on this historian in residence's silo door, in walked Nora Ouzts, biological mother of James and Joyce. She said, "I know that you're involved in important work, Mr. Akers. I am sorry to disturb you." She wore her gym instructor's outfit of black rubber shoes, dark blue stretch-band shorts, and a gray T-shirt. I'd brought along my dice and made a pact with myself to actually work on Gruel's family tree once I rolled a straight. Not that I believe in superstitious signs, but I looked down to see two fours, two deuces, and a one, which, of course, added up to thirteen. Nora Ouzts said, "I know you know what only I know. I can tell. So to be more truthful, I know you know what, at one time, only my first husband, your parents, and I knew. Now it's you and me. And it shall remain so, I hope. There are things we know, and things we know that others know we don't know."

Had she been reading Leo Strauss? I thought. What kind of political philosopher had Nora Haughey become?

Her feet didn't appear to touch the cement floor as she, always the ballerina, floated inside the silo. I said, "How're the PE classes going? I bet the students really love you. How long have you been at Gruel Normal? Have any of your students gone on to study PE in college? It's too bad we're not big enough to have sports teams. When I first got approached about my position here I thought it might be cool to start a lacrosse team, but I guess that might take some time, seeing as we'd need a larger enrollment. I like track anyway. As a matter of fact my brother and sister became such great distance runners..."—my inner voice said Shut up, shut up, shut up, shut up, but I kept going, of course—"... that they ran back to Ireland, their original birthplaces. Is it 'birthplaces' or 'birthsplace'? I have these writing books back where I live that have some commonly misused words, like mothers-in-law, sergeants at arms, and secretaries of state. Anyway, I'm doing pretty good here. Pretty *well*. I have no idea what you're talking about."

Now go watch the movie *Whatever Happened to Baby Jane?* starring Bette Davis, and come back to this scene.

Nora Ouzts said, "I know that you've seen birth certificates, Novel. It's not like I don't stay in touch with anyone still living in Black Mountain. Milson Willets at the old Black Mountain College Research Archives, for example. It's not like he never called me and said I needed to come up there to retrieve my papers. According to Milson I showed up right after you did. I knew that your good mother kept the real and original birth certificates of Joyce and James. I only hoped that I'd be dead before anyone found out."

Here's what I thought, no lie: In real life, people do not speak to each other in long, long soliloquies. They don't banter monologues. It's in more than one of those writing books. Now, it's okay in the world of drama. A character on stage can speak for five fucking minutes to another character, then the second character may respond for five full minutes. As opposed to real life, or in novels, soapboxes might actually be encouraged and rewarded in a play. Go read *Happy Days* by Mr. Samuel Beckett, then come back.

NOVEL

How old are you, Ms. Ouzts? Those papers I retrieved from Milson Willets came from about fifty years ago. You don't look older than fifty now. Fifty-five at the most. Fifty-nine.

NORA

Call me Nora. That's quite a compliment. Call me Nora. The great thing about teaching in a private school is that there's no age discrimination. Call me Nora.

NOVEL

Nora.

NORA

I came here today to tell you that you're not crazy. I got home the other night with Derrick and thought about how you must think all of this is some kind of cosmic joke being played on you. I mean, you've come back to a town where your ex-wife may or may not have killed off some of her loved ones, where her loved ones may or may not've killed off some people, where your stepbrother and -sister may or may not've ended up being your half brother and sister, and so on. What would it be like, I thought the other night, to wonder why one got put on this planet?

NOVEL

That's another one. It's not two *steps-sibling*. It's two *stepsiblings*. I think. I'm almost sure. (*Coughs. Coughs uncontrollably. Clears*

275

throat and runs fingers through hair.) Derrick? How old is Derrick? If you're as old as you say you are, then—and I'm not being an ageist—I imagine Derrick's at least that old. Two years one way or the other. But he looks young! He looks, also, to be fifty. Like you. Well, anyway, how did you ever meet good old Derrick Ouzts? You know, when I say his name in my head it comes out "Dairy Coots." I think about all these little bugs on a cow.

NORA

At Black Mountain College. I know it's hard to believe now, but back then he could've become one of the most recognizable abstract expressionists in the twentieth century. At the time, though, he carried around his own easel and copied from the masters—charcoaled boring still lifes, and so on.

NOVEL

I don't want to hear any of this. I must ask you to leave. I have too much work to do if I want to finish this biographical sketch.

NORA

I didn't mean to upset you. You appear upset!

NOVEL

Tell Mr. Ouzts that I'm not not unhappy. That I'm not not not not not disunsatisfied.

After Nora Ouzts left me to "do research" I took out my notebook filled with possible activities Gruel could attract. The Annual Disabled Persons Festival, I thought, but it appeared that it would only bring in the cave-living phantoms. I wrote down, "DNA Fair—bring in a bunch of scientists and let's see who shouldn't ever couple, seeing as they're related." I wrote, "I'm afraid that Gruel, South Carolina, cannot properly be labeled a town. It's not a city, of course, but it's not a suburb, village, hamlet, or crossroads, either. It's not best described as a community, in strict sociological terms. No, the area known as Gruel should be viewed as one thing only: family."

There. That would be the opening to *Gruel: A Biography*. It could be photographs from there on out, as far as I cared. Anyone in a bookstore could match beady eyes and high foreheads to connect the dots, fill in the blanks, put two and two together, make their own conclusions, fit the puzzle pieces together, and every other cliché performed by logicians.

My job, at this point it seemed, was to find a suave and relentless escape plan.

30

IN OR ABOUT 1973 my father put his index finger to his lips for me to shush. This might've been February. Ice-crushed snow stood on the ground. Walking in the front yard required a high step known mostly to predominantly black southern college halftime marching band members—clarinetists, trombonists, saxophone players who not only had to play their notes but to stamp in geometric patterns so that, as a family, they could spell out something meaningful. My father jerked his head once for me to follow him out of our Black Mountain house where we lived with my two adopted Irish orphans and my mom. Right out of the front door Dad said, "I got something to show you. This is between you and me. Or you and I—I forget correct English. This might be something you need to know."

He spoke in a whisper, and of course I couldn't wait to do something James and Joyce and my mother would not be in on. My father wore boots, a plaid Pendleton shirt, one of those flap-eared hats. As I recall, I wore footie pajamas, but looking back this couldn't be truthful. More than likely I wore jeans and a flannel shirt, a watch cap, rainsuit, galoshes. I probably looked like the Morton Salt Girl's crazy brother.

We trudged out of the yard, walked past our frozen Oldsmobile stuck in the driveway, and turned left toward downtown Black Mountain. We walked down the middle of the rough-paved road outside our home, up one hill and down the next. Please understand that—May through October—I had investigated this entire region. We walked by at least two creeks where I unrocked salamanders, picked them up, held them long enough to make my skin crawly, then put them back. We passed a place where, later, I'd take a pellet gun, shoot and kill a blue jay, and feel so bad that I would never pick up a gun again.

"Are you going to kill me?" I asked my father. We slid and slid on the blacktop.

"What? Now why would you think that, son? Good god, no, I'm not going to kill you. Where'd you get a dumb idea like that?" We walked and slid and fell uncontrollably. I had recently read an article in one of my mother's magazines concerning the Bataan Death March.

I said, "I don't know."

My father put his arm around my shoulder in a way that would make Norman Rockwell wonder why he even tried. Dad said, "Goddamn it to hell, sometimes I can't figure you out, Novel. I'm doing the very goddamn best I can, considering. What are you—ten, twelve?—go back and ask your buddies how often their fathers take them out on bad, miserable, frozen days for walks where they learn something. Son of a bitch." My father, ex-pianist, patted his pant pockets, his two-pocket Pendleton shirt, the bottom sides of his polarized coat.

I said, "Last week I was the only one in school to understand a trick. My math teacher asked how we could do three coins to

279

add up to a quarter, one of which wasn't a nickel. Three coins. Everybody said, 'You got to have two dimes and a nickel.'"

My dad walked like a penguin, or how I'd seen penguins walk on one of those *National Geographic* specials. He said, "The other's a dime. The other one's a dime. Easy. It's still two dimes and a nickel. One of them's not a nickel means that one of the dimes isn't a nickel."

I said, "Yeah. That's what I said. I got an A. I got a gold star. No one would talk to me afterwards. There's a problem with being smart in Black Mountain, isn't there."

My dad pulled out his left arm and said, "I think this is the right path."

We took a slight slim trail through spruce, pine, and rhododendron. My dad and I stepped sideways. We must've gone a hundred yards until we approached a twelve-by-twelve shanty, surrounded by hutches.

I said, "My feet feel froze."

"Here we are. You want a rabbit for a pet? I wanted to get you a pet rabbit for Christmas, but I never got around to it. I thought you might want a bunny. Instead of a dog or cat."

A man walked out on his porch. At first I didn't notice that he didn't own a right arm. No, I only saw him in coveralls, his beard hanging down past his sternum.

My father said, "Shake hands with Mr. Payne, Novel. Shake his hand. Go ahead and shake his hand."

I stuck out my right arm proud as any fourth grader asked to meet the mayor's wife. The one-armed rabbit salesman offered his left arm, and we performed that awkward sideways shake — hands sideways, hands upside down — until my father slapped me upside the head. "When you see a left-handed man, boy, you shake with your left hand. There's no other choice. There's no other proper way. You stick out your left arm immediately and pretend like there's nothing better or different in the world. That's what you do."

Mr. Payne said, "It doesn't mean a fuck to me. It ain't like this ain't happened before. Y'all want a white rabbit? They make good pets. Y'all want a Angora?—you want one these floppy ears? Make good pets and y'all can spin they yarn."

Make good pets and y'all can spin they yarn, I thought.

My father asked Mr. Payne, "How much do you want for your merchandise?"

Your *merchandise*! If I'd've known that my father would've died in the Everglades I might've said something at this point, something like, "Be careful or you might end up having your rib cage act as *merchandise* for an alligator at one point in life."

My father held me by the neck, pretty much. The one-armed man said, "I get two. Two dollars each."

"I got me a Havahart trap, put peanut butter in, catch rabbits every night."

Rightly, the one-armed man said, "Then do."

My father said, "I might."

And then he drug me away. I think I said, "I want one of those calicos, I want one of those calico rabbits." My feet drug through the crushed frozen path leading back from Mr. Payne's house. I said, "You promised me a rabbit you didn't get me for Christmas."

My father stopped at the corner of Mr. Payne's path and our road home. "There are many lessons to be learned here, son.

First off, don't believe everything your old man tells you." My father reached down in the snow, picked up a piece of gravel, handed it to me, and said, "Don't say I never gave you anything, boy."

We walked back home rabbitless. I didn't pout at all, I promise, as far as I remember. Halfway home I said, "Is it hard for a pianist to play when his fingers get cold?"

My father said, "I imagine."

We walked in the center of the macadam. I said, "Playing a piano with frozen fingers would be hard. I couldn't do it. A great pianist should keep a rabbit with him at all times in order to keep his hands warm."

My father stopped and looked at me. He sidestepped into the bough-draped woods, ice-heavy limbs pointing south. My father snapped off one limb and shook it, snapped the ice off on his thigh. Right away I knew that he didn't want to walk with a cane, that he wanted something nearby to pop me on the hamstrings whenever possible.

I ran onward. I wished that I had followed my brother and sister in regards to distance running. My father chased me. He yelled, "I'm not going to hit you, I'm not going to hit you," over and over, but I turned around and saw him brandishing that rough bark-covered limb.

I ran on. After I passed our house I yelled back to him, "I bet that old one-armed Mr. Payne can play piano better than you."

That night, his head filled with mucus, he said, "I don't know who came by here selling me a fifty-five-gallon drum of snot, but here I am with it."

My mother said, "Maybe you need a martini, babe."

I took note.

◆ ◆ ◆

When I refused to learn how to swim, my father took to hand-knotting a fishing net. I'm not sure what he used for a template but he gathered a few thousand feet of cord, twine, shoelaces, and rope. Somehow he strung together a net that, when thrown properly, covered a good eighth acre. He sewed a variety of weights to the edges: spoons stolen from a Morrison's Cafeteria down in Asheville, a couple of broken windup clocks, two or three bicycle chains, a slew of giveaway church keys. The net must've weighed three hundred pounds.

James and I helped my father load the net in his refrigeration truck's back, and when James said, "Let me go, Dad," my father said, "No, no, we won't have room on the way back."

I didn't understand his motives whatsoever. My father said, "Instead of just buying shrimp to bring back, I'm going to rent a boat down there, catch my own shrimp, and come back. I've checked into all this." My mom walked out in the driveway at this point. My father found it necessary to repeat, "I've checked into all this. A boat rental ain't nothing compared to buying shrimp wholesale. Anyway, after Novel and I fill up the back of the truck, we'll need to ride home with the net between us. There won't be room for anyone else."

I didn't think to ask my father how we'd get a wet net back in the truck, seeing as it took the three of us nearly six hernias to haul it from backyard to bumper. James said, "Does this make me the man of the house?"

My mother said, "You're always the man of the house, James," which, too, should've tipped me off about things not being copacetic in our household.

"So we'll leave now, drive for six hours, spend the night in the truck, shrimp tomorrow, and get back, I'd say, around midnight tomorrow."

My mother held up her left hand halfheartedly. I thought of one-armed Mr. Payne, but said nothing.

My father and I drove in silence over Highways 64, 74, down 501, and finally got to 17. We pulled up in Murrells Inlet and my father rented what most people might consider a "johnboat" at best. "In the morning we'll take this down to the inlet. Then we'll get some old boy to help us get the net in. There's always an old boy hanging around at five in the morning."

I said, "Good night."

"And then we'll go out about two hundred yards into the bay and throw the net out. I don't know how long we'll have to wait, but maybe we can watch some of those shrimp boats and figure it out."

"Good night," I said. I turned in the passenger seat and pulled a blanket around me.

"We don't get any shrimp, we'll come back in to one of the creeks and do some crabbing. I got chicken necks! I got string!"

"Yessir."

"Here," my father said. "Here, Novel." He pulled out a flask. "You're old enough now. In case you're worried about your fingers freezing off in a way that'll keep you from ever playing the piano."

That's the last I remembered. In the morning my father shoved a life jacket on my torso and led me to the boat, and taught me how to row. He dropped anchor and, luckily, some-how, threw the cast net out by himself in one great motion without tipping over our dinghy.

"Good thing we didn't take Mr. Payne with us. I hope his legs never go out. A one-armed man with no legs can only circle around in a wheelchair on dry land."

I'm talking it was colder than a Junior Leaguer's titty. There in the bay no waves piled in, but the wind cut us not unlike a man sprinkling ammonia throughout a closed-ended room. I wore my mittens and watch cap. I wore a bad fake-fur-collared coat bought at Sears. Chattering, I said, "Shrimps aren't like mammals. They can't feel the cold."

My father said, "Goddamn it to hell." He pulled in his net line. "I don't think the net made it to the bottom. Take off your life jacket and pearl dive down to see if the net reaches bottom."

I was old enough to discern my father's crazed look, as opposed to how he looked after yoga club. "I can't swim," I said. "I'd drown." My father jerked the life jacket over my head—I still have scars beneath my armpits from the strap burns—and threw it in the water.

"Damn you, Novel. I didn't plan on your being such a pussy." He threw the net back in, took off his own preserver, and jumped into the Atlantic. I'm not proud to admit that my first thought involved rowing back to shore immediately. Before Dad surfaced—and this might've been two seconds after he submerged—I constructed an elaborate explanation and/or alibi that involved a giant freakish tidal wave, the anchor coming loose, my riding the flat-bottomed boat sans net all the way into shore like a surfboard, and so on. I considered a shark attack, too, of course.

"Help! Help me, Novel!" my father yelled out when his head popped back up twenty yards away. He reached his arms out, and this particular facial expression—maybe he took an acting course or two at Black Mountain College—held pity, despair, anguish, helplessness, profound loss, sincerity, unrequited love, improbable hope, and determination all at once. I don't know if Hollywood's ever distributed a motion picture production of Johnny Appleseed, but I can't envision Jimmy Stewart, James Arness, Charles Bronson, Bruce Lee, Wally Cox, Peter Lorre, Peter Sellers, Woody Allen, Alan Hale, Jr., or Meryl Streep invoking the exact same face that my father so professionally exposed.

I jumped in. I swam to him as if my arms were regular paddle wheels, and didn't notice that he swam toward me. When we met he took me by the torso and drug me back to the boat. After maybe five minutes of trying to get back in without tipping the thing over, we managed to get ourselves back in: Dad held the side of the boat as I crawled up, then I sat hard on one side so he could extricate himself from a cold, cold death.

We chattered hard together, and flinched with Jimmy-limbs. "Help me pull the net back up," he said. When it felt no heavier than the first time, meaning that we had no shrimp, he said, "Screw this," and dropped the rope overboard.

We rowed back in together—a nice rite of passage, really—and left our boat on the beach. Inside the truck, heater on high, I said, "Well that was a mistake."

"You can swim now, can't you?"

My father drove us back to the campground. We showered and redressed. I think it was about in the town of Rockingham on the drive back with no merchandise in back to sell later, where Dad pulled over at a roadside bar he knew and insisted that we go inside, do a little drinking, and play the house spinet for tip money.

◆ ◆ ◆

My mother thought it would be a great idea to play charades during my thirteenth birthday party. Even mountain kids didn't play *charades*. Mountain kids raised by pseudoartistic parents who made their entire family read aloud to each other didn't play charades. Hell, thirteen-year-old children didn't even have birthday parties in Black Mountain.

"And now it's time for charades!" my mother yelled out. She had invited most of my friends' parents, which only made it more embarrassing. The men stood around drinking Dad's booze, smoking pipes, and exaggerating what their latest paintings sold for. The women sat down on our ugly pastel furniture, drank booze, smoked Tiparillo cigars, and exaggerated their *children's* accomplishments, after saying things like, "I've been asked to audition for some kind of musical up in New York, but I can't do it without feeling guilty about leaving Purpose," or Synchronicity, Raven, Cedar, Megadose, Latitude, Diopside, Sensitive, Thrombin, Rhododendron, Tritheism, or Razor Clam—some of my poor schoolmates named by drug- or karma-addled young parents.

I think my mother expected a giant "Yah!" like that.

"We want to play kickball in the front yard," I said, even though we really wanted our parents to fucking leave so we could play a game I'd recently made up called "Where's My Finger?" I had a thing for Megadose Norris, whose parents both gave up careers early on in ceramics in order to concentrate on a dual and symbiotic relationship involving bats, guano, and farming and inculcating microbiotic far-eastern vegetable needs here in the southeastern United States, things like bamboo shoots, kimchee, gingerroot, wasabi, bok choy, water chestnuts, and podded soybeans.

"Everybody write down the name of a song, movie, or book title. We'll do boys against girls." My mom opened two brown paper bags, one with a pink dot on it, the other blue.

I looked at my classmates. We all looked at each other and said nothing. I don't know if, in our DNA, we possessed a skewed version of ESP, but already I knew that this little game of my mother's would, indeed, be a charade.

Cedar McKenzie, a girl, extracted a slip of paper from the boy's team bag. No one would ever know what she truly pulled out. My mother went through all of the standard charades clues: pulling on her ear for "sounds like," flipping open prayer hands for "book title," reeling in her eyeball for "movie."

Cedar opened her hands and looked at her teammates. That was it. Raven yelled out, "*The Adventures of Huckleberry Finn.*"

"Damn," Cedar said. "That was fast." She tore her paper in tiny bits before anyone could look.

My brother, stuck at a little kids' party, went next. He checked his paper, did the movie clue, and I yelled out, "*It's a Mad, Mad, Mad, Mad World.*"

"All right, little brother," he said, tearing up the sheet.

This went on through three sets. Whatever anyone spouted out, the cluegiver said, "Uh-huh" right away. My mom, frustrated that neither she nor any of her friends got to play, said, "This is *so* uncanny! Are y'all watching this? I've never seen anything like it in my life! Remember when we used to play back in college? Sometimes it might take an entire *night* to figure out the right response."

Somebody's father said, "Yeah, but you must remember that we delved in more complicated and cerebral ideas. We chose quotes from the world of philosophy."

As my friends and I ran outside to play "Where's My Finger?" my sister Joyce said, "And don't forget that y'all were stoned."

I thought she only meant that they were drunk. "Come over here, Megadose," I yelled. I stood behind a giant tulip poplar. "Close your eyes." For some reason I felt exactly no fear of rejection. It might've been because I knew how to shake hands with a one-armed man, and I could swim with my head above water.

31

BEKAH TOOK Maura-Lee to some kind of Baba-lovers' retreat down in Myrtle Beach in order to recruit possible yoga gurus to live and teach where I'd finally considered my home, so I had no other option but to break into the old Cathcart antebellum mansion and snoop around. I awoke early on a Friday morning mid-May—Gruel Normal's students traveled to Ghost Town in the Sky up in Maggie Valley, North Carolina, in order to witness a real-life Cherokee Trail of Tears production as part of their history/social studies/drama/world lit component. It didn't bother me, as I drove the step van over, that it wouldn't be difficult to finger an intruder's getaway car if he drove anything other than a midsize American sedan.

The front door had not been locked. I turned the handle and let myself in. A cup of what I first thought to be water fell on my right hand—I'd done this little joke in college—but after I sniffed my back palm I sensed gasoline. I thought one thing only at the time: Maura-Lee and Bekah must be out of money if they've foregone normal burglar detection devices in order to delicately balance a wax-paper cup of gas. "Stay away from open flames," I said aloud. "There might not be working water here."

I don't want to say that the place was a disaster zone, seeing as I'd lived in one since moving to Gruel, but there barely existed a path to walk through. Not only did stacks upon stacks of Barry and Larry's forged iconic oil paintings glut what should've been the foyer, hall, and dual parlors, but so did industrial baker's racks, ovens, and stainless steel rolling carts. Old man Cathcart's giant mounted heads—every possible antlered being—still stared down from the walls. The ex–Gruel Inn furniture piled up randomly, along with all the items I had recovered—gimcracks and treasures both Jeff the owner and Victor Dees supposedly sold to people at the Pickens County Flea Market in my presence: the Picayune cigarettes, knives, spent cartridges, book matches, perfume bottles, the pleas for help scrawled out on a variety of papers, and so on.

I felt like I had no choice but to get my hammer, cat's-paw, and crowbar out of the van in order to check out what remained hidden in *these* particular walls. In the upstairs bedrooms there was nothing. I hammered ancient nails back in the best I could. The bathrooms, laundry room, mudroom, parlors, living room, downstairs bedroom, and closets held nothing outside of cobwebs, dead bugs, a couple mouse carcasses, and mishandled nails. I found no "Help Me" summons, no fingernail-scratched "I'm still alive" dictums that would certainly be displayed in a top-rate B-movie horror film.

Behind a Hobart automatic dishwasher shoved beside the fireplace, though, I peeled back Sheetrock to find a twine-wrapped scroll. Let me say right now that this wasn't a hand-made paper document rolled up like some kind of old-fashioned diploma or land deed. Because I had no expertise in the tanning process I couldn't positively distinguish deer, cow, horse, or sheep skin from that of human derma. For some reason, though, I understood the odd document to be nothing but shaved back skin from a small, small Homo sapiens. Let me tell you that I cringed, and got creeped out, and felt the hairs on my neck stand as I picked up this flesh tube and rolled it out, expecting to read a list of every dead Gruel orphan ever used and abused by the Cathcart machine.

An ambulance went by on its way, I assumed, to Graywood Regional Memorial. I jumped. Who fell sick enough in Gruel to be transported thusly? I wondered. Everyone either humped out their sicknesses—from stroke to heart attack—or flat-out died. A minute later I heard Victor Dees driving crazy, palm pressed hard on the horn, he being Gruel's only serious volunteer firefighter.

I turned back to the hidden scroll to read, "You are here. Write here."

Well I don't have to elaborate any about how I got the fuck out of the house immediately, as soon as I replaced the Sheetrock, hammered in new threaded nails, patched over all the minor indentions with compound, mixed some latex Porter paint to match the yellowed tint of Bekah's walls, took out an old bandanna to wipe down all of my fingerprints, replaced all of the major bakery appliances to their original positions, and checked every corner for hidden cameras that might need destruction. Then I slid out of the house, closed the door with my elbow, and kept my face to the ground should any of the Vicksburg descendants be up on Gruel Mountain with their old-timey eyepieces.

I forgot to replace the cup of gas.

In the distance I heard Victor Dees's makeshift siren he'd

salvaged from an MP's Jeep, according to him. I got in the step van and drove up Old Old Greenville Road, watching an isosceles triangle of smoke that, as it turned out, emanated from Gruel BBQ and Pig-Petting Zoo. I pulled in behind Dees, who could only watch the structure fall in on itself. "You should've heard the squeals an hour ago, Novel. I guess old Brother Scott is gonna throw himself a bake sale tomorrow. A fire sale."

It stunk, in a you-overcooked-the-pork-shoulder kind of way. I said, "What happened? What's the story with the ambulance that flew by right before you did?"

Dees pulled out the walkie-talkie clipped to his belt and said into it, "I'mo be incommunicado directly for an unspecified time. This has officially become an arson investigation, ten-four," and turned the dial to *off*. Who knew which man or woman did or didn't stand on the other end, or why? To me Victor Dees said, "I didn't drive by the motel, Cuz. Where were you seeing a convoy of ambulance and me?"

Fucking A, I thought. There's no way I should admit to breaking into Bekah's house. I said, "What?" stalling.

"I didn't drive by the Gruel Inn, and I didn't drive by Gruel Normal—plus all those people outside of you are gone off to a field trip, Bubba. Where were you?"

I said, "Well you know, Victor. I needed to take a walk. You drove by me a hundred miles an hour, right there on the square. Me, I stood there looking at Colonel Dill's statue—as you well know I'm writing the official unabridged historical biography of Gruel, its people and environs—and you drove past me."

He said, rightly, "Bullshit. I took a defensive driving class a few years before you came into our midst. I know how to train my eyes in a way that involves everything peripheral. I got my

293

side mirrors locked in all ways to view what I passed, you know. I got my rearview stuck in a way to understand what went by just. You weren't there, pal. *I think you might've burned down the Gruel BBQ and Pig-Petting Zoo. There's no one else in town today. There's no one in town. You.*"

I said, "No. No, no, no, dickhead. I'm a lot of things, but I ain't an arsonist."

"I smell gas on your hands, buddy. I don't smell gas on *my* hands. I'm no master of rational thought, but I might think — or the guy we're going to bring in from the South Carolina arson investigators might think — that you have something to do with this particular fire. Hmmmm — let's see." Victor Dees put his index finger to his temple, like any situation comedy actor might do. "No one's in town outside of Novel Akers. His hands reek of a flammable liquid. I never got the opportunity to take a college logic course, but this seems almost too easy."

Again, the building smouldered and flamed and fell in on itself right in front of us. Victor Dees stood beside his empty five-gallon drywall bucket. "Is the Forty-Five Volunteer Fire Department showing up any time soon? Is this how y'all do it here — one man, one bucket?"

"We spend our money otherwise," Dees said. "And we urge our residents not to burn their houses down. That's about it."

No churches existed in Gruel, I knew. Did they burn down due to fire-and-brimstone preachers? Did lightning strike and eradicate them before real firefighters could show up? I said, "I got gas on my hand when I needed to siphon from my van in order to fire up the lawn mower."

Dees stared at me. I kept hard eye contact. Victor Dees said, "You can't tell lies to a professional liar. That's an impossible task." Brother Scott's propane tank blew up about this time. I don't know if pig or metal flew straight up in the sky, but Victor Dees and I watched it, just like in a slow-motion movie. He said, finally, "I've voted for some things that we shouldn't've done. I'll admit it now. Everything else I've thought would work out, worked out. Anyway. I didn't think you'd go so far as kill the pigs in order to distract everyone from what you really have on your mind."

"I didn't start the fire, you fucking idiot, and you know it."

Victor Dees tried to stare me down again. He tried to see if I'd avert my eyes or develop a nervous twitch. I pulled my shirt up over my nose in order to eradicate the smell of burning flesh. "I know. I know that. I'm playing with you." He said, "There are people who want to see you fail and fail. There are people among us think you're a little highfalutin, having your own autobiography due out any day now from Harcourt. That's the word, right? That's what's happening."

Another trick, I thought. I said, "Harcourt's the word, if that's what you mean."

Dees rested his hand on the camouflaged truck. Above us, buzzards circled like they normally did above Gruel Mountain. "I don't think Graywood County Fire and Rescue owns a map of the county, taking this long to get here. I called them up two hours ago."

What sounded like firecrackers going off emitted from the barbecue stand. "There's no telling," I said.

"Listen." Victor Dees picked up his walkie-talkie, held it to his mouth, and said, "I'm back, ten-four," like that, though he never turned the *on* switch up. "Listen," he said to me. "There are people."

"I didn't start any fire. As a matter of fact I'd broken into Bekah's house looking for anything I could find concerning me and mine. Or at least me. Me and hers, what with that odd upbringing. There are human remains in the wall over there, I tell you. There's a rolled-up tanned back side of somebody, and they've written a note to me on it. It's like a giant curled pork rind, I swear to God."

Victor Dees looked off somewhere in the distance—I swear to God—and yelled, "Cut! Cut! We got the truth out of him."

From the back side of Gruel BBQ and Pig-Petting Zoo Brother Scott stood up. He said, "I hope this was worth it all, goddamn it. I got to sue somebody for smoke inhalation."

"Oh fucking shutup," Victor said back. "You'll get enough insurance money just like everyone else did. You'll either be able to retire forever or rebuild a real barbecue joint worth going to."

It wasn't difficult to understand how my fellow citizens had plans of their own outside my historical Gruel biography. I said, "I'm wearing a tape recorder! I've got a tape recorder!"

Victor Dees said, "Oh shut up, Novel. No you don't. We got you pegged. You're too stupid to do something like that. Your parents should've named you 'Short Story,' if anything. Or 'Poem.'"

Brother Scott came up and shook my hand, smiling. "Well that was fun. I have to get on the horn and call a contractor to come rebuild. Who's hungry?"

◆ ◆ ◆

I drove my step van over to Roughhouse Billiards and parked sideways right in front. No one lolled on the square, and I knew it only meant that people used this day of nonchild leisure to procreate, which I thought to be a sad, myopic occasion.

"Hey, Novel. I thought you'd be up in Maggie Valley today," Jeff the owner said. He reached in the cooler for a PBR.

"Nice try."

Barry and Larry stood like idiots before their pool table, no trick-shot paraphernalia evident in their midst. For the first time ever I noticed that these brothers weren't speckled in old paint. As a matter of fact, their arms appeared to be *singed* somewhat. I took my beer and said, "How's about that Gruel BBQ and Pig-Petting Zoo burning down?"

Jeff the owner shrugged. "I didn't hear about it."

"What about y'all, Barry and Larry—if that's y'all's *real names*—what do you think about the barbecue place burning down? What a shame. All those nice pigs."

They stood like minutemen holding pool cues. They both slanted their eyes to the left immediately. Barry said, "I ain't heard."

"*You ain't heard,*" I said, getting up off my barstool. I walked over and picked the striped eleven ball out of the closest middle pocket. "*You ain't heard.* Well I'm of the belief that y'all set the place on fire. I'm of the belief—this isn't paranoia—that some people want to peg me for it. I'm of the belief that Gruel will keep burning down, establishment by establishment, until I'm gone. I think *some* people don't want *other* people to know the truth."

Immediately I wished that I had had time to rehearse my little speech. "Establishment by establishment" came off weird metrically. It also sounded forced, and one of those how-to-write textbooks warned about forced-sounding writing.

"What did you say?" said Larry.

I held that eleven ball back up like a pitcher faking toward first base. "You know what I'm talking about."

Jeff the owner came up behind me and tried to grab the ball. "That's enough. We don't want no fights. We might be called Roughhouse, but that don't mean we want any."

I hate to say that I shook. There's got to be some kind of physiobiological term for what happens when a person gets to that am-I-really-about-to-do-what-I'm-about-to-do point. I was there, baby. Would I cock my arm further and hit Barry or Larry with the eleven ball square on the forehead? Would I gain enough strength to turn the pool table over? Or would I realize that perhaps I should pack up my few belongings and slouch my way out of Gruel? I said, "Thank you" to Jeff the owner, like a big baby.

Barry said, "*That's right*. I don't think you want to mess with us."

I turned to Jeff and said, "Please. Please. You can keep the ball. I won't use the ball, I promise."

"I'd kind of like to see this," he said. "What the hell."

And then I was on those boys like tarnish on silver.

◆ ◆ ◆

Maura-Lee and Kah showed up at the Gruel Inn. Me, I'd bedded down in room 11, thinking it was some kind of sign. I came out the door and looked down to who knocked on the office entrance. I yelled out, "I'm here. What do y'all want?" from however many feet away.

Let me say now that I knew that these two women loved each other, and held a lesbian relationship that they didn't want

298

anyone in Gruel to know about. Let me say that it didn't bother me, that I never felt emasculated, and that I wished for them nothing but the best in South Carolina.

I yelled out, "Hey you two lesbians, come on down this way and give me a show!" like a fool.

Maura-Lee and Bekah looked at each other, and looking back on it all now I understand that they smirked. They walked up my way. They didn't hold hands, but they kept up one of those side-to-side kind of walks best used by tired weight lifters. Maura-Lee looked out at Gruel Mountain. Bekah said, "I'm not a lesbian, Novel. Maura-Lee's not gay, Novel. We just like each other."

"Yeah, yeah," I said.

Maura-Lee said, "Hey, Novel. I'm writing a book. I'm writing a book about all the things I think might help people live better, like in a different light. There will be recipes, of course. But there will be other things in between. Like jokes and conundrums. Say, why do you think when you pull olive loaf out of a package, all the olives fall out? And then, at the end of the resealable container, how come there aren't a hundred olive slices stacked up?"

I couldn't tell if she offered a joke or a riddle. I said, "You finish that book up and I'll put in a good word to my agent."

The women walked into room 11 and gyred around. Bekah said, "This place looks so much better than it did after you tore all the walls out being nosy."

Now, I couldn't remember fully if Bekah had ever come into the Gruel Inn after its innards got refurbished after my demolition work. How did she know how it looked before my townmates showed up on a volunteer basis to refurbish the place for possible gurus? I said, "I can only surmise deductively—and you know for a fact that I'm able to do so, after successfully passing a graduate school course called 'When Statesmen Refuse What Seems to Be Apparent, and How'—that you've been inside my abode at a time when I toiled over archival Gruel photographs."

Maura-Lee touched the wall. Bekah said, "Well that certainly might be a crime, Novel. That's an odd and weird and scandalous accusation. Because *someone* broke into *our* house as of late. Fortunately I installed one of those home protection movement cameras in the fake eyeball of a mounted dik-dik. Technology's amazing, isn't it? It keeps so little from being a mystery, Novel."

Right away I knew that Bekah couldn't've made all this up off the top of her debt-collector head. The fucking dik-dik, I thought. When I looked around the rooms it never occurred to me that she might desacralize one of her father's prized stuffs. "Well," I said. "Maybe I'm just trying to figure out what bizarre deus ex machina plopped me down here in Gruel, you know." Damn me to hell for being the kind of person who wants to understand tragic flaws, past-life indiscretions, or doomful predestiny.

Maura-Lee said, "I'd almost bet that our yoga gurus will want these rooms painted in pastel shades of green. That's the best color for tranquillity. Maybe we should paint the whole town in pastels."

"Or take a vote and change its name," Bekah said. She held one eyebrow up and kept a smirk.

I could only think about how I would honor my Gruel Normal contract, then slip out of town on my way to write speeches for a state whose lieutenant governor needed help, a place like Alabama, a place where my tragic flaws might be recognized and ballyhooed.

32

I COULD NOT have worn blinders for the next few weeks and been more focused. At home—no matter what room I chose— I read over all my how-to books again and again. At work inside the silo I stacked articles and photographs in chronological order: starting with news of Gruel's own Colonel Dill's heroic escapades, ending with a November 1984 report in the *Forty-Five Platter* on the inexplicable and unlikely occurrence that no one showed up to vote in the presidential election. Victor Dees, of all people, got quoted in the article as he told rookie reporter Bob Murray, "I guess we all had something to do that day. Tuesdays are important in Gruel. Most southern towns, it's Wednesdays, what with night church. For some reason it's always been Tuesdays in Gruel. I believe—don't quote me on this—that Colonel Dill himself designated Tuesdays as days of constant labor, way back in 1866 or thereabouts. He believed that only good luck happened if people worked a sixteen-hour Tuesday. Something about Gettysburg or Antietam. Or the battle of Franklin. I forget. Don't quote me on all this." Bob Murray's page B4 article went on to list out how every white-majority precinct—like Gruel—didn't garner a vote. Murray

301

ended his item with a quote from Victor Dees, which went, "So. Who won?"

Then I arranged the photos of Gruel residents by way of forehead and eye-beadiness. I never studied genetics, anthropology, Darwinism, or models who specialized in close-up facial shots, but it appeared logically possible—from an amateur "maxillariologist's" point of view—that Gruel's residents would one day have two touching eyeballs and a hairline not dissimilar to the average wolfman.

Oh, I shuffled and blind-picked, and played fifty-two pickup with forty-five thousand documents. And then I closed my eyes and pulled what I thought may be the most important Gruel pieces. I didn't really close my eyes. That's both "hyperbole" and "exaggeration." The how-to books point out not to use clichés, and that it's proper to stretch the truth, aka "lie."

I took everything home, to my approximately fifty-two-hundred-square-foot brick trailer, and wrote this prologue:

Gruel, South Carolina, might be a template for small-town southern America. In these pictures and news items you will come to understand how hardworking people strive and strive to become the good, honest citizens in a world gone cynical. From Civil War to trickle-down theory, learn how a small town—a village, a spot on the Rand McNally atlas—slowly progressed from thump-on-heads proletarians to economically vibrant members of the merchant class. Live and learn. Come on down. There's a place for a person like you in Gruel.

That's all I wrote. Then I proceeded with everything I'd seen in the silo.

"Well," said Derrick Ouzts. "That's something. That's a little something. Do you think your publisher would be interested and amicable about all this?"

As you know I had zero publishers. I said, "Uh-huh. Indubitably. As a matter of fact, with so much information left over in the silo that I couldn't use, I'd be willing to bet that they'd be interested in a second Gruel book." Students walked back and forth in their small, weird, plaid outfits. We stood outside. "I'll do what I can do. I imagine they'll want to do this in paperback, what with the cost of cloth-covered, perfect-bound productions. Cloth-covered means hardback. Perfect-bound means not saddle stitch. Saddle stitch means stapled, really."

My ersatz boss put his hand on my shoulder. "I'm not an idiot, Novel. I've seen books in my life. I've even read a couple. Listen, I'll tell the committee that you're well on the way."

My mind could only race about a year ahead. Nobody, I knew, would ever purchase a book of useless small-town tidbits titled *More Gruel, Please*. I said, "There'll be a bona fide ISBN number and cataloging-in-publication data. I'm thinking about either dedicating the book to Colonel Dill or to all the orphans who passed this way." I looked up at what appeared to be a pterodactyl flying overhead. I said, "Who's, exactly, 'the committee'?"

"Again, everybody, you know. The whole town. Except you, I guess."

I knew that answer, but stalled in order to make some mental notes—I needed to find a print shop that wouldn't mind me using a real publisher's name on the spine. I needed to put my money earned from being Gruel Normal's historian in residence in a mutual fund for three months and hope for 20 percent interest in order to pay for a thousand copies.

And then I planned to escape. I would get out of Gruel before anyone learned that no bookstore in America carried the biography—either mine or the town's.

I said, "What?"

"Everybody except you, I guess. *Hey*, I'm betting that you haven't met the whole town. Why don't we plan a big party sometime next week. You can announce that the book's done, and maybe we'll take some prepublication orders. You writers get anything you want for free, don't you? We can go ahead and see how many people want one for them and theirs. It'll be a coffee-table-sized book, right?"

Again, I daydreamed about getting the stupid history camera-ready. I said, "Writers don't get their own books for free, believe me. Oh, we get a big discount, but nothing's free. Listen, I'm going to need a few days off doing grunt work. I'll need to make some phone calls. I might even have to drive up to New York City. Sometimes, from what I've learned, you got to pressure these people to send a contract before you die."

I went on and on, lying. Derrick Ouzts walked off saying, "Do what you have to do. You're the historian, Bubba."

I could've plain flat-out left, my wallet filled after closing up an account at the Graywood County Bank. Don't think that I didn't consider any of this. Hell, those thoughts began right about when Maura-Lee Snipes left the Sneeze 'n' Tone in order to perfect Jesus crust.

I yelled out at Derrick Ouzts, "I'll put in an acknowledgment page thanking you and Mrs. Ouzts, you know."

❖ ❖ ❖

Bob Murray, in a matter of only fifteen years, had risen from cub reporter at the *Forty-Five Platter* to full-fledged Lifestyles editor. "Lifestyles" might've been somewhat misleading for the people of Graywood County: There existed no fashion, movie review, book review, visual arts review, or recipe page. Pretty much the "Lifestyles" section included anything not included on the obituary page. Letters to the editor congratulating the stupid, talentless cast of *The Sound of Music, Oklahoma, The Music Man, H.M.S. Pinafore, Our Town,* and *Grease*—mostly lawyers, bankers, high school drama teachers, and gene-impaired wealthy Forty-Five long-standing landowners—got published nonstop, all lauding the performers, the director, in addition to pointing out how fortunate all of us were to live in such a vibrant, open-minded, meaningful, fulfilling, and lustrous community. In between stood articles about the latest Sonic Drive-In opening or a man who taught nighttime home decor classes at the new Lowe's.

Mr. Bob Murray, maybe my age, wore a buzz cut. Front-page headlines, torn out unneatly, half floated away from the Scotch-taped anchors on the wall behind him. It didn't take me five seconds to notice that each one held a horrific and execrable typo: MAN LANDS ON MOAN!, NIXON RESINGS!, U.S. HOKEY TEAM WINS!, CRATER BEATS FORD!, BUSH BEATS MANDOLL!, and so forth. I'm not lying. There were hundreds of them, most of which meant more to the locale, and were less emphatic: TRACTOR PULLLL AT FARGROUND, LION'S CLUB ANNUAL ROOM SALE, LIBARY HOLDS LITRACY DRIVE.

I pointed. Murray didn't turn around. "This is a family-owned business. It's been a family paper since it started. My editor Frankie Mundy—who insists on writing the goddamn headlines for each item—happens to be the great-great-great-whatever grandson of our founder. This boy has a degree in phys ed from Anders College. Half the time when we're pushing deadlines and need help you can find him in his office conjugating imaginary football plays that would never work." He said, "Are you all right? You don't look like you hail from around here. Hey, why're you even here? I don't write stories about the plight of the homeless in Lifestyles. Go talk to Glenn Flack over in Metro."

I'd not thought about getting a haircut. I only shaved once a week if and only if my face itched. Perhaps the hygienic regimen I employed while writing scripts for lieutenant governors, and while feigning herpetologist status, fell off inexorably, I don't know. I said, "I've been living in Gruel for too long. The town could use a barber and a haberdasher."

Bob Murray looked behind himself. I scanned his desk at this point: a glass paperweight with seashells inside; a Mr. Peanut figurine; a bag of peppermint stars; two of the same photographs of Bob and what I supposed was his wife and son, all of whom wore grins and short, short hair; a postcard of Samuel Beckett, oddly. "Gruel," he said. "I know Gruel. Back in the day my Little League team got trounced by Gruel all the time. They had kids living there, then."

I kind of lied about my role. "I'm just trying to figure out some facts," I said. "You know—about the people. The place."

"I'll tell you about Gruel, my friend. First off, don't go there. Second—if for some reason you get stuck with a flat tire or whatever, run. Run at a diagonal from the sun. Or moon. Get away. Do you know how many people considered 'missing' are probably buried in a Gruel shallow grave? Fucking A—do you know how many people considered missing actually moved to Gruel so that no one would ever find them? The answer to both questions goes a little like this: too many to count."

The chair in which I sat might've been a reject. The legs seemed six inches too short all the way around. I sat there stupid like a man asquat in a public restroom. I said, "There are some strange people living in caves up on Gruel Mountain, from what they tell me."

Bob Murray said, "*Strange?* There are felons living up there running a gaming industry that makes Las Vegas look like a place to shoot marbles. Whaddya got for me, man? Whaddya know?"

"Not much. You know more than I."

"I've been trying to hire out a detective, Novel. Absolutely no one will take this project on. One day a couple months ago I took a hike upside the mountain from the old, closed-down Gruel Inn site." I didn't say anything about the new Gruel Inn's inside opulence. "Well I walked and hiked and trudged until I found what I thought was an open grave. The weird thing was, someone had laid down a bunch of carpet up the trail, as if asking anyone to follow it. Anyway, luckily I'd brought along a backpack, and in it I had a collapsible retrenchment tool I'd bought at Victor Dees's army-navy store, along with water. And my AK-47."

I said, "Huh," and felt my face turn red.

"Well what I dug up was *this*." Before Bob Murray turned around, opened up a file cabinet, and pulled out a metal fire-proof lockbox, I knew that he would pull out my pathetic memoir in rhymed couplets. He did. Luckily I'd been smart enough not to type a title page with name and address—something the how-to books said a writer should do, along with word count. "The people living up on Gruel Mountain keep some kind of history of themselves and evidently bury their records for future generations to discover. I'm no archaeologist or believer in UFOs, but I'm of the mind that those people up there might be readying for an alien invasion. Or a mass suicide."

I looked at my sorry excuse of a manuscript and foresaw what would drive me straight out of Gruel on a giant wave of ridicule and embarrassment. "Whatever you do," I said, "don't publish this thing in the *Forty-Five Platter*. It'll only cause a general panic. Anyway, what I came to you about was this history of Gruel book I've been contracted to write, and I wanted to know your thoughts on why no one there voted ever."

Change the subject, change the subject, change the subject, I thought.

Bob Murray thumbed through my sad, odd tome. "Hell, I don't know. Maybe no one remembers voting day. Maybe no one cares. From what I can gather, those people hold a grudge against the government. Ours, and the old Confederate one."

I pretended to listen as he went on to tell me what I already divined, but to be honest I could only think about stealing back my epic poem and burning it. Unfortunately, though, he replaced the thing in the lockbox, replaced the lockbox in the lockable file cabinet. I said, "Well thanks for your time."

"Hey, if and when your book comes out, let me know. I'll write a piece about it in Lifestyles. I don't think we've ever done anything on a book, you know."

I told him he'd be the first person I would contact.

On my way out of Forty-Five I stopped at the Dixie Drive-In and ordered two chili cheeseburgers. Looking back, I figured that I had a death wish, that I wanted to clog my carotids, undergo a stroke, and lose that part of my brain that stored short-term memory. Or I simply wanted to faint, get sent to Graywood Regional Memorial, and die from unknown causes.

33

"I GOT A CALL from a man named Murray over at the paper,"
Bekah said. She showed up unannounced at the Gruel Inn. I
couldn't tell for sure but I swore that I saw someone hunch
down hiding in the backseat of her car.

I said, "Why'd he call you?"

We sat in the office, and I offered her a cup of special coffee
I'd bought in Forty-Five, a little something I couldn't get anywhere in Gruel. I offered her some fucking Folgers. "Bob Murray's daddy and my daddy were friends. I guess he knew I'd
come back. How or why he called me up isn't the question,
though, Novel-baby. The question is, why were you over there
snooping around more than you need?"

Let me say right now that I'd only seen Bekah bow up fighting mad a few times during our marriage, and two of those occasions occurred during our honeymoon. "I need to know some
things if I want to write a true account. I need to know some
things. I need to know. A true account is what it's all about, am
I right or am I right?"

Bekah crossed, uncrossed, and recrossed her legs. "You
know enough. You know more than enough. That's why I voted

against this whole project long ago. I knew you weren't the right man for the job years ago."

My wife stood up to leave. I said, "What?" and thought about a philosophy course I took in college revolving around free will and nothing else. Well about free will and predestination.

"I thought you'd puzzle out this mystery, Novel. Before now. Maybe you fried too many brain cells working for those lieutenant governors I never knew about, I don't know. It seems to me it wouldn't take a history major to understand how you and I ran out of—years ago—romance, Novel. Maura and I have been lovers since something like the eleventh grade."

It's not like I hadn't figured it out, kind of. When I look back now and think about how she returned to her hometown too often—even if it was to run the forgery business—something about the rug burns on her knees and chin should've told me something. Or how when we made love she always wanted me to tuck my pecker between my legs and hump her pelvis.

I said, "Maybe I should've written more speeches promoting gay unions. Maybe I should've fessed up about my real job, and gotten the lieutenant governor to give speeches about the importance of softball in the schools. Why the hell did you marry me in the first place? Were you bisexual back then?"

Bekah rolled up the sleeves to her lumberjack shirt, which I thought was a little too warm to wear in mid-May. "You confused me. Back then it hadn't been all that long since you stood on the side of the road with your daddy, selling shrimp."

That hurt, I have to tell you. At this point I understood how Bekah prospered as a debt collector. I said, "That's politically incorrect. You can't say something about how lesbians are attracted to the smell of fish. That's just not right, Bekah."

311

She said, "Get ready to move out of here. The gurus are coming to take you over."

◆ ◆ ◆

The stomping emanated from atop Gruel Mountain minutes after Bekah left. I reconsidered Supergluing every outside doorknob again. I thought about stuffing everything from cotton balls to those nickel slugs found lying around near electrical outlets on newly built house underlayment into my ear holes. I tried to talk myself into believing high blood pressure caused the throb-throb-throb that drove me paranoid. Maybe it's the sound of my *heart*, beating, pounding, surging oxygen into my brain in order to allow me to think some rational thought, finally, I thought.

I looked out one of the new venetian blinds only to see pure darkness. Cicadas! I tried to talk myself into believing. Tree frogs, crickets, locusts, one of those bad urban child bands banging trash-can lids.

I walked in circles and found myself thinking about how I could only write my autobiography after leaving Gruel, and that as hard as it would be to "willingly suspend disbelief"—a term mentioned over and over in all the goddamn how-to-write-a-novel books—I would have to forgo ages one through Gruel: I'm talking leave out my entire upbringing, the sad college years, and then the snake education/speechwriting years.

Forget the course I took on predestination and free will, Bubba. Bubbette.

Right as I walked into my parking lot in order to drive far, far away—or at least to my silo hideaway to *really* finish up the bogus and encompassing biography of Gruel, South Carolina—maybe twenty black men met me from across the street.

I said, of course, "I'll be damned. Y'all are the first black people I've seen all this time in Gruel."

"They talk about us still, I'm sure," a man said, a man I considered the spokesman, the leader. He stood in front of his vee of comrades. On closer view, he looked more sandy than black. More gray-skinned than bronze.

I walked across the road. "What's the noise y'all have been making?" Let me say that I wasn't surprised, scared, or taken aback by these fellows. I said, "They say y'all are the descendants of Vicksburg cave dwellers. Is that true? From what I understand, from my voluminous reading on the Civil War — or what some people insist on calling the War between the States — only white people migrated to the hilly guts of Vicksburg. So you might need to explain. Are y'all like melungeons?"

This is what I wanted to discover. As a history buff, I could see that these people provided a missing link, of sorts, that explained everything in regards to Americana.

"We've been watching you, Novel. Good lord. We're getting a little impatient. From the beginning we thought you were our only hope, mister. We had you popped as a compatriot."

"Well I'm doing all that I can try to do," I said.

As I looked closer, these people looked less gray than flat-out worn-out and haggard. Were they descendants of the Lost Colony? Were they a mix of Cherokee and African slaves, or the ancestors of Francis Drake, Chief Skyuka, Mississippi plantation owners, and runaway ex-Dinka tribesmen? "My name's Mac McAdams," the leader said. Was that a slight Scottish brogue? I thought. Did he stutter?

I said, "Novel Akers," and stuck out my hand.

Mac McAdams turned to his people and said, "Somebody

go tell the women and children it's all right." To me he said, "You wouldn't be opposed to some company tonight, would you? We might have a mutual reason to become, well, *associates*, I guess is the best word. We've been watching you for over I don't know how many fortnights. We read your poem before it got desecrated."

One of the how-to books stressed "Know of what you write." This particular "scholar" professed that a certain amount of "method acting" should ooze into the writing process, that if one wished to write about bank robbers then one should rob a bank, et cetera. At least that's how I read it. So I, eager to gain experiences that might nudge me toward writing *something* worthy of the history books—an aside, at least—said, "Bring 'em on down. Maybe we'll have a big cookout."

Oh. Perhaps this isn't exactly "linear." There might seem to be a missing step in the "logical continuum." Maybe I should mention—in case anyone's keeping tabs to my solemn and thoughtful and completely rational movements—that when I bought the Folgers Coffee in Forty-Five I also happened to pick up a dozen racks of ribs, a dozen pork shoulders, a dozen whole fryers, all on sale. I didn't ask the butcher if they came from Gruel BBQ and Pig-Petting Zoo.

When the good citizens of my domiciliary chipped in to renovate the Gruel Inn for yoga instructors, they furnished each room with a minifridge-freezer combination. I guess Victor Dees, Jeff the owner, Bekah, Maura-Lee, Barry and Larry et al. wanted their new guests—the contortionist men and women who'd bring Gruel back to legitimate financial bases—to feel comfortable in regards to safely storing their prized *foogath*, nasturtium salad, kumquat chutney, raisin bran tea, buckwheat pie, wild rice fritters, turnip waffles, German watercress codfish balls, sanitarium Vitrogen pudding, gingerroot soufflés, buttermilk muffins, curry chutney, prune milk shake, parsnip pancakes, lima bean marmalade, beet fritters, date chutney, bean sprout soup, and Yellow River poached mackerel.

But that's only a theory.

Research!

◆ ◆ ◆

Mac McAdams led thirty-six men, women, and children back at nine o'clock. There seemed to be a good five generations present, from a couple of octogenarians down to toddlers. I'd started four fires over open pits I had completed long before, right after salvaging all of the hidden outdoor treasures and secreted pleas for someone to strong-arm his way into the Gruel Inn and free the hostages. I made a variety of barbecue sauces inside my office: ketchup-, mustard-, and vinegar-based, each with jalapeños, habaneros, and the slightest hint of bourbon.

Mac McAdams's people wore uniforms. The men seemed split evenly between Johnny Reb tattered grays and army-issued Yankee blues. The women sported those ankle-length corset-waisted dresses. All of the kids kind of looked like models for a Tootsie Pop wrapper.

And they all looked *familiar* to me. I'm talking these people appeared to be straight out of the history books, not merely folks I'd run into in the sad, crowded family waiting rooms at Graywood Regional Memorial. It had nothing to do with their garb, either, please believe me. What I'm trying to make clear is this: Even in the harsh bright, spattering light of a barbecue pit piled high with pork butt behind a twelve-room motel of questionable integrity I felt like I'd stared at these people in vivid black-and-white photographs before.

Mac McAdams pulled me by the bicep and said, "There's no possible way that you know how to cook meat on a grill as well as we do, aye? Have you ever heard of a certain Charlie Vargas over in Memphis, aye? Where do you think his people learned, aye? The Rendezvous, aye?"

Mac McAdams might not've added all those "ayes," but he spoke in such a melodious dialect that "aye" kind of came out understood. I said, "Okay."

"Everyone take care of the food. We'll have a celebratory feast for breakfast!" Everyone else took their places as if on cue. I allowed McAdams to lead me back inside.

He smelled, but not like you'd think—not of sweat, body odor, booze, gunpowder, woodsmoke, red clay, domesticated animals, and/or pipe tobacco. Mac McAdams emitted a, I don't know, *chemical* scent, something between isopropyl alcohol and formaldehyde. I took him inside the motel office. McAdams checked the door lock and closed the venetian blinds. I said, "Are y'all professional Civil War battle reenactors?"

McAdams held his head directly toward me, though slanted down a bit. His massive forehead could've been used for a hand-ball court. "I'm of the belief—there's one man in Gruel who 'accidentally' divulges information to me—that you already know about the forged religious icon paintings and whatnot. That you understand Gruel's money flow."

I said, "I've learned some things I wish I never uncovered."

McAdams went to the refrigerator, pulled out two cans of PBR, and, in the light, looked exactly like Robert E. Lee in that famous pose. I don't want to come across as some kind of soothsayer or visionary, but at this particular point I could've held up my palm and told Mac McAdams to say no more, that I understood the whole monologue that would follow.

We popped our beer tabs. McAdams said, "Right before the Civil War a young Scottish fellow came through named Alexander Gardner. He'd originally teamed up with Mathew Brady, the most famous chronicler of the Civil War through his photographic images. Brady, as I'm sure you know, pretty much followed the union forces in the Civil War, Novel. He got his subjects to pose there stock-still for minutes at a time.

"Well, Mr. Alexander Gardner came down Vicksburg way, and he needed assistants. My great-great-great-great-grandfather and two of my great-great-great-great-uncles got jobs with him. Mr. Gardner had developed a process that didn't use copper and silver basic to daguerreotypes. He used a glass plate covered with a light-sensitive coat of chemicals. The term my ancestors learned was 'collodion,' and it yielded a positive photo that reduced exposure time by 90 percent. People only had to stand still for about three seconds."

Put a bunch of "aye?s" in the above paragraphs. I tried to concentrate on McAdams's story, but found myself tuning in on a couple women out back screaming "Dry rub! Dry rub!"

"Okay. So my ancestors learned. And then union blockades kept them from receiving the necessary chemicals needed. Alexander Gardner went back up North—you might've even seen those great photos of the Abraham Lincoln conspirators."

I said, "Spangler, Arnold, Payne, Atzerodt. Hanged July 7, 1865." I knew and remembered some shit, somehow.

"Yes. Well. So. As you recall—and the people of Gruel are correct—my ancestors in Vicksburg took to the caves. And some

317

of them emigrated east. *Some went west*—but we can only believe that they successfully infiltrated and commingled with the Anasazi Indians out there.

"My people, according to our oral history, meant to trek all the way to New York, Maine, maybe Nova Scotia. But they stopped here because of the wonderful reception given and offered by Gruel's own war hero, Colonel Dill.

"My great-great-great-great-grandfather brought what followers he had up onto that hill, and found similar caves in which to hide. I am aware that the people you've met—your wife, for example—insist that we all still live in various holes, chasms, minor indentions, and alluvial outcroppings, but that's an exaggeration. If you'd've spent another half hour walking up the path when you buried your beautiful Robert Burnsian epic poem, then you would've encountered my home, a twelve-room stucco house with handmade, kiln-fired terra-cotta roof tiles. How do you think the rest of our people know so much about running a barbecue pit out back?"

A fearsome paranoia took over me about this point. I foresaw my soon-to-be guru-relocated abode burning down, my poem printed in the *Forty-Five Platter* by Bob Murray, and my moving atop Gruel Mountain in order to undergo some kind of arranged marriage with one of Mac McAdams's nieces in order to enhance the gene pool, among other disastrous personal events. I envisioned someone from either side saying, "Welcome to science fiction, Novel."

Mac McAdams took another beer from the refrigerator. "I've heard of Pabst Blue Ribbon. It's not that bad. Up where we live we kind of make our own double-run peach bounce. It's not that hard. Not that I want to sound like a cookbook, but all you need is a crop of corn, a steady fire, some water, and sugar and yeast. Peaches."

I said, "I'm worried about the meat outside. Are you sure everyone out there knows when to turn the pig? Me, I usually keep a timer."

Mac McAdams said, "Good segue. A timer. We have a variety of timers up where we live. Like I said, I live in a regular house. It might be more than regular if four thousand square feet qualifies such. Anyway, we've been using the caves as darkrooms. What our ancestors learned and passed down, we have used to our advantage. Now. Whereas the Cathcarts began selling forged paintings, all of us started selling Civil War photographs. You've seen that picture of Robert E. Lee with Traveler the horse? That's probably me. Oh, they might have an original in Washington and Lee University, but about five hundred people think that they have the original. My relatives and I pose, and we take old-fashioned pictures that don't succumb to carbon-14 dating.

"Any of those still photographs of ex-soldiers staring straight ahead? Go outside. You'll find Stonewall Jackson, Jefferson Davis, Pierre Gustave Beauregard, George Blake Cosby, and Secretary of the Treasury Christopher Gustavus Memminger. Hell, boy, you'll find Scarlett O'Hara. Here's what we do, and what makes those snot-nosed elitist portrait painters so angry: We have backdrops up there, we take our flash photos, and then we go out to flea markets, fairs, reenactments, swap meets, conventions, NASCAR stock car races, ACC basketball tournaments, every catfish 'feastival,' chitlins festival, boll weevil festival, Claxton fruitcake festival, and peanut celebration. Maybe people think they're buying originals, and maybe they think it's a simple reproduction. I don't know. I've never taken a survey. We set up a tent, and we say, 'Wouldn't you love a photo of,' say, 'John Singleton Mosby?' and then I point to an eight-by-ten that they've probably seen in one of the history books. Maybe my still shots have gotten half faded, wrinkled, and/or cracked and crazed in the week or ten days since I took the shot.

"No one asks me questions, and I don't offer explanations. Anywhere from twenty-five to a hundred dollars. So you can see why the people in Gruel have a hard-on about us. It's been going on since photography came on the scene. Painters *hate* photographers. They see themselves as better than us, and think we take away honest work from them. But you don't see my group setting up to pose for a *Last Supper* photograph, do you? I believe it's time for this little petty war to end. And I'm of the hope that you can arbitrate the situation."

More than likely I missed most of what he said because I kept thinking about how people don't speak more than two or three lines of dialogue at a time. I looked at my watch and was surprised to find that we'd not eased over into the next year. I said, "Well that's a fascinating story, Mac McAdams. Do you want me to include it in my forthcoming book *More Gruel, Please*?"

Mac McAdams said, "I'm usually not a betting man, but I would wager that none of your books ever sees a bookstore shelf. Especially that long poem."

He reached into his uniform coat pocket and pulled out what appeared to be freshly printed Confederate paper money.

34

MAYBE I FELL ASLEEP slumped down by the ex-check-in desk, next to my refrigerator, near the table where I finally officially collected the history of Gruel. Maybe. One minute Mac McAdams told me the long-winded and highly unlikely story of how his people suffered more than a hundred years, and the next thing I knew some lady wearing a Zouave uniform rang a goddamn cowbell in my ear and said we could eat barbecue breakfast, lunch, and supper.

Mac McAdams said, "This may be your day, Novel. You should spring to your feet."

He stood as erect as a gray tiki doll and either didn't seem to suffer from sleep deprivation or just awoke. I said, "My day. My day. What's that supposed to mean?"

The sun rose as slightly as it's prone to do, and a slick of dew rose and hovered where orphans once conjured up impromptu games. Mac McAdams's minions ran around with tongs, forks, and skewers. Oh man there was chicken, pig, and beef, all creeping toward rare. I looked out back and tried not to think about how a clan of people up on Gruel Mountain might possess evolved and frost-hardened gastrointestinal tracts that resisted trichinosis better than the average carnivore.

At first I thought that one of the children whooped or screamed, then another, then some of the women. Who pulled out the bagpipes? I thought. Mac McAdams reached into his left boot and extracted a tiny pearl-handled derringer the likes of which I'd only seen women use on 1960s TV westerns. I said, "Hey. Hey, hold on a minute. I'm on your side, if anything. This isn't my day to *die*."

"That's old Victor Dees coming out here," McAdams said. In profile he looked like Stonewall Jackson holding a cap gun. "That's the Gruel Volunteer Fire Department, plus about everyone else, I'm betting. They must've seen the smoke." Mac McAdams opened the back door and yelled to his people, "Today's the day. Today's the day." He pointed at a man who had to have been the eldest and said, "Papa, you're in charge of photography."

The sirens neared, and understand that I don't mean this in an *Odyssey* kind of way. I made out Victor Dees's regular-sounding horn—the one I heard when he passed Bekah's parents' house that day as I encountered the tanned human-flesh scroll—and then a couple London air raid–sounding *eee-aww-eee-aww-eee-aww*s. I could never prove it, and no one would make an admission, but I'm pretty sure I delineated Bekah, Maura-Lee, Barry, Larry, and Jeff the owner, Dr. Bobba Lollis, Derrick Ouzts, Nora Ouzts, and maybe even that couple with their flat tire in my parking lot months before, *all* whoo-whoo-whooing with their heads out the driver's window. I focused, caught Bob Murray, and in my mind saw all those cars, Jeeps, pickup trucks winding their way down Old Old Greenville

Road, then Old Old Augusta Road, and right up to what might or might not have been safe-from-firing distance, both ballistically and photographically. When they all arrived it didn't take a textile management major from Clemson to understand how Victor Dees attired everyone in his leftover helmets—regular World War II caps mostly, but some of those flat, flat doughboy things, and a couple nice German head coverings. Listen, and this is the truth: Bekah and Maura-Lee sported those nice kaiser-pointed chapeaus.

But unlike Victor Dees they didn't have two swaths of thirty-aught-six bullets across their chests.

Oh, the smoke sifted behind the Gruel Inn heavily and one of the strange photographer-to-be children yelled out, "I want coleslaw on my barbecue, I want coleslaw on my barbecue!" like that, somewhere between pleading funny and crying outright.

I said, of course, "Well this doesn't look good."

"You're in charge of Papa Locke. You got a ladder? You and Papa Locke get up on the roof and espy what battle might or might not ensue. This is finally the day! We've been expecting this confrontation for, aye-aye-aye-aye-aye-aye-aye-aye lo these many decades, aye."

What else could I say but, "Papa Locke should've started up a locksmith company. Get it? Like, if you accidentally closed your car door locked with your key in the ignition, he could come out with one of those shims. Pop-a-lock. Hotdamn."

Mac McAdams didn't exactly keep eye contact with me. He looked elsewhere, namely at the stretch of Gruelites, or Gruelists, or Gruelons lined up pissed off that photography forgers infiltrated painting forgers. McAdams said, "We know you have a ladder. You and Papa Locke get up on the roof. We might need witnesses. Corroborators. Biographers. You've kind of pickled up that responsibility right till this moment—now's your day."

Let me point out a few things: One, I foresaw gunfire and I didn't want to get shot in the middle of it; two, Papa Locke, I thought, might have some words of wisdom, even it he stunk horribly from a full night of smoked pork; three, I couldn't remember if I dug a fire pit too close to the propane line going into the Gruel Inn, et cetera; four, who knew what taxidermic genes remained dormant in Bekah's being?; five through about forty, again, I foresaw gunfire.

From above it looked like two regular stupid armies standing length to length. The Gruel Mountain cave dwellers stood straighter than liquor store bottles awaiting selection. The other half of what I understood to be Gruel scammers stood fifty yards away, dressed in motley, looking as though they'd rather be ordering sausage biscuits for breakfast at a fast-food chain that would never be near this area.

Papa Locke wore a tam-o'-shanter. His eyebrows grew downward and seemingly covered his vision. On top of the roof he said, "Have you ever boiled some eggs, and cleaned your silverware with polish, and taken a gigantic dump in your outhouse all at the same time? Well that's what odor's coming from this situation." Papa Locke smacked his lips up and down a good fifty times in a way that sounded like year-old Bubble Wrap popping. He said, "Uh-huh. I tell you something else, but this is good— boil eggs, soak them in buttermilk, wrap them in sausage, then deep-fry the bastards. Scottish eggs."

You'd've thought that—after at least one hundred years of tyranny and utter seclusion—the man might start throwing shingles. Instead, he sat down on his sits bones like some kind of guru. He breathed in and out better than any oxygen machine in Graywood Regional Memorial. Papa Locke looked like he could go into a trance presently.

Like I said, everyone lined up facing each other. I would've gone down the ladder and retrieved binoculars I picked up at the army-navy store back about the time I overordered MREs, but it didn't take magnified-enhanced vision to delineate two people—a man and woman—wearing green and white sweat-suits, jogging in place right between Maura-Lee and Bekah.

My bastards: James, Joyce. I yelled out, "I thought you got killed somewhere along the way!" to my brother. To Papa Locke beside me on the rooftop I said, "This is the biggest intervention ever."

◆ ◆ ◆

We played this game as a child: who can hit the softest. I didn't catch on until maybe age twelve, when James and Joyce readied themselves to escape North Carolina, the United States, all of North America under the false impression that they possessed Irish blood unknown to the people of Black Mountain, though Scottish and Irish blood, certainly, coursed our capillaries, et cetera.

It went like this: "Hey, Novel, I bet I can hit softer than you can."

"What do you mean by 'softer'?"

"I can hit you so softly you'll barely feel it. Come on, let's bet a dime. Let's bet a nickel."

"So you're saying that whoever hits softest—and you got to at least touch skin—wins the bet."

"You go first."

Early on I should've figured out that history wasn't my forte, seeing as James and/or Joyce continually tricked me with this mean ploy, something that I'd've done, too, if Bekah and I ever had children, or if I'd've taught history at a private religious school in the 1990s where corporal punishment still existed.

I always went first and barely brushed my particular sibling's bicep. Sometimes this happened in one of our bedrooms. Sometimes it occurred in the backyard while my parents either smoked pot or went off on one of their "only us" biannual honeymoon runs buying off shellfish in Murrells Inlet. Out in the middle of the driveway. The street. Somewhere on the school playground. In the car, or refrigerated truck. On Main Street in front of the candy store. Inside the boys' dressing room at Belk's department store every August when we got new blue jeans and shirts that might've been in style a decade earlier for the rest of America.

I clenched my fist and pulled back an inch or two, then at the velocity of a fireplace ash floating to the ground I would barely whisper whatever thin blond hairs poked from my siblings' outer triceps. "That was a good one," my brother or sister might say. "That one was epic, Novel."

And then either James or Joyce would cock back halfway to West Virginia and clobber me to the point of a four-knuckle charley horse. "You win," they always said. "I don't have a nickel on me right now, but I'd rather owe you than beat you out of it."

Call me a slow learner. What small muscles I showed off ages six through twelve were mostly swollen hematomas risen from my shirtsleeve, kind of off-kilter biceps.

I looked down from the Gruel Inn roof at my now-middle-aged brother and sister. "I thought you were dead," I said.

My sister grabbed a bullhorn from Victor Dees. "Don't jump," she said. "Come off the roof slowly. We're only here to help you, Novel. You have love from the entire community, Novel. And we're willing to teach you self-help, Novel. Please back away from the edge."

Okay, listen: The motel, as you know, wasn't but one story high. Falling or jumping off meant a sprained ankle at most. Back in Black Mountain I regularly jumped off our roof into the pile of leaves and pine needles I scooped from our gutters and threw down to clump up wet in the haphazard front yard. "I'm not committing suicide," I yelled back. I cupped my hands to my face and yelled, "I'm not committing suicide. Y'*all* might be. I'm just watching." To James I hollered, "Hey, James, tell me what happened to you the last time you were here."

In a fake, though pretty reasonable and obviously well-rehearsed Irish accent he screamed back, "What last time, Novel?"

I said, "I can't believe it's really you. Hey. Hey, I've done pretty well for myself outside of writing lies for politicians, having a weird sexless marriage, viewing the death of my in-laws, running a useless and incomprehensible writers retreat, and devoting my time to detailing the ins and outs of Gruel, South Carolina, without telling the truth, and some other things."

Barry and Larry stood way off holding their cue sticks. I could make them out. Bekah held up a newspaper and said, "Is this your memoir? Is this what we all hoped you'd get famous for? For which you'd get famous?"

I looked over at Papa Locke. He sat forward, squinted, and said, "The *Forty-Five Platter*. Some kind of poem."

"It's your life story. Bob Murray here says he undug it," my sister yelled.

Fucking A, I thought, even though I had no idea what the term meant—something about the army? That would make sense. I looked below me at Mac McAdams and his troops standing there stoic. He yelled across, "Let me say again, as my ancestors have admitted, that we're sorry about how the photographic image has replaced the need for realistic paintings." But it came across thus: "Let me . . . say again . . . as my ancestors . . . have admitted . . . that we're . . ." You get the picture, no pun. He could've been Franklin Delano Roosevelt pushing Social Security, or JFK espousing what we could do for our country, et cetera.

I watched crazy Mac McAdams, so I couldn't quite tell who barked back, "This isn't about you, Bubba. It's about the novel."

Hell, I couldn't even distinguish whether the voice was male or female. Was that Bekah? Was it Jeff the owner, or Derrick Ouzts? I stood on the roof and said, "Hey! Hey, let me tell y'all that *I'm* not nuts. Everyone *here's* crazy, except for me. And from what I can tell—through my thorough and relentless investigations—I'm about the only man in this county who hasn't either killed a person or sold a piece of artwork under false pretenses."

Bekah held up the *Forty-Five Platter*. She said, "Say that again about false pretenses." Somebody from the Gruel side added, "Photography's not art."

I said to Bekah, "That poem's not the same as lying. It's how it ended up, that's all I have to say."

But it didn't matter.

They were on each other.

Papa Locke said, "Good barbecue downstairs." I shrugged.

◆ ◆ ◆

Right before I met Rebekah in Chapel Hill, I went to a presidential election party. My guy hadn't won the Democratic nomination, but it didn't matter to me as long as those dumb sons of bitches who shoved trickle-down down our throats and offered free government cheese as a consolation prize got voted out of power. Somebody in the history department actually *qualified* for a hoop of cheddar—*all* of us did, unofficially—and brought it to the shindig. Oh, we took out our daddy's inherited Case knives and sliced into that orange wheel. We had thrown dollar bills and quarters into a pile, and garnered enough money to purchase a couple gallons of cheap white wine, a case of Milwaukee's Best, a case of Schaeffer's.

"Novel, are you still of the belief that Jefferson's king of the United States?" this boy named Grover asked me. He'd never faltered from a Marxist bent.

I said, "Good architect."

"Bad coin. Bad profile."

I raised my plastic cup and laughed. At the time I owned what the latter generations might label a "mullet." Thomas Jefferson wore one, by god, when he let his hair down, to either Mrs. Jefferson or Sally Hemings.

We watched the television set. Reagan won again.

Me, I decided to pretty much kill anyone in my way. That New Year's my resolution was to make a resolution every year to take no prisoners the next 365 days. "Take no prisoners!"

329

understand, was my resolution from then on out. By this time you know me, so don't think that I'm a bad person, or that whoever publishes any of my future memoirs—again, let's pretend Harcourt—wishes to slant poorly on the vicious, irrational, immoral Republican Party. "This isn't a good thing," I said to anyone who'd listen at the losefest. "Motherfucker. What's going on in this country? I'm going to get a job as a speechwriter and work from the inside."

"No you won't," Grover the Marxist said.

"Watch me."

Someone changed the channel. We started watching a bunch of guys hanging out inside a bar, then we left to go down Franklin Street, burn or tear up any Reagan-Bush or Jesse Helms bumper stickers aptly applied to sidewalk garbage cans, and pretty much made nuisances of ourselves.

We walked on over, as I remember—maybe a dozen of us, all sad Democratic voters—to Cat's Cradle, not knowing that the UNC Young Republicans would be holding their celebration inside. And we lined up across from those red bow tie, blue oxford shirt, khaki pants–wearing accountants-to-be. I swear it looked like every one of them had gotten a fresh haircut within the hour. This one fellow named Driscoll—he's probably out of federal prison now for fraud, embezzlement, and insider trading—pointed at us losers and said, "Too late to register with us, Cuz. But we appreciate y'all coming down here to congratulate us."

Now, this episode in my life hadn't come to memory until I saw the sad fistfight below me. Back in Chapel Hill, the Republicans mostly slapped and kicked and pulled our hair. My buddies and I were so wasted that our windmill punches only took us to the slimy bar floor. Later on, though, a couple boys in the physiology department on our side stuck their fingers down their throats and released what cheap white wine and government cheese burbled in their alimentary canals, right onto the jubilant mass of lemmings. I swear to God I heard one of them yell out, "You're going to be getting a dry-cleaning bill for this!" as we got thrown out onto the sidewalk by a 120-pound kid with a railroad spike in his nose.

Which brings me to what went on in front of the Gruel Inn. Papa Locke and I descended. He walked over to a sizzling rack of ribs, tore off about four, and started eating.

Me, I rounded the back side of the motel and told myself not to get involved. No, I would only participate in this sad melee as a referee of sorts, as an arbitrator. Not fifty yards away I heard screams and accusations from both sides: "You're not a real artist, you're a human photocopier," for example, though I couldn't tell if it was photographer or forger speaking. The same went for, "You bunch of backward poseurs!"

And I would've continued toward the people I knew — James, Joyce, Bekah, Maura-Lee, Jeff the owner, Derrick Ouzts, Bob Murray, Victor Dees, the men and women who posed as, or with, General Robert E. Lee — but I stopped and thought, Another fucking rhyme.

And then one of my ungrateful, bitter, taciturn, released copperheads, probably out of its winter hole for only the second or third time since spring broke — a big, thick four-footer in search of field mice and anoles — didn't cotton to my foot being so close to its head. When he struck, when he sank two inch-long fangs into my lower right calf, I only thought bramble, bee sting, or briar. But when I reached down instinctively and the same snake hit my inner wrist, I knew.

Not that I possess a complicated and twisted system of veins, capillaries, and arteries in my right arm, but that goddamn copperhead's fangs, somehow, got tangled up in such a way that made him go into an alligator-like death roll, trying to release himself.

I screamed out the only primordial, subconscious language that I could muster, namely, "This ain't how my life's supposed to end! I got other things to add, I got things to do!" like that.

❖ ❖ ❖

Bekah started the step van. She cried, and helped me into the passenger seat. My wife blurted out, "I'll admit a lot of this got planned long before we met, Novel. But we didn't mean to have anyone get hurt. You have to believe me. I come from a long line of tricksters." She put the van in first gear and stuttered forward. Everyone quit fighting, they waved good-bye to me, and in the rearview I saw them walk side by side to the barbecue out back. I can't say that I squinted an eye in disbelief, but I should've. Instead I watched my arm and ankle swell to the width of prize-winning gourds. As Bekah took Old Old Augusta Road toward Old Old Greenville Road I said, "My heart's beating two hundred times a minute. This isn't good."

"I only hope they have antivenin at Graywood Regional Memorial. There's no telling. They might have to airlift you to Greenville or Atlanta." She didn't seem to be pushing the accelerator very hard. We traveled down the cobbly asphalt maybe thirty-five miles an hour.

"You ever going to tell me what's really going on in this town? There's something. Are your mother and brother really dead, or was that some kind of life insurance fraud? I didn't see them in the crowd back there."

"Look at your wrist. It looks like your skin might peel away. You must be allergic to poison or something."

I don't want to say that I saw that light at the end of the tunnel like all of those freaks say on talk shows and religious programs. Nor do I want to admit what might've been a hallucination: My parents weren't dead due to unpredictable reptiles. All of those click-click-clicks poured through my mind as to how James almost died from a heart-attack-induced snake encounter, et cetera.

I said, "I meant to make good on my personal vow," but my Adam's apple didn't clench up. "This is only a lesson. It's only a lesson, that's all. There's too much more I'm fated to deliver." *Fated*, that's right. I'm not too proud to admit I said "fated," just like Euripides might've, Sophocles, Aristophanes, the rest. Goofballs Marlowe, Shakespeare, and Beckett. I said, "I've never been to the capital of New Hampshire. Do they have a governor and lieutenant governor there? That would be a nice place to write speeches. Hey, Bekah, keep an eye out for stray dogs. I don't want you hitting any strays."

I thought, Maybe I could write a fucking play.

Bekah eased up on the accelerator more so and said, "This turned out way worse than I imagined."

When I jumped out of the step van—for some reason I thought that I could run thirty-five miles an hour and kind of veer my way through a field and out of sight toward a new life— and when I rolled and rolled, I couldn't remember if I should tuck my head in, go sideways like a log down a hillside, or try to stop and drop. I thought about *bowling.* I remembered watching a documentary one time on the migration of *armadillos.* Later on, I knew, I would come back to this fallow field I had chosen and measure off the length of my impromptu side trip.

I don't mind if it was the poison coursing through my veins, or the sheer terror of being admitted to Graywood Regional Memorial, but instead of my life flashing before me—from gold panning to roadside shrimp sales, to a speech I'd once written for the lieutenant governor wherein he predicted not only international factories in North Carolina but also *alien* industrial complexes in and around the Research Triangle—I foresaw the future.

Bekah sped onward, either unaware that she'd lost her cargo or convinced I'd be found dead and ruled a "natural cause" by Graywood County deputies and coroner alike. Back in Gruel I envisioned the townsfolk and the Gruel mountaineers congratulating each other, slapping backs, laughing on their way to a celebratory shindig picnic that might last until the next failed outsider got duped into performing whatever odd tasks he or she agreed to undertake. I imagined those poor upcoming Myrtle Beach gurus.

I didn't see my parents anywhere in this vision, though.

When my momentum stopped, I remained still. You better get across the state line as soon as possible, I thought. Write up a résumé. Find someone from back in the old days whom you never double-crossed or tricked or embarrassed publicly. Never return to South Carolina.

More Gruel, Please, I thought.

But the soil felt warm and soft and welcoming. This particular spot would've been a perfect place, I thought, to bury anyone's autobiography, their lucky tales.

I drug myself away, though, limping, swollen, crouched, confused—yet lucid enough to tell myself, Don't try this again, Novel. I thought, A *way a lone a last a loved a long* the way I must've done something mean-hearted in a previous life, and hoped it didn't involve any of Gruel's ancestors, for I didn't want to be remembered by these people ever again—in photographs, on canvas, or in words.

I knew that I had stories.

ACKNOWLEDGMENTS

I wish to thank my agent Liz Darhansoff for never saying "novel" to me either; everyone at Harcourt—especially Patty Berg; Julie Marshall; Evan Boorstyn; Jen Charat; Tricia van Dockum; David Hough, maniacal copy-editor; philosopher Jim Edwards for letting me skip over that "we must pass over in silence" bit of Wittgenstein's; and Glenda Guion for letting me drive South Carolina aimlessly, cursing.